WINTER WARRIOR

WINTER WARRIOR

THE WOLF OF KINGS
BOOK THREE

RICHARD CULLEN

HEAD
of ZEUS

An Aries Book

First published in the UK in 2025 by Head of Zeus,
part of Bloomsbury Publishing Plc

9 7 5 3 1 2 4 6 8

A catalogue record for this book is available from the British Library.

ISBN (PB): 9781801102100
ISBN (E): 9781801102094

Cover design: Mark Swan (kid-ethic)

Typeset by Siliconchips Services Ltd UK

Printed and bound in Great Britain by
CPI Group (UK) Ltd, Croydon CR0 4YY

MIX
Paper | Supporting
responsible forestry
FSC® C171272

Bloomsbury Publishing Plc
50 Bedford Square, London, WC1B 3DP, UK
Bloomsbury Publishing Ireland Limited,
29 Earlsfort Terrace, Dublin 2, D02 AY28, Ireland

HEAD OF ZEUS LTD
5–8 Hardwick Street
London EC1R 4RG

To find out more about our authors and books
visit www.headofzeus.com
For product safety related questions contact productsafety@bloomsbury.com

He cut down many in his vengeance; destroyed the lairs of others; harried the land and burned homes to ashes. Nowhere else had William shown such cruelty. Shamefully he succumbed to this vice, for he made no effort to restrain his fury and punished the innocent along with the guilty.

Orderic Vitalis, *The Ecclesiastical History of England and Normandy*

Place Names

Alba – Scotland
Axholme – Isle of Axholme
Berchastede – Berkhamsted
Bràigh Mhàrr – Braemar
Bretagne – Brittany
Brune – Bourne
Cildeford – Chilford
Cornualge – Cornwall
Cunecsheafod – Consett
Danmọrk – Denmark
Drifelt – Driffield
Dun Holm – Durham
Éire – Ireland
Ely
Ferebi – Hessle
Gippeswic – Ipswich
Goat's Head – Gateshead
Grentebrige – Cambridge

Grentebrigescire – Cambridgeshire

Hagenesse – Hackness

Hagustaldeséa – Hexham

Litelport – Littleport

Mameltune – Manton

Norwic – Norwich

Notingeleia – Knottingley

Picheringa – Pickering

Roeskildia – Roskilde

Saint Peter's Burgh – Peterborough

Scireburne – Sherburn-in-Elmet

Suafam – Swaffham

Waruic – Warwick

Willingaha – Willingham

Wintanceastre – Winchester

Yorke – York

Prologue

Mameltune, England, Autumn 1067

How they loved to hear their own voices, these Franks. Their mirth filled the longhall as they feasted on the ale and meat they had stolen. Grease moistened their chins, spittle flecking the table as they bawled and japed, heedless of the misery they had wrought. All the while she gripped tight to the jug in her hands, filling tankards for the new lords of this manor without complaint. But what use would it be to complain to these animals? It would just mark her as a malcontent. Another mouth to be silenced. Another victim to be punished.

She glanced across the hall at the three other women serving these brutes. Stout Osgyth laid meat in their trenchers, her jaw set as though it were the grimmest of duties. Begilda ensured their tankards were full as she forced her smile, taking every lascivious jest as though it were the sweetest compliment. Nearest was young Winfrith, tears in her eyes as one of the Franks tugged on her skirts, eager for her to sit upon his lap. The knight was insistent, despite her obvious discomfort.

All three had suffered enough, but she would need just a little more time before the entertainment began. Just a few more moments of suffering, before these men were far enough into their cups for her to act.

She moved to Winfrith's side, grasping the girl's arm and pulling her clear of the amorous knight.

'Apologies, my lord,' she said to the drunken sot, before pressing her empty jug into Winfrith's hand and taking the half full one from the girl's grip. She fixed Winfrith with a determined look. 'Dry your eyes and fetch more ale. And while you're there, see to the hounds.'

Winfrith nodded obediently, before scurrying off to do as she was bid. A sudden cheer went up as one of the knights slid back his chair and raised a flagon to the rafters.

'We have been remiss,' he announced in the language of the Franks. A language she knew well, though now she wished she had never been cursed to hear it. 'We sit in this hall, our bellies full, and not one of us has yet offered thanks to the man who granted us this hospitality.' That brought smirks of delight from the dozen others around the feasting table. 'A toast, to the former master of this estate. To Lord Eskil.'

The men cheered, and some laughed as they stood on unsteady feet, their flagons raised toward the crossbeam above the fire. She should not have looked but it was impossible to resist. Glancing up, her eyes caught sight of the severed head mounted where before a set of stag antlers had been nailed in pride of place. His eyelids drooped, mouth hanging slack, face so wan it barely resembled the man he had been in life. Still, it was unmistakably the head of Eskil. The head of her father.

The Franks laughed again, slapping each other on the back before slumping in their seats. She ground her jaw so tight it almost cracked her teeth, squeezed the jug in so steely a grip she felt the pewter bend. All she could do was resist the urge to howl her rage at this injustice, to scream in their faces that he had been her father, that she would have her vengeance, that damnation would be too merciful a fate for them all. But they could not know who she was. Not yet.

A tankard clattered noisily as it was knocked off the table. When one of the knights bent to pick it up he slipped from his seat, and landed on his arse, to the merriment of his fellows.

'This ale is damned strong,' one of them shouted.

'Aye, and we need more of it,' growled another.

The time was near. She felt fear churn in her gut but pushed it down. There would be justice for her loss, and it could not wait another night.

Catching Osgyth's eye she nodded, and the woman offered a wink of acknowledgement in return. Taking Begilda by the arm, Osgyth made for the door at the rear of the longhall. Quietly they bolted it behind them. Now the only way out was the great northern entrance, double doors crafted from solid oak and bound in iron.

She was alone with these killers, and the temptation to flee through those doors almost stripped her frayed nerves to nought but threads. Instead, she stood at the end of the feast table, tall and proud, as those Franks continued to holler and carouse.

'My lords,' she announced, but her voice lacked conviction and was ignored amid the clangour. 'My lords.'

This time louder, stronger, powerful enough to quiet them, and they glared at her as though she had just insulted their precious king.

Under the gaze of these ogres she could barely catch her breath, but she could not falter now. Not so close to the end.

'I would play a song for you, my lords. If it would please you, of course.'

A laugh of disdain from one, as another spurted ale from his mouth in amusement. She thought that perhaps they would chastise her for her boldness, but the one at the head of the table, the one who had lifted his cup in a mock toast to her father, raised his hand for the others to be quiet.

'A song would be fitting, I think. What say the rest of you?'

He raised an eyebrow, glaring across the table as though challenging any of them to disagree. If any did, they lacked the nerve to speak it.

On the wall beside the doors hung a lyre, and next to it a hunting horn. She took the instrument and sat at the end of the table, ignoring the smirking knights as she took a deep breath.

With one finger she caressed the strings, a single note calling the longhall to order. Then with her right hand she plucked a chord, before following it with an intricate refrain. The knights fell silent, realising they were watching a skilled minstrel. She began to play 'The Seafarer', a lilting tune she had learned when nothing but a girl. It would have been fitting for her to also sing that poem, but her voice was lost in her throat, and all she could do was tease each note and chord, remembering well how she had played it for her father on so many happier nights.

A tear threatened to break across her cheek, but she

ground her teeth, concentrating on that melody, conscious that all the while these men were watching, perhaps thinking of far-off family, perhaps just glad for a moment to be carried away by the music.

From the corner of her eye she saw one of the men slump forward, overcome by his excesses as another reclined in his chair, closing his eyes. By the time she finished, these men, these beasts who had come for murder, looked more like children listening to a mother's lullaby.

Slowly she stood, and the one at the head of the table began to clap his approval. When she turned toward the doors, the others joined in, calling for more.

'Another,' one of them demanded. 'Play another.'

She unbarred the doors, swinging them wide, letting the chill autumn breeze blow through the hall. Her hand trembled as she placed the lyre back on its hook and grasped the hunting horn from its place on the wall.

'I will play you another,' she said, turning to them. 'I will play you one last dirge… to mark your passing.'

The horn resounded as she blew with all her might, filling the longhall with a lament so long and loud one of those knights clapped hands to his ears. It heralded the sound of barking hounds, stirred into a frenzy by the horn's signal. The first of them swept by so swiftly her skirts were whipped in a flurry. It leapt on the nearest knight before he could think to rise from his stupor, a snarl on its lips as it latched jaws to his throat.

More hounds followed, her faithful alauntes, one after the other till they made a score, growling and barking as they fell upon their prey. All night she had filled those flagons, strong ale from solid oak barrels. But that was not all. Each cup had been laced with henbane to keep these bastards pliant, and boar's blood to act as bait and drive her alauntes into a fury. They had smelled the scent of their game all night, and now they were unleashed.

How she would have loved to watch as they ripped and tore, dragging men from their chairs to tear at their flesh, but instead she stepped through the open doors. As the screams and snarls echoed behind her, she took up the bow she had hidden above the lintel, along with a quiver full of newly fletched arrows.

With care she plucked the first arrow and nocked. One of the knights had managed to rise, a hound latched to his arm but still he had drawn his blade. The bowstring creaked as she drew it to her cheek and let fly. It whipped the air, thudding into his chest, and he fell, for her dog to finish its sport.

A second arrow nocked as she scanned the hall. One of them had freed himself from the chaos, running to the locked door on the hall's eastern wall, only to find it was bolted. His fingers tore at the handle, but it would not open. She loosed, the arrow piercing his neck and he stumbled, eyes widening in panic as he realised his life was over.

One after the other she nocked and loosed those arrows as the tumult subsided. She did not stop until the quiver was empty. More than a dozen men had come this night to laugh and make merry in the hall of a butchered thegn. Instead, they met their end, screaming in terror as Eskil's dead eyes watched each one perish.

When the hall finally fell silent but for the sound of feasting alauntes, she placed her bow down on the table and trod through the carnage. At the head of the table still sat the leader of these men. His eyes stared as he gasped in the last of his breath, an arrow in his ribs, arm torn down to the bone. A sword lay discarded on the ground, and she picked it up before moving to his side.

'Who sent you here?' she asked, pressing the blade to his chest. 'Which Frankish cur ordered you to take this estate by force?'

His eyes wandered for a moment before they focused on her. She could see the disbelief in his eyes, the fear. 'It was… it was Lord Frederic. It was all him. Please… Please I—'

'Who?'

'Frederic. He is brother by marriage to the Earl Wilhelm of Warenne. Please, wait—'

She sank the sword deep, taking her time as he gasped his last, eyes widening before his head slumped forward. No one else was breathing but for her faithful hounds. The only ones left to feast in her father's hall.

Outside the night was still, the cold air matching the chill in her heart. She had done murder here, but it had been righteous. Her father could rest, but there were still so many others left who would suffer. This was not the end of it. Not the end by far.

'Hereswyde.'

She turned at the sound of her name, seeing a man step into the torchlight wearing the vestments of an abbot. He was bent by his years, bald pate shining atop a kindly face.

'Uncle Brand,' she whispered. 'I warned you not to come.'

'And yet here I am. And this is what I find. Slaughter, most foul.'

'Of our enemies. Would you prefer it if I was the one slain?'

He lowered his gaze. 'You know I wouldn't.'

'Then rejoice, and thank the Lord that justice has been done.'

Brand regarded her with a frown. 'Justice? You think this is what Eskil would have wanted?'

'Of course. He was my father. It was my duty—'

'And he was my brother, Hereswyde. I know he would not have wanted you to endanger yourself like this. Not for him, nor any amount of duty.'

She turned back to the longhall. Her hounds were still gorging themselves inside, though some now lay glutted from their feast. 'Yet here we are.'

'What will you do now?' Brand asked. 'Run? Hide? Take up the life of a silvatici in the forest?'

'I will run for now,' she replied. 'But I will not hide forever. I will fight. And there are others who would fight with me. This Frankish king will not sit easily on his throne. I will make sure of it.'

'Then there is nothing I can do to protect you,' Brand said, and she could hear the sadness in that voice.

'There never was,' she answered, turning to him once more. 'Go back to Saint Peter's abbey. Say your prayers. Watch over your flock.' Hereswyde stepped forward and kissed her uncle on his cheek. 'I have my hounds to gather. This hunt has just begun.'

Part One

A Reckoning

I

It had rained that morning, as it seemed to do every morning, and the ground was soft underfoot as he waited at the bottom of the mountain. Half a dozen men stood at his shoulder – hulking men, hair braided, skin scarred and stained with woad. But Styrkar had stood beside fearsome men before. Fought with them and against them. There was no one here who gave him any pause.

The wounds he had suffered at Yorke were all but healed. As he stood, stripped to the waist along with the rest, he felt stronger than he had for many months. Styrkar had built himself anew, in body as well as spirit. Now was his first chance to put it to the test.

'Hearken, men of the glens.'

Máel sat atop his horse, staring down at them. The great chieftain was a formidable sight bedecked in his furs, his thick hair ruffled by the inclement breeze. His eyes bore into them as they waited, but there was a wide grin beaming from his bearded face.

'I have gathered you here at the foot of Creag Chòinnich to offer you a chance to prove yourselves. And you have answered, from Dynbaer and Moreb. From Athall, Aonghas and Gallowa. Proud warriors of Alba. At each other's throats as often as not, but you are not here to fight. As the *ceann mor* I would see us united, for there is a more wicked foe to face in the south, and we must join together if we are to defeat him.'

The men cheered as one, though Styrkar kept his silence. He had been asked to join in this contest as an honoured guest. To represent all the earldoms of the south in King Harold's name, and it was an opportunity he had been unable to refuse.

'You are the bravest and the best of your clans,' Máel continued. 'And with this contest I would hope you can play out your rivalries in a manner befitting. With honour. My token lies at the top of this mountain. Whosoever reaches it first, and brings it to me on the other side, will take pride of place beside me at the feast table tonight. But remember, we will all sup together, no matter who is the victor. I would see your clans united in brotherhood. So do them bloody proud.'

Another cheer from the men, louder than the first. Styrkar could see the zeal in some eyes, and wondered if they were indeed as united as Máel would have liked. This was a victory they all hoped to claim, and most of these men looked willing to shed blood in the seizing of it.

The king of Alba raised a meaty fist to the cloudy sky. Every man at Styrkar's shoulder crouched in anticipation, glaring at Máel, willing him to give them the signal. When his arm came down in a slicing motion, they were off, with Styrkar bolting alongside them.

Ahead, the mountain was covered by a thick forest of pines. There was no trail to lead them to the summit, and Styrkar could only hope the token that awaited was easy enough to spot. But before that he would have to be the first to reach it, and he concentrated on forging ahead as they splashed through a narrow stream before clawing their way up a slope toward the treeline.

To Styrkar's right was a thick-set warrior, growling from his throat as he raced ahead of the pack. To his left, a slim young man opened his rangy gait to catch him. Styrkar was already breathing hard as they reached the trees, but he refused to be left behind, striding on, using the trunks of the pines to propel himself forward.

Once within the darkness of the wood, the three of them began to leave the pack behind, setting a quick pace despite the constant steepening of the slope. They raced through the ferns at their feet, and occasionally Styrkar had to swat at the midges that threatened to choke the air from his lungs. He could see ahead that the bulky warrior was losing his lead to the lanky youth, and it only served to spur him to greater effort. His thighs burned, breath coming in sharp gasps as he refused to be left behind.

Up he struggled, further into the darkening wood. As he dodged another tree he lost sight of the leaders, quietly cursing through his gritted teeth. But he would not give in, would not succumb to defeat until he reached the finish.

A glance over one shoulder and he could see the rest of the contenders were far behind, struggling to pull themselves up the slope. Only three dogs in the race, but Styrkar had work to do before he caught the leaders.

No sooner had he turned back toward the summit, than the thick-set brute stepped from the shadow of a pine. He was fast, head striking forward, butting Styrkar on the bridge of his nose.

The sharp snap of violence rocked him back and he went tumbling back down the slope. When his sense returned, Styrkar was staring up at the boughs, hearing the sound of the others gaining on him. That hairy bastard had confounded him, but the Red Wolf would not be beaten so easily.

Wiping blood from his nose, Styrkar dragged himself to his feet and began to lope on up the hill. He felt himself become incensed, quelling his fury, his need to kill that trickster. This was not the thick of battle – it was a contest between rivals, nothing more. Styrkar had to remember that, lest he go too far and lose the favour of Máel altogether.

His pace quickened, his anger compelling him forward, legs pounding as he charged up the slope. Toward the summit the trees thinned out, revealing a flat clearing dotted with rocks. As he burst from the trees, he heard voices snarling gutturally. The young lad and the brute were wrestling one another amid the rocks. Though the heavy-set bastard looked the stronger, the young lad was holding his own as he wrestled his foe with wiry limbs.

Styrkar caught sight of something lying on a rock nearby. A chain of iron links – the one Máel often wore around his neck as he strode about his court. This must be the token he had spoken of.

Ignoring the two fighters, Styrkar lunged forward,

snatching the chain from the rock. As the men struggled behind him he dashed for the trees to the north and the descent beyond. Before he could reach it, he stopped. The men fought on, snarling and spitting their fury. If no one stopped them they might do one another irreparable harm, and Máel's alliance would be cast to the four winds.

Styrkar darted toward them, grasping the youth who had managed to pin his opponent to the ground and shoving him aside. His squat opponent lurched to his feet, a curse on his lips that was cut short as Styrkar butted him full in the face. The man fell, nose askew, blood flecking his face as he collapsed. Styrkar turned to the boy, and they stared at each other for a moment. It was silent challenge the lad was unwilling to take up.

More noise came from the trees. The rest of the pack was almost upon them, but Styrkar had his prize. He dashed away from the clearing, leaving the rest behind and delving into the woodland once more, consumed by the pines as he raced down the hill.

Descending the slope was nearly as difficult as climbing it, and Styrkar was almost unbalanced several times, but he managed to avoid tumbling through the ferns. He could hear the gathered spectators waiting for them beyond the wood at the foot of the mountain. Not too much farther and he would be able to claim his victory.

But should he? This was not his victory to claim. Máel had gathered these men of the clans to form an alliance. If Styrkar won this contest it might only cause contention between them that a foreigner had stolen their glory.

He stopped just inside the treeline, spying the crowd beyond it, Máel standing tall among them, waiting for the victor to appear. The sound of tramping feet made him turn, and Styrkar saw the young warrior still in pursuit. He came to within a few feet of Styrkar and stopped, breath ragged as he eyed the iron chain he had almost claimed for his own.

'Take it,' Styrkar said, offering Máel's token. 'You deserve it, boy.'

If he felt any humiliation that he was being gifted the prize, he did not show it. Instead, he snatched the chain from Styrkar's grip and sprinted from the woodland. Styrkar stood and watched as the crowd cheered when their victor appeared, quickly surrounding him and slapping his back in congratulation.

The rest of the contenders appeared through the trees, some almost fit to collapse from their exertion, and Styrkar walked with them from the woods. He stood and watched as the men and women of their clans greeted the gallant losers in their own way. Some offered words of consolation, while others chided them for laggards. Pipes began to play as the young victor was hoisted upon shoulders, raising his prize aloft for all to see. As Styrkar took in the sight, he felt a hand squeeze his shoulder.

'Don't feel too bad, Red Wolf,' Edgar said above the sudden noise. 'You have been through much these recent months. I'm sure on your best day you would have won victory with ease.'

'Maybe you're right,' Styrkar replied, offering Edgar a knowing wink.

It brought a smile to Edgar's face and he clapped Styrkar on the back. 'When you have recovered your breath, we must speak with the earls. Our time is almost upon us.'

'Then lead on,' he replied. 'I have breath enough for all of them.'

Edgar nodded, offering a wave to Máel, who was regaling the winner with praise. Edgar's sister Margret was close by the king's side, offering her own words of congratulation. Since Styrkar had come to Alba he had seen the bond of affection strengthen between her and Alba's chieftain. He could only imagine that soon there would be talk of marriage. It would only consolidate Edgar's alliance.

He followed Edgar away from the crowd as it prepared for the coming feast. Tents had been erected all around the foot of the mountain, and the aroma of spitted deer drifted across the encampment. All thought of feasting left Styrkar's mind as they approached an awning pitched toward the edge of the camp. The earls waited there – the cousins Waltheof and Gospatric, and Maerlswein by their side looking well recovered from the wound he had suffered at Yorke. A tall man was among them, one Styrkar did not recognise. A fur cloak was wrapped about him, beard spilling over his broad chest, his head shaved to the scalp.

'Red Wolf,' said Maerlswein as they drew closer. 'Enjoy your sport?'

'Well enough,' he replied, eyeing the newcomer.

'This is Lord Siward Barn,' Edgar said. 'A thegn of renown in the northern shires. He has come to join our cause and bears no love for the king in the south. He brings more warriors to swell our growing numbers.'

'I have heard of him,' Styrkar said offering his arm.

'And I have heard of you,' Siward replied, gripping Styrkar's arm. 'There's not a man loyal to King Harold doesn't know the name Red Wolf.'

Maerlswein stepped forward with a grin. 'And now we are all acquainted, to business. We have waited long enough. The time to cross back over the border and take the fight to the Franks is almost upon us.'

'Aye,' said Gospatric. 'With the help of the ceann mor we will strike back at William's army and retake our lands. King Máel will raid deep into the northern territories, while together we will take back Yorke.'

As much as Styrkar felt his blood run hot at the prospect, he had his doubts. 'We took Yorke once and could not hold it. What makes you think this time will be any different?'

Edgar grinned. 'Because, my friend, while you were recovering from your wounds, I have not been idle. My messengers crossed the sea to Danmork, sending word of our fight against the Bastard. They returned just this morning with news that King Sweyn has offered to help us, but we must travel there in person to entreat his aid.'

'A ship is readied at port,' said Maerlswein. 'Edgar and myself will set sail on the morrow. But if we had a true Dane with us, it might help us better persuade Sweyn to our cause. What do you say? Will you come and meet with this Danish king?'

It was an easy question to answer. 'I say yes. If it will help us bring down the usurper, then it is a journey worth taking.'

Edgar laughed, slapping Styrkar on the back again. 'Then it is settled. We sail at first light. But before that, it would be churlish of us not to take advantage of Máel's hospitality one last time.'

The earls raised their voices in agreement, and began to make their way back toward the sweet smell of roasting deer. Styrkar followed, thinking on what might await him in Danmørk. Sweyn was a powerful man, that was for certain. A man who might have been Styrkar's own king, had fate not brought Harald Sigurdsson to his home all those years ago. Soon, Styrkar would judge for himself if he would have made a worthy one.

2

Roeskildia, Danmǫrk, July 1069

The crossing was rough, but Styrkar had weathered storms before. He could only hope it was not an ill portent of what awaited them in the court of King Sweyn. As the sun shone over the port ahead of them, he could not shirk the feeling of disquiet. Even with Edgar and the irascible Maerlswein at his shoulder, he knew they might yet be sailing into danger.

His cloak billowed as they cruised toward the harbour, the air crisp, gulls screeching their welcome. The high-sided fjord they had rowed along for miles opened out onto flat land, and the capital of Danmǫrk sprawled ahead of them. He had expected some memories of his childhood to flood back on returning to his homeland after so many years, but all he saw was the port city of yet another foreign king. Much like Dublin, this one churned with bustle, the seafront awash with traders. In the distance, beyond the thatched roofs that lined the shore, a huge building of stone was under construction. No doubt a cathedral of the Christian god, slowly rising to dominate the landscape.

Once the ship had drifted up to the jetty and its mooring ropes were secured, Styrkar spied half a dozen warriors waiting ashore. Their helms glinted in the sun, embroidered cloaks blowing in the breeze as they looked toward the newly landed ship.

'Looks like we're expected,' Maerlswein grunted.

Edgar jumped from the boat and onto the jetty. 'Then let's not keep the king waiting.' He glanced over his shoulder toward them. 'And let me do the talking.'

Maerlswein and Styrkar followed him up toward the harbour and the waiting housecarls.

'Do you think this could be a trap?' Styrkar whispered, tightening his hold on the axe he carried on one shoulder.

'Every chance,' Maerlswein replied matter-of-factly. 'It could better serve Sweyn's purpose to ransom us to the Bastard rather than fight him.'

'I'll be ransomed to no man,' Styrkar replied, lengthening his stride as Edgar exchanged words with the men ahead.

Before he could reach them, Edgar turned with a smile, gesturing that they both follow him. The Danish housecarls led them along the harbourfront to a road that cut through the middle of the city. They didn't have to follow it far before they reached an opulent longhall – its beams, rafters and even the stone footings embossed with intricate carvings, animals of every kind rendered into the thatch. The doors stood open, and a welcome aroma of spitted pig drifted from within.

Styrkar followed Edgar and the housecarls inside, seeing the hall was filled with men and women awaiting their arrival. From the opulence of their dress they were jarls and magnates King Sweyn had summoned from every corner of Danmork to greet his esteemed guests. Still, it did little to put Styrkar at ease as they made their way deeper into the hall. He gripped tight to the axe at his shoulder, anticipating danger, but surely if the Danish king intended them harm he would never have allowed them to enter bearing weapons.

The crowd moved aside as the housecarls led them through the press to reveal a throne raised on its dais. Upon it sat a man of fifty winters, his long blond hair and moustache flecked with grey. He watched them intently with piercing blue eyes, and as Edgar came to stand before him, he smiled in greeting.

'The Aetheling,' Sweyn said, his voice deep but giving nothing away as to his intentions.

A hush had descended on the hall. Styrkar noted a man standing not far to the king's right, hand on the pommel of his sword. Such was his resemblance to Sweyn that Styrkar thought they could be twins, only this one looked younger, his hair lacking the grey that marred the king's.

Edgar bowed his head, as did Maerlswein. Despite his reluctance, Styrkar found himself overcome by the occasion, and he too bowed in respect.

'King Sweyn,' Edgar said. 'I am honoured you have invited me to your court, to hear my entreaty for aid.'

'How could I commit to your cause without first measuring your worth? Without seeing the boy who considers himself a king?'

If the insinuation was intended to provoke it did the trick, and Edgar took a step toward the throne, his chin raised. 'I am no boy, as you can see. I have fought for the right to wear the crown of England. I have bled for it.'

Sweyn raised his eyebrow with scepticism. 'Yet it still sits atop another man's head.'

'And that is why I have crossed the sea to be here. The Bastard did not win the throne of England alone. He beseeched the aid of his allies to do it, and to defeat him I would do the same.'

'Indeed he did,' Sweyn replied with a nod. 'And rewarded them handsomely for their help. So tell me, Aetheling: what would be Sweyn Estridsson's reward for helping you? Will it be land? Riches?'

'Both, should you wish them,' Edgar said, perhaps a little too quickly. 'And you may keep what you plunder. I would have your warriors harry the coast to the south while I return to the north and gather my followers for an attack on the northern city of Yorke. There are rich pickings there. Even for you, great king.'

Sweyn considered the offer for a moment, before fixing Edgar with a stern glare. 'So my reward is land and plunder? And you would offer me a portion of your kingdom? You would bargain with me for only half a throne?'

Styrkar could see Edgar's jaw tighten in frustration. 'I would take what is mine under God. The Franks have no right to it.'

Sweyn shook his head. 'If our Lord God agreed, you would already wear the crown. If he did not think the Franks worthy of it, then surely it would still rest upon Harold Godwinson's brow. But he fell before the might of the Bastard Duke.'

At the mention of his former master, Styrkar felt his anger boil. Edgar had come to entreat the Danish king's aid, but here he was being belittled. Now it seemed as though King Sweyn was approving of the Frankish usurper's claim to the crown. What right had he to do that? This Danish king who had failed to defeat his own enemies, yet still kept his crown?

Styrkar took a step forward, mindful of the surrounding housecarls placing hands on their weapons. To his credit, Sweyn did not move a muscle, despite the axe still resting on Styrkar's shoulder.

'And I fought with Harold that day,' he announced to the king and anyone else who cared to listen. 'I bled, and I fell alongside him. But I was spared death. Not by my gods and not by yours. The gods do not decide who lives and who dies, nor who wears a crown. It is men who decide such things. I have seen how fearsome this Frankish king is. Faced his knights and their warhorses. And you should fear him too, King of the Danes, just as you feared Sigurdsson.'

Silence, before he heard Maerlswein let out a long sigh of resignation. If Sweyn took the outburst as an insult, it could well mean death for all three of them.

The king rose, his face a sullen mask as he took a step down from his carven throne. He limped on his right leg – most likely a wound from battle. Possibly a battle fought against Sigurdsson himself.

Sweyn stood before Styrkar, almost as tall, staring into his eyes before his mouth creased in a smile. 'Does the Red Wolf try and shame me?' he barked. 'And in front of my own court?' There was nervous laughter from among the gathered crowd. They, like Styrkar had no idea what to expect next. 'Yes, I have heard of the Red Wolf – your reputation has even reached these shores. One of our own countrymen, taken as a boy to serve King Harold of the Saxons.'

Styrkar shook his head. 'It was not Harold who took me. It was Sigurdsson who burned my town and made me a slave. King Harold set me free.'

Sweyn nodded knowingly. 'Then we both had good reason to hate that dog. But he is dead, and we are both alive. And in another life it might have been me who profited from the Red Wolf's loyalty – for who does not know how faithfully you served your king? So tell me,' he gestured to Edgar, 'are you just as loyal to the Aetheling?'

'I am,' Styrkar replied without hesitation.

Sweyn took a step back and regarded Edgar. 'Then he must indeed be worthy. And for that I will aid you, Edgar who would be king under God.'

A rousing cheer of approval echoed through the longhall. Immediately all tension seemed to leave the cloying confines, and Styrkar found himself loosening his grip on the axe at his shoulder.

'Asbjorn!' Sweyn called above the noise. The warrior who stood beside the king's throne took a step forward. 'My brother here will sail with his fleet at your behest, Aetheling. He will set the south of England aflame and burn the Franks from their lair. Then, before they can even bury their dead, he will meet you with your army in the north, and together you can take back Yorke. Will that satisfy you?'

Edgar bowed. 'It will, King Sweyn. We will sail back

on the morning tide and prepare for his arrival, where the Black River meets the sea.'

The king gripped Edgar's arms. 'Then tonight you will be my honoured guest. There will be a feast in celebration of our alliance later – you have had a long journey, I am sure.'

After bowing once more, Edgar and Maerlswein turned to leave, but Styrkar could not join them, not yet. He held Sweyn's gaze, conscious that others were watching him, not least of all the king's brother Asbjorn.

'Is there more the Red Wolf has to say?' Sweyn asked.

And there was. He had crossed the sea to a homeland he had not seen in almost twenty summers. Now he stood among his people it was difficult to leave so quickly.

'There is, King of the Danes. I would ask a favour of my own.'

'Then speak it,' Sweyn said.

Styrkar turned to Asbjorn. 'I would join your brother on his raid. I would sail with his fleet and bring death to the Franks alongside my countrymen.'

Sweyn nodded his approval along with Asbjorn, before turning to Edgar. 'And does the Aetheling approve?'

Edgar stepped forward and clapped a hand to Styrkar's shoulder. 'He does. Though I would be a fool to refuse – it is a brave man who tries to keep the Red Wolf leashed when he smells blood.'

'Then it is decided,' Sweyn said with a grin. 'I am sure my brother will be only too happy to have the Red Wolf sail with his fleet.'

Styrkar nodded his thanks, before turning to say his goodbyes to Edgar and Maerlswein. As he did so, a steward approached the king, whispering a message in his ear. The king nodded his acknowledgement before turning to Styrkar once more.

'It seems your arrival in my court is welcome news to one of my guests. They would speak with you, Red Wolf.'

'And who is this guest?'

'Why, the Lady Gytha has resided here under my protection for some months now.'

Styrkar felt his mouth go dry. Lady Gytha, the mother of King Harold. And she wanted an audience with him. It could only be to chastise him – to castigate Styrkar for his failure to protect her son. For betraying her grandsons. Although he did not fear that she would do him harm, Styrkar knew she was a woman of formidable reputation, more likely to damn him for shame as anyone. But he was the Red Wolf, and he would endure this battle as he did all others.

'Very well,' he replied. 'Take me to her.'

With a nod of farewell to Edgar and Maerlswein, Styrkar followed the steward from the longhouse. He was led out into the crisp air and then north through the streets. The cathedral stood ahead of them, and though it was not yet fully built it still loomed ominously. The steward stopped at the entrance and beckoned for Styrkar to proceed through an open archway. He paused at the threshold, before leaning his axe against the stonework and striding inside to face his fate.

It was dark within, the candles that flickered in their sconces doing little to penetrate the long shadows dominating the interior. There were a few priests going about their business, but Styrkar's eye was drawn to a woman on her knees before the altar, head bent in prayer. He walked toward her, his footsteps echoing before he stood and waited for her to finish. All the while he prepared himself, waiting for her to vent her spite. For her to lash him with her grief and hate.

Slowly the woman stood, bowing before the altar and turning to face him. Styrkar let out a breath as he saw this was not the Gytha he had expected. It was not King Harold's mother who regarded him with sadness in her dark eyes... but his daughter.

'Styrkar,' she said quietly.

'Gytha,' he replied, taking a step forward to embrace her, before stopping himself. 'What are you doing in this place? How did you get here?'

'My aunt Ealdgyth thought it safest for me to be brought to the court of King Sweyn. He has been a most gracious host. At my aunt's request he has arranged a suitable husband for me. I am to be wed very soon.'

'Wed? But to who?'

'I am betrothed to Volodymyr Monomakh, Prince of Ruthenia.'

Styrkar's hand was shaking, and he found it difficult to speak. All his fear at meeting Harold's mother was gone now, only to be replaced with guilt.

Gytha moved forward, taking his hand in hers. He almost snatched it back as though her touch might burn him.

'Be happy for me, Styrkar. It is a good match; I could not have hoped for more. I will be a queen. My sons will be kings and princes all.'

He gripped her hand tight, and she squeezed it back. 'It is just... I...'

'Do not torture yourself over what happened, Styrkar. You are but one man. And an army could not save my father that day.'

She was right. But did she know of his other misdeeds? How he had betrayed her brothers for the love of Gisela? How he broke his oaths and fought against them?

'I am not the man you think I am,' he whispered.

Even now, when faced with all he had done, he could not admit the truth. The shame of that cut deeper than any blade.

'None of us are what we thought we would be, Styrkar. But we must accept our fate, or the thought of what could have been might destroy us. Know that my sister, Gunhild, is safe in an abbey. My brother, Ulf, resides under the protection of a Frankish lord. All is not lost.'

'But I should have defended them to my death.'

'No,' Gytha said, so forcefully it reminded Styrkar of the grandmother after who she had been named. 'You are not to blame yourself. This was none of your doing. It was not you who came across the sea to destroy. It was the duke.'

'I don't know what to say to you.'

She forced a smile on her face. A face so young with innocence but with the eyes of a woman grown. 'I only wanted to see you, that I might ask you one thing, Styrkar.'

'Anything,' he replied.

The smile shrank from her lips, brow furrowing with determination. 'I know you are to return to England. I know you will continue the fight against the usurper. So I would ask only one thing of you, Red Wolf. Will you act as my hand of vengeance?'

Suddenly none of his betrayals seemed to matter. With

that one question she had offered him a way to absolve himself for his treachery against her brothers.

Styrkar gazed deep into that young girl's eyes. That girl who would one day be a queen.

'I will.'

3

He thought he would be used to the smell by now, but this city somehow managed to stink morning, noon and night, no matter how long he was exposed to it. At least it was safe now. Or at least relatively.

The great gate at Yorke's southern extent had been rebuilt, a steady flow of traders and travellers making their way in and out. Knights and men-at-arms guarded the way, keeping the peace. And here was Ronan – thrust among them, reduced to the role of sentry. It was an ignominious duty, standing at the main thoroughfare, watching through that gateway to the green fields beyond, and doing his best to ignore the stink of shit behind.

This posting might have been less taxing had he friends about him to alleviate the tedium, but Ronan had no friends here. He had always been shunned. Disrespected. Ignored. But for Aldus, he had made no real friends in either Frankia or England. Earl Brian might have been considered a friend of sorts, but where was he now? Were he the friend

Ronan had thought, then surely he would have sent word to Mallet that Ronan was needed to the south in Cornualge. He could have travelled to those greener pastures and helped Brian defend his new castle. But no, there had been no word. He had been left in the service of a madman in the north. A handsome smiling tyrant, only concerned with his own betterment.

Though weren't they all?

Ronan tried not to think on that now. It seemed his dreams of a lordship were further away than ever, as he stood ankle-deep in the mud, ignoring the niggling pain in his leg. How long he would be able to endure this, who could say? Certainly it was no worse than being captive to the Saxons. To running for days through the freezing cold. Although at least then he had been fuelled by the thrill of escape. The joy of being free. Now it felt as though he had been bound once more. Forced to abandon any ambitions he might have harboured, in order to follow the desires of his betters.

'Ho there!'

Ronan was distracted from his misery by the voice of a gate guard standing nearby. He had stopped a cart at the entrance to the city, its driver pulling the reins to cease the relentless plodding of his weary carthorse.

'What are you bringing in?' the guard asked.

The driver motioned lazily to the back of the cart that he'd covered with animal hide. 'Barley for the brewer.'

Ronan moved closer to the cart. It was his job to oversee security at this gate, and he may as well do it right.

'Where have you come from?' he asked.

The driver took his cap from his head and wiped the

dewdrop from the end of his nose with a sniff. 'Farmstead over at Rudeston. It's just barley for the brewer.'

'Yes, you said that,' Ronan replied as he pulled back the hide.

The man was right: it was indeed barley piled high in the back of the cart. Two of the other gate guards were paying an interest now, one shoving his spear deep into the piled crop. With every thrust, the driver of the cart flinched a little.

'Nothing here,' said the guard with one final stab.

The driver pulled his hat back onto his head. 'I already said, it's just barley—'

'For the brewer,' Ronan finished, digging his hand deep into the cart's load.

His fingers touched sackcloth, and he grasped it, pulling it free of the barley. Wrapped in the cloth were half a dozen swords, newly worked.

Ronan held them up for the driver to see. 'Are these for the brewer too?'

The man's eyes went wide and the reins fell from his hands. Before he could think to flee, one of the other guards grabbed his coat and dragged him from the wagon. He went sprawling in the mud, taking a firm kick to the ribs before he could rise.

'Bastard,' said one of the guards, before giving him another kick. 'Rebellious fucker.'

The other men were emboldened at the violence, rushing forward to join in.

'We should perhaps question him?' Ronan said above the sudden ruckus. 'Maybe find out what he... Oh forget it.'

The driver was squealing as he was kicked bloody by

the guards. There was no way Ronan would be able to stop them before they'd had their sport, and the driver was unlikely to be able to tell them who the swords were intended for if he was dead. Maybe it *was* just the brewer.

A short man made his way toward them, slopping through the mud. Ronan recognised him as one of the castle stewards. He glanced down his nose at the scene of violence before focusing on Ronan.

'The castellan wishes to speak with you,' he said, quite out of breath.

'For what?' Ronan replied.

The steward shrugged. 'That's all I know.'

Some bloody help he was. Shaking his head, Ronan left the steward and the sound of a man being kicked to death behind him, as he trogged his way through the streets toward the newly rebuilt fort.

Curse this posting and curse his inability to refuse it. But how could he? Sheriff Mallet had been most insistent, and Ronan still had the burn scar on his chest to prove it. The only consolation was that he had not seen that mad, grinning bastard for days, so busy was he in other parts of the shires. How Ronan would love to have fled, to have gone back south to Brian, but this was his burden to bear. His curse – to be at the perpetual behest of men more powerful and ambitious than he.

By the time he reached the keep, his leg ached with the damp and the effort. Scorch marks still marred the outer stones of the building, where it had been set aflame by the Saxons, but its wooden structure had been replaced. It was heavily guarded, armoured knights standing vigilant at the door, but it was hardly surprising after the slaughter those raiders had unleashed upon Yorke not five months earlier.

Ronan struggled up the stairs to the entrance. None of the men on guard deigned to help him, but neither did they block his path. One advantage of his position at least. The warmth of the interior was a welcome relief from the miserable northern weather, and when he reached the chamber atop the keep he found a fire blazing. At the other side of the room, behind a desk covered in scrolls and missives, sat the castellan of Yorke.

Giselbert of Gant was small for a knight. He was a man of little repute on the battlefield, but he had not attained his position because of his martial prowess. In his thirty summers he had proven himself a skilled tactician, a clever bureaucrat and cunning negotiator. Even as Ronan waited, Giselbert's attention was fixed on the parchments before him as he pored over records of taxation and trade, or whatever it was he organised in this kingdom's northern extents.

'One moment,' he said raising a finger.

'Take all the time you need,' Ronan whispered back. What could he expect other than to be a lower priority than some piece of parchment? Besides, he was just grateful to be inside next to the warmth of a fire.

Giselbert dipped a quill before adding his signature to the scroll he was reading. Then he looked up and smiled.

'Thank you for coming, Ronan. I have important business to discuss.'

'With me?' Ronan replied, feigning humility. 'I am honoured.'

If Giselbert saw through the sarcasm he made no issue

of it. 'I have received word from the king. There have been attacks on the ports of Dover and Sandwice. A vast fleet of Danes making their way north and pillaging what they can from the coastal towns. It appears that Sweyn Estridsson has suddenly decided to add to King William's troubles.'

'May the Lord God curse him by bell, book and candle for the devil he is,' Ronan replied with little enthusiasm, wondering what any of this had to do with him, but still getting an all too familiar pang of dread in the base of his gut.

'Indeed. But in the absence of God, the king must rid himself of these savages in his own way.'

'Why do I get the feeling he won't be doing it alone?'

A smile curled up one side of Giselbert's mouth. 'He has requested aid from every knight and lord loyal to him. The eastern ports must be fortified. We are to send a contingent to Norwic. If this Danish fleet is targeting ports of value, it will inevitably attack there.'

'And I will be waiting,' Ronan said with a sigh.

'That is just the kind of foresight that makes you the natural choice to lead our contingent of men.'

Ronan touched a hand to his chest. 'Once again… honoured.'

Giselbert rose to his feet, his eyes downcast. Was that a look of sympathy? 'You are a man who knows how to get things done, Ronan. The natural choice. Accomplish this, and repel the Danes, and who knows what rewards might await on your return?'

'With all respect, castellan, I have heard that kind of thing before.'

Giselbert took a deep breath. 'Yes, I am sure. But try not

to worry. By the time you get there, there's every chance the Danish fleet will have taken its fill of plunder and passed by Norwic altogether.'

'We both know that's unlikely.'

The castellan nodded. 'Yes, we do. And under normal circumstances you could refuse. But the king's missive came via Mallet himself. I think we both know what that means.'

Ronan nodded. 'Indeed we do.'

It meant he was fucked either way. Refusal was not an option.

'Your men will be ready to leave by morning,' Giselbert said. 'I suggest you get some sleep – it's a long road to Norwic and you'll be riding hard to beat the Danes.'

Ronan bowed. 'Like the wind.'

He turned, and limped from the warmth, down through the fort and out into the drizzle. It was time to prove his worth once more on the promise of a reward he knew was not forthcoming. The best prize he could hope for, and not for the first time, was simply to survive.

4

The sun was setting behind him, casting a long shadow across the beach. Twelve-score boats were lashed together on the shore, bobbing gently on the evening tide. Asbjorn's fleet was a sight to behold. As large as the one Sigurdsson had brought when he defeated the northern earls and took Yorke. This time though, it was not conquest that had brought these invaders across the sea, but plunder.

Styrkar had no idea what he'd expected when he pledged himself to the Danish king so he could join these raiders. Perhaps some connection to his past. A chance to live a life that might have been, had things been different, if only for a few days. Whatever his ambition, it rang hollow now.

They had pillaged the coast all right, ravaged Frankish forts and slaughtered when they could. More importantly, any ships they had found harboured had been set afire. That way, when they eventually reached their rendezvous point in the north, there would be no way the enemy could launch a counter-attack with any speed. But despite their success, they had suffered casualties. Only today, thirty of their number had been killed as they assaulted the fort. Styrkar had watched men die as these hulking Danes failed to breach the walls at Gippeswic. Still, they celebrated as though it had been a great victory.

He could hear them now, just beyond the grass-covered rise. Kristian, the stout bishop of Aarhus, was saying his prayers. Showering those huge Danes with blessings, reassuring them that despite their losses, the god they worshipped still watched over them. Styrkar was not so sure. Regardless of the corpses they had made, and the treasure they had looted, they had still set themselves a difficult task. There would be much more death to come before they faced the Franks at Yorke. More still before they could confront the usurper. Styrkar could only hope that the king of the Danes would stay true to his word until that day came, and his men loyal to Edgar.

No sooner had the bishop finished his sermon, than the noise of the Danes rose on the evening air. Despite losing brothers, they were in good spirits, looking forward to the plunder that lay ahead. But then, men of violence often treated death as a minor inconvenience, only looking to the rewards their brutality might win them.

Styrkar turned, walking up the grassy hillock to see the encampment before him – fires already lit as the Danes hunkered around, sharing cured meats and the drink they had brought or looted. With every step he took through the camp he was greeted with a nod of acknowledgement or toasted with a raised cup. It was no surprise; Styrkar had more than proven his worth alongside these veterans. None among their number had slain more Franks than the Red Wolf.

He passed the brooding form of a jarl named Thurkill, seated beside his sons. His face brightened at seeing Styrkar, and he offered a nod of respect. His name was mentioned in quiet reverence as he moved among these warriors. They recognised him as a kindred soul, a man who might have been one of them had fate treated him differently. But the Red Wolf was not one of them – he was alone in this, as he was in all things. He might have fought beside them, taken the lives of their shared enemies, but he would never be a true Dane. His real master was dead, his adopted country stolen by invaders. All he had left was his unquenchable thirst for a reckoning.

A young warrior moved to block his path, a smile on his face but his eyes keen. He held out a cup.

'Drink, Red Wolf?'

Styrkar nodded his thanks, taking the cup before the man stood aside. He lifted it to his lips, tasting the rich apple wine. They had plundered barrels of it from the settlement at Dover, and Styrkar found it to his taste, unlike most ale or mead. For a moment he considered staying, joining in with the merriment around him, but he knew he did not belong here. Better that he leave the Danes to their feasting before he found himself enjoying their company a little too much. Edgar was his man now, not the king of Danmork. Styrkar knew from hard experience that allies you made at dawn could well be enemies by twilight, and he was loath to make friends with men he might later have to kill.

At the other side of the camp was another grassy hillock, this one rising to a stand of trees that sheltered them from any prying eyes inland. Styrkar sat himself among the tall grass, laying his axe down before he took another sip of the wine. The camp would soon become more raucous as they celebrated their dead. They mourned with curious jubilance, these Danes. No lamenting the passing of their brothers, and Styrkar could not bring himself to consider it was the wrong way.

As he sat, and the sky darkened to night, a tall figure approached him from the camp. Styrkar recognised the broad silhouette of Asbjorn making his way closer, but did not feel the need to stand and greet the Danish prince.

'Red Wolf,' Asbjorn said. 'May I sit with you a while?'

'Not revelling with your men?'

Asbjorn shrugged his big shoulders before sitting himself in the grass beside Styrkar. 'I am getting no younger, my friend. I find these days it is better to rest when there is still fighting to be done.'

'A sound philosophy.'

'Besides, this has not been our best day by far.' Asbjorn sighed, not hiding his frustration. 'I lost a ship's contingent. Warriors. Brothers. It is almost as though the Franks knew we were coming.'

Styrkar nodded. 'Yes. Word of our raid will have travelled fast. From here to the north the fighting will be harder.'

'Ach, hard fighting is part of the reason I came. My brother sits with a crown upon his head, so what is a second son to do but carve out his own name in glory?' Asbjorn's eyes flared in the light of the campfires. 'And Yorke will bring riches all its own when we finally reach it. As long as your friend Edgar is good to his word.'

'Do not worry on that score,' Styrkar replied, sensing Asbjorn's doubt. 'He is young, but he has already proven himself a man who can be trusted. He will honour his debts to your brother.'

'And what about you, Styrkar? What has this Aetheling offered the Red Wolf that he would follow so faithfully? Are you due your own lands and riches?'

'I have asked for nothing. Other than a chance to kill the Franks and drive them from these isles.'

Asbjorn considered the answer for a moment, before he barked a long loud laugh. The sound of it cut across the camp, but he stopped when he realised Styrkar had not spoken in jest.

'You're serious, aren't you. Even though you know it is impossible. You could never slay every last Frank in this kingdom. It will be the death of you, and yet you'll try anyway. You must have truly loved your dead king.'

'I did,' Styrkar replied. 'But he is not all I have lost since the Frankish duke sailed to this island.'

Asbjorn scratched at his corn-yellow beard as he considered Styrkar's words. 'A woman then? Yes, I have seen that look before in the faces of other men. Grief and loss can turn us mad with the red hate, and I see it in you often. Now I understand.'

Though the Danish prince was close with his assumption, he could not know the depths of Styrkar's anger. He had lost more than Gisela. More than his king. He had lost Edith who had been as a mother to him. Lost his brothers due to his own betrayal. Lost the daughter he would now never see.

'I was unsure of you, before you joined us,' Asbjorn continued. 'I had heard of the Red Wolf's deeds, for sure, but I did not know if you were really one of us. A true Dane. Now I know it beyond doubt.'

Styrkar turned to regard him. He appreciated the words, and perhaps years ago they would have meant much. Now they were nothing but empty praise. 'I would once have been proud to call myself a Dane. Now I no longer care for homelands. For crowns. For kingdoms. I belong nowhere.'

Asbjorn shrugged. 'We all need to belong somewhere, my friend. We all need family. Something to fight for.'

Styrkar looked out over the camp, listening to the songs being sung and the merriment made over the dead. He would have had a family – something to live for, to fight for – if only he had made a better choice and fled England with Gisela. Now that was all gone.

'Vengeance will be enough,' he said.

Asbjorn sighed, before rising to his feet. He laid a hand on Styrkar's shoulder. 'I hope so, Red Wolf.'

With that, the Dane left him alone on the hillock, looking out toward the sea. Asbjorn needn't have worried – vengeance would have to be enough. It was all he had left.

5

He had brought a hundred spearmen, but even behind the newly built walls of the fort, Ronan still wasn't sure it would be enough. They were fighters all right – seasoned in battle for the most part – but they were not knights. This was no conrois he was a part of. Ronan could only hope the rest of Norwic's defenders were worth their salt. Or better still, that the raid they all anticipated with such fear would never happen.

Along the parapet Ronan watched as the earl spoke to his men. Ralph of Wael was a proven leader, and one of the most powerful in the land now the king had gifted him this eastern territory. Still, he looked nervous, gripping tight to the sword at his side as he glared out toward the coast.

Norwic could have been a stalwart bastion, but it was hastily erected. The castle that stood atop its bailey was still not fully constructed, the parapet surrounding it untested. Though the river meandered by to the east, protecting it from attack, the harbour to the south was still vulnerable from the sea. All eyes had been fixed upon it for the past two days, and at any moment they had expected that Danish fleet to come sailing right at them, sails unfurled, brawny raiders pulling at their oars with zeal. So far, nothing.

'Any sign, Dol-Combourg?'

Ronan drew his eyes from the darkness to the south to see Ralph by his side. He scratched at the stubble of his jaw, which he had been too preoccupied to shave these past days.

'None,' Ronan replied. 'Perhaps God is with us, and the Danes have moved on to riper pastures. Were they to attack we would see their ships from miles away.'

'I hope you are right, my friend.' Ralph clapped a hand to Ronan's shoulder. 'But if not, I am glad you're here, and our past disagreements forgotten.'

It was an empty gesture. They were not friends and never had been. Less than five years before, Ralph had sided against Ronan's father during an uprising in Bretagne. Rivallon of Dol had fought against Duke Conan of Rennes at the behest of William, when he was still just Duke of Normandie. It was a bloody conflict that only ended when Conan was found dead from poisoning. Ralph had picked the wrong side then, but clearly in following William on his crusade against the Saxon king he had reconsidered where his loyalties lay. Loyalties he was no doubt questioning now.

'Of course,' Ronan replied with as convincing a smile as he could twist onto his face. 'We are all servants of King William. All brothers together.'

With a smile and a nod, Ralph moved on along the battlement. Ronan couldn't even bring himself to look at the turncoat as he gazed back over Norwic. The place was quiet. All but abandoned after news of the Danish threat. Ronan could hardly blame them. This was a town of potters and fishermen. It was unlikely they'd be much use against a fleet of savage pirates.

'To the north!'

The cry echoed across the fort, cutting through the silence and striking Ronan right in his gut. Every head turned toward the northern parapet where one of the defenders was gesticulating wildly.

Ralph rushed along the walkway toward the man, and Ronan followed, in no mood to be left in the dark. A murmuring of disquiet was spreading as he limped past archers and spearmen. When he reached the northern side of the palisade, he could see what had provoked the man's panicked cry.

The light of a single torch was making its way from the woods in the distance. It was followed by another, then another until there were too many to count, those beads of light closing in swiftly on the fort.

'Damn those devious curs,' snarled Ralph, gripping the sharpened wooden stumps atop the parapet. 'They have abandoned their ships and seek to assault us from the land.' He turned, and Ronan could see the fear in his eyes. 'Archers! To the northern defences.'

As Ralph's men raced to bolster the rampart and began to crank their crossbows, Ronan watched as those distant lights drew ever closer to the surrounding settlement. A torch was flung atop one of the houses, the thatch catching quickly. Then another, the town starting to blaze as a scream cut through the night.

The first whip of a crossbow string echoed from along

the parapet – too soon, firing at nothing. It didn't stop half a dozen others unleashing their quarrels into the darkness. Ronan heard the whip of an arrow as the Danes returned the favour, their aim much better than that of the defenders. A gurgling cry came from further down the line as one of the archers staggered back, the shaft of an arrow buried in his throat.

Ronan drew his sword. Breath coming in short gasps as he awaited the inevitable. Those Danes had most likely brought ladders. Most likely half of them would scale the walls with their bare hands if they had to, so savage was their reputation. All he could do was stand and wait for that first brutish face to show itself.

Nothing.

As he stood in the brooding quiet, he could feel the tension mounting. Ralph stood amid his men, spears held at the ready. Would there be enough of them to defend this fort? If the rumours spoke true, the Danes had come aboard two hundred ships – there could be thousands of them making ready to wash over the wall, bringing their steel and their bloodlust.

The silence was ended by a cry from across the fort. He glanced to the south, where only a few men remained at the wall. One of them was pointing, gesturing frantically.

'The harbour,' he cried. 'They're attacking from the river.'

Ronan limped across the walkway as quickly as his cursed leg would allow, his heart beating so fast he thought it might burst through his mail. Ralph was by his side as they reached the eastern parapet and glared out onto the night.

Through the gloom he could just make out the silhouettes

of a dozen ships cruising toward the harbourside. In the darkness beyond he knew there would be more.

'They're after our fleet,' Ralph yelled. 'They intend to fire the fleet.'

It seemed he was right about one thing at least.

'What do we do?' asked one of his men.

Ralph turned to Ronan. He was trying to look commanding, but there was terror behind those eyes. 'Dol-Combourg, take your men, defend the harbour. We must protect our ships.'

Ronan glanced back to the south. He had only brought a hundred men. What could they possibly do against a thousand Danes?

'Are you insane?' Ronan replied. 'They cannot be stopped.'

Ralph grasped his shoulder. 'That is the king's fleet,' he bellowed. 'It must be defended. You were sent here to help me, Dol-Combourg. Surely a man like you would not shirk his duty?'

Was it the mention of the king? It couldn't have been the mention of duty that made him think it not such a mad idea. Whatever it was, Ronan suddenly saw the spark of an opportunity. Perhaps a way he could raise himself back from the depths to which he had sunk. To restore his reputation, and earn a chance at glory.

Then again, it was a sure way to end up speared on a Danish lance or beheaded by an axe.

Before he had a chance to consider the worst of all outcomes, he had turned to his men waiting in the courtyard below. 'All right – gather yourselves.'

He limped down from the parapet, ignoring the screaming ache in his leg as he made his way toward the gate. If any of his spearmen thought this a mad idea they didn't think to mention it as the gates to the fort were unbarred and hauled open before them.

Ronan raised his sword, signalling for them to advance, and they marched along the flying bridge, through the smoke and ash drifting down from the burning huts. As he crossed the bailey he saw darkness ahead, but knew those Danes would be waiting. How he would have loved to be on horseback right now, to be riding with his conrois. He would have pushed back those barbarians with ease, smashed them into the sea, but all he had was a hundred men on foot. It would have to be enough.

As they made their way past the fishermen's huts toward the harbour he could see a ship was already on fire, flames crackling in the night and licking at the black sky.

'Brace shields,' Ronan shouted, trying his best to sound valiant. To his credit his voice did not waver.

His men locked their shields, forming a wall as they marched forward relentlessly. Before they even saw the first of the Danes, a volley of arrows hissed from the blackness. Someone screamed behind, and the sound of a man falling to the ground only made Ronan more determined. They ignored the fallen spearman, carrying on relentlessly toward the harbour. There would be time enough to see to their casualties later. For now they had an enemy to face.

More ships were lit on fire as they neared the wide river. Ronan could see hulking figures moving across the harbourfront as every ship was being doused in pitch, torches flung with glee and catching alight. Ralph was right about one thing – the king's fleet would be nought but cinders if the attackers were not stopped. But how to stop them?

At the sight in front of him, Ronan's steely nerve began to fray and drift away on the night air. This was madness. What was he thinking to lead his men in this assault? He had seen all this before and knew how it would end. A bloody fight, as these savages fell upon them with all the hellish lust of their kind. There would be no end that did not result in his death or worse – capture. And then what? The thought did not bear considering.

'The fleet is gone,' Ronan shouted, the strength in his voice now so much ash, just like those ships. 'All we can do is hold them here and defend the fort. Form a barricade.'

At his order, the men obeyed, a group of them moving abandoned carts to block the road up to the gate. Together they hunkered behind the defence, watching, waiting as those flames turned to an inferno on the harbourside.

Ronan still had his sword drawn, but it felt useless in his hand. He had no intention of fighting anyone, especially not these hulking brutes. The Danes were shouting at one another, stirring themselves into a hate-fuelled frenzy. With any luck they would fire the fleet and it would be enough to sate them.

'We have to stop them,' one of the men shouted. 'We must charge. Take the fight to the enemies of the king.'

On any other day, Ronan might have admired the man's bravery. Right now he could only think such overwrought courage would get them killed.

'Hold the line,' Ronan snarled desperately.

He could sense the men around him growing agitated, keen to act, quelling their panic and replacing it with zeal.

'We are men of Bretagne,' the man continued. Ronan didn't even know his name, but then he had not bothered to learn who any of these men were. 'We have conquered these lands. We are not cowards who hunker behind carts while our enemies run rampant.'

Ronan could sense the rest of his spearmen were roused by those words. A couple of them even cheered their assent. Without warning, the man stepped forward and clambered atop the wagon, raising his spear.

'Follow me,' he cried. 'Follow me to victory. For the king!'

Ronan was suddenly reminded of that day at Senlac Hill, when Duke William had been unhorsed. Panic had spread as rumours of William's demise had almost caused his army to rout. But he was not dead, and he had thrown off his helm to show his army he was alive – a man to be followed. A hero. Now this nameless man atop the wagon was doing his best to emulate that heroism. It was a brief reminder of how a man could inspire courage, even when all seemed lost…

A hulking shadow loomed behind the man as he stood there on that barricade. Before he could turn to face it, there came the glint of an axe in the flames. It swept the spearman's head from his shoulders in a single mighty blow. As he fell, a huge warrior stepped forward, his face a mask of fury, teeth shining as he grinned a death's head grin.

No, it could not be. Not now… not here…

The Red Wolf had come.

His axe swung again, smashing another helm. Someone should have struck back, but the men around Ronan were already staggering away in the face of such unbridled violence. Styrkar appeared as a devil in human form. A beast unfettered, and unleashed upon its prey. Before Ronan's men could rally themselves, more Danes leapt up onto the wagon, their axes hacking down at the hapless spearmen.

Ronan was stunned, unable to move, unable to speak. The first of his men turned, dropping his shield and fleeing in the face of such wanton barbarity. Then another, and another, as though they were all suddenly afflicted with cowardice.

Someone knocked into Ronan and he stumbled, feeling that familiar searing pain in his leg. It served to galvanise his thoughts – there was nothing to be won here. He had to run.

As more Danes surged over the wagons, Ronan and his spearmen fled. Arrows flitted past them, the sound of death bellowing from behind as those not quick enough to escape were hacked down by the fearsome Danes. All Ronan could focus on were the open gates to the fort up the bridge ahead. Some of his men were already rushing through, but before Ronan could reach them the desperate defenders within the fort began pushing those gates closed.

No. He could not be left out here. Not to the mercy of the Red Wolf. Not again.

The prospect of that only spurred him to greater effort. His leg screamed in protest, but on he pushed, and it was with relief that Ronan managed to stagger over the threshold before the gates were slammed shut and barred behind him. He breathed heavily, his hands shaking as he gripped his worthless sword, fighting the urge to vomit. When he had gathered his breath, he looked up to see Ralph of Wael glaring at him.

'What's happened?' he barked. 'What's happened to the ships?'

Ronan felt his fear drain to be replaced by a red fury.

He took a staggering step toward Ralph, their noses almost touching. 'Those bastard ships are gone,' he growled. 'By morning they will be kindling.'

Ralph looked incensed. 'The king's fleet is—'

'Fuck the king's fleet,' Ronan spat. 'And fuck you.'

He staggered away from Ralph, who had thankfully nothing more to add. Nearby was a stable, where his horse awaited, already saddled. With some effort, Ronan mounted the steed, urging it across the courtyard toward the gate so recently barred.

'Let me through,' he shouted. The men at the gate looked at one another, unsure of what to do, until Ronan drew his sword. 'I said open the fucking gate.'

Perhaps they thought him about to make one last heroic charge at the Danes, or perhaps they thought him mad with fear, but the men did as they were ordered. The gate opened, allowing the light of the distant fires to illuminate his way. In the distance, the Danes still milled about the harbour, but thankfully there were none lurking at the threshold of the fort. They had only come to burn the king's ships, and burn them they had, but they would not stop here. Those Danes would ravage the coast all the way to the north, and Ronan knew exactly where they would go next.

He kicked his steed and galloped from the safety of the

fort, reining it toward the north-west. As the fires burned behind him he knew those Danes would soon be back aboard their ships and moving swiftly. Ronan could only hope he would beat them to Yorke, and be in time to warn its castellan of what was coming.

6

The mouth of the Black River yawned wide, inviting them back home to the turbulent shores of the north. They had spent the past weeks ravaging the coast, plundering all they could, but still their ships were only half laden. As Styrkar worked the oar, Asbjorn stood at the bow, hand on the steerboard. He looked pensive, as though the past days of raiding and slaughter had done little to sate his thirst for glory. His quest to prove himself as mighty a man as his brother, the king of the Danes, was not done with yet.

Beyond him, in their wake, was the rest of the fleet. Styrkar could see Jarl Thurkill standing at the prow of his ship, as eager to land as Asbjorn. Above the sound of the wind and the keening gulls he could also hear the distant voice of Bishop Kristian bellowing a prayer of thanks that they had reached their destination in one piece.

Asbjorn steered the ship toward the fishing town that lay on the northern shore of the Black River. Men were already waiting to greet them, armed and armoured, spears and helms newly polished. Styrkar squinted across the water at those unfamiliar faces, his instinct for caution nagging at him. Only when he recognised Maerlswein's broad and bearded face among them did he allow his tension to ease.

They raised their oars, some throwing ropes to the waiting hands at the dock, and as the ship was lashed, Asbjorn was the first to debark. Grabbing his axe, Styrkar was quick to follow as the leader of the Danes was met by the waiting Saxon warriors. Maerlswein greeted Styrkar with a firm grip of the hand and a firmer slap to the shoulder.

'Good to see you've returned safe,' said the beaming warrior. 'Has all your recent raiding slaked that appetite for battle?'

Styrkar offered Maerlswein a solid slap to the shoulder in return. 'Slaked? No, my friend. But whetted? Perhaps.'

Maerlswein barked his deep sonorous laugh. 'Thank Christ for that. If we're to see off the Franks from Yorke we'll need that axe of yours sharp and eager.'

Styrkar followed Maerlswein from the tiny harbour toward the town. Asbjorn and his men trailed close behind, and there was an immediate shift in the mood at the dock. Fishermen stopped working their nets and hunched their shoulders, none too keen to become the focus of attention. Women moved their children behind their skirts as the towering Danes made their way along the muddy path from the harbour.

Before he'd even reached the first of the stone-built huts, Styrkar could hear the discordant ring of hammer on anvil. This was more than just a single blacksmith at his work. This was a settlement preparing for war. Those hammers duelled one another above the bustle of the port

– a discordant racket that only served to stir Styrkar's hunger for more bloodshed, just as Maerlswein was hoping.

They passed groups of fighting men, Maerlswein offering the occasional nod of acknowledgement. Most looked like fyrd, their armour little more than leather hide, weapons crudely forged. But among them were some who looked like warriors, mail and helms bereft of any scuffs or dents, as though only recently forged.

The townsfolk watched them in small gaggles, and Styrkar heard the occasional cheer of encouragement as they greeted the debarking Danes. He could only wonder how genuine those shouts of encouragement were. Experience had taught him that the ordinary folk of these lands cared little for who ruled them. Only thegns and ealdormen had anything to gain in this age of rebellion, but oft-times it was the ordinary folk who ended up sacrificed on the altar of their ambition. Most likely they only saw yet more raiders on their shore and considered it best to welcome them with open arms, lest they suffer as so many settlements along the English coast had already suffered.

A longhouse stood at the centre of the mess of huts – a modest affair, much like the rest of the town – and Maerlswein led them inside. Fire burned in a pit at the centre of the room. Edgar, Gospatric and Waltheof sat awaiting them, as Siward Barn stood apart with some of his men. When Styrkar entered, Edgar stood and smiled in greeting.

'The Red Wolf returns. I trust you enjoyed the hunt.'

Styrkar locked arms with him. 'I did. But there is still more game to be slaughtered. And I have brought friends to help in its tracking.'

As though on cue, Asbjorn stepped into the longhouse, joined by Thurkill and the bishop Kristian.

'Welcome,' Edgar said. 'It is good to see you again. Please, sit. There will be meat and mead for all. News of your victories along the coast have already reached us. The Franks must still be reeling in terror.'

'We have done our part for now, Aetheling,' Asbjorn said as he warmed his hands beside the firepit. 'But ravaging ports on the coast will not see your kingdom won.'

'No, it will not. Which is why we must act swiftly. Now you are here we will move toward Yorke. Most likely they will anticipate our attack, but with luck they will have no idea of the size of our host.'

Asbjorn's blond brow creased in a frown. 'That's your plan? Strike hard and fast, and hope the Frankish king has not already fortified the city?'

Waltheof stepped forward before Edgar could answer. 'It's as good a plan as any. Are you with us, Dane? Or have you already glutted yourself with your raiding?'

The room fell silent. Styrkar could sense the tension – the suggestion that Asbjorn was craven and might not join the attack on Yorke hung over them for a moment. From what Styrkar had seen, the Danish warrior was anything but a coward, and Waltheof was treading dangerous ground.

Asbjorn regarded Waltheof blankly. If he felt challenged by the ealdorman's implication, he didn't show it. 'The ships of my fleet still sit high in the water. I would see them filled before I travel back to Danmǫrk. There is much more blood to be spilled before I am glutted, Saxon.'

'Then it's settled,' Edgar said quickly, trying to calm the

air. 'Together we sail for Yorke. And you will have more plunder than you can carry, Asbjorn.'

'And what then?' Asbjorn asked. 'Once we have sacked Yorke and sent the Franks scurrying south? How do you intend to hold the city?'

Edgar's eyes flitted around the room uncertainly. Was he looking for someone to give him the answer? Finally his gaze settled back on Asbjorn.

'Perhaps together, Saxon and Dane, we can hold Yorke against the Franks indefinitely.'

Asbjorn gazed back into the fire. 'What are you offering me, Aetheling? A piece of your kingdom? Just like you offered it to my brother?'

Now it was Gospatric's turn to step forward. 'Hold on, Edgar. We have already decided how our earldoms will be divided. We asked the Danes for their help in return for spoils. Not lands. The best we can hope for is to force King William into an agreement, that he give us control of the north in return for no further rebellion. Our holdings get smaller if we start handing it away to every man who raises a sword beside us.'

Asbjorn looked up from the fire, and this time there was a smile on his grim features. 'And how did it work out the last time you took Yorke? Were you not forced to flee like cowards? It sounds like you need me more than I need you. What price is a few plots of land for the return of your earldom?'

Gospatric's eyes widened, his nostrils flaring in rage. 'We don't need any bloody help from—'

'That's enough,' Styrkar growled, stepping in between the men. 'Asbjorn has come here as our guest. He has pledged himself to aid in our attack on Yorke, but all you can do is question him? If he helps us take the north, he deserves any reward he asks for. I have bled beside him. Only I among you know what he is worth, and I would give him as much land as he asks for. What have you done, Gospatric? Other than piss and moan?'

Gospatric could not hold the Red Wolf's gaze for long, and took a step back beside his cousin.

'First we must take Yorke,' Edgar said. 'Talk of land and plunder can wait. The question of how we hold the city is one for another day.'

'Perhaps not,' Asbjorn said, still staring into the flames. 'I am not the only Dane keen to see you victorious, Aetheling. You promised my brother land and plunder. He will not have forgotten. And so, should we whip those Frankish dogs from the city of Yorke, there is every chance he will come to help you hold it.'

Now it was Edgar's turn to look troubled. 'King Sweyn will come here soon?'

Asbjorn nodded. 'He may. And unless I have missed my guess about the Franks, I think you may need him.'

'Indeed. Should we take Yorke again it is sure to draw King William north. And he will bring all the might of his armies with him.'

Silence, until it was Siward's turn to step forward. He gazed across the gathering, his bald pate shining in the firelight. 'Good. That's good… isn't it? We will have another chance to avenge King Harold. Another chance to rid these shores of those foreign bastards.'

Maerlswein clapped Siward on the shoulder. 'As much as we admire your enthusiasm, lord, you haven't yet faced his knights in battle. Asbjorn aside, we have. And we all bear the scars to prove it. Even with King Sweyn beside us, it will be no easy task to see the Bastard defeated.'

Asbjorn was grinning as he shook his blond head at Edgar. 'I was not expecting such a worrisome bunch of fishwives. I thought I had come to meet with warriors. The Aetheling will not gain the crown without facing the king sooner or later. Or are your northern earls right – you only want to bargain for his scraps?'

'There will be no bargaining,' Styrkar said, bored of their quarrelling. It was time for them to unite. 'The Aetheling will have his crown, or we will all fall. Yorke will be liberated. If it brings Sweyn from his court in Danmørk then all the better. But if not, it is no matter. All I need is another chance to face the Bastard king on the field. When I have slain him, there will be more than enough land to go around. These petty squabbles, this waggling of cocks, it ends. From now we are brothers. We will shed blood at one another's side. If any of you disagree, then there is your way out.'

He gestured to the poorly hung door of oak behind him. The men gathered about did not even look in its direction. His words had stirred them enough that they were all nodding their agreement.

'The Red Wolf speaks harshly,' Edgar said. 'And as usual, I'm of no mind to disagree with him. What say you – do we take Yorke together? As brothers?'

One by one they nodded – first Siward, then Waltheof, then Asbjorn and Gospatric.

'God be praised,' barked the bishop Kristian, and immediately their animosity was forgotten.

The warriors gathered within the modest longhouse were

joined together in agreement, but Styrkar only felt a sudden twinge of sorrow. They were all as brothers in this, but it failed to rouse him as it should. It only reminded him of the brothers he had lost. Of Godwin. Of Edmund. Of Magnus. They should have been here, but instead they were miles away across the sea. Or worse, lying in some anonymous grave.

An alliance had been struck all right, and soon they would attack Yorke. But Styrkar also knew well how such alliances could fracture. Edgar might soon win his victory, but it would take much more than one battle to win his kingdom. Before that could happen, the Red Wolf had a king to kill.

7

At first the road north seemed to never end, but now Ronan recognised the rolling hills ahead of him. He was almost there.

Earninga Strǣt, the locals called it. A virtually endless thoroughfare originally built the last time these lands had been conquered by invaders. Ronan had to hand it to them – they knew how to build a road all right. He wasn't so sure his horse appreciated it, though.

Beneath him the beast huffed and limped its way ever onward. He would have patted it encouragingly, whispered soothing words, but it would get to rest soon enough. Ronan, on the other hand, was cursed with his perpetual labours, and as he saw the city of Yorke looming in the distance, he realised those labours were about to get harder than ever.

The stench of woodsmoke drifted thick and swift on the morning air, blown by errant winds. On its own, that might not have been a cause for concern, but as he squinted across the undulating land south of the city, he was sure he could also spy a rooftop burning within the shadow of the city wall.

Had he come too late? Were those relentless Danes already here, setting their fires and pillaging the place? He could hear no screams of anguish that inevitably accompanied the violence of a settlement under siege. Men milled about the houses to the south of the city, but were those…? Yes, the unmistakable surcoats of Frankish knights.

Ronan spurred his steed to one final burst of effort, forcing it into a trot along the last half-mile of road. Drawing ever closer he realised it was his own countrymen who were setting fire to the dwellings that surrounded the perimeter of the city, rushing here and there with torches raised, as if they were besieging Yorke themselves, rather than defending it. As though to remind him of the danger, the wind whipped up, the flames atop those buildings agitating.

'What's going on here?' Ronan called as he slid down from his saddle, desperately trying to ignore the ache in his arse cheeks, and the sudden burst of pain in his leg.

He was ignored, as those men carried on their burning. The wind gusted again, the flames that consumed one roof starting to spread, setting light to its neighbour. If this gale kept on blowing, it would disperse the fire all across the city.

The peasants who had occupied these dwellings were standing by, helpless. None of them raised a hand to help, but neither did they try and stop the torchbearers. Probably wise, all things considered.

'Stop,' Ronan cried. 'You're going to—'

'Dol-Combourg!'

Ronan resisted the urge to shiver as he recognised the voice that had called his name. From the open gate of the city strode Guillam Mallet, his usually pristine hair windswept, and his face marred by soot.

'My lord,' Ronan said, taking a stumbling step toward Mallet. 'What is happening? This is—'

'Never mind that,' the sheriff replied, waving toward the rampaging fires with a dismissive hand. 'What word from Norwic? Why have you returned alone? Where are your men?'

Ronan swallowed, tasting the acrid smoke in the air. 'Norwic still stands. But its complement of ships is destroyed. I returned with all haste to—'

'Warn me of the coming Danes? You needn't have bothered. I know they are approaching. Scouts from the east have reported their ships are sailing along the river toward us as we speak.'

Ronan gestured helplessly to the fired houses. 'Then why are you setting the city aflame?'

'To give them no shelter when they attack the walls, of course. Clearing the houses gives us a killing ground all around the perimeter defences.'

'But the fire is spreading,' Ronan growled. 'Can't you see?'

Mallet looked toward the fires, as though for the first time. He squinted through the smoke, billowing ever thicker. Already thatched roofs were aflame. Where the ancient stones had collapsed, leaving breaches in the curtain wall, cinders were blowing through into the city. A cry of alarm from within served to galvanise the threat yet further.

'Oh shit,' Mallet breathed.

'Put down those torches,' Ronan shouted at the knights surrounding them, who were now staring with concern at the flaming huts. 'Buckets. Get buckets and fill them from the river.'

Another cry went up from within the city. Ronan limped toward the open gate, Mallet striding alongside. When he peered through the vast arch he saw the worst had indeed happened. The wind had blown embers across the threshold of the city, and the thatched roofs at its perimeter were already smouldering. Panic was starting to spread.

'We must get to the river,' Ronan yelled above the shouts of alarm.

Mallet nodded, setting a brisk pace. The fire was spreading from the east, but as Ronan peered over the rooftops to the north he was sure he could spy more distant flames.

The throng began to thicken, as men, women and children rushed from their houses. His feet slopped along the muddy pathway, boots growing more clogged, his crippled leg screaming at him.

Mallet was yards ahead now, his rangy gait making fast progress through the boggy street. Before Ronan could call for him to wait, a burly peasant barged into Ronan's shoulder. It put him off balance, a sharp twinge lancing up to his knee, and he snarled in pain, falling forward into the mud.

Dirt spattered his face, the shit-strewn ground filling him with revulsion. He tried to push himself up, but someone trod on his back, driving him head-first into the stinking mud. Gritting his teeth, he pushed himself back up again, covered in grime and dung. God damn this place and all its unruly denizens. He should have left it to burn, but knew that he couldn't. If this place fell, how would they defend themselves against the coming onslaught? He had already faced those Danes at Norwic. The prospect of doing it a second time, among the charred cinders of Yorke, was not a prospect he relished.

Ronan staggered to his feet. The smoke was cloying now, taunting the back of his throat as he limped on through the street. Someone raced toward a burning building, water sloshing over the lip of the bucket he was struggling to carry. The man hefted it, flinging the water up the side of a burning house. He may as well have tried to blow out the flames, for all the good it did.

'An axe,' Ronan snarled. 'Get me a damned axe.'

No one took any notice, so stricken were they with panic. Still, Ronan had to do something, and he glanced about, desperate for some way to bring down these burning buildings. A forlorn-looking knight raced past him like a frightened mare, and he grabbed the man by his jerkin.

'We need axes. We have to tear these buildings down – it's the only way to stop the fire spreading.'

The man's eyes were wide with fright, but he nodded anyway. For endless moments Ronan was forced to watch as the city folk vainly tried to curb the inferno rising up to consume their homes. The more water they flung, the more the smoke thickened, until it was impossible to see more than a few feet.

'Here,' shouted a voice.

The knight had returned with more of his fellows. Half a dozen of them all carrying axes.

Ronan took the weapon he was offered. 'This entire row has to come down. Quickly, before the flames take.'

He was irritated at the panic in his own voice, but this was like walking through Hell itself. Still, he and the others began their work, hacking at the wooden structures, battling against the billowing flames, as they desperately tried to collapse the burning houses.

Ronan grunted again and again as he swung, his eyes streaming and stinging from the smoke. As they worked, they were joined by more peasants, emboldened by the knights as they hacked at the wooden walls, but it was all in vain.

Staggering back, he squinted through the cloying grey, seeing that despite their efforts the fires had continued to spread. It was obvious the city was lost.

The axe fell from Ronan's grip as he stumbled north toward the river. Surely it couldn't all be like this – surely the whole of the city had not been consumed by flame. But the further he staggered through that choking cloud, the more he realised his worst fears had come to pass. Yorke was damned. And with no defences the city would fall.

As he gazed out across the river, to see the rooftop of the great church smouldering, he knew there was no way they could ever defend this place from the approaching army.

The river lay just up ahead. Scores of armed men stood alongside the men of Yorke, an endless trail of buckets being handed from one to the other. It was a defiant gesture, but it would never stem the tide. All they were doing was sending yet more clouds of smoke billowing high into the sky. Showing the approaching Saxon army where their next conquest would be.

Mallet stood on that shore, marshalling his men as best

he could. Further up the riverbank was Giselbert, but he was looking on with a forlorn expression on his pinched features.

'We must abandon the city,' Ronan said, as he staggered down the muddy bank. 'It is lost. There is no way we can—'

'We do not flee,' Mallet snarled, still glaring out across the river. 'The king has tasked me with defending his northern territories. I will not fail him. I will not be the man who lost Yorke for a second time.'

'Defend what, Mallet? Look, man. See what has become of the city. There is nothing to save.'

Mallet turned, regarding Ronan with disdain. It was an expression he had seen many times before, on the faces of many men. On Mallet's it bore a particular scorn.

'You are a fucking coward, Dol-Combourg. Why did you even come to these shores? Just to gain land? Riches?'

'We all did,' Ronan replied. His defiance surprised him, but then he had suffered enough at the hands of Mallet and his ilk. He was done with being lectured to.

'Yes, we did. But most of us were prepared to fight. To bleed so that we could keep what we have gained. You though, Ronan. You want to ride on the backs of other men. Earl Brian. Robert of Comines. The king. Me. You would stand in the shadows, watching as other men shed blood so that you can hold out your hands and take a share you have not earned.'

'I have fought as hard as anyone,' Ronan said through gritted teeth. 'You think I have not bled? I have shed as much blood as any of you. More, damn it. I just have the sense to know when we are beaten. When it is time to retreat.'

Mallet sneered, shaking his head. 'Had the king retreated

at Senlac, the Saxon dogs would now be walking on our corpses. We won because we faced them, despite the fury of their swords and axes. You are not worthy of that armour, Dol-Combourg. Go. Run if you must. But pray I never see you again.'

Ronan's jaw was clenched so tight his teeth ached. He would have screamed in Mallet's face, told him he was a madman who would lead this city to its doom. But did he even care anymore? Damn Mallet and his zeal. Damn his loyalty to the king. And damn Yorke to its fate.

Glancing up the riverbank he saw Giselbert still staring at the rising flames north of the river. It looked as though he was as lost as the city.

'Don't worry,' Ronan replied. 'You won't.'

If Mallet heard him, he didn't acknowledge it.

Ronan turned, almost falling as he slid in the mud. With some effort he clawed his way back up the bank, fighting the urge to cough up his guts. The smoke had become so cloying his eyes were streaming, the burning thatch raining ash all across the city. The distant screams of panic had faded away, most likely as the city folk had fled the boundary of Yorke.

A horse. He needed his damned horse, but there was no sign of it. Before he could wonder how to escape, he saw someone had tied a mule to a post close to the southern gate. It pulled against its rein but was secured tight, unable to escape.

'Fear not,' Ronan said, as he untied the beast. 'We're both leaving this doom behind us. For good.'

Bringing the mule under control, he clambered atop its back. It needed no urging to take the road south, away from the rising flames. Ronan was only too happy to cling to its back for as long as he could. Two cowards running to escape their fate.

But at least they would live.

8

Yorke, England, September 1069

They stalked the muddy pathways and alleys, swift hunters on the prowl. Their prey was close – Styrkar could hear the panicked cries in the distance, shouts of alarm in that language they had brought with them across the sea. The last words they would ever speak, once his eye fell upon them.

Edgar had led his attack by land, crossing the open ground swiftly and assaulting the scant defences of the city. At the same time, Asbjorn had led his fleet along the river to strike at the heart of Yorke. It would have been a swift and devastating strategy even had the walls been reinforced, but the city was woefully unprepared.

Yorke was already half burned to the ground as soon as they had debarked at the river. The great church of Christ that had once dominated the skyline stood dark and black in the distance, and the deeper Styrkar and his fellow Danes trod, the more devastation they saw. They would have set fire to all in their path, but the few wooden dwellings that still stood were supported by already crumbling timbers. Not that it stopped them trying. The alliance of Saxon and Dane were doing their best to set the rest of the city aflame, and smoke billowed thick across those scorched rooftops. They had bloodied their weapons quickly, and now looked for more worthy opponents.

A cry of alarm steeled them. A Frankish voice bellowing so close. It stirred the Red Wolf's ire, and his mouth filled with saliva at the noise. There had to be more. Had to be someone left within this wreck of a city worthy enough to face him…

Ahead, he caught sight of men in mail, domed helms dulled by soot, spears held aloft, but they were not racing to fight. They were fleeing.

Two Danes broke from the pack to give chase, but Styrkar kept his steady pace. Despite his bloodlust he had the sense to reserve his energy. He was sure he would need it soon enough.

A groan from further along the path. As the smoke cleared, Styrkar saw a Frankish warrior crawling toward the gutter. His legs were hacked, mail bloodied. For a moment the Red Wolf gripped his axe tighter, wondering if to spare him his suffering, then thought better of it.

'A spear,' he growled. Thurkill stopped close by, then flung him his spear. Styrkar glared down at the man, still crawling through the mud. 'This one is not worth my axe.'

A single thrust into the man's side and he grunted, before going still. Styrkar wrenched the weapon free, before throwing it back to the jarl. More noise from up ahead, and he felt his stomach lurch in anticipation.

They increased their pace, Asbjorn at the head now,

moving with haste. Another gust of wind, a swirl of smoke, and they could see Franks desperate to surrender at the edge of a market square. The Saxons who surrounded them were in no mood for clemency, and their pleas turned to cries of panic, to be followed by swift swings of both axe and blade, and the thrust of spears. By the time the Danes reached the slaughter it was done.

As they moved on it became obvious there were few townsfolk left to witness their passing – most having fled. Those who remained looked on with hate. War had come to their city yet again, and Styrkar could not blame them for their anger. Their once magnificent city had been reduced to a husk, and it was doubtful they could now tell invader from liberator.

A scream – long and loud from across the rooftops. Styrkar glanced up in time to see a mailed warrior plummet from the high tower in the distance. Was he friend or foe? It mattered not. All that mattered was that this place had been put to the torch and the Franks scattered. But when their path was cleared by a billow of wind, Styrkar realised that task was not done yet, and he bared his teeth in anticipation.

The vestige of a defensive shield wall lay ahead of them. Spears by the dozen stood proud across the thoroughfare. It was silent though – no shouting, taunting Frankish voices here. Only silence as they blocked the way ahead.

Asbjorn came to a halt, Thurkill and Kristian and all the rest stood in a brooding mob as they viewed what remained of the Frankish army. Without their warhorses these knights were just ordinary soldiers come to fight on a level field. Come to die.

'Are you ready, warriors of Danmǫrk?' Asbjorn growled,

breaking the pensive silence. 'Let us show these Franks once more what it means to fight true warriors.'

There were barks of assent. A couple of the Danes smashed axe against shield. Styrkar glared through the grey mist, tasting the bitter air, seeing that despite the few who stood against them, making a desperate last stand, their shield wall was resolute. They could not be underestimated.

Before Asbjorn could give the order to attack, Styrkar raised his axe high. 'Come! Follow the Red Wolf. I will show you how these dogs bleed.'

He was running. In front of him, the wall of shields braced, locking together as the Franks saw what was coming. Their spears were levelled. Someone roared behind Styrkar as the Danes were swift to follow, in no mood to be robbed of their share.

Those spearheads began to waver the closer he got. The men behind their shields standing stalwart, despite their terror.

Styrkar swept his axe upwards, hacking aside a spear shaft, before barging into the first shield. He expected resistance, but the wall buckled as soon as he smashed into it. Two men fell back, stumbling in the filth. His axe swept left, clanging off a helm and sending another Frank to his knees.

No sooner had he struck than he heard the deafening knell as the Danes fell upon that wall. A Frankish knight stared up at him, fear writ on that soot-stained face. He did not even try to rise, before Styrkar hacked him in the chest and blood spewed from his mouth as he coughed one final breath.

The Franks were already running, only a few of them

brave enough to remain in the face of the Danish onslaught, and it only served to anger Styrkar further.

'Stand,' he bellowed. 'Face me. Fight me.'

But their taste for battle had fled. Around him, the violence was all too brief, and shields clattered to the ground as their enemy bolted, but the Red Wolf had the scent of blood in his nostrils. He could not let his quarry escape until he had tasted more.

Asbjorn led the way this time – in no mood to be beaten to the slaughter twice. Styrkar followed, close to his shoulder. The feet of the Danes made a thunderous sound as they charged along Yorke's main thoroughfare, caught up in the frenzy of the hunt.

For a moment, Styrkar remembered once before when he had seen men caught up in such a hysteria. At Senlac, Harold's fyrd had broken their line to chase down the fleeing Franks. It had ended in their defeat that day, but this was no trap. This time the Franks would not lure them into the lances of towering horsemen. This time they would die.

One of their prey fell in front of them, but Styrkar barely acknowledged the man as he was swiftly hacked to pieces. His cries stirred no sense of mercy within the Red Wolf. The last time he had fought at Yorke, the Saxons had been shown no clemency by the Franks. This time there would be none offered in return.

Ahead rose the great southern gate – the Myglagata – the breach Styrkar had defended a few short months ago. These very Franks had ridden through that gate bringing fire and death with them that day. It was only right that he send them fleeing back through it with death of his own.

The fleeing knights rushed through the stone arch, out

toward freedom, but as Styrkar followed them, gripping his axe, ready for his reckoning, he saw that it was not salvation that awaited them.

Earl Waltheof was waiting with his own war host. The housecarls of the north stood ready, axes sweeping in merciless arcs to greet the routing mass. In their midst, howling his fury, was Waltheof himself, singing for death, taking the head of any Frankish knight who dared to run close enough.

Asbjorn was in no mood to be left out. He and his men attacked from the rear as the Franks met Waltheof's murderous hunting party. Crushed within this millstone of fury, the knights stood no chance.

Styrkar halted, his battle lust fading, as the noise of laughing cursing Saxons and Danes rose to a tumult. This was not a just reckoning. This was cruel slaughter. Butchery – and the Red Wolf would take no part in it. Besides, he hungered for rarer game, and it had not yet arrived. As the last of the Franks were crushed, Styrkar could only yearn for the day his nemesis would come. The day the usurper would return to face him.

The smoke that hung over the city drifted away as the afternoon wore on. Hundreds, perhaps thousands had been slaughtered amid the burned bones of Yorke, and when it was done, Asbjorn stood with Styrkar at the southern gate, as Edgar watched over the looting of Frankish corpses.

'A good day,' Asbjorn said with a grin. The only trophy he had to show for the day's victory was a cut to his cheek.

Edgar nodded back his acknowledgement. His face was unmarred, as though the slaughter had all but passed him by. 'A good start, my friend.'

'You were vicious today, Red Wolf,' Asbjorn said. 'But I sensed your thirst for battle waned at the great gate. What ails you?'

Styrkar's immediate reaction was to deny the fact. It was almost a suggestion of cowardice, but Asbjorn was right. He had lost his battle ardour at the end.

'My axe spilled enough blood. More than most. But I seek a greater prize. Until I meet the king on the field, I will not be satisfied.'

Edgar grinned wickedly. 'You will meet him soon enough, Red Wolf.'

Before they could continue, Waltheof made his way toward them through the gate. Some of his men were with him, corralling two prisoners, as Gospatric brought up the rear. They drove the sorry-looking Franks to their knees, but Styrkar could tell from the cut of their well-made tunics that they were men of import.

'Stewards of the city,' Waltheof growled, gripping tight to his axe, its blade still stained red. 'Or so the townsfolk say.'

One of the men bore a forlorn expression, doing his best not to tremble in fear, while the other hung on to his noble bearing, if barely.

'We should take their heads,' Waltheof continued. 'Spike them atop the gate.'

Gospatric stepped forward. 'I've told you – we have to ransom them. King William may well pay generously to get them back.'

The more defiant of the prisoners began to babble in the Frankish tongue, as though his contribution to the conversation mattered. Waltheof rewarded him with the haft of his axe to the jaw, and the man fell silent.

Asbjorn stepped toward the prisoners, glaring down with disdain. Now the braver of the two looked much less sure of himself.

'I will take them,' Asbjorn said, before turning to Edgar. 'With your leave, of course.'

'Now wait a minute,' Gospatric replied. 'If there's a ransom to be had, it should be shared among us all.'

Asbjorn regarded Gospatric with all the casual regard of a man in full control. 'I was promised spoils, in return for my help taking this city. You have had my help.' He gestured to the two men. 'Now I will take the spoils.'

Waltheof and Gospatric looked as though they might argue, but thought better of it.

'Of course, the prisoners are yours,' Edgar said, before the situation soured. 'And they are less than you deserve. Do with them what you will.'

Asbjorn nodded his appreciation, before gesturing his men. He and the rest of his warriors bundled the prisoners toward their waiting ships. Waltheof and Gospatric looked unhappy with the deal, but they did not voice their discontent as they too left to see what other treasures could be salvaged from the carcass of Yorke. They bore enough respect for Edgar to not argue with his decision, and Styrkar felt relieved at that. The Aetheling would need their support if they were to face what would soon be heading north.

'Do you think we can rely on those Danes?' Edgar asked, as they both looked out onto the endless road winding its way south. 'Will their king honour his alliance, now we have taken Yorke?'

There was no way to know, and Styrkar could only shrug his broad, aching shoulders. 'One thing I can be sure about is that King Sweyn had best come quick. King William will not take this insult lightly. Not a second time.'

'No. As soon as he hears of this he will make his way northward with all haste. And you will have another chance at his head.' Edgar slapped a hand to Styrkar's shoulder, before leaving him alone.

As he stood, wondering how long they would have to wait, Styrkar winced at the sudden dry keening of a bird atop the stone gate. He turned, seeing a sleek raven glaring down at him. It cawed again, its throaty cry echoing southward.

Was the bird some omen of ill tiding? Or perhaps it was trying to warn him of something?

No matter. If all that approached from the south was his doom, Styrkar would face it. He would not run a second time.

9

A crisp breeze drifted in through the shutters, but the chamber was warmed by the flames of a fire. Ronan listened to those logs crackling, revelling in the comfort of the bed. And the comfort of his sleeping companion.

Wuna was a big-boned girl but possessed of more vigour than any warhorse Ronan had ridden. Her enthusiasm had kept him occupied enough to forget his recent woes. An enthusiasm that her father had most certainly not shared, from the look on his face when Ronan first arrived, though he'd made little objection. But then, why would he? When Ronan had come to this backwater and demanded the Saxon peasants provide him all the hospitality he deserved, they had been too afraid to refuse.

'Morning, my lord,' Wuna breathed in his ear.

Ronan smiled at the sound, feeling her breath against his cheek. 'Morning, my dear.'

'What will it be today, my lord? A hearty breakfast, or something... else.'

She moved her hand down beneath the woollen blanket, and Ronan felt a familiar tingle in his loins. He could easily have got used to this, but after the previous night's exertions he was parched.

'Perhaps a little milk and honey first. It may help perk me up a little.'

She kissed him sweetly on the cheek. 'Your wish is my command, lord.'

Yes, this was a life he could definitely get used to. And one that he had surely earned.

When she slipped from the bed, he let out a deep sigh, resting the feather pillow over his eyes. His head was still dulled from the ale he had guzzled the night before, and if Wuna was as demanding today as she had been yesterday, he would need all his strength to satisfy her.

Still, there was a nagging feeling that this could not last forever. Best he enjoy himself while it did, and damn the consequences. He took a deep sigh, breathing in the scent of her hair that lingered on the pillow. Three years he had been in this godforsaken country, and was this the first time he had been given any opportunity to appreciate it?

A memory, quick and sharp, entered his mind. Gisela and her child, in his care.

No, this was not the first time he'd had something to appreciate, but that previous joy had been fleeting. It had taught him to grasp what pleasure he could whenever it presented itself. To not invest too much hope in the future. *Here* was all that mattered. *Now* his only concern.

Footsteps approached, heavy on the wooden boards. Damn she was a big one, but Ronan had found that alluring. Ample about the hips, and a bosom to match.

Besides, she was a pretty enough thing, and he had never been partial to skinny waifs anyway.

'That was quick, my love,' he whispered. 'Couldn't stay away from me?'

Silence.

Was this some kind of new tease? Wuna certainly hadn't been so coy up until now.

'Are you going to make me beg for—'

He lifted the pillow, seeing it was not his buxom bed mate standing at the foot of the bed, but two towering knights. Their armour was mud-spattered from the road, faces grim as they regarded him there, with nothing to defend himself but a sullied sheet. Where had they come from? Had Mallet sent them to find him and drag him back north?

No – Yorke was nothing but a shell. By now the Danes would have ransacked its rotting corpse and slaughtered everyone left within its fire-blackened walls.

'What the fuuuu—'

One of the knights tore the sheet aside while the other grabbed his leg – his crippled one, naturally. Ronan howled as he was dragged from the comfort of the bed and fell heavily to the wooden floor.

The second knight grabbed his other leg. No time to protest as they dragged him naked across the floor, an errant splinter slicing his arse cheek and provoking a squeal as they kicked open the door. Ronan vainly snatched at the doorframe, a harsh gust of wind chilling his clammy body, as he was hauled across the threshold and out into the mud.

More knights waited in the crisp morning air, watching on as he was dragged by, the cold earth freezing him to the core. Row upon row, most tending their horses and offering him only casual regard. Others pointing, grinning as he slid across the muddy ground.

'Wait,' he howled, as they found his discomfort more and more amusing.

Among the throng of knights he recognised Wuna's father, his previous scowl now replaced by a grin of delight. Of his enthusiastic lover there was no sign. Most likely she would receive a scolding from her father for her lack of chastity, but Wuna's problems seemed insignificant in comparison to his own right now.

One of the knights shouldered open the door to a haybarn, and Ronan was pulled inside before being unceremoniously dumped next to a bale of straw. He looked up at the two knights, their faces bereft of sympathy.

'I am one of you. There is no need for any of this.'

The taller of the two took a threatening step closer. 'You're a damned coward. There is rebellion in the north, and here you lie with some Saxon whore.'

It seemed a harsh assessment of Wuna, but Ronan was in no mood to set the man straight. 'My name is Ronan of Dol-Combourg.' He winced as he pulled a troublesome splinter from one buttock. 'I am—'

'Dol-Combourg of Bretagne?' The knight stooped to look closer. 'The cripple?'

'Yes. Dol-Combourg the fucking cripple. That's what I'm trying to tell you.'

'The only knight to live through the massacre at Dun Holm?'

Fame at last. 'Yes. The very same.'

Now it was the other knight's turn to step forward for a

closer look. 'Didn't you survive by hiding with pigs in their pen?'

'Erm… that's not exactly how it happened, but—'

The knights began to chuckle, but before Ronan could set them straight, the door to the barn swung inward. Another warrior in mail strode in, carrying his helm in the crook of one arm. He peered down, and Ronan allowed himself to breathe a sigh of relief.

Hugo of Grentmesnil was tall and lean, with a mop of dark hair cut in the common horse knight's style, but he was anything but common. Born of noble stock he was a close companion of the king. Ronan wouldn't have called him a friend, but they were known to one another, having crossed the sea from Frankia on the same ship.

'Thank God, Hugo. I was trying to explain to these idiots who I am. Tell them—'

Hugo raised a finger to his lips for Ronan to be silent, then he turned and opened the door. Stooping beneath the lintel entered a man who could have silenced any room in the realm.

King William looked about the dingy haybarn with casual regard, as though he owned the place, but then Ronan supposed that he did. He wore a regal red cloak about his shoulders, but it appeared he had seen fit to leave his crown behind on his journey north.

Hugo and the two knights bowed as soon as the king entered, but Ronan struggled to bring himself to rise. He was damned whatever he did now. The best he could hope for was exile. At worst… who knew?

For his part, William gazed down at the naked man in front of him, before raising an apple to his mouth to take a crunching bite. Ronan struggled to his feet, wincing in pain, before bowing to his king.

'Sire, I…'

He had no excuses. Nothing to say as he was locked within that grim gaze.

'Dol-Combourg, is it?' William said. 'I have heard of you. Brian of Penthièvre has spoken favourably of your exploits. Says you are a man who can be relied upon. Is he correct?'

Ronan was suddenly all too aware that he was shivering and filth-ridden in a backwater haybarn. 'In the current circumstances it may not look like it. But I can assure you, sire, that he is indeed correct.'

'No. It does not look like it. Only a few miles to the north Yorke lies in ruins, our countrymen slaughtered, and here you are enjoying the hospitality of the locals.'

'I… I was merely recuperating after a recent ordeal. Then I planned to make my way south with all haste.'

'Recuperating?' William gestured to Ronan's pale and naked frame. 'You don't look wounded.'

'What can I say? My swift recovery is a testament to the care given by my nursemaid.'

The king raised a dubious eyebrow. 'I'm sure she was most… tender.'

Not the word Ronan would have chosen. 'Yes, indeed she was.'

William took another bite of his apple before chewing noisily then swallowing. 'So, moving south, eh? Back to Earl Brian's side?'

It hadn't even crossed Ronan's mind, but he nodded enthusiastically, nevertheless. 'Indeed, I was—'

'Why?' William asked.

Now there was a question. Though Brian was supposedly his friend, staying loyal had certainly done nothing to enrich Ronan so far. 'I have served at Brian's side for—'

'You have. And in his turn, Brian serves me.'

Ronan bowed his head. 'As do we all, sire.'

'Do you?'

It appeared his loyalty was in question, and under the circumstances that suspicion was well placed. Ronan glanced toward Hugo, but from the blank look he received in return there would be no help there.

'Most certainly. You are the rightful king of England as ordained by God. You have my—'

'Good.' William flung the apple core away and planted his hands on his hips. 'Then you will not object to joining my retinue. The north is in full rebellion, and I may have need of a man with your... reputation.'

Ronan was about to bow again, to thank the king for his most generous offer, when William turned and left the barn. He was followed by the two knights, but Hugo paused in the doorway.

'We leave at dawn tomorrow. I suggest you get dressed. And I hope during your... recovery, you did not lose your horse and armour.'

Ronan winced. 'I'm sure I can find my armour, but a horse...' He thought how ridiculous he would look besieging Yorke upon the mule he had stolen.

Hugo rolled his eyes. 'I will see what I can find.' He leaned forward and sniffed. 'In the meantime, find somewhere to wash.'

Before Ronan could offer his thanks, Hugo had swung the barn door open and stepped outside.

He shivered in the cold, suddenly all too aware that he was naked and filthy. That he was most likely heading back into another battle against both Saxon and Dane. But this time it was in direct service to the king. This time he was no longer servant to privileged lords and earls. He answered to the most powerful man in all the land.

Strange how fortunes could change.

How despair could so quickly turn to an opportunity to prove oneself...

But he had not proven himself yet.

IO

After days of dry weather, the clear skies were beginning to darken. Soon there would be rain – a torrent that would wash away the filth that covered the burned city.

They had rebuilt the wall as best they could from what rubble lay within the boundaries of Yorke. Ancient stones worn smooth by the passing of years, tarnished by smoke and dirt, piled high upon one another. At least it would look as though their defences stood strong, though in truth a stout wind could have blown them over.

From atop the southern gate, Styrkar watched as all across the city, the people of Yorke teemed among the ruins like ants. This was not the first time they'd had war forced upon them, and again they had to rebuild.

Gone were the cheering joyous faces he had been greeted by last time. But then he supposed they did not feel the rapture of liberation as they had before. This time they knew what was coming from the south. Knew that their fight had only just begun.

'You think this will be enough?' said Siward Barn, leaning heavily on his spear.

Styrkar had spoken little to the northern ealdorman since joining with Edgar at Ferebi, but so far the man had proven himself a solid fighter, and his men were loyal enough.

'We will need more than high walls to defeat what is coming,' Styrkar replied.

Siward ran a meaty hand across his bald head. 'But you have faced the Franks in battle before. You must think we have a chance, otherwise you wouldn't be here.'

Styrkar turned to regard him. There was no fear there, but Siward's words were laced with apprehension. Understandable – even the bravest of men feared death when it was charging toward them.

'The king has sealed victory in every battle he has fought on these shores. I would say our chances are slim. But I would gladly face certain defeat if it gave me one more chance at William's head.'

Styrkar expected Siward to balk at the notion they had little chance, but instead he smirked. 'I wish I shared your thirst for death, Red Wolf.'

'If you don't, why are you even here?'

Siward looked out onto the city. 'Because this land is worth defending. It is worth dying for.'

Styrkar could see little but ruins. 'I abandoned any thought of dying for land and kings long ago.'

'No. The Red Wolf fights for vengeance. And that is as good a reason as any.'

Before Styrkar could think further on that, he heard the distant sound of galloping hooves coming from the south. He squinted out over the flat land to see two riders approach from the woods. They rode with all haste, and Styrkar knew instinctively that the tidings they brought could not be good. Neither rider paused as they approached the gate, and as they passed beneath the stone archway, Styrkar recognised them as two of Asbjorn's Danes.

'Trouble?' Siward asked, as he watched them gallop deeper into the city.

Styrkar knew it must be, as those horses headed toward the river, where Asbjorn's fleet was moored. Both riders dismounted, one of them calling out for his jarl. Asbjorn appeared from one of the ships, listening intently to his messenger before turning to one of his men and snarling an order. A horn blew, long and loud over the rooftops.

There was frantic activity by the river, as the Danes began to gather. It became obvious that they were loading their ships as fast as they could.

'They're leaving,' Siward said. 'Why are they…'

It couldn't be true, but as Styrkar watched, it was more and more obvious Siward was right. Asbjorn and his warriors were making ready to leave the city of Yorke.

Styrkar rushed down the worn stone stairs of the gatehouse, closely followed by Siward. They made their way along the main road through the city as quickly as they could, seeing that more Danes had gathered by the river. At the bank, Edgar had come, summoned by the sound of the Danish horn, and was already arguing with Asbjorn.

'You cannot leave. We had a deal,' the Aetheling growled. 'I had the assurance of your brother that you would help defend—'

'Look around you, Aetheling.' Asbjorn watched his men

readying the ships with his arms folded. 'There is nothing to defend. This city was lost before we even arrived.'

When Styrkar drew nearer, Edgar gestured toward him desperately. 'Red Wolf, talk to your fellow Dane. Tell him he cannot abandon us now – not so close to victory.'

Asbjorn regarded Styrkar solemnly. The two of them had fought together – days of raiding, of shedding blood side by side – but now Asbjorn's eyes were downcast, perhaps a moment of shame.

'We can make a stand here,' Styrkar said. 'Even without your brother. But if you abandon us—'

'Make a stand? This city is lost. This land belongs to the conqueror now. Even if my brother were here there would be no chance of victory. Do not take my word for it.' He gestured to one of his men. 'Arnketil, tell them what you saw.'

The man drew closer – one of the riders Styrkar had seen cross through the gate. 'We scouted south. The king is close, and he brings a war host the likes of which I have never seen. Thousands, mounted, armoured, bearing more banners than we could count.'

Styrkar looked back to Asbjorn. 'So there is nothing that would make you stay and fight with us?'

'I am not ready to die yet, Red Wolf. I will take my ships back along the Black River. If my brother comes, then perhaps we can strike at the Franks again. I suggest, Edgar, that you take your army back north and wait for word.'

'But we have to hold this city,' Edgar snarled, taking a threatening step toward Asbjorn.

Maerlswein planted a restraining hand on the boy's shoulder. For his part, Asbjorn did not move a muscle.

'His mind is made, lad,' Maerlswein said.

Edgar and Styrkar could only watch as the Danish ships were quickly loaded. Some of them had already pushed off from the bank and were rowing their way east back along the river.

Just as Asbjorn climbed aboard his own boat, Waltheof and Gospatric arrived to discover their Danish allies finally abandoning them to their fate.

'Damn them,' Edgar said through gritted teeth as he watched the last ship make its way downstream.

'They've left us?' Gospatric said. 'What the hell do we do now?'

Edgar looked at the thegns and warriors surrounding him. Maerlswein and Siward. Waltheof and Gospatric. Finally to Styrkar. 'Nothing has changed. We still hold the city. We will fight.'

'Agreed,' replied Maerlswein immediately.

'Aye, I will stand with you Aetheling,' Siward said.

Gospatric raised his arms. 'Are you mad? Did you not hear him? The king travels north with a vast army. They took the city from us last time and we had walls to defend us. Now we stand within a charred ruin.'

'My cousin is right,' Waltheof said. 'If we stay here we may as well open our throats to the Franks. This city cannot be defended. Not without allies to help us.'

The gleam in Edgar's eye dimmed. He knew they were right. Even if Gospatric and Waltheof stayed with their housecarls and sworn men, they had little chance. But it was more likely they would flee before the Franks arrived, and then Edgar would be left with only a few to face the fury of the king.

'All right. We withdraw. Find a more defensible position north of the River Eyr. With luck, King Sweyn will come with a war host of his own. In the meantime, we will lead the Frankish king a merry dance. He will not find us so easy to defeat this time. Make ready.'

Siward, Maerlswein and the northern earls nodded their assent, before heading off to gather their fighters. With the Danes gone, it was unusually quiet beside the river, and Edgar watched it flow by. He wore a troubled brow, now that his plans to defend Yorke had gone awry, but he was not beaten yet.

'I imagine you wanted to stay, Red Wolf? To fight? You think me a coward?'

Styrkar would gladly have stayed, even though he knew it would be suicide. 'I have had my fill of running, yes. But you have no choice, Aetheling. If this host is as large as Asbjorn's scout claims, we stand no chance. If you are to wear the crown you must act with wisdom. Not rashness. That is what led to King Harold's end. You should not make the same mistake.'

It brought a grim smile to Edgar's face, and he nodded his appreciation. As though compounding the ill tidings they had received, the dark sky grumbled.

It hurt Styrkar to abandon the city he had won for a second time, but he would have a chance to make amends. The Franks were coming. This time they would not give up until all resistance to their rule had been stamped into the cold northern earth.

But they would have to defeat the Red Wolf first.

Part Two

Crimson Winter

II

The rain was relentless. Days and days, a deluge Styrkar had never experienced, and there seemed no sign that it would stop. It had soaked through their armour, their jerkins, and everything was heavier with the burden of it. The sun had not shone for days as the river had swollen its banks – but that had been to their advantage. How long that advantage would last was a question no one could answer.

Styrkar knelt behind the wooden parapet, or at least what remained. It stretched along the southern extent of the town, a once robust perimeter now studded with arrows and smashed in places. His shield was raised, the torrent tamping off his helmet. That tinny sound had almost driven him mad, but there were worse things than madness to be mindful of right now.

Maerlswein grinned at him from nearby. The bearded warrior looked half drowned. Strange that he still possessed enough mirth to smile.

'What's so funny?' Styrkar asked.

Maerlswein shrugged. 'Can't a man enjoy the weather?'

Perhaps Maerlswein had succumbed to the maddening effect of the relentless rain. Still, Styrkar couldn't help but grin in reply.

An archer at his shoulder risked a glance over the parapet, before rising to his feet and loosing an arrow. No sooner had the bowstring hummed its song, than the man was struck in the chest. A four-foot ballista bolt knocked him off his feet, propelling him back off the parapet. He didn't even have time to howl in pain.

'Loose, damn you,' Maerlswein bellowed along the defensive line.

Usually his commanding bark would have been heeded, but this time the archers remained hunkered behind the wooden palisade. Men were shivering in fear, rain pouring down their faces as they gripped their bows and quivers, vainly trying to shelter them from the rain.

'We're running out of arrows,' someone called mournfully.

Maerlswein grumbled in response, but there was little he could do to chastise his men. It was a surprise they had not already fled after what they'd endured these past days.

Gingerly, Styrkar leaned forward and peered between a gap in the palisade. He squinted through the wooden struts and across the fast-flowing river. It was difficult to see, so torrential was the rain, but he could still make out the endless row of siege machines the Franks had brought north with them. Perhaps they had intended to use them to retake Yorke. Maybe they had been constructed in the last few days. Either way, they were putting them to good use now.

They were unleashed relentlessly, despite the deluge, loaded with huge four-foot spears and rocks. Styrkar guessed that had the elements been more favourable those missiles would have been set alight, but at the moment the weather was with them – one small thing in their favour. Despite the fact Edgar's forces had held this side of the river for almost three weeks, their morale was waning. And the rain would not last forever.

No time to wonder when it might stop, as the cry went up from across the river. The Franks began to hurl their projectiles, one after the other.

Styrkar watched as a missile, more spear than arrow, was launched and headed straight for Maerlswein's position. Instinctively he leapt, grasping the old warrior, and they both fell to the floor as the shaft lanced through the parapet where he had been crouching.

Before Maerlswein could offer a word of thanks, the wood of the parapet exploded nearby, showering them in splinters. The missile that had been flung rolled to a stop near them.

'What in Hell are they flinging at us now?' Maerlswein growled, as Styrkar helped him to his feet.

As the rain clattered down, Styrkar saw the severed head of a bull was lying close to them, one horn snapped off, its battered face slack and rotten.

'Looks like they've run out of rocks.'

Maerlswein grinned once more as someone shouted from behind. Looking down from the palisade, he could see a rider gallop into the compound, hooves splashing through the mud before he drew up his panting steed. The scout wasted no time, jumping down from the horse and calling for Edgar.

'Trouble,' Maerlswein grunted.

Styrkar couldn't think it was anything but. 'Then we'd best go and see what he has to say.'

Both men made their way down from the parapet as more missiles flew overhead. They kept their heads down as they slopped through the mud to a wooden shelter that had been erected within the boundary of the settlement. Edgar crouched within, Gospatric, Waltheof and Siward with him, listening to the scout relay his news.

'They have crossed ten miles upriver, my lord. Managed to bring their warhorses with them. It won't be long before they have a big enough force to attack us. Maybe a day, longer if we're lucky.'

Silence in the shelter, as the Saxon leaders considered those words. The only thing that had spared them from being overrun was the river stopping the king's mounted knights. Now he had overcome that barrier, there would be no holding him back.

Edgar slammed a fist against the table that sat in their midst, overturning a cup. 'Damn it. We have come so far. Now we have to run again.'

'There's no other choice,' said Gospatric. 'The Danes are not coming. King Sweyn has abandoned us. Our only choice is to make our way north and join up with Máel. He will help us.'

Edgar gazed across at Styrkar, then Waltheof and Siward. 'What say you?'

Siward shook his head. 'This place is already collapsing around our ears. Once the rain stops they'll be launching more than rocks. We'll be burned out, then there'll be nothing to stop the Bastard running us down beneath the hooves of his horses.'

'Aye,' Waltheof agreed. 'Retreat is the only answer.'

Edgar shook his head. 'No. I won't believe the Danes would just abandon us. Not after they've fought this hard. Maerlswein, send some of your men. Find them along the Black River. They have to meet us further up the coast where we can rally our forces and plan a counter-attack.'

Maerlswein nodded. 'Aye, Aetheling. It will be done.'

Edgar turned to the scout. 'Signal the men. We withdraw now. The rest of you, gather your housecarls and start moving north.'

They nodded and did as they were bid. Once they'd gone, Edgar was the only one left with Styrkar under that meagre shelter.

'I am sorry, Red Wolf. I know you would rather stay and fight, but I cannot sacrifice these men in a last stand. Once we're back north, beyond the king's wrath, we will think again. When the winter has passed, those Danes will be hungry for war once again.'

Despite his words, Styrkar could tell Edgar's own appetite for battle had waned; cut short by bombardment and the relentless rain. He would have offered words of encouragement, but he had none to give. Edgar's fight was over for now, and perhaps he would return in force. But first they had to reach safer ground. There was no way the Franks would let them withdraw unharried.

As the horns sounded outside, signalling their retreat, Styrkar knew they were not safe yet. Not by a long way.

12

Axholme, England, November 1069

The further north they had travelled, the more incensed the king had become. He was more angered by the cold, the dark skies, the barrenness of the landscape with every mile they rode. By the time they reached Yorke, fire-blackened and all but abandoned, he was ready to ravage every burgh and hamlet on his own.

As it was, he set his knights to that task instead. A task they executed with all the zeal and fury Ronan had come to expect.

Even now they were burning and pillaging their way across the north in pursuit of the rebels and their errant leaders. The rebellious earls had fled, but it was doubtful they would get far or find shelter. Ronan didn't envy those Saxons, but they had brought this all upon themselves. Why could they not just kneel? Defiance had not worked at any time in the past three years, there was no reason for them to think it would work now.

Indeed, those Saxon lords had condemned themselves,

and would be damned for their defiance. For Ronan, however, damnation might come for quite the opposite reason. Loyalty could well be his downfall.

The king had offered him a very specific task. One suited to his talents, or so William had said. He had not been too specific about what that talent was, and as they rode along the banks of the estuary, Ronan began to wonder if *talent* had been the word the king had meant. Surely *expendability* might have been more appropriate.

Ronan was to follow the fleeing Danes along the Black River to where they had moored their fleet. Once there, he was to negotiate a deal. To pay them off, if possible. Ronan had been assured this was a simple task. That the Danes had for centuries been in the habit of raiding these shores only to be offered silver to sail away in the end. Still, it did little to reassure Ronan that this time it would be so straightforward. Hard experience had taught him that these things were rarely so cut and dried.

At least he wasn't alone in this. Hugo of Grentmesnil had offered Ronan two of his most loyal knights to accompany him in his mission. Wymon was grim and iron-jawed. His nose flat to his face, eyes pale like a fish's. Ronan would never admit it, but the man gave him an unnerving chill. Serle was less silent, less brooding, but looked an equal danger with his ratty features and his habit of always fiddling with a small knife. At any moment it felt like he might stick it in something, just to test if it bled or not. Ronan could only be grateful that both these men were on his side... for now.

Despite their threatening nature, he couldn't think of anyone more suited to taking care of the silver they had brought. Their horses were laden with sacks of it – a gift from the king. And there would be much more where it came from, if the Danes agreed to leave these shores for good.

The moon lit their way along the Black River, reflecting off its surface. Ronan would have been fearful of bandits, or worse, but his companions provided some reassurance. They passed a town on the shore, giving it a wide berth as they continued toward the coast. It wasn't long past that town they saw what they had come for.

A fleet sat amid the vast estuary – two hundred boats or more lashed together, torches winking in the distance as the sound of singing and laughing drifted across the water. Before long, Ronan and his companions came to a small shack by a jetty – a single rowing boat moored at it.

He dismounted, handing the reins to Serle, before approaching the shack. He couldn't hear a thing within as he rapped on the door. It was answered quickly, the man within holding a lit candle in his hand.

'Bloody late to be knocking,' he said, squinting out into the night.

'My apologies,' Ronan replied unnecessarily. He could have just taken that boat, but there was no use in starting trouble where it wasn't needed. 'Your boat – is it for hire?'

The man looked puzzled, before glancing across the murky water toward the Danish fleet. 'You thinking of… going over there?'

'That is my intention, yes.'

'You do that, not likely I'll get my boat back.'

'Do not trouble yourself on that score. I have a gift for them that will cool their temperaments.' Before the man could argue further, Ronan fished out a shilling, newly minted with King William's head.

The man held the coin up to his candle, then eagerly gestured toward his boat. 'All yours.'

Ronan nodded his thanks before signalling for Serle and Wymon to follow him. They dismounted, untying the silver from their saddles and making their way along the jetty. After dumping the booty in the boat, both men took up oars as Ronan took his place at the prow.

They were deathly quiet as they crossed. Those Danish voices grew louder, and Ronan began to get an all too familiar feeling of dread in the pit of his stomach. He should have brought a torch, made it obvious they were approaching with good intentions, but it was too late now.

Sounds of alarm echoed from aboard the nearest ship, as it became clear they'd been seen. Ronan struggled to stand at the prow, gritting his teeth as he fought to balance on his accursed leg. He raised his arms to show he meant no harm, but as they drew closer he could see the Danes were rousing themselves, grasping spears, drawing blades.

'I have come with no ill intention,' he called in the language of the Saxons, hoping at least one of these Danes might be able to understand him. 'I am here at the bequest of the king.'

Wymon and Serle ceased their rowing and the boat drifted toward the nearest ship. Gently the prow bumped against the hull, and in the torchlight Ronan could see a score of grim faces watching him.

Without waiting to be invited, he stepped across and onto the deck, wary of the dozen spearheads levelled toward him. 'I would speak with your chieftain. I come with an offer. A bargain you would be wise to heed.'

Just as he thought he might be run through by one of

those spears, a gap appeared among the hulking Danes and a tall, grizzled warrior stepped to the fore. He regarded Ronan casually, but there was still an air of imminent violence about the man. Blond hair cascaded down his broad shoulders, and his thick arms hung at his sides, one of them close to the sword at his hip.

'Do you speak the language of the Saxons?' Ronan asked.

'Some,' the warrior replied.

'I am Ronan of Dol-Combourg, here on behalf of Duke William of Normandie, the rightful king of these lands.'

'And I am Asbjorn,' the man growled. 'Rightful lord of these ships. Speak your king's words fast, Frank. Lest my men grow tired of waiting.'

Ronan tried to relax, to seem in command, but with so many Danes eager to run him through it was a tough ask. 'His message is a simple one. He offers silver, and in return he asks that you leave these shores and go back to your homes, never to return.'

Asbjorn looked suddenly tempted, much to Ronan's relief. 'He would offer us Danegeld?'

Ronan was familiar with the term. Treasure in return for a swift departure. The Saxons had offered it so much to these raiding Danes that it even had its own word. He signalled to Serle, who reached into the bottom of the rowboat and hefted a sack of shillings. With a grunt, he threw the sack onto the deck. Ronan stooped with some difficulty, before lifting the sack and wrenching it open. He reached in and produced a fistful of shillings, which he let fall through his fingers to tinkle on the boards. Asbjorn could not quell a grin, as his men began lowering their weapons.

'And there is much more where this came from. As long

as you vow to leave this place unsullied, and abandon your alliance with the Saxons.'

The huge Dane stared down at the gold, then back at Ronan. 'More where this came from?'

'Much more.'

Asbjorn's grin widened. 'Then how could I refuse?'

He turned to his men, barking something in the language of the Danes, and they jeered their approval. One of them snatched the bag from Ronan's hand, and he turned, nodding for Serle to throw the remaining silver on board.

The atmosphere changed in a heartbeat. Now those Danes were laughing, smiling, and their weapons didn't look quite so threatening. They almost seemed a friendly bunch, but Ronan was mindful that only a few short weeks before they had ravaged the coast and almost killed him at Norwic.

As his men began their celebrations, Asbjorn stepped closer to Ronan. 'I have one request, Frank. With the king's leave we would winter here, before we risk the seas back to our homeland. And since he is in such a generous mood, perhaps he can also provide us with supplies with which to eke out the cold months.'

It seemed a request too far. One Ronan wasn't sure if he had the power to grant. 'King William is indeed benevolent. But his generosity is not limitless. What might you offer in return?'

Again, Asbjorn turned to his men, this time barking in his foreign tongue. The call was relayed across the lashed ships, and eventually Ronan saw movement across their decks. Figures came closer in the stark torchlight – two men dragged with little ceremony across ship after ship. They were driven to their knees before Ronan, and it took him a moment before he recognised them.

Giselbert looked fearful, his face bruised and bleeding, clothes torn. Beside him Mallet was defiant to the last, despite his cut face and dishevelled hair, but then what could Ronan expect.

'A gift for your king,' Asbjorn said. 'The stewards of Yorke, returned unharmed. Or close enough. Will they suffice?'

Ronan did his best to quell a smile of satisfaction at seeing Mallet on his knees. 'I am sure the king will be most grateful.'

Asbjorn signalled for the two prisoners to be placed aboard the rowboat. After a gracious nod to the Danish chieftain, Ronan followed. This time as he sat himself at the prow, he gazed in pleasure at the two men.

Wymon and Serle began to row back across the water. Giselbert was shivering, too stricken by his recent capture to speak any words of gratitude. Likewise, Mallet had nothing to say, but he stared back at Ronan as though it had been him who had held him in bondage and not the Danes.

'I imagine you're curious as to why I am here,' Ronan said. 'Why I have been sent to secure your freedom.'

Mallet sneered. 'I assume it is because you have managed to wheedle your way into the king's circle.'

'Good guess. But then the king is an excellent judge. He has an eye for men of quality. Brave men such as I, who are willing to risk their lives and entreat with the savages who stand against us. Still think I am a coward, Mallet?'

He had nothing more to say, dragging his gaze away to look out over the dark waters of the Black River. They continued in silence, until the little boat bumped up against the shore. Ronan was the first to stand, and limp up onto the bank.

'See them back to the camp,' Ronan told his men. 'I will ride ahead. The king will be eager to hear the news.'

Wymon and Serle, nodded, helping the two former captives from the boat. Ronan couldn't mount his steed quick enough, offering the boatman standing in the doorway of his cabin a cursory nod before pressing heels to flanks.

As he galloped back along that dark road it was all Ronan could do not to laugh. He had faced the Danes, served the king, and to top it all now Mallet himself owed him a debt. How quickly fate had turned his fortunes on their head.

Only a few miles further and he could see the lights of the encampment. As he slowed his horse at the perimeter, the men on guard recognised him. Was that even a nod of respect? Ronan could not quell the pride that swelled in his chest. He had truly become the king's man, and acquired all the privileges that entailed.

Fires burned throughout the camp to keep away the chill of encroaching winter. At the highest point stood the king's tent, the smell of cooking pig wafting down from it as Ronan dismounted. He made his way up as fast as he could, pushing his way past the knights who stood about the fire over which the pig was spitted. King William stood the closest, staring into those flames hungrily, awaiting the first cut.

'Dol-Combourg,' the king said as Ronan bowed. 'What news?'

'The Danes have accepted your offer, sire. The deal is done, though they have requested they be allowed to winter on the waters of Axholme before returning to Danmørk. They also… requested provisions, in exchange for the return of prisoners.'

'Prisoners?' The king looked at him now, his eyes lit in the flames. 'Who?'

'Giselbert of Gant. And Guillam Mallet, sire.'

William nodded. 'A fair trade, I suppose.'

'Then should I have the supplies gathered and sent to their fleet?'

The king looked back to the fire, before stepping forward and drawing his knife. He hacked off a juicy slice of pork from the pig's rump, before stuffing it in his mouth. All around them, the men had gone silent.

King William chewed the meat before swallowing it down. Then he looked at Ronan and grinned, the juices still running down his chin. That smile turned to a laugh, the laugh to a raucous bellow. It was taken up by the men surrounding them, until it sounded like the whole camp was joined in merriment.

No. It looked like the Danes would not be feasting this winter.

13

They had marched for days across the flat forested land, sheltering where they could from the winter snows. At first they had pulled their carts by horse, but soon the gnawing approach of starvation had forced them to slaughter the beasts one by one. Now those carts had been abandoned, and what remained of Edgar's army carried their meagre supplies on their backs through the wooded wilderness.

Though Styrkar had done his best to remain stoic against the elements and the ignominy, he knew that even he must have looked a sight as they approached the clearing ahead. He felt relief when he saw Edgar had stopped amidst the wide-open space, his men slumping exhausted against the surrounding trees, and dropping down upon the snow-dusted earth.

There they stood, breath misting as they waited for the rest of their band to catch up. A band that had dwindled over the days, but Styrkar could hardly blame them. Edgar had gathered fyrd and ceorl from all across the north, and now they were forced to flee in the face of the Frankish onslaught. It was foolish to think they would all have remained by the Aetheling's side.

'This is the place,' Edgar announced, his voice echoing amid the surrounding woodland. He sounded hoarse, his eyes shadowy with exhaustion. 'We make camp here. Gather the supplies.'

Some of the men looked confused. They had seen no sign of food nor ale for days, while others were already sifting through the patchy earth. One close by kicked aside some leaves, stooping to grasp a rope before dragging a wooden cover along the frozen ground. Within were barrels and sacks of supplies that Edgar had been wise enough to store before all this began. Had he expected defeat? Left this treasure here for their inevitable retreat? It mattered little now – Styrkar could only be thankful for the boy's forethought.

On seeing more supplies revealed, the men fell on them like dogs on a downed stag. Edgar looked as though he might order them to relent, but there would be no stopping these men, half-starved as they were.

Gradually more men entered the clearing, carrying their weapons and what armour they had. Gospatric and Waltheof still had their faithful housecarls, while Siward and Maerlswein led their own bands. Despite the loyalty of their followers, all four had seen their numbers dwindle, and when they were all gathered, Styrkar guessed there were fewer than a few hundred of them left. Not much to take on the might of the Frankish cavalry in their wake.

Styrkar waited his turn as the supplies were dealt out. Fires were lit, high and furious, the wood wet and billowing smoke into the sky, but none of them cared. If they were not kept warm through the winter nights it would not be the king's hunters who killed them but the cold. If they were too frozen to defend themselves they would be easy meat, and Styrkar was determined to go down fighting if they were caught in the open.

As night fell and the surrounding forest was cast in darkness, there was a sullen silence across the camp. Men who hadn't eaten for days were suddenly full, and it put many of them in a stupor. A harsh voice from across the glade suddenly stood out starkly, and Styrkar could see it was Gospatric who was once again stirring discontent.

Styrkar approached, seeing Edgar once more listening intently, though he looked weary as he stood. Their leadership was growing fractious, but what could Styrkar do to heal the scars now they were all but beaten?

'We have to bargain,' Gospatric snarled, trying to keep a hushed tone and failing. 'We have to fall upon the king's mercy now or all is lost.'

Waltheof nodded his agreement, but from the hardness around Edgar's eyes it was clear he disagreed. 'How can we do that now? We have no position from which to bargain. We hold no lands or cities. Defend no fort but these woods. Our last hope is the Danes. If they—'

'We'll be dead before the damned Danes come,' Gospatric growled.

The silence that followed was uncomfortable, made worse by the fact that Edgar had no argument. As much as it sickened Styrkar, he knew that Gospatric was probably right.

Siward moved to stand between the men, his bald pate

covered against the chill by a fur hat. 'Perhaps we can find somewhere further north. A town to defend. A fort perhaps. Northumbria is still loyal to us; the Franks have not crushed the spirit of its folk yet.'

'Maybe not crushed,' Maerlswein replied. 'But they have struck fear into their hearts. Every gate will be barred to anyone standing in opposition to the king, if not now then soon. Already the Franks burn their way north. We could make a stand at Dun Holm, but will we reach it before the king's knights?'

Edgar shook his head in frustration. 'There must be somewhere closer. Maybe on the coast. Somewhere the Danes could rally to us.'

Styrkar had heard enough. Their situation might be dire but he for one had faced worse odds. He took a step forward, making sure they could all see him.

'Before we joined together, I fought alongside another rebel. Eadric the Wild struck against the Franks from the Marcher Lands. He had no city, no castle, no knights, and yet he still made the king's men bleed. He established a safe haven in the Long Forest, beyond the reach of the very same enemies who now search us out. We can do the same in the north.'

Styrkar hoped his words might stoke a fire in these men, but even Edgar looked little enthused by them.

'You would have us become silvatici in the wilds, Red Wolf?' Gospatric said, contempt dripping from his mouth. 'I am Gospatric, son of Maldred. Ealdorman of Northumbria. I am no forest savage. I will not hide in the woods and strike like a coward from the shadows.'

'No.' Styrkar leaned in close. 'Instead you would kneel

and beg for mercy from the man who has robbed you of your lands. Sooner or later you will have to fight for the title that was taken, whether you are the son of Maldred or the spawn of a dog.'

Gospatric's eyes lit, his lip curling. He stepped forward, not fearful of the Red Wolf, not backing down from the challenge. Styrkar felt a sense of satisfaction that he had managed to stir Gospatric to action, even if he did have to kill him.

Before any steel could be drawn, they heard the sound of hooves approaching across the hard ground. A horse bolted into the clearing, causing a moment of panic, before they saw it was one of Maerlswein's scouts who had returned to join them in the dead of night.

As the man jumped down from his horse, stumbling on unsteady legs, Maerlswein moved to greet him.

'What news?' he asked. 'Where are the rest of you?'

The scout shook his head. 'Dead. Fled. I know not which. I rode north as fast as I was able, and the news is not good, my lord. The Franks are on the move again. Pushing north. Burning everything in their path and leaving nothing but slaughter and ash in their wake.'

'What news of the Danes?' Edgar asked. 'Did you manage to find them? To tell them to rally with us further up the coast?'

The man took a drink from the skin he was offered, before shaking his head. 'Asbjorn and his fleet are not coming, Aetheling. The Bastard has paid them off. They winter at Axholme and will leave at the first spring thaw.'

'Treacherous bastards,' Gospatric snarled.

Edgar's shoulders sagged. 'Then that is the end. Our only

hope is to return to Alba and hope Máel can protect us from our pursuers.'

Styrkar had only seen Edgar look this cowed once before, in Berchastede, when he had been touted as king. Now he looked much the same as that scared boy, and it only served to stir fury within the Red Wolf.

'No. We will not run. We will fight. I will not take another step back.'

His fists were clenched, teeth gnashing, and the silence that followed told him his outburst had struck fear in these men. But surely that was what they needed – to be more afraid of the Red Wolf's wroth than that of the Franks.

'How do we fight?' Edgar said, his voice calm, staring down Styrkar's anger. 'Look around you. These men are beaten. But if we flee there may be a chance they can fight another day. If you stay, if you fight, Red Wolf, you will surely die. And you made me an oath. You owe me a crown, and I promised in return I would give you a chance to take the head of King William. Do you remember? It is a promise I intend to keep, but for now we must take the road north.'

Styrkar felt his anger wane, as the cold winter night crept deeper into his bones. He glanced about him, seeing that there were no men here with an appetite for war.

'Very well. We go north. But I will hold you to your oath, just as you hold me to mine.'

The Aetheling, seeing he had curbed his rampant wolf, turned to the rest of the camp.

'Slaughter the horse. Tonight we will dine as kings. At first light, we must run.'

14

Yorke, England, December 1069

It was a ruin, and yet they still sat within its blackened confines. Ronan could smell the bitter tang of charred wood, the roof having all but burned away. The rafters of the Minster had been hastily replaced, and thatch shielded them from the bitter wind, but he could still see stars through it. Thankfully enough fires had been lit that the chill wasn't too bad, but Ronan was grateful for the fur cloak he had pulled tight around his shoulders.

The king thought it fitting that he spend Christes Maesse in Yorke, and what other place to hold this hallowed celebration than the Minster? Here, he could show his people that it was not just the south that he presided over. Even in the north, the hand of his benevolence reached out.

Ronan had to suppress a smirk at that notion. There would be no benevolence here. Only might. Only dominance.

Lords loyal to the king were still filtering in through the great doors to the church. It had been laid out like a feast hall, the altar pushed aside for the king's table, though he was absent for now. Ronan was sure he would want to make an entrance.

Instead, through those doors walked Giselbert and Mallet, looking somewhat more themselves after their ordeal at the hands of the Danes. Ronan tried to look as gracious as he could as they took their places at the table nearby.

Was that a nod of appreciation from Giselbert? Would wonders never cease? As Mallet took his seat with a barely masked scowl, it became obvious they would.

'I hope you are both feeling better,' Ronan said, raising his cup.

Giselbert raised his own, though it was empty. 'Yes, Dol-Combourg. And thank you, once again.'

Mallet didn't even reach out a hand to his own cup. He simply sat, with that bruised face, trying to look anywhere but toward Ronan.

Three loud knocks, as one of the king's retainers pounded the stone floor with the butt of his spear. The signal for them all to stand and receive their king.

The door was opened ceremonially, allowing a stark breath of winter air to blow in. It heralded King William, walking with all the regal solemnity his position warranted. He was dressed in full regalia; red cloak trimmed with white fur, golden crown upon his creased brow. But there was a glint of mail beneath that royal garb. A show of brute power as well as regal authority.

As the king took his place upon the chancel, Giselbert leaned in closer to Ronan. 'Is all this pomp really necessary? Why have we been gathered here, in this place? It seems wholly inappropriate considering the... state of it.'

Ronan gestured to the doors that were still lying open. 'It

may well be our king is demonstrating a show of strength. See, he has invited honoured guests.'

In the king's wake shuffled a dozen or more ragged-looking Saxons – their hair unkempt, their cloaks looking wholly insubstantial considering how cold it was outside. The thegns of the north, invited here to benefit from the king's generosity. As they were corralled to a small table, burned black and displaying no cups or trenchers, it appeared their status as 'honoured guests' might have been overstating it.

Ronan expected speeches, but instead through those doors came a line of peasant serfs carrying platters on their shoulders. The king was first to receive his bounty – a roasted chicken, surrounded by braised coneys brought from their homeland, lamprey marinaded in red wine, and a haunch of venison to finish the plate.

As the king began to eat with enthusiasm, platters were brought for his guests, though Ronan noticed the table before the Saxon lords was conspicuously bereft of fare.

Nobody waited on ceremony, and the king's closest began their banquet. Nearby, Giselbert began to dig in. He had always been a wiry individual, and Ronan had never seen him eat so much as a morsel before. Since his ordeal at the hands of the Danes he was clearly taking every opportunity to gorge himself. Mallet, on the other hand, picked at his meat as though he had no appetite at all.

Giselbert looked up from his meal, still chewing on something. 'So, Dol-Combourg, you are now a man in the know. What word of the latest rebellion?'

Ronan wiped grease from around his mouth and placed his chicken wing back on its trencher. 'From what I know, the rebels who took Yorke have fled into the northern hills. Their Danish allies still reside at Axholme, but they are in for a tricky winter. As far as I am aware the north is secured.'

Giselbert nodded his approval. 'That is good news. I for one feel safer knowing the king has curbed these foreign pigs.' He glanced over to where the Saxon lords still sat, looking hungrier with every passing moment.

Ronan couldn't help but agree with the sentiment. He'd more than had his fill of gallivanting around the country putting out fires... and igniting them. Surely the Saxons had learned their lessons. They had been sent scurrying into the hills, their corpses littering every back road, dell, and marsh. There could be no more fire left in their bellies.

With luck, the kingdom was now firmly in the king's control, and Ronan could leave the north behind him and return to Brian's side. His friend would greet him with open arms. The country quelled. Their future assured.

Another bang of the spear haft on the stone floor, and all Ronan's daydreams of a brighter tomorrow were blown away on the chill air. The imperious form of Hugo of Grentmesnil towered beside the king as he sat.

'I would have your attention,' he yelled, his voice echoing through the vaulted interior of the Minster. 'The king has gathered you here this Christes Maesse, to receive the generosity of his table. He would now address this joint gathering of magnates from both these isles and the distant shores of Frankia, brought together at this celebration of our Lord.'

Hugo took a step back. King William continued to nibble at the bony carcass of an eel, slurping down the jelly as though he hadn't heard his announcement. No one was of a mind to hurry him along.

Eventually he dropped the bones onto his trencher and looked up, seeing for the first time that all eyes were upon him. Wiping his hands on the white fur trim of his cloak, he rose to his feet. Those piercing dark eyes took in the room – his followers, his guests. It was a stony gaze that did not alter, even when he forced a smile on his narrow face.

'Thank you all for coming,' he said in the Frankish tongue. The notion that any of them had a choice in their attendance almost made Ronan laugh out loud. 'I hope the banquet I have provided is adequate for you all?'

The lords he had appointed, who had followed him across half a kingdom, murmured their gratitude. The Saxon magnates, unable to understand him, offered no response.

'Ah, my apologies,' William continued, gesturing to the Saxons at their empty table. 'I am afraid I have not yet learned any of the languages native to these islands. Dol-Combourg.' He motioned for Ronan to stand. 'Do the honours, if you would. Tell them I am grateful they are here.'

All attention now on him, Ronan gingerly rose to his feet. He glanced across at the Saxons, who gazed back in confusion.

'My lords,' Ronan said. 'The king offers his thanks that you have come.'

If they were grateful for the king's acknowledgement, they made no remark on it. More likely they were still wondering why they alone had not been fed. Ronan was wondering it too.

'From the first day I landed on these shores,' William said, as Ronan repeated his words in the Saxon tongue, 'I have tried to find an accord with the people who live here. Tried to persuade them of my rightful claim to the throne. That it is in everyone's best interest if I am accepted, peacefully, without fuss. As you might have heard, I have had little success.'

Silence. Then the king burst out laughing. At first few got the joke, until some of his men laughed along, soon joined by those Saxon lords.

William calmed his laughter, wiping a tear of mirth from his eyes. 'I have offered gifts of land. Of authority. Tried to atone for the corpses I have left in my path. But at every stage it has been thrown back in my face. Even now, rebels haunt the northern dales and forests. Striking under cover of dark. Murdering my appointed officials. Causing me no end of trouble.'

He still laughed, but Ronan could sense the mood beginning to shift, as though they had suddenly veered from stony ground onto marshland. Though the Saxons were smiling, they were nervously glancing toward one another. Ronan almost felt sorry for them as he did his best to translate the king's words as he continued.

'And who aids these rebels? Offers them shelter and sustenance? The very people who smile and bow and offer me their fealty. The thegns who pledge themselves to the king with one breath, and whisper conspiracies to unseat him the next. They are aided by *you*.'

William slammed a fist on the table, all his mirth gone. Ronan could see those Saxons squirming in the resultant quiet. One even went so far as to open his mouth to protest, but William raised a hand for his silence.

'No more excuses,' the king growled. 'I have endured

enough of your lies and disloyalty. Offered too much clemency. Now all I offer is ash. I will take my armies north. We will salt the earth. Kill every animal, burn every farm, slaughter any bastard who dares to look us in the eye.'

As Ronan repeated the words he could see the growing dismay among those northern thegns. See their fear. Their realisation that this was what they had wrought with their treachery. They knew this was no idle threat. This was the end, explained for them in detail.

'Food,' William yelled. 'A banquet for my honoured guests.'

At his word, more serfs entered carrying more platters. But these were not piled high with roasted meat and vegetables. Here were scraps of days-old meat and the rotting bones they still hung from. Without ceremony, the scraps were dumped on the table before those Saxon lords.

'Act like dogs,' the king said. 'Eat like dogs.'

Some of the thegns looked upon the table with disgust. Others looked forlorn, as though they had been caught in a lie, and now had no idea how to get themselves out of it.

'I said eat!' screamed King William, stabbing his knife into the wooden table.

His voice resonated up to the sparsely thatched roof – a fire that seared away the chill of the room. Ronan saw those magnates flinch, before reaching forward with trembling hands. It turned his stomach to see them pick at the remains before them, and despite his satisfaction at witnessing these traitors brought low, he all of a sudden lost his appetite.

The king regarded the rest of the gathering. Every eye was on him, wondering who the next target of his ire might be.

'As for the rest of you... I suggest you eat heartily this night. Tomorrow there will be no rest. We strike north. We will root out every rebel left in this northern wasteland. Pursue them to the gates of Hell itself. Or Alba – whichever comes first.'

With that he wrenched his knife from the table, swept his red cloak back, and strode across the Minster toward that open door. Men stood and bowed as he passed, Ronan one of them.

So much for this being over. While those Saxon lords retched and gagged as they ate, and the harsh northern cold blew in through the doors, Ronan knew it had barely started.

15

Though it shamed him, the Red Wolf ran. Through the storm of arrows and flame he fled, dodging past trees, eyes streaming from the smoke. The sky above the treetops was black with it, and it looked as though the Franks had set the whole forest alight. Still they pursued them, the sounds of their cries and the hooves of their horses thundering through the dense woodland.

Shouts up ahead. Saxon voices. All Styrkar could do was keep running, try to meet up with his fellows. He could barely remember how this battle had even started, how he had found himself separated, but if he didn't find an ally soon he would surely die alone in the shadow of this cursed forest.

Movement ahead through the pall. Styrkar gripped his axe as he heard the desperate yells of men locked in violence. A Saxon fallen on his back, a Frankish knight standing over him. Their shields had been abandoned and now they battered one another with the hafts of their broken spears.

Styrkar dashed into the clearing, axe gripped in both hands as he raised it high. The knight didn't even see him before he stoved in the back of his helm. Styrkar didn't pause to gloat over his kill, instead holding out his hand – and the Saxon warrior gratefully took it.

The man staggered as he rose, favouring the weight of one leg, and Styrkar grasped him about the waist as they both struggled through the thick smoke. It was cloying as they stumbled on, arrows streaking overhead to pepper the ground around them. The warrior snarled as they stumbled further, biting back the pain, as Styrkar gritted his teeth, desperately trying to put distance between them and the rampaging enemy.

A hiss, before the telltale thud of arrow piercing mail. The man went heavy in Styrkar's arms and he couldn't hold him up any longer. He slumped to the mossy ground, shaft protruding from his back, but there was no time to feel sorrow. He had to keep moving. Had to survive.

More arrows fell as he left the dead man behind. Before he could begin to feel any despair, he heard voices ahead, men he recognised. A shout above the noise of violence as Edgar did his best to gather his scattered army.

'To me,' he shouted in that thick accent of the Rus. 'Men of the north, rally to me.'

Styrkar burst from cover. The woodland rose up to rocks, upon which the Aetheling stood. On seeing Styrkar he nodded his acknowledgement, eyes greeting him with relief. Not for long as he realised how few of his men remained as he beckoned them on from the woods.

Together they mounted the rocks, running toward the rising sun and out of the smoke-choked forest. Styrkar heaved in the fresh air once they had broken the cloying confines of the woodland, but their chase was not over yet.

Edgar led them through brushland, and down another slope to a shallow river. There they hunkered down as they moved along the bed, desperate to avoid the watchful gaze of pursuing horsemen. The river led them northward, until they could see a settlement ahead. The burgh was on fire, flames burning low as black smoke trailed off into the pale sky.

'Where are the others?' Styrkar whispered, as they edged their way closer to the settlement.

Edgar didn't take his eyes off those burning huts. 'Just to the north of that town, if God is with us.'

'He has not been with us so far, Aetheling.'

Edgar looked at him and grinned. 'Then we are overdue his attention, Red Wolf.'

He led them on, and Styrkar was encouraged that despite all they had lost, how much they had bled, he still had the will to see them through this. They followed the boy as he struck out from the river, toward the edge of the burning town. The ground had been churned up by the hooves of so many horses, every hut and barn set afire, the thatch blackened.

The deeper they delved into the settlement, the more the merciless nature of their enemy became evident. Not a thing had been left alive. Every sheep, pig and even dog lay gutted. Men were sprawled alongside their women and children, as the remnants of their lives smouldered. It was with grim silence that Edgar led them through this, and even Styrkar was struck by the needless brutality of it.

It was a relief to leave the place behind them as they kept

on north toward yet more woodland. Styrkar avoided a last glance back, as they delved into the trees, striking quickly into the forest before they were seen by the very men who had done this.

Would he have wanted that confrontation? A chance at a reckoning? Though the Red Wolf stirred inside, Styrkar was not sure even he was up to that fight now.

As night drew in, they reached their rendezvous, and the rest of the survivors. No one offered a word of challenge, these men just as wan and silent as the ones Styrkar had escaped with, their hair and beards bedraggled, many of them carrying the wounds they had suffered after days of fighting and running.

Edgar led them to the centre of a makeshift camp where Gospatric was sitting. With no healer to aid him, he was tending to a wound in his leg, doing his best to wrap fresh cloth about it after discarding the bloodstained bandage that had covered it previously. From the scant number of men who surrounded him, Styrkar had to assume he had all but been abandoned.

'Thank the Lord,' Gospatric said, when he saw Edgar approaching. 'I thought we were the only ones left.'

'Don't thank him yet,' Edgar replied. 'We are not out of this by a long way. Where is your cousin?'

Gospatric shook his head. 'Waltheof has gone. He and his men have not been seen since yesterday. And neither have Maerlswein or Siward.' He winced as he tightened the sorry-looking bandage. 'So what do we do now?'

Edgar squatted, leaning his back against the trunk of an oak. 'Now? We rest. Tomorrow, we carry on northward to Máel.'

If Gospatric thought it a wild idea he made no argument of it. But then none of them, least of all Styrkar, knew what else to do. Even in his days in the wilds he had never run so far. Never felt more hunted than hunter.

He sat himself close to Edgar, as the men shared what little food they had managed to forage. As night finally fell, and it seemed they were alone, Styrkar took his moment to lean into the Aetheling.

'With Waltheof gone, Gospatric won't be far off fleeing himself. He will surely abandon you at the next sign of trouble. Perhaps even betray you to save his own skin.'

The news only seemed to amuse Edgar. 'My friend, I have never trusted any of these ealdormen, be they from the north or the south. I was a token to be bargained before. Morcar and Edwin. Waltheof and Gospatric. All would have sold me to the Franks in return for a seat at King William's table. I do not trust them any more now than I did then.'

'Good,' Styrkar replied. 'Then know you only have to give the word, and I will take that bastard's head for you.'

That widened Edgar's grin. 'I will keep it in mind.'

Night deepened, and the meagre fires they had built dwindled, but Styrkar was still a stranger to sleep. As he stood to stretch his aching legs, he heard distant rustling through the bracken, as a group approached. Warnings were hissed across the camp, and men scrambled for their weapons, but as Styrkar stood staring into the dark of the wood he heard a familiar voice.

'Stay your hands,' Maerlswein called, as he appeared from the black.

Other men were at his back, looking as weary as the bearded war hound who led them.

'Glad to see you, friend,' Styrkar said, clapping Maerlswein on the shoulder.

'And I you. But we don't come alone. We have a gift for you all.'

Styrkar could see more men following behind. The tall figure of Siward appeared, his bald head reflecting the moonlight, as his men dragged a prisoner along with them. The Frank was beaten half to shit, hands bound, breath coming in fevered gasps, but Styrkar felt little pity.

'Bring him,' he ordered, before leading them back toward the centre of the camp.

Edgar and Gospatric were waiting, looking relieved to see that more of their allies had survived the flight. On noticing they had a prisoner in their midst, Gospatric asked if anyone spoke enough of the Frankish tongue to question their prisoner.

'I do,' Edgar replied, stepping forward and kneeling so he could look the beaten Frank in the eye.

'Ask him where their main force is,' Gospatric said, tottering on his wounded leg. 'Ask him where they're headed, so we can avoid them on the way north.'

Edgar ignored him and his weasel words, looking deep into the eyes of the prisoner. Did that Frankish knight see any mercy there? He certainly looked as though there might be some hope for him.

The two exchanged brief words in that foreign tongue. Styrkar watched as Edgar's questioning became more urgent, and the knight spoke faster, almost seeming to panic, so desperate was he to live.

'Well?' Gospatric asked.

Edgar rose to his feet, letting out a long sigh. 'The news

is not good, if this man is to be believed. He says the king has had his fill of rebellion. He comes north personally to oversee the quelling of the populace. The north is to be razed. Every farm and burgh put to the flame. He intends for us to receive no aid or succour wherever we run.'

'No. Not even the Bastard would do something so drastic. This man's lying. He's trying to put the fear of God in us to save his own skin.'

'This man is too afraid to lie, Gospatric. I believe him. William has shown us mercy time and again, but his patience is spent. Did you not see the town to the south? Before long the entire north will suffer the same fate, and we will suffer along with it if we tarry.'

'So what do we do?' Gospatric's voice was small, like a child lost and alone.

'Our plan does not change. We continue north, meet up with King Máel and rally our armies. He will help us. He will provide more warriors; this is not finished.'

'There's more,' said Siward, stepping into the light of the campfire flames. 'My scouts to the east have sent word that Máel is no longer in Alba. He has struck south, and from what they tell me, he now waits along the river in Goat's Head.'

'What?' Gospatric said. 'Goat's Head is part of my earldom. Why is he there?'

Siward shrugged his broad shoulders.

'Perhaps he comes to our aid,' suggested Edgar. 'He must have heard we are in need of reinforcements and rides to meet us.'

Gospatric looked doubtful. 'Aye, perhaps. Whatever the reason we should move at first light to meet him.'

'Agreed. For now, get some rest.'

The men were not about to argue with that. As they dispersed to find a warm spot in the camp, the prisoner they had captured began to murmur. Maerlswein raised his axe and silenced him.

Styrkar barely noticed such a casual act of violence. He had no pity anymore, but then none of them did. Neither had they the appetite for war, even if Máel had come to help them in their fight. But had he?

All these lords were self-serving, be they from England or Alba. Or Danmǫrk for that matter. Had they decided to work together long ago, unite themselves under a single leader, then perhaps they might have had a chance to defeat William. Now, it seemed they were just as petty and greedy as they ever had been.

But maybe Edgar could change that. Styrkar had gambled much on it. He was not ready to admit he had lost yet. He had seen the Aetheling's quality, his steadfastness, his strength. It reminded him of King Harold more than he cared to admit, and more than that, the young warrior symbolised hope. A way for them to regain what they had lost. To wrest the crown of England from the grip of a tyrant and begin anew. And while that hope still kindled, Styrkar would follow.

16

They ravaged their way north, their fires burning with such a rage they sent the snow running in rivers, mixing with the blood, before setting to ice once more. All this Ronan had watched with an ever-waning sense of zeal. At first he had been caught up in the king's determination to end the rebellions that plagued his reign. It had seemed the most expedient path. The reality of it had soon painted an altogether more sickening picture.

It was not stout and hardy rebels who now suffered as he stood amid the carnage of another pillaged settlement. It was the peasants of the north. Common folk sent screaming into the night, as their livestock was slaughtered and their crops destroyed.

At least Ronan wouldn't have to watch them starve, and the warmth of the burning buildings kept the cold away, at least for a while. But then, he always thought it best to try and look on the bright side, since his fortunes had changed.

Besides, this was a means to an end. What mattered the

lives of a few peasants if it ultimately meant peace? Even if he objected to the constant pleading and murder, what could he do? Complain? No, that would only cause him to lose face, and after spending so much time and effort gaining it, he wasn't about to lose it all for the sake of a few foreign farmers.

The wood of a nearby hut crackled. Smoke billowed as snow turned to mist then to cloying black cloud. It stirred a long-suppressed memory. Of those first days he had been in this accursed country, and the souls damned upon his order. How he had embraced William's methods, and looked forward to what he might gain from them. Ronan had changed since then. Had embraced a different kind of hope, only to see it taken from him.

What would Gisela think of him now?

He dismissed that thought. It would not do to dwell on it. Ronan of Dol-Combourg was the king's servant now, and all those prizes he had been told were beyond his reach might yet be his, if only he served with faith.

Just as his leg began to ache too much to bear, he saw Wymon and Serle appear from the smouldering barn. At first Ronan had winced at the sound of them hacking those sheep apart, but it hadn't taken long for the sounds of the distressed beasts to fade into the background with everything else.

Both men were covered in blood, Wymon carrying the carcass of a sheep over one shoulder. Despite their booty, both men looked as dismal as Ronan felt. Clearly their appetite for all this was waning too.

'We're done,' said Serle.

'Very well,' Ronan replied, turning to where their horses were tethered. 'Best be off.'

As he limped away from the heat of the burning hut, he could hear other sounds in the distance. Other men, burning other buildings. Causing havoc in other parts of the settlement. They all had their duties to perform.

'How much more of this before we're finished, you reckon?' Serle grumbled as they mounted their steeds.

'As much as the king decides, I suppose.' Ronan wished he had a more definite answer, but truth was none of them knew when.

They tugged on their reins, heading toward the west of the town where the king had ordered they set up camp. As they left the warmth of the burning barn behind them, Ronan gave off a shiver.

'We must have curbed the north by now,' Serle continued to grumble. 'This place is finished. We've left nothing – these people will starve for sure.'

Glancing back at yet another burned settlement, Ronan couldn't help but agree. 'They will starve. But the king is far from done. He wants his prize.'

'Those rebels, you mean. Wherever the hell they are. Well, the king's going to struggle on that score if he keeps pushing us like this.'

Ronan turned to regard the rat-faced knight. 'What is that supposed to mean?'

Serle sniffed in the cold. 'You mean you haven't heard the griping? The malcontent? None of us want to die in the cold, just so the king can have his prize. What's our prize?'

Indeed, this was the first grumbling of discontent he had heard. But then he had no wish to mix with the rest of the men, now he was close to the king. 'You're talking of mutiny, Serle. What exactly have the men been grumbling about?'

He shrugged. 'Just about the cold. The food. The endless trekking through this shitty winter. Won't be long before men start riding off and leaving this mad crusade behind.'

'I do not imagine such a raw display of disloyalty will go down well with our king.'

'Me neither,' Serle replied. 'But he's blind to it. Blinded by his mad urge to find Edgar and those other Saxons, and punish them. And what does he think that will achieve? Most likely it will only fan the flames of yet more rebellion.'

Ronan was surprised by how insightful Serle was. He'd thought the man a mindless thug, but here he was reading the land and its people like a native.

'More rebellion is not our concern. That is for William to worry on. All we need do is obey, and we will see the rewards. Rest assured.'

Serle didn't look convinced, but before he replied Wymon let out a long and loud yawn, then said, 'I'm bloody hungry.'

They were the first words Ronan had heard him say. 'All right, best we get back to camp and set to cooking that mutton.'

He spurred his horse to a canter, and the three of them continued along the riverbank. The longer he spent away from the burned huts, the more the cold infested his bones. When he spied the king's encampment ahead, he was relieved to see that fires already burned in wait for their arrival.

They dismounted, a couple of squires taking charge of their steeds, as Wymon carried the sheep carcass to a waiting table. He did the skinning and gutting himself as Ronan stood close to a fire.

There were comings and goings in the camp. The usual bustle. Riders returned in their groups, conrois sent to pillage the local area, but they looked little enthused by their labours. When all this had started, there had been a zeal about it. Now it was obvious that was waning. Ronan hadn't noticed until now, but it was obvious Serle was right. Their campaign was only spreading discord, the king's followers beginning to grow disillusioned with the endless slaughter. As he shivered again, despite the flames, Ronan remembered how the shitty English weather could do that to any man.

As Serle and Wymon returned with the mutton spitted and ready to go on the fire, Ronan felt the sudden urge to know just how bad things were. Despite the cold, he left the warmth of the fire, and limped through the camp.

It didn't take long before he was struck by the discontent. Not a smile to be seen. Not a tale told of what these men had done, of what they had pillaged. Certainly no talk of how they would crush this rebellion. Every eye looked weary. Every face pale and drawn. If there was no end to this soon, it might not just be a Saxon rebellion the king had to worry over.

Closest to the river stood the king's tent. Ronan wandered nearer, hearing voices inside, the sound of the king's deep brogue. More plans afoot?

Ronan ducked as he stepped within. Men surrounded the king as he listened, and Ronan could see Hugo of Grentmesnil standing in the centre. At William's shoulder was Thurstan, known as the White, his standard bearer. Even these men of import looked grim as they relayed their news.

'Our forward pathfinders have returned with news of the Saxon rout,' said Hugo. 'The enemy is scattered, Edgar and his rebellious earls still flee to the north.'

'How far ahead?' the king asked, running a hand over his thick stubbled chin.

'They are days away, perhaps four.'

William clenched his hand into a fist. 'Then we must move faster. We will hunt every last one down. Grind them into the hard winter earth.'

If the king had been expecting mumblings of assent, he was sorely disappointed. Not one of his lords spoke in support of the idea.

'What is wrong with you all?' William said, rising to his feet. 'Victory is almost ours.'

Ronan knew full well what was wrong with them, but he was in no mood to enlighten the king. He watched as Thurstan and Hugo shared a knowing look, silently bargaining for who would be the one to speak. Eventually it was Hugo.

'Sire, the men are spent. They will not suffer much more of this endless chase and the northern cold.'

William's brow darkened, but what could any of them have expected. 'Dissent?'

'We are farther north than we have ever come, my king. Isolated from any castle. From any help, should we need it. The men are weary, cold, hungry. The rebels are beaten. They are—'

'Beaten,' William said quietly, but the word still held menace. 'They are not beaten until they are driven before me in chains. Or dead and frozen in the snow.'

'Your men would disagree,' Hugo said. It was brave of

him to contradict his king in such a manner, but someone had to do it. Ronan was just relieved it wasn't him.

'Would they?' William stared across the tent, and no man could hold his gaze. 'Then I would have you remind them that they are my subjects. And they will do as I command.'

'Your subjects?' Hugo replied, finding some courage. 'You brought them here to help you in claiming your crown, sire, but they are still free men.'

Ronan could see a fire light in the king's eyes, but his jaw was clamped shut, lest he rage at such defiance. Did he see the truth in Hugo's words? That his army consisted of free men he had brought here who were his equals, not his serfs?

'Thurstan,' William said, turning to his standard bearer. 'You have fought beside me since the beginning. What say you?'

All eyes fell on Thurstan, but he remained uncowed. 'I have followed faithfully, sire, as have we all. And I offer the respect you are due as rightful king of these lands. But we are men of Normandie and Bretagne, not English vassals. We fight by your side on the promise of reward. And I see little reward in carrying on north, heedless of the hardship.'

William nodded at his standard bearer's wisdom, eyes scanning the gathered men once more before settling on Ronan. 'And you, Dol-Combourg. What have you to say?'

There was a sudden lump in Ronan's throat as the gathered knights glanced toward him. Days ago he had been a pariah – now he was being asked his opinion by the king himself. He could imagine how they would expect him to want an end to this hardship. Maybe best not to plead his own case and confirm their belief that he was a coward.

'There is… discontent among the men. I do not see them suffering this cold much longer. The winter has been hard, but they are still loyal. However, I would question whether there is enough fight left in them to quell these rebels even if we hunt them down.'

Slowly, William lowered himself back into the chair. His jaw was working, eyes fixed on the ground as he considered his options. It was obvious he had few.

'Then it seems I am a king without an army. I can hardly fight these rebels alone.' He gazed up at his gathered knights. 'Very well, we will make our way back south and hope that the chill of winter cools the rebellious temperaments of these northern thegns.'

Ronan could sense relief. The king did not need to speak to dismiss them, and Ronan followed as the rest of the knights filtered from the tent. As he made his way back toward Wymon and Serle, he smelled a sudden alluring aroma and was relieved that he could deliver welcome news.

17

With every mile they marched closer to the town, the higher the smoke had risen in the morning sky. No one spoke their fears, but Styrkar knew what these men were feeling, what they were thinking. Their flight had been cursed with ill fortune since the day they had left Yorke. Their numbers dwindling every day. Now, as they approached Goat's Head, they all knew their god had abandoned them completely.

Less than a mile from the town, Edgar drew them up. Gospatric stood at his shoulder, looking forlornly toward the place that was supposed to be their salvation. It looked far from welcoming now.

'They've beaten us here,' Gospatric said gravely. 'Somehow the king has marched his army ahead of us. Burned the place down. He's waiting there somewhere – we must turn back.'

Edgar ignored his craven words, glaring toward the remains of the town. 'Turn back where? There is nowhere left for us to run.'

Styrkar took a step forward. Though he was weary, he knew he still had strength enough for one final fight. One last reckoning that he had walked so far to face.

'The Aetheling is right. We must forge ahead now, for good or ill.'

Part of him hoped the Franks might still be lurking nearby. That he would see an end to this one way or another. He was done with running, despite his oath of loyalty to Edgar.

Over his shoulder, he saw that what remained of their army looked anything but ready for a fight, but still they drew their weapons, clutching their spears as much for support as to face the enemy. Only Maerlswein – that implacable bear of a warrior – looked anything close to prepared for a battle.

'What are we bloody waiting for then?' he said, pushing his way to the fore, and leading them on along the eastern road.

Styrkar followed, surprised when the rest did not pause. Together, the last five hundred or so of their number loped toward the town, starving wolves on the hunt. When they were within a hundred yards of the main gate the air became heavy with the bitter stink of woodsmoke. Bodies littered the path ahead of them, stripped and naked in the road. The gates lay open, although it looked as though they had not been battered down. There was no sign of arrows peppering the palisade. It looked as though the town had opened their gates to the enemy, and let them ravage their way through unhindered. That in itself was curious – Styrkar had been led to believe these northerners were hardy in the extreme. They would never have allowed the Franks to pillage their homes so readily.

They entered with caution. Styrkar gripped his axe tight, eyes scanning for any sign that there might be someone, anyone left to fight. All that awaited were corpses, the only sound the faint crackle of smouldering wood.

He could sense the relief around him, and turned his attention to the ground. Despite the hardness of the earth, he could still tell that there had been scores of attackers, but not a single horse among them.

Resting his axe on his shoulder, he began to walk deeper. Some of the other men quickened their pace, eager to find any spoils that remained among the carnage.

'Where is everyone?' Siward breathed. 'There's not many corpses. The Franks don't take slaves.'

'Most likely they have fled to the hills,' Maerlswein said. 'Scattered by the king, to starve in the wilds.'

'Here!' someone shouted from across the settlement.

Styrkar saw one of Gospatric's men waving frantically, and they made their way closer, all caution now abandoned. The man and a few others were staring into a hastily dug hole in the centre of the burgh. Half-naked corpses had been flung inside, all men, all grim and bearded. If they were the raiders who had attacked this place they certainly weren't Frankish. These men were all shaggy and bearded, not one of them bearing the tell-tale cropped hair of foreign knights.

'The rest must have departed in a hurry to leave them like this,' Maerlswein said, as he gazed upon the dead.

'And gone where?' Styrkar wondered.

The man who had beckoned them nearer raised a tattered banner. 'We found this among the corpses.'

It was burned at the fringe and filthy yellow. Upon it

could still be seen the red lion rampant. The symbol of the king of Alba.

'Máel's war banner,' Gospatric breathed. 'That treacherous fucking bastard. Why? Why would he do this? We are supposed to be allies.'

'Calm yourself, Gospatric,' Edgar said. 'There must be an explanation.'

'Explanation?' Gospatric's face had reddened, spittle flecking his chin. 'It's easy enough to work out. That scum has taken advantage of us. Used our absence to invade my lands and pillage what he can, like the dog he is.'

Edgar raised a hand to try and placate the ealdorman. 'There must be a reason. Perhaps the—'

'Fuck your reasons, Aetheling, and fuck you.' Gospatric took a threatening step toward Edgar. 'You led us to this. You promised us victory and look where we are. I told you we should have bargained with the king, but no. You knew better. Your lust for the throne has led us here.'

'You forget your place, Gospatric.'

'My place? My fucking place?' His nose was almost pressed to Edgar's, his hand on his blade. 'I put you where you are, boy. I am Gospatric. Son of Maldred. Ealdorman of—'

Styrkar moved in his path, glaring down, seeing Gospatric's enraged expression waver. 'You are ealdorman of nowhere. You are cast down. Your only hope is to beg on your knees and hope the king forgives you. Scraps are your only legacy.'

Gospatric glanced toward Edgar, unable to hold Styrkar's gaze. 'Is this how it ends, Aetheling? Is this how I am to be treated after we have fought so hard together? After I raised you up to challenge for the crown? You'd be nothing without me.'

Edgar shook his head. 'You only offered aid for what you could take in return, Gospatric. For the power it would give you. Don't pretend this wasn't all for you, and you alone.'

'This is treachery,' Gospatric replied, backing away. 'You and Máel are betrayers both. I should have left you where I found you. A boy with no followers. No army. No claim.'

His hand was still on his sword. Styrkar stood waiting for him to draw an inch of steel and give the excuse he had waited so long for. Instead, Gospatric stepped away, before turning and yelling for his men.

There might have been more violence, the air was tense with the promise of it, but the ealdorman gathered his men about him and ordered them to follow east from the destroyed settlement. Styrkar felt rare and welcome relief as he watched them go.

'So what now?'

It was Maerlswein's voice, and for the first time Styrkar sensed doubt in it. Despite how stoic he had been since that first day they'd been reunited at Dun Holm, now he looked beaten.

Edgar gazed toward the south. 'This raid may not have been King William's doing, but he is sure to be close.'

'You think we can trust Máel to help us against him? After what he's done here?'

Edgar gazed at the carnage. 'That, my friend, seems unlikely now.'

Siward was leaning heavily on his spear. 'Will he at least offer us shelter?'

'Now Gospatric is no longer among our number, I am sure he will. So we continue north to his fortress at Scoin.'

His answer seemed to satisfy the two warriors, but it did little to offer Styrkar any relief. The last thing he needed was more running, despite the fact that Edgar's rebellion was done for. There was nothing in Alba for the Red Wolf other than more empty promises of victories to come.

Before Siward and Maerlswein could begin to gather their remaining men, Edgar regarded Styrkar with a look of sadness. Or perhaps resignation.

'Are you coming, my friend?'

Styrkar looked back at him, thinking about all that could have been. He had followed this youth with faith. Had put much by his promises of overthrowing the evil that had overtaken this land. Of a worthy king on the throne. But now all that had winnowed to ashes.

'No.'

Edgar let out a long slow breath that misted in the cold air. 'I thought not. But you should know that there is still a chance that Máel will—'

'I am sorry, Aetheling. Sorry for what you have lost, despite how much you deserve it. Were you perhaps older, with wiser and stronger men in your service, then you could have united all the enemies of William. But you would have needed all the kings of Alba, Danmork and Eire to seize the throne. There is not a man alive who could have united those kings. I can think of only one who could have accomplished the deed, and he is dead.'

And it was true. Although he had seen much of King Harold in Edgar, it was clear this young warrior was not meant to rule. Not now. And because of that, the Red Wolf had to find a new master to serve. One who might offer him what he sought.

'Then this is goodbye, Styrkar.'

'It is, Aetheling. May your god watch over you.'

All Edgar could offer was a stern nod of the head, before turning to gather his men.

Siward likewise offered his nod of farewell before following Edgar, but Maerlswein remained. His eyes looked tired, and perhaps a little glassy from the cold.

'Well, lad. I always knew that Edgar could not keep the Red Wolf as his faithful hound forever. I just hoped we might have had a chance to avenge our king before we parted ways.'

'Clinging to a lost hope is for lesser men, my friend.'

'That it is,' Maerlswein agreed. 'Good luck to you, lad.'

'And you,' Styrkar replied, but Maerlswein had already turned, already following where the boy who should have been king led him.

Styrkar gazed toward the east, seeing the remainder of Gospatric's party disappearing into the winter haze. Northward, Edgar, Siward and Maerlswein led their beleaguered army toward the shelter of Alba. All that remained for the Red Wolf was the long journey back south toward the king he was still determined to kill.

There was still an oath to honour. One he had made in Danmork to the daughter of his fallen master. He would at least keep that final vow…

Or he would die.

18

The fires raged like the pits of Hell, but after what they had endured for the past few weeks, Hell bore little fear for any of them. Ronan only welcomed the heat, and as he sat at the edge of the feast hall, wine cup in hand, he almost forgot the searing pain that infested his leg at this time of year.

There was laughter. He'd almost forgotten the last time he'd heard it. The noise should have filled him with mirth, but after what he had seen on their expedition north he wondered if he might ever laugh again. As it was, he kept to himself among the august company, watching as the jongleurs played.

They performed a jolly tune – one plucking away at the gittern as another kept time with his tabor. All the while the piper whistled a refrain that kept the room humming along. Ronan had no idea what the songs were they played, but it didn't matter. He was more captivated by the bear that was dancing among them. They'd dressed it in a doublet of motley and balanced a straw hat upon its head. Occasionally it was poked and prodded with a stick, stirring it to greater effort. From what Ronan could see, the bear alone had secured them more coins in its sack than the minstrels.

A glance across the hall, and it was obvious it was doing the trick. Gone were the sullen faces Ronan had seen on the road. Now his fellow knights smiled and laughed as they dined, though the fare they consumed compared poorly to the feast they'd had at Christes Maesse. Now there was barely a bag of grain or wing of foul to be found in the whole city.

But not all were pleased with the largesse. At the head of the room, upon a seat of polished wood, sat the king. He was sullen, cup held limply in his hand as he viewed proceedings. Ronan guessed that only rebel heads juggled in front of him would have seen his humour lifted, but that chance was gone. Surely he should have been satisfied. Surely the devastation he had left in his wake as he travelled back from the north should have been enough to satisfy his thirst for domination.

Ronan shuddered despite the heat of the room. Despite the laughter and the music. They weren't laughing in the north. For the common folk there would only be tears and grumbling bellies as they buried their dead.

The journey back to Yorke had been a long one, but uneventful, and they had faced no opposition as they marched south. Seen no trace of rebellion. But then how would they? The rebels had fled north to the king in Alba, and any support they might have found on the way quashed to nothing. No beast had been left alive. No burgh left unburned. It would leave a mark on the north of William's kingdom that might never be cleaned. A stain that would tarnish all their souls… if any of them possessed one.

And what next for soulless Ronan of Dol-Combourg? What now there were no more rebels to quell?

As he watched these men, these knights, laugh at a dancing bear, he knew that there would be more rebels soon enough. Conquerors in a foreign land never got to rest easy for long.

'You look as sullen as our king, Ronan.'

A hand clapped to his shoulder, and he flinched. Hugo looked down at him, a smile creasing one side of his face, his eyes glassy from too much ale.

'Oh, I am laughing on the inside, Hugo.'

'Come now.' He motioned across the boisterous hall with his cup, slopping ale onto the floor. 'This is a time of celebration. We have won. The north is ours, and with it, the country.'

Ronan wasn't so sure. 'And look what we had to do to secure it.'

Hugo's brow creased in confusion. 'I never took you as squeamish, Dol-Combourg. Rumour has it you would sell your own mother if it bought you a lordship.'

Ronan gritted his teeth at mention of his mother. With any other man he might have taken issue, but as ever he had to endure the insult.

'No, not my mother.' He regarded Hugo with as stern a stare as he could muster. 'But perhaps yours.'

Hugo glared back as though he didn't quite understand the jibe had been poked right back at him. Then he grinned, slapping Ronan on the shoulder once again.

'That's the spirit. There's the cripple we all know.'

Yes – the wicked cripple. The self-serving dog of a knight. Barely any use to anyone but himself in days gone by, but things had changed. He had made himself useful. Just the fact he spoke the Saxon tongue made him valuable now the fighting was over. And his value to the king would only rise, as that of these boorish knights diminished.

'So what next for you, Hugo?' he asked, keen to move the subject on.

The knight shrugged. 'I have been granted land to the south. I will take it with gratitude and hold it for the king. I imagine you will do much the same.'

If Ronan had been granted any lands, the king had not yet seen fit to tell him. 'Were that offered, I would.'

'Ach, only a matter of time, I am sure. Although I imagine the last thing you want is to sit in your hall growing fat. You wouldn't want to give up this life. From what I've heard you are a man of action.' He grinned again. 'When you're not being kept prisoner.'

If only he knew. If only Hugo could imagine what Ronan was willing to give up. And he had almost done it. Almost sailed away from these cursed shores and lived in peace.

But no. That had been a dream. Gisela had told him herself; she would never have been his.

Before he could offer Hugo any kind of reply, the door to the hall opened. Most of the revellers barely took notice, but Ronan watched the man, filthy from the road, a fur cloak draped over his shoulder, coif pulled down tight over his ears to ward off the cold. His eyes scanned the room before they fell upon the king, and he began to push his way through the crowd.

Ignoring Hugo, Ronan moved along the side of the hall,

eager to reach the king before this messenger. Who knew what he had to report. Perhaps the rebels they had thought defeated had rallied. Maybe they were even now descending on Yorke with the king of Alba's army at their back.

The messenger made his way to the king, dropping to his knee and bowing his head. Ronan managed to limp close enough to hear the exchange as the man spoke.

'Sire, we have received word of the rebels in the north.' That was enough to stir William from his malaise, and he sat up to attention on his wooden throne. 'Ealdorman Waltheof has offered his surrender. He is willing to pledge his continued fealty to you in return for mercy.'

Slowly a smile of satisfaction spread across the king's face. 'These are good tidings indeed. And with the fall of one, the others are sure to follow. Any word of the other treacherous bastards?'

The messenger looked awkward as he shook his head. 'I am sorry, sire. But Edgar and the remnants of his army have not been heard from.'

'None of them?' William's smile quickly faded. 'Not even Waltheof's cousin, Gospatric? Surely that craven dog has turned his back on Edgar by now.'

'We have heard nothing else.'

King William looked as though he were searching for a way to blame the poor wretch in front of him, but as he considered the news he thought better of it. 'Very well. Then I suppose we should be grateful. Waltheof is a powerful man. His capture will show the rest of these Saxon upstarts that defiance is folly.'

The messenger stood for a moment. Ronan couldn't help but notice his expression of discomfort deepen.

'What?' the king asked. 'Is there more?'

The messenger nodded, glancing at the men surrounding the king – Ronan, Hugo, Thurstan and others. 'Yes, sire. I bring word from the northern clergy. Several bishops have sent their blessing, and with them a… request.'

William leaned forward in his seat, struggling to hear over the sound of the minstrels. 'Speak it.'

'The north has been ravaged, sire. Its townsfolk left in deprivation. Starvation is rife. They merely ask that supplies of grain be brought from the southern earldoms to stave off a famine.'

'Do they?'

Again the messenger looked at the other faces watching, before nodding to the king. 'Yes, sire.'

'And did those priests come to my support when the north was in full revolt? Did they offer prayers when the Danes pillaged the coast? When the Saxons sacked Yorke? Did they think about their poor northern peasants then?'

Ronan saw the messenger's throat bob as he swallowed. 'N… no, sire.'

'Fucking no, sire,' William screamed, rising to his feet, the wooden chair toppling behind him.

The music came to a stop. The man with his pokey stick, prompting the bear to dance, jabbed a little too hard. The bear snarled, rearing on its hind legs. It took a swipe at the dance master, who reacted on instinct, striking out with his stick. Quickly incensed by the attack, the bear roared, leaping upon him. He fell screaming as the animal began to maul him, the rest of the jongleurs rushing forward to help, but there was nothing they could do.

As the man screamed, his body clawed to the bone, the

knights watching laughed and clapped their appreciation louder than ever.

William stepped closer to the messenger, who took a step back in fear. 'Tell those shit-eating priests they will have nothing. Tell them to eat the dirt and the snow if they have to. Those rebellious northern pigs will have nothing from me. Hunger will be their penance.'

The messenger nodded his agreement, but something in Ronan could not stay silent. He had seen the misery the king had wrought. Surely it was no fault of those ordinary folk in the hamlets and burghs.

'Sire, if I may?'

William turned to regard him, the fire of rage still in his eyes. 'Dol-Combourg?'

'Are you sure this is the wisest course?' He was conscious that all eyes were now on him. He was dancing on a knife edge, dallying with the king's ire. 'Starving the populace will not be seen with sympathy by your allies. I understand your enemies must know the consequence of defying you but...'

He could tell the king was unmoved. No need for more words – they would have been wasted.

'The cripple wants mercy?'

'I was just—'

'Have I misjudged you, Dol-Combourg? Have I put too much faith in you?'

Ronan glanced toward Hugo, seeing he looked as surprised as the rest. 'No, sire. Of course, your judgement is law. Forget I spoke.'

There was a resounding crack from across the hall,

followed by the sound of something heavy slumping to the floor. One of the knights had clearly grown bored with the mauling and seen fit to dispatch the rampant bear.

William turned his attention back to the messenger. 'Where is Waltheof now?'

'He is south of Yorke, sire. Awaiting word of your... clemency.'

'Then he shall have it. Send word that I accept his surrender. Have him taken to Wintanceastre. I will meet him there and he can beg his forgiveness before God.'

With a bow, the messenger left as quickly as he had come. Someone picked up the chair William had knocked over, and he sat himself down in it once more.

'What happened to the music?' he bellowed, not even noticing the corpse of the bear.

Reluctantly, the minstrels struck up another tune. To Ronan's ear, it sounded like a dirge. Considering the fate of the north, it was only fitting.

19

Picheringa, England, February 1070

Styrkar wandered half-starved through the desolate fields. The sky was a dreary blanket of grey, the colour washed from the world around him. This had once been fertile farmland, but the ravenous Franks had left nothing alive in their wake. The few trees that still stood were charred husks, branches reaching upward like bony fingers begging for salvation.

His stomach growled. It had been two days since he'd eaten anything substantial: a handful of withered berries scavenged from a thorny bush, a few mouthfuls of brackish water cupped from a stagnant pond. He knew he needed to find shelter and food soon if he hoped to continue his aimless journey southward. But fortune was due him sooner rather than later... thankfully sooner.

In the distance he spotted a small shack nestled in a copse of trees. Smoke wisped faintly from the chimney, the first sign of life he had seen in some time. He hesitated. In his experience, survivors this far north were as likely to be foe as friend, but the gnawing ache in his gut compelled him forward.

Styrkar crept toward the shack, moving as silently as his large frame and the fatigue would allow. The door hung ajar, the single window shuttered. He peered inside but could see little through the gloom. The hut was abandoned, but someone had tended that hearth recently, the cinders still glowing.

He pushed open the creaking door. 'Hello? Is anyone here? I mean no harm.'

No answer. The filthy boards underfoot showed signs of imprints, still fresh. Whoever had made them could not have gone far.

Styrkar stepped inside, moving closer to the waning fire in the stone hearth, burnt down to embers. He leaned his axe and shield against the wall, grabbed a few logs from a neat pile and stirred the fire back to life, relieved as warmth began to fill the modest room. If the owner returned, perhaps Styrkar could reason with them, and share this meagre shelter for a night. Bargaining had never been his gift, but a fight was the last thing he needed right now.

Before long, his empty stomach urged him away from the flames. The scarred wooden table sitting in the centre of the room held a few crumbs and a bowl with traces of thin gruel, but nothing of any substance. Styrkar's stomach grumbled angrily. He would have smashed the table to splinters if he thought he might wring some nourishment from it, but that would hardly win him any friends should the owner return.

Heavy footsteps echoed outside, and Styrkar tensed, ready to fight or flee. The door creaked open and a large, bearded man entered carrying an armload of firewood. He stopped short when he saw the hearth's flames licking higher.

'Who the hell are you?' The man dropped the wood, pulling a long knife from his belt. 'Looking to rob me? I've got nothing worth taking.'

Styrkar raised his hands. 'Peace, friend. I mean you no harm.' He glanced about the bare room. 'And you're right about that.'

The man looked unconvinced, gripping his blade tighter. Styrkar recognised the desperate glint in those eyes all too well, and was conscious that his axe was only a few feet away still leaning against the wall.

'I'm just a traveller seeking shelter. I can be on my way if you wish.' Looking out onto the frigid landscape outside, he did not relish the prospect.

To his relief, the man seemed to relax slightly. 'Where you headed?'

'South.' A vague answer was safest. This man could be loyal to the Franks or scared enough to give Styrkar away to them.

The man nodded slowly. 'Well, I suppose no use turning aside a starving man. Name's Godart.'

Styrkar felt some relief as the man sheathed his knife. 'I am Styrkar. And yes, I haven't eaten in some time.'

'Not much to spare, but better than nothing.' Godart knelt, prying up a floorboard with bony fingers. Reverently he plucked a small sack from its hiding place and opened it up. Styrkar watched, as patiently as he could manage, as

Godart scooped a handful of wheat bran into a pot, added water, and hung it over the now crackling fire.

'No milk, sadly. Damn Franks slaughtered every cow for miles around.' Godart shook his head bitterly. 'Bastards.'

'Aye, they've left quite a trail of ruin,' Styrkar replied.

They ate in silence, spooning up the thin, saltless pottage. To Styrkar, it was a feast. Godart studied his guest closely, perhaps noticing the scars that marked him and the mail he wore under his threadbare clothes. Styrkar avoided his gaze, letting the man make his own assumptions.

'I am grateful for your hospitality,' Styrkar said, pushing back his empty bowl.

Godart shrugged. 'Got to help each other out these days.' A knowing look crossed his eyes. 'Especially those of us who tried to stand against those Frankish devils.'

Ice trickled down Styrkar's spine. Did this man know who he sheltered? Despite Godart's generosity Styrkar was still not willing to trust him.

'I did my best, though it wasn't enough. Now I am looking to find others who still have the courage to fight.'

Godart smiled bitterly. 'Aye, courage and defiance are in short supply of late. Can't say I blame folks for keeping their heads down. The Franks have made any rebellion damn near suicidal.' He studied Styrkar closely again. 'But you look like a hard man to kill. Reckon you've got some fight left in you.'

Styrkar met the man's gaze steadily. 'I'll breathe my last with sword in hand and a cry of rage on my lips. Of that you can be sure.'

Godart nodded. 'I do not doubt it. You're welcome to bide here tonight, friend. Hard telling when we'll get another peaceful night's rest with so many of those bastards abroad.'

'You have my thanks.' Exhaustion had been creeping up on Styrkar like a serpent through the weeds. It had been many days since he had slept without fear of ambush.

Godart gestured to a pile of ragged blankets in the corner. 'Get some rest. You've travelled a hard road, I'd wager.'

Styrkar's limbs felt leaden as he wrapped himself in the musty blankets. Within moments, his breathing slowed, and he sank into dreamless oblivion...

A metallic tang filled Styrkar's mouth. His stomach heaved, and he lurched upright, vomiting bitter bile onto the dirt floor. The room swam around him as he realised...

Poison – the treacherous cur had poisoned him.

Through blurred vision, he saw Godart looming over him, a glint of light from the blade of his knife. With a roar, Styrkar seized his wrist before the blade could plunge downward. They struggled, crashing into the table. Styrkar smashed his forehead against Godart's face and felt cartilage crunch.

Howling in pain, Godart staggered back, clutching his gushing nose. Styrkar tried to rise but could barely summon the strength to crawl. His head pounded, guts clenching viciously.

'Fucking bastard,' Godart spat, blood streaming into his bushy beard. 'I'll see you in Hell.'

He staggered forward, knife poised to finish the job. Styrkar's hand reached out, finding only an empty wooden bowl on the floor. With no other weapon, he flung it with all his might. It cracked against Godart's skull and he stumbled in shock.

Styrkar rushed outside into the pre-dawn air, legs shaking beneath him, hands trembling uncontrollably. He crouched in the dirt, retching helplessly, the poison coursing through his veins with unrelenting malice.

He heard Godart groan within the hut, already recovering from the blow. Styrkar would make it no further than this. The end he had so long evaded would find him here, alone and unmourned. Murdered by some hermit in the wild. But the Red Wolf would not go meekly into the dirt.

Godart stumbled out of the hut, clutching his throbbing head. Styrkar's vision cleared as he rose swaying to his feet. The poison had taken a firm grip on his body, but his resolve would remain unbroken.

With a guttural cry, he lunged at Godart, fuelled by desperation. Despite the tremors racking his body, Styrkar's grip on Godart was unyielding, and they crashed to the ground in a tangle of limbs.

Godart had the knife in his hand, stabbing out with it, but the Red Wolf was faster. He caught Godart's wrist and slammed it to the ground, the knife spilling from his grip. Styrkar's vision blurred, his breath laboured as the poison continued its merciless assault. Every moment was agony, but he could not relent.

Summoning his last ounce of strength, Styrkar grasped Godart's hair with his free hand, slamming his head into the ground. Again he bashed that skull into the hard winter earth, seeing Godart's eyes roll as he was dazed by the onslaught. He groaned before Styrkar clenched trembling fingers around his throat, cutting off all sound. Steel fingers squeezed, as Godart vainly tried to grasp Styrkar's wrists and pull his hands clear. It would do him no good. It would be Godart who died on the hard cold earth this night, not the Red Wolf.

A small cry pierced the haze of poison afflicting Styrkar's senses – the wail of a child.

He was suddenly unmanned enough to release his foe, and Godart coughed as he tried to fill his lungs with air. Another cry caught Styrkar's attention. A young girl, no more than five, stood to the side of the hut clutching a toddling boy. Their faces were smudged with grime, eyes wide with terror.

'Please…' Godart choked out beneath him. 'Spare me… they have no one else…'

The girl found her courage. 'Don't hurt Papa!' she shrieked, dashing forward. 'Please don't hurt my papa.'

Styrkar hesitated. Godart had wronged him, but these children were innocent. As the boy began wailing pathetically, his thirst for blood waned. Could he orphan these children out in the wild? They would surely die if he did.

Grudgingly, Styrkar released his grip on Godart's throat. The traitorous wretch gasped for breath, scurrying across the frozen earth to grasp his children close.

'Why?' Styrkar demanded. 'And don't lie to me again.'

Godart held the whimpering children close. 'We were starving. After the Franks came our livestock was slaughtered. What choice did I have?'

'What choice for what?' He took a threatening step forward. 'Speak, man.'

WINTER WARRIOR

'We are starving,' Godart blurted through his tears. 'What choice do we have with no other meat to feast on?'

Styrkar felt disgust roiling in his gut. It seemed in so short a time since the Franks had ravaged this land its populace had become truly desperate in their need to survive.

'Where is their mother buried?' he growled. 'Or did you devour her too?'

Godart flinched at the accusation. 'She died when the Franks razed our village. It's been just us since.' He looked up pleadingly. 'They would have perished if not for what I've done. Have mercy, I beg you.'

Styrkar glanced toward the man's daughter. Her eyes were a piercing blue, perhaps as blue as those of his own daughter. The girl he had abandoned all hope of seeing. But if he ever did see her again, would he not go to any lengths to protect her, just as Godart had?

Styrkar picked up the knife, discarded on the ground. He strode forward, grabbing Godart by the hair and pressing the blade's edge to his throat. One quick slash would grant him vengeance.

The boy began wailing again. Styrkar stopped, in that moment realising how he must have looked to these helpless infants. Nothing but a murderous savage.

With a snarl, he shoved Godart aside and cast the blade away into the bushes.

'I thank you for my life,' Godart gasped.

'Do not thank me,' Styrkar replied coldly. 'You deserve death. I spare you only for the children's sake.'

Godart dabbed at his still-bleeding head with his sleeve. 'I wish I could offer something in return. Some way to repay your mercy.' He paused, thinking. 'The Isle of Eels – have you heard of it?'

The name meant nothing and Styrkar shook his head curtly.

'It's in the south, a fortress in the marshes of Grentebrigescire. You said you were looking for others with the courage still to fight. Last I heard, some rebels still make their stand there against the Franks.'

'How do you know this?' Styrkar asked sharply.

'Rumours mostly, but they say the local lords cannot defeat the rebel leader. A man called Hereward. He plagues them from the marshes like a ghost.'

This was valuable knowledge. Enough to curb the Red Wolf's ire. Or at least to spare Godart's life.

Styrkar stripped off Godart's cloak. 'I'm taking this. You'll find another.'

He walked back into the shack, collecting axe and shield before storming away without a backward glance at his bewildered poisoner.

The taste of bile lingered in Styrkar's mouth for most of the morning as he walked. The sickness gradually passed, but a sense of failure still festered within him. He had won nothing on this long southward trek except his own life.

As night fell, and he reached sparse woodland he heard a familiar noise. Looking up, he saw that a raven watched from an oak's skeletal branch, cawing mournfully. There was something familiar about it, as though it were the very same one he had encountered at Yorke.

The more he regarded the creature, the more he convinced himself it was the very same. Was it the poison still numbing his senses that made him think so? Or was this a valravn of legend, waiting for the day the Red Wolf would fall?

Not this day though. Not yet.

If rebels yet defied the king at this Isle of Eels, he would join them gladly.

Once he had his vengeance, the valravn could have its due.

20

Heavy mist hung over the city, blanketing it in a veil of grey. Outside the looming edifice of the abbey, Ronan stood sentinel, the early morning chill creeping through his jerkin. He shifted his weight to favour his left leg, the old pain flaring up from the bone-deep ache.

In the pre-dawn light, he could just make out the silhouette of the abbey's square central tower against the leaden sky. The hilt of his sword dug into his palm as he tightened his grip, steeling himself for the ceremony soon to take place within the abbey's hallowed nave. Since dawn, he had watched a procession of magnates, abbots and knights file through the arched entrance, their whispered conversations drifting on the mist. The implications of this day would be felt across the country; he could feel it in his marrow.

At last came the toll of the abbey bells, sonorous and leaden, signalling that the congregation had gathered. It was time.

Ronan passed beneath the shadow of the vaulted ceiling and through the abbey's western door. As his eyes adjusted to the dim interior, he was greeted by a sea of hushed faces illuminated by the flicker of candles.

Though the nave could have easily accommodated over a thousand souls, the assembled numbered scarcely two hundred. Word of this ceremony had travelled only by whispered rumour, each attendee vetted with meticulous care. Even now, beady eyes tracked Ronan's progress up the central aisle, most flitting away as he met their gaze. Reaching the crossing, he took up position in the south transept, affording him a clear view of the chancel and altar.

The candle flames danced, casting waving shadows that seemed to give the statues of saints and apostles a semblance of restless animation. Ronan's hand once again found the hilt of his sword, though what good steel would do in a house of worship, he couldn't guess. Despite the sanctity of the venue, he could feel the undercurrent of tension in the room as palpably as the chill in the air.

Footsteps echoed from the gloom of the ambulatory behind the altar. Two priests appeared, taking up positions on either side of the chancel steps. Last to emerge was the archbishop himself, Lanfranc of Pavia, a new appointment made in part because he was not a duplicitous Saxon dog. With an air of grave solemnity, he took his place before the altar.

All attention was drawn to the western door as it groaned inward on protesting hinges. Two knights entered, hands resting on the pommels of their sheathed swords. Between them walked a third man, clad in a simple woollen robe, his feet bare against the cold flagstones. Though his wrists were unbound, the slump of his shoulders marked him unmistakably as a prisoner. Waltheof, the fearsome rebel who had very nearly tipped the balance of power in the north. He looked far from fearsome now.

The man's aspect was so transformed that, were it not for his distinctive flaxen mane, Ronan might not have recognised him. Word had it that at the battle of Yorke, Waltheof had cut a ferocious figure, bellowing oaths and curses as he cleaved through men like a farmer through wheat. Now he shuffled meekly between his captors, eyes downcast, deprived of mail or weaponry. As they reached the crossing, the guards gave the prisoner a rough shove, sending him to his knees before turning smartly on their heels and retreating from whence they came.

Ronan half-expected Waltheof to leap up and rage against his oppressors. Yet the man simply knelt in supplication, head bowed as if resigned to his fate.

The king entered alone. Even at a distance, Ronan could sense the aura of authority surrounding him. William wore no crown, yet held himself with the surety of one who expected obedience as his divine right. His keen eyes swept impassively over the assembly, craggy features set in their accustomed stern lines, as he strode down the nave's central aisle. Reaching Waltheof, he gazed down imperiously at the kneeling man, then proceeded to the altar. There he stood in wait as a heavy silence enshrouded the sanctuary. With a gesture from the king, Waltheof stirred, rising slowly to his feet. He approached the altar as one already condemned, coming to a halt before William's towering form.

Lanfranc stepped forward, holding a gilt-edged Bible, and with a reedy voice took on a singsong cadence as he led Waltheof through the Oath of Fealty. Ronan spoke little Latin, but he gleaned enough to understand that the former rebel was pledging his unconditional loyalty while renouncing all other earthly allegiances. The words of surrender were unfamiliar, yet their import clear enough. Should Waltheof renege on his vow, dire consequences would follow.

As the last words of the oath died away, Ronan felt an unexpected lightening in his chest. Since coming to this accursed isle, barely a day had passed without bloodshed. Pacifying the belligerent Saxons had proven a far greater challenge than anticipated, but perhaps William's patience had won out in the end. If even the battle-hardened Waltheof bent the knee, others would surely follow. Unity would replace enmity; peace would supplant strife. At long last, Ronan might know a measure of peace.

At the altar, Waltheof sank slowly to his knees, bowing his head before William in final capitulation. The king gazed down with pitiless eyes, his craggy features etched in stone. For endless moments, ruler and rebel locked stares. The surrounding nobles looked on with evident discomfort, Saxon and Frank alike shifting awkwardly at this abasement.

In the end, even the proudest men could be made to kneel. All that mattered was who held the whip.

Rising from his supplicant's pose, Waltheof extended a hand as if anticipating a conciliatory gesture from William. The muscles in Ronan's neck tightened with apprehension as the silence stretched. Then William drew himself up to his full height, disdain etched on his features. When he spoke, his voice rang out with diamond hardness.

'You kneel before your rightful lord, yet think to receive my hand in friendship? No, Ealdorman, that I will not give. Not until every last rebel lays down his arms and bends his knee as you have done this day.'

Murmurs swept the crowd at this cold pronouncement. There was little chance Waltheof could understand the language of the Franks spoken by his king, but he got the gist, letting his outstretched hand fall slowly back to his side.

'I accept your vow, but do not mistake this for forgiveness. There will be no mercy for those who persist in treason. Ringleaders will dangle from gibbets, their lands forfeit, their lineage erased. Follow their lead at your peril.'

He swept his arm to encompass the entire assembly.

'Let that stand as warning to all. The king will suffer defiance no longer. The word of law in England comes from my lips alone. Swear faith to me and no other, or face swift justice.'

A tense silence hung in the air as he finished. Saxon and Frank alike stood frozen, transfixed by the authority in the king's tone.

William eyed the assembly with flinty dispassion, before pacing through the nave in the echoing silence. At the altar, Waltheof stared after William with haunted eyes, shoulders hunched. Once the king had crossed the threshold and left the abbey in silence, the congregation began to move. One by one they stood, following the king out into the cold air. Ronan watched them go, until finally it was only he and Waltheof left under the judgemental eyes of Lanfranc.

Was the former ealdorman to suffer yet more lecturing? If he was, it might perhaps be best the two were left alone.

Outside, Ronan limped down the abbey's limestone steps, his leg aching fiercely after standing motionless for so long. The day had turned clear and crisp, the damp chill burning away under a climbing sun. Blinking against the glare, he spotted a familiar athletic frame striding in his direction.

'Well met, Hugo,' Ronan hailed his fellow knight. 'That was quite the spectacle, no?'

Hugo of Grentmesnil shrugged his shoulders. 'I've seen better mummery at feast day fairs, truth be told. Though I'll allow; Waltheof played the penitent convincingly enough.'

Ronan smiled. Hugo liked to portray himself as perpetually unimpressed. In truth, he was as anxious as any of them to see this vexing rebellion quashed.

'At any rate, it is finished.' Ronan sighed. 'With Waltheof kneeling in submission, and his fellow rebels fled, surely the peasants will disperse to their hovels, cowed by our king's show of strength.'

Hugo squinted at him. 'You sound pleased by the prospect, Dol-Combourg. I had heard you were a man who thrived on... action.'

'Don't believe everything you hear,' Ronan replied. 'This rebellion drags on, while I remain little richer than when I arrived. I am ready to collect what I am owed, and retire to a warm hearth and a soft bed.'

'Retire?' Hugo snorted. 'We are warriors, you and I. Peace will never sit comfortably upon our shoulders.' He turned and gazed at the rising spires of the abbey. 'Still, you aren't wrong. It would be pleasant to see the last of this accursed isle for a spell.'

'You think this will be enough to snuff the last embers of uprising?' Ronan asked.

Hugo pursed his lips. 'If not, rest assured William will employ more… forceful methods. The man is like a hound on a hare when it comes to ferreting out dissent. I would not envy the next Saxon rebel who rears his head.'

Ronan grimaced. In the preceding months, they had witnessed the full measure of William's wrath unleashed upon the seething Saxon populace. Such wanton cruelty served its purpose, but the memories still left a bitter taste.

'Let's hope cooler heads prevail,' Ronan muttered, thinking of the suffering he had seen in the north. 'This country has bled enough.'

'Some would say not nearly enough,' Hugo replied darkly. 'Not until the Saxons are fully cowed. Still, you are not wrong. The land and its people have suffered through this storm of swords. And winter's bite continues.'

Ronan thought on all the scarred fields and grain stores put to the torch. 'Revolt or submission, famine looms. The people will starve regardless. This is a bleak victory we have claimed.'

Clasping Ronan's shoulder, Hugo straightened with a rueful grunt. 'Keep your spirits up, man. Our fortunes will turn. The Saxon winter cannot last forever. And William's gratitude will be lavish for those who serve him faithfully through the darkest nights.'

Ronan couldn't help but think he'd heard all this before. 'From your lips to God's ears.'

As Hugo left, Ronan turned toward the abbey gates. Passing beneath the arched entrance, he paused for a moment to savour the crisp spring air, scouring the last vestiges of stale incense from his nostrils. Overhead, the sky shone a tranquil blue, scattered with only the faintest wisps of cloud. Slowly he became aware of birdsong and the cheerful din of voices from the town beyond the abbey walls. The world was regaining its colour after the bleak ceremony. Ronan stood a moment listening to the sounds of cartwheels and merchants hawking their wares, the everyday chatter of humanity persisting despite wars and kings.

He walked slowly through the narrow, mud-churned lanes, oblivious to the press of townsfolk that ebbed and flowed around him. Ronan could not evict the worm of doubt that continued to gnaw at his guts. Waltheof's submission changed nothing; would-be kings yet schemed, and commoners still simmered with resentment toward their foreign overlords. Perhaps the ealdorman's gesture of fealty would convince William that England was finally his, but Ronan knew that a land quashed beneath the heel of occupation could never be truly ruled.

Unbidden, the image came to him of a particular rebel, face contorted in berserk fury: that damnable red-maned Dane who had nearly unmanned him outside Norwic. As long as warriors like the Red Wolf stalked the wild reaches of this land, rebellion could flare again as quickly as a spring grassfire.

Ronan shuffled to a stop, realising his aimless wandering had led him back to the fortified manor he had been billeted at. Smoke curled enticingly from the kitchens and he shook off his dour musing. The morrow would present its own trials; for now, he could only attend to his rumbling stomach and pray for respite from pointless slaughter. Steeling himself, he trudged toward the entrance and the comforts within.

Part Three

Isle of Eels

21

Brune, England, April 1070

The fire crackled and popped, casting flickering shadows across the dim interior of the longhouse. Styrkar stared into the flames, frustration gnawing as his mind turned again to the rebels he'd heard tell of, but who remained so elusive.

For days he had searched to no avail, questioning villagers and townsfolk across these frigid lands, only to be met with fear in their eyes and silence from their tongues. He had wandered the woods and fens where it was rumoured they hid within their island fortress, but found no trace of them.

Styrkar rubbed his hands before the flames, trying to cast off the chill that had settled into his bones after long nights sleeping rough. This was not what he had envisioned when he left Edgar behind. He had sworn to keep his oath to Gytha – to take vengeance against the king for all that he had lost, but alone, without allies, what hope had he to complete his vow?

A creak of timber roused Styrkar from his brooding. He tensed, gripping the haft of his hand axe as he listened. More creaking, accompanied by heavy footfalls. The door swung open, and Styrkar felt every muscle tense as four hulking, grim-faced men entered the longhouse. Their scarred faces and shaggy beards marked them as Saxons but that was still no guarantee they were friends. His eyes searched for any other way to escape, but he cursed his lack of care as he realised he was cornered.

Silently they gazed at him, sizing him up no doubt, deciding if he was a threat. Styrkar kept his hand on his axe haft, ready to use it in a heartbeat. He had no wish to slay these men, but if they came with violence in mind he would have no choice.

'Who are you?' one of them rumbled at last. His yellow beard spilled over his chest, matched by the mane of yellow hair erupting from beneath a leather cap.

Styrkar considered his response. Best not to seem a danger, though that was difficult given his size and the axe that lay near his feet.

'A wanderer on the road,' he said at last. 'Nothing more.'

The Saxon's eyes narrowed, unconvinced. 'You have the look of the raiders who plagued the eastern coast not so many months ago. And you sound like a Dane.'

'I have shed blood beside the Danes, yes,' Styrkar admitted. 'But only in common cause against the bastard king. My loyalty lies with my Saxon brothers, with all who would see these lands freed from the Franks. I seek a man, a rebel lord named Hereward. I would join with him in his defiance of the usurper.'

Silence. The only sound the popping of the flames between them. Then the bearded man turned to his companions and grunted. In unspoken agreement, they moved back toward the door.

'Best you find somewhere else to warm yourself, Dane,' he said. 'You'll find no brothers here, nor any rebel lord.'

With that they trooped from the longhouse, leaving Styrkar alone again but for the noise of the crackling flames. He released his grip on the axe haft and flexed his fingers. Things might have turned ugly, things still could, but perhaps fate had finally led him to the rebels he sought.

He stood, his earlier frustration burned clean by his determination to find allies one last time, and lifted his axe before striding for the door. Whatever it took, he would make these warriors accept him as one of their own. His vengeance would not be denied.

The cold night air bit through Styrkar's tunic and mail as he stepped outside the longhouse. A half-moon cast faint silver light over the silent village, the road empty now but for the wind. He glanced about, wondering which direction the rebels had gone, when a voice rang out from the inky shadows.

'Not so fast, Dane.'

Styrkar turned, axe haft gripped tight as the four Saxons emerged from around the side of the longhouse. So they had not strayed far.

Again they spread out in a half-circle before him, blocking any escape.

'You're a stubborn bastard, aren't you,' said their leader, hands on his hips as he stared. 'But how do we know you really are looking for brothers to join with, and not just some turncoat looking to betray us for Frankish silver?'

Styrkar met his gaze unflinchingly. 'I have walked a

long road to find your people. I will not leave here tonight without pledging myself to your cause.'

The Saxon regarded him with narrowed eyes. 'Our cause? You can know nothing of it.'

'I know you resist the invaders. That you alone have the desire to fight them still, where every other army has been vanquished or fled. And I would lend my axe.'

'Axe or no, you're still just a Dane. How do we know you won't betray us for Danegeld if the tide turns against us?'

Anger kindled in Styrkar's chest at the insult. 'Do not judge what you do not know. I have shed blood beside your people, against the Franks. Bled for this country and her rightful king.'

'There sits no king in England now, rightful or not,' spat the Saxon. 'Only a tyrant.'

'And I would see his reign ended, if you would take me to the one they call Hereward.'

The Saxon exchanged curious glances with his fellows, as though Styrkar had made some jest. At last he sighed.

'Aye, Hereward might wish to speak with you. But only if you throw down that axe first. I'll not bring an armed man before him unbidden.'

Styrkar hesitated. Once he handed over his weapon there was no way he could hope to survive if these warriors intended him ill. But what choice was there?

'Very well,' he said, throwing his axe down to stick in the earth between them.

The leader nodded, picked up the weapon, then turned and strode toward the outer dark. After a brief hesitation, Styrkar followed, the other three men falling in behind him.

Despite being unarmed, he did not fear these men. He sensed no malice in them, despite their grim appearance. Only caution born of the need to survive in the wilds, beyond the notice of their Frankish enemies. Caution he understood too well.

They walked in silence through scrub and sparse woodland for some time. The village disappeared behind them, and with it any second thoughts Styrkar might have held about following these strangers into the night. His path was set now for good or ill.

Eventually they came to a thickly wooded hollow. Shadows moved between the trees, and a hushed voice called softly that all was well. Styrkar's guides were welcomed into the hidden camp by men who eyed him with interest bereft of warmth.

Fires dotted the hollow, warming cloaked and bearded men who sat sharpening blades or fletching arrows by their light. Though they appeared a ragged bunch, Styrkar glimpsed the glint of mail beneath their cloaks and well-made helms and shields stacked nearby. These were well-equipped warriors, despite their woodland guise.

'Lightfoot,' the leader greeted one man by a fire. 'I've brought a new ally. Says he's keen to cave in Frankish skulls with this great bloody axe of his.'

Lightfoot's eyes glinted with interest as he looked Styrkar up and down. 'Then he's come to the right place. Though he looks less a rebel and more a damned hermit.'

This brought chuckles from the men nearby. Styrkar allowed himself a smile. The mood in this camp was not what he'd expected from outlaw rebels. There was an easy humour between them that reminded him of his days in King

Harold's household. For the first time since abandoning Edgar weeks ago, he felt at ease.

'Let's not be hasty with this one,' said an archer, as he paused in fletching an arrow. 'Could be a spy for all we know.'

'I am no spy,' Styrkar assured them. 'My name is Styrkar, the Red Wolf, and I have fought against the Bastard Duke since Senlac.'

'He gave up his weapon willingly when I bade him, Ouri,' said the leader. 'And claims he wants only to kill Franks with it.'

A rumble of approval from the camp. Styrkar sensed he was already winning their trust.

'Then what can we do but offer him the chance?' Ouri chuckled.

Styrkar raised his chin, emboldened by their enthusiasm. 'Tell me, where might I find the one called Hereward? I would pledge myself to him and prove my worth as soon as I am able.'

'Eager, aren't you, Styrkar the Red Wolf,' said Lightfoot. 'We'll take you to him soon enough. For now, warm yourself, friend. You've had a cold journey by the look of you.'

Gratefully, Styrkar joined them around the fire, shedding his damp cloak and holding his hands out to the crackling warmth. Though these men were strangers, he felt he had found kindred spirits. A new brotherhood to replace the one he had lost.

As he warmed his travel-chilled bones beside the campfire, he studied the faces of the rebels around him. Lean, bearded faces, weathered by long months in the wild, but lit by camaraderie and shared purpose. These were not the desperate outlaws he might have expected, but disciplined fighters waging a crusade against tyranny from their hidden refuge. In their eyes, Styrkar saw his own defiance reflected. His own unquenchable thirst for vengeance.

After grabbing two legs of a cooked rabbit from a nearby fire, the leader sat beside Styrkar. He offered a piece of meat and Styrkar took it gratefully.

'Lightfoot, Wenoth, Ouri,' the man said, gesturing to the other warriors sitting about the fire. 'The rest you will get to know in time. I am Wulfric, called the Heron. So what's your tale, Red Wolf? You look a fierce bastard right enough. How'd you end up over here wanting to do murder so far from Danmork?'

Styrkar considered the question. Should he speak of his loss and betrayal these past years? No, those memories were still raw wounds no salve could heal. Better to keep his past locked away, and look only to the future.

'I was loyal to Harold Godwinson,' he said at last. 'When the Bastard took the crown and began doling out lands to his foreign lapdogs, I lost everything. Now I wish only to see every Frankish bastard in England fed to the crows.'

Eyes glinted with approval around the fire. They'd all seen villages put to the torch, no doubt. Watched invaders claim lands their father's fathers had worked for generations.

'Well said,' growled Wenoth. 'Seems we're of like minds on the matter.'

'You'll find no shortage of those here,' added Lightfoot. 'And beyond this place. Hereward has gathered quite the band of fighters, all thirsty for foreign blood.'

'Then I am eager to meet him,' said Styrkar. 'To join his rebellion, if he'll have me.'

They exchanged amused glances across the fire. Then the Heron nodded and rose to his feet.

'Come on then. We'll take you to him.'

22

Styrkar crept through the shadows, following close behind his new allies. The night pressed in, dark and damp, the air thick with fog that swirled about his legs. Somewhere nearby, an owl hooted, its cry echoing eerily across the gloom. The marshlands stretched endlessly in all directions, a foreboding maze of reeds and bogs. Pools of dark water glimmered beneath the moon's wan light. Strange wisps and rustles sounded just out of sight, hinting at unseen fauna lurking in the murk.

Ahead of him, the four shadowy figures moved swiftly and silently, cloaked forms blending into the mist. There was no way to tell where they were leading him. He could only follow and hope it wasn't to his doom.

After what felt like hours creeping through the fen, they arrived abruptly at a tiny jetty jutting from the mire. Tied to it was a rowboat, paint flaked and peeling, looking older than sin. Without a word, the Heron clambered in and gestured for Styrkar to follow. The boards creaked ominously beneath his weight as he stepped onto the vessel and sat at the prow, hand gripping the axe these men had returned to him. Lightfoot and Ouri took up oars in silence and as one they dipped the blades into the murky water and propelled the decrepit boat forward.

The sedge closed in oppressively on all sides. Long strands of algae trailed through the boat's wake like ghostly fingers. Somewhere in the distance, a bird cried a desolate lament. After what felt like an age, the hulking silhouette of an island loomed out of the darkness ahead. A fortress built upon a rise of earth amid the endless fen. Its wooden battlements and towers stood grim and defiant against the night sky, and Styrkar eyed the approaching island warily, wondering at the secrets it held within. With luck Hereward awaited. The rebel lord who would give him one last chance to satisfy the oaths he had made. One last chance at redemption. At vengeance, before he perished on a Frankish blade.

The boat bumped gently against a hidden dock on the island's shore. Silent as phantoms, his escorts leapt ashore and hurried to make fast the mooring ropes. Styrkar followed them onto land, his hand still tight upon the haft of his axe.

All around, the island bristled with fortifications, designed to turn back any hostile force. Great wooden palisades surrounded its perimeter, the sharpened tops jutting skyward. Watch fires flared at regular intervals atop the walls, grim sentinels scanning the darkness. The Heron led him quickly toward a postern gate set deep within the palisade. It creaked open just wide enough for them to slip through, and within four bowmen stood guard, swathed in shadow. They watched Styrkar pass with narrowed, suspicious eyes, and once inside, his guides moved swiftly across a maze of timbered walls and moats. The entire island was a fortress, layered with cunning defences to confuse and dismay any invaders. Styrkar saw archers patrolling the parapets, blades glinting in the firelight. Like ghosts they passed, silent as the marsh mist.

They emerged abruptly into a wide courtyard. All around stood the trappings of a rebel army – smithies, barracks, storehouses. Men moved with purpose, intent upon various tasks, and some saw Styrkar and offered hard, appraising looks before returning to their duties. The ring of hammers shaping steel echoed from a smithy. The welcome smell of baked bread wafted from a cookhouse opposite. At the far end of the ward stood a squat, circular tower, its stones black with age. To one side, a set of worn steps climbed to a derelict chapel that crowned the small island's summit.

The Heron made straight for the steps and Styrkar followed, axe held loosely in his grip as he gazed about. The steps led up to an empty arch, its wooden door long since rotted away. The Heron stopped, gesturing for him to continue alone. Gripping his axe haft tight, Styrkar passed into the shadowed chapel, teeth clenched as he prepared to present himself to the lord of this island fortress.

He hesitated after crossing the threshold. The chapel interior was murky, what little light there was muted by narrow windows choked with grime. His eyes took a moment to adjust as strange shadows crouched in the corners, and to all intents it appeared he was alone.

Warily, he loosened his grip on his axe haft, letting the weapon hang loose in his hand. Its familiar weight gave some small comfort against the oppressive gloom as, step by cautious step, he moved deeper into the derelict chapel. The flagstone floor was worn and cracked beneath his feet, his footsteps echoing faintly.

Styrkar stopped on seeing a lone figure, half-cloaked in shadow, knelt before a weathered shrine in the apse. A whispered voice echoed faintly beneath the groined arches as they recited fervent prayers. He hesitated, watching the kneeling form and, after a moment, they rose fluidly to their feet and turned to face him.

It was a woman, clad in a robe of undyed wool. Though her head was shaved at the temples in the manner of a nun, she wore leather armour beneath her habit and a long seax at her hip. Her piercing eyes gleamed like steel as they fixed upon Styrkar.

'Welcome, Dane,' she said, her voice strong and clear. 'I received word of a visitor. Red-haired and fearsome.' She glanced to the axe still clutched in Styrkar's grip. 'Now to see if you have come bearing ill will or good.'

Styrkar blinked in surprise. This was no nun, but could only be the infamous rebel leader, presumed by all to be a man. He had not thought to find a woman commanding an army from this desolate fenland refuge, but her gaze was stern and fearless as she regarded him. About her lips hovered the faintest smile, as though she discerned his thoughts.

'You did not expect to meet a woman, I take it,' she said dryly. 'Yet here we stand. My name is Hereswyde. And yours?'

'Styrkar,' he replied quickly, trying to hide his surprise. 'Known as the Red Wolf. And I have come to join your fight. To take Frankish heads, as many as I am able.'

Hereswyde gave a grim nod, her eyes glittering. 'Then we have common purpose.' She glanced back at the weathered shrine, her expression growing stern. 'But I would have you swear it upon the relics of our patron, Aethelthryth. All who fight beneath my banner are bound by sacred oath to serve her cause.'

Styrkar frowned, shaking his head. 'I'll swear no oaths to the saints of your Christe. My loyalty is my own, and my banner is vengeance.'

Hereswyde studied him intently, her eyes like flint. 'Without an oath, I cannot trust you.' She rested a hand upon her seax hilt. 'And I permit no one here that I do not trust.'

They stood unmoving, gazes locked in silent challenge. Styrkar's grip tightened on his axe. The rebel leader looked ready to draw her blade in an instant as the chapel's shadows crouched expectantly around them.

Finally, Styrkar lowered his weapon. 'I need no oaths to prove my worth. I would have you judge me by my deeds, not my words.'

For endless moments, they hung poised on the brink of violence. Then Hereswyde relaxed, though her eyes remained watchful.

'So be it, heathen,' she said coldly. 'Just spill Frankish blood, and we will have no quarrel.'

Styrkar gave a terse nod. This narrow-eyed woman was hardy and pragmatic, qualities he could respect, even admire. Clearly, she would let no principles stand in the way of her cause.

'You have nothing to fear on that score. I will bring you more heads than you can stake upon your walls.'

Hereswyde's stern look softened a fraction. 'I hope so. We are sorely outnumbered, and stand as a last bastion of resistance to the foreign scourge. I'll turn away no man willing to fight them, creed be damned. So, heathen, you will stand with us?'

Styrkar met her piercing gaze. 'While breath remains in this body, my axe will drip Frankish blood.'

A fierce light entered Hereswyde's eyes. 'Together, we shall make the usurper rue the day he dared despoil our home.'

Styrkar grasped Hereswyde's offered arm in kinship. She was strong, determined. It offered Styrkar a glimmer of hope he thought never to feel again.

'Come, I will show you what we have built here,' she said, before leading him from the derelict chapel onto the exposed roof of the circular tower.

A bracing wind keened across the fens, tearing at his cloak. Styrkar gazed out at the surrounding marshlands, the island's defences, the scores of grim-faced rebels preparing tools of war.

'From here we can strike out against the Franks, then melt away before any reprisal,' Hereswyde explained. 'We are ghosts in the mist. The dark shadow of their nightmares, for how can they fight what they cannot see?'

Styrkar turned the concept over in his mind. His lust was for open battle, to stare his foes in the eye as he struck them down. Yet he could not deny the cunning of Hereswyde's strategy.

'Attacked by shadows and phantoms, the Franks will grow evermore fearful. You will plant a seed of terror in their hearts that will spread like poison.'

'Just so.' There was a note of relish in Hereswyde's voice. 'Together, we will bring Hell to their door.'

Styrkar's battle-hungry spirit stirred at her words. Here at last was a chance to unleash red vengeance against the usurpers.

'When do we begin?' he asked.

Hereswyde's grin was fierce. 'No time like the present, Styrkar the Red Wolf.'

23

Ely, England, June 1070

His knife cut delicate slivers into the wood, slowly revealing the hidden figure beneath. It seemed so long since he had last carved anything, he thought he might no longer have the knack for it. He needn't have worried, and with every slice and whittle he grew more confident. Styrkar had forgotten how much peace the simple act brought him.

Before the sun had reached its zenith he held a small carving of a wolf in his calloused palm, for what else could the Red Wolf have crafted for himself? He had made its like before, so long ago, but that one had been lost to him. Now he took the time to craft a new one, and it offered some comfort to occupy his solitary moments with this simple act. The last few weeks had seen him perform work of an altogether different kind, and he needed this diversion, if only for a little while.

Styrkar had been quick to adopt these eastern flatlanders as his brothers in arms. At first it had struck him as odd how they gave themselves such curious names – Lightfoot, the Sickle, the Dodger, the Black, the Red, Kite, Hedge-Sparrow. Quickly he had learned that these names helped disguise their real identities, if not protecting the outlaws themselves then at least their families.

They had wasted little time in striking out from their island fortress and bringing violence unto their enemies, but the blood they had spilled was far from the largesse he craved. As he looked around at the solid wooden walls of the fort, he considered them painfully bereft of Frankish heads. He had promised Hereswyde more than she could count, but quickly realised that despite their dedication these rebels were few in number and for the most part lacking in experience. There was little they could do but strike swiftly in the night, setting supplies afire and killing those they could, before retreating to the safety of the marshlands. It would never be enough.

A grim atmosphere hung over the island as he took in its sprawling extents, and it felt like the men and women he had fallen in with shared Styrkar's frustration. A kind of doom hung over the place, mixing in with the scent of damp earth and woodsmoke. As though they knew they were killing time until the inevitable. Until the king brought his army and found a way to assault this place. Then there would be no running into the shadows. Then there would only be fire and death.

Still he could see them going about their business. Sharpening their blades, linking their mail. Some even went about making remedies and tinctures, the scent of the herbs wafting across the courtyard. It reminded Styrkar of what a superstitious band he had fallen in with. How these people of the fens respected their saints and idols, but also the old gods and the old ways. Nevertheless, faith and worship would not see them victorious.

Before Styrkar could lament further on the fate that awaited them, a monotone ring of metal pealed from the northern gatehouse. Someone rang the bell with zeal, warning the fortress of someone coming along the waterway.

He stowed his wooden wolf within the leather pouch at his belt and grasped his axe. Men were already running to see what had provoked the commotion, and by the time he reached the gatehouse there were twenty of them peering into the sunlight at the boat's approaching.

When he recognised the intimidating prow of a dragon ship, Styrkar tensed every muscle. The sight prompted enthusiastic noises from his fellows, for this was not a Frankish boat, but Styrkar knew well that was not a sign that they were out of danger. It wasn't until he recognised the broad features of Wulfric the Heron standing at the ship's prow that he felt the fire in his belly winnow just a little.

'Men of Ely,' the Heron cried, smile beaming from within his thick beard. 'The Heron has returned, and he has brought new friends.'

The rebels at the gatehouse cheered as the ship cruised toward the shore at the foot of the fortress wall. When Styrkar recognised the white and scarlet sail hanging limp from the mast, he could not share their enthusiasm for newfound allies.

A shout went up for the gates to be opened, but Styrkar was already moving down from the parapet to greet the new arrivals. Hereswyde was waiting, Duti and Ouri at her shoulders, and Styrkar moved close to her, glaring at the gates as they were pushed wide for the man who had come from across the sea.

He walked with a slight limp, tall and blond and kingly, as was his right. Sweyn Estridsson looked very much out of place in this fortress of wood, far from his throne in Danmǫrk. The sight of him stirred some emotion within Styrkar, but it was nothing compared to that provoked by the man next to him.

Asbjorn stood just as tall as his brother, if a touch broader about the shoulders. His gaze did not fall upon Styrkar, but then why would it? He would not have expected the man he had abandoned, along with his other allies, to be in such a place as this. It was all Styrkar could do not to bark his accusations at him. To call him a coward in front of everyone gathered. Instead, he kept his silence as King Sweyn came to stand before them.

The Heron gestured to the new arrivals, nodding his head as though unsure of whether to bow or not. 'We are honoured by the presence of Sweyn, King of Danmǫrk. He has crossed the seas to join us.'

Light glinted in Sweyn's eyes as they fell upon Hereswyde. 'I have heard of a rebel lord who stands alone against our mutual enemy. I came to search him out with an offer of alliance.'

Hereswyde regarded the king in silence. Styrkar had watched her lead these rag-tag rebels. Watched her command their respect. Now they would see how she held her own against a king.

She stepped forward, standing a full head shorter than Sweyn but not breaking his gaze. 'And you have found your rebel lord, King of Danmǫrk. What do you offer?'

A grin spread across Sweyn's bearded face. 'I offer an army. I offer hope.'

Hereswyde regarded the men Sweyn had brought from his single ship. They were all tall, broad in the shoulder, thick in the arm. If she was impressed she didn't show it.

'And what do you ask in return?'

Sweyn looked deeper into Hereswyde's eyes. 'Only that once the Bastard has fallen, our alliance continues. Yes, I would seat men in English lands. But I would form a bond with a new Saxon king. One I will never have with this upstart Duke of Normandie.'

Hereswyde's stoic expression faded until she mirrored Sweyn's wide grin. Clearly she had heard enough to persuade her, but Styrkar could hold his tongue no longer. He stepped forward, axe held loosely by his side. Still, the warriors King Sweyn had brought flinched, not least Asbjorn, whose eyes widened with shock on seeing one of the men he had abandoned to the Frankish scourge.

'I have heard such promises before,' Styrkar said. 'When you sent your brother to aid the Aetheling in his war for the crown. Promises that were abandoned in favour of gold.'

For a moment Sweyn's expression turned stern, before he offered a warm smile. 'So, the Red Wolf lives. And remembers my oath.'

'I do.' Styrkar fixed Asbjorn with a deathly glare. 'And I remember it broken.'

Asbjorn stepped forward, hand to his sword. 'You call me oath breaker?'

Hereswyde was quick to stand between them. Though each man towered over her, it was enough to stop them both coming to violence. 'Enough, Styrkar. These men have come to offer us aid. What has passed is gone. I would offer my feast table to these men. I am sure an accord can be met.'

Styrkar shook his head, still holding Asbjorn in his sights. 'I would urge caution. Do not be so quick to offer your table or your trust. It might not end the way you wish.'

'I'll hear no more,' Asbjorn snarled, drawing his sword a foot from the scabbard before his brother the king grasped his arm.

'This is not why we have come,' Sweyn said through gritted teeth. 'Peace, brother.'

'And you, Red Wolf,' Hereswyde said.

Before Styrkar could think whether to obey her or not, there was a commotion from behind. Someone shouted and all heads turned to the south. Someone pushed their way through the crowd before Lightfoot appeared, to stand before Hereswyde.

'What news?' she asked.

Lightfoot fixed her with a mournful expression. 'Ill tidings from Saint Peter's Burgh.'

'Speak it,' Hereswyde urged him.

Lightfoot seemed reluctant, lowering his eyes to the ground. 'The abbot... your Uncle Brand. He has taken his final breath.'

'The Franks?' she spat.

Lightfoot shook his head. 'No. It was his time, or so I am told.'

Hereswyde placed an arm to his shoulder. 'Ill tidings indeed.'

'But not all,' Lightfoot replied. 'Word is, the king has appointed a new abbot to replace him. A foreigner named Turold. A man of base character, if the rumour is true.'

Hereswyde considered the words. 'Base character or not, it is still an insult to our forebears that the position be handed over to the Bastard's lackey. An insult that will not stand. Turold may take the abbey, but I will leave him no treasures. He will gain no gold from its coffers. We will travel there with all haste and strip the place of its relics before this Turold can lay his hands on them.'

Grunts of assent from most of the men surrounding her, but the Heron had other ideas. He shouldered his way closer, shaking his huge, bearded head.

'Saint Peter's Burgh is sacred. A holy place like few others. It would be a sin for us to ransack consecrated ground. You would damn us all.'

The noises of assent waned as others agreed with the Heron's fears. For the first time since he had come to Ely, Styrkar could sense tension between Hereswyde and the men who followed her. She eyed them earnestly, as though sympathising with their doubts, before turning her attention to Sweyn.

'What say you, King of the Danes? Should I allow this foreign priest to take my uncle's seat without challenge? Or should I provide him discomfort before he has a chance to swear his churchman's vows?'

'I think this is your land, lord. Or is it lady?'

'I am neither. I am both. I am whatever I need to be. And right now I am rebel and robber. My uncle held Saint Peter's Burgh sacred, as my men attest. But he is dead. I will not see it fall into the hands of the enemy without first claiming what is Saxon by right. The only question, King Sweyn, is whether or not you will aid me in the task?'

The king shrugged his shoulders. 'I am a godly man. But

you are right; the abbey should be plundered. Better its riches are in our hands than those of William and his lords. You will have my help.'

A cheer rose up. If any of Hereswyde's men had harboured doubts they were gone now the king of Danmǫrk had offered his aid. Only the Heron looked apprehensive, but he was one face among many.

For his part, Styrkar remained silent. He did not trust King Sweyn, and certainly not his brother Asbjorn, but he also knew that Hereswyde could not hope to prevail against the Franks without allies. At least this way, Sweyn might prove himself useful, if not loyal to their cause.

As the cheering subsided, King Sweyn fixed Styrkar with a wry look. 'And what about you, Red Wolf? Can you bring yourself to fight alongside your countrymen once more? Can you and my brother Asbjorn forget your grievance?'

Styrkar could not bring himself to look upon Asbjorn again lest he be moved to anger once more. 'I have pledged my axe to Hereswyde. Promised her Frankish heads for her fortress walls. It is a promise I intend to keep.'

'Settled then,' Sweyn bellowed. 'Tonight we feast. Tomorrow we set sail for the abbey and salvage its riches from grubby Frankish paws.'

More cheers at the prospect of a feast and the treasure that might follow. Styrkar stood at Hereswyde's side as her men led their new allies off to be fed and watered. When finally they were alone, and the northern gate closed to the reed swamp, she looked up at him. There was a hint of concern behind her dark eyes.

'You don't think we can trust the Danes?'

Styrkar watched them leaving, seeing their zeal for the

feast, as strong as their need for battle. 'To fight for us? Yes, I trust them to do that. To stay loyal? No.'

'But you are a Dane. I trust you to be loyal.'

'I am only a Dane by birth. I was raised by a Saxon king. I learned loyalty from him.'

'Then I am glad you are here, at least,' she said, before striking out to join the feasting warriors.

Styrkar watched her go. He had no stomach for a feast. Not when there would be blood to spill so very soon.

24

One hundred and fifty men. He had never commanded so many. They called it an honour, but as he rode at their head, Ronan wasn't so sure. This now meant that he was responsible for his actions. That there were definite expectations laid upon him. No more lying with whores and drinking himself into a stupor. At least not until the work was done. And what esteemed work this was.

He had been tasked with accompanying the recently appointed abbot of Saint Peter's Burgh to his new residence. God's work, as well as the king's, and a high honour indeed. As he rode ever farther across the flat eastern landscape, he didn't feel particularly honoured.

'Christ, this place is bleak,' Serle whinged, and not for the first time.

He had made his feelings about the empty English countryside plain for all to hear, loudly and often. At first his discomfort had been amusing. Now it was beginning to put Ronan's teeth on edge.

'Not long now, my friend,' Ronan replied. In reality, he had no idea how much longer they would be riding along this lonely road.

Wymon plodded along at his other shoulder. As usual he was silent on the matter, his sullen expression offering no notion as to his feelings. Likely he was as bored as the rest of them, since they had been ordered to travel swiftly and leave the land unharried. Ronan doubted any of them had the stomach for pillage anyway, after what they had done in the north only a few months before. Besides, it was best they did not provoke these fenlanders any further. One hundred and fifty armed men sounded like a lot, and certainly looked menacing enough as they rode in a column, but Ronan had heard the stories.

There were still rebels abroad, and not like those they had faced at Yorke. These were organised raiders who did not gather as an army at the behest of northern lords. They travelled in smaller groups, striking from the shelter of the forest, fast and merciless, before retreating into the night once more. This place was a hive of rebellion, the bees well hidden, their stings lethal, and Ronan was under no illusions about what danger he was in. Esteemed this new position may have been, but it could so quickly turn into a curse if he were to provoke the swarm.

The road led on, winding through sparse woodland that filled Ronan with unease. When they came out at the other side, he felt relief at seeing a lonely hamlet on the flats, a tall stone church rising from its midst.

'Please tell me that's the place,' Serle grumbled.

Ronan couldn't say for sure, but he set his heels to the horse's flanks, spurring the column to a trot in his eagerness to find out. When they reached the hamlet, the villagers appeared none too pleased to see them, shutting themselves in their hovels, or straying far from their path. By the time they reached the church, a trio of reed-limbed priests was waiting for them, smiles forced in greeting.

'Welcome,' one of them said, as Ronan reined in his steed. 'Welcome all, to the Priory of Saint Mary.'

'We have come to meet with the new Abbot of Saint Peter's Burgh,' Ronan announced. 'Are we in the right place?'

'Oh, most certainly,' the priest said, his fellows nodding their affirmation too, as though one of them wasn't sufficient. 'He waits within.'

Friendly enough, and all going to plan, but Ronan couldn't help but feel a little unsettled. 'And he doesn't see fit to greet us himself?'

The smile on the priest's face wavered. 'He is currently… indisposed. But I'm sure—'

'I'm sure he won't mind me making an introduction.'

Ronan climbed down from his horse, limping past the trio of holy men and into the priory. Inside was the nave, nothing unusual about it apart from the stink of damp. To his left a door stood ajar, and he heard the tinkling sound of female laughter. Now that was unusual.

No sooner had he pushed the door wide, than a woman came running out, half naked, clutching a bundle of clothes to her otherwise bare breasts. Once she fled the priory, a second woman rushed from a chamber further down the corridor, forcing Ronan to step aside as she stumbled past. Little wonder why those priests had looked so uncomfortable.

Undaunted, Ronan made his way toward the room, from where he could hear a tuneless humming. The door stood wide as he reached the threshold, and looking inside he caught a sight he could well have done without seeing.

A portly man sat naked on a bed, balancing a bowl on his knee. With his other hand he was wiping at his nethers as he sang a tuneless drawl. The chamber stank of sex, and not the pleasant kind.

'Ah,' the man cried, unworried at an armed stranger entering his bedchamber. 'You must be my escort.'

Ronan thought about bowing his respects, but decided it was far from appropriate. 'And you must be the abbot of Saint Peter's Burgh.'

'That's right.' The man beamed, as though the idea were new to him, and he liked the sound of it very much. 'Abbot Turold.'

'I am Ronan of Dol-Combourg. Here with a guard of one hundred and fifty lances.'

That widened Turold's eyes somewhat. 'Really? Seems a lot of men just to accompany one priest.'

'A priest who clearly has the king's favour.' Though looking at him wiping his ballocks with a wet rag, Ronan began to wonder how.

'Yes, I suppose I do. But still, all those men and horses to defend a church. Bit of a waste, if you ask me.'

No one was, but Ronan felt compelled to point out the obvious. 'The fenlands surrounding Saint Peter's Burgh are dangerous territory. Its people unpredictable and...'

Ronan paused as Turold stood up, the hair on his back and chest matted with sweat, every pimple and sore on his flesh clear to see. How those women had been able to lower themselves was a mystery Ronan would never solve.

'Unpredictable and…?' Turold asked as he squeezed himself into a priest's robe.

'And violent. Unruly. Rebellious. Take your pick, Abbot.'

Turold pulled the grubby cassock over his belly and loins, finally offering Ronan some relief from the hideous sight. 'I'll take your word for it.'

'Good. Then we leave with all haste. With luck we'll reach the abbey by high sun tomorrow, if we ride hard enough.'

'Now?' Turold looked incredulous. 'But I haven't bathed. Or eaten. No, you'll stay the night and we'll leave at first light.'

The prospect of staying overnight in a damp priory with a hundred and fifty stinking knights was not one Ronan relished.

'No. We leave now.'

Turold stared. Obviously a man unused to having his authority questioned. Ronan thought he might try and leverage that authority, but instead Turold shrugged his fleshy shoulders.

'Very well, Ronan of Dol-Combourg. I suppose I have suffered worse in my time. Give me a chance to gather my belongings and we shall ride like the proverbial wind.'

This time Ronan did bow before leaving Turold to prepare for their journey. Outside the bright sunlight did little to lift his mood. Most of the armoured men had dismounted, some tending to horses, others taking the opportunity to stretch their legs. Ronan wondered for a moment if it would have been better to let them stay here the night, but doubted they would have thanked him for it.

'Well?' Serle asked. 'Is the abbot as pious and pompous as you expected?'

Ronan glanced toward the three priests who still stood nearby, looking more awkward than ever. 'You did see the two partially dressed whores who fled the priory a moment ago? That should give you a clue.'

Serle laughed, slapping Wymon on the arm. 'Yes, we saw them. This abbot is a man after my own heart. I doubt there'll be many blessings said for our journey, but I imagine it won't be boring.'

Ronan pressed the flesh of his nose just between his eyes, hoping to stifle the headache he was getting. He would gladly settle for a boring journey as long as it was uneventful. And the sooner he could rid himself of the lascivious Turold and return to more important things, the better.

No sooner had he thought it, than the abbot appeared carrying a saddlebag and a large sack that jangled suspiciously. At his barked order, the priests quickly brought his horse, holding the bridle as Turold struggled up onto its back. They carefully strapped his belongings to the saddle, and if that jangling was riches purloined from the abbey, none of them had the nerve to question it.

'Come on then,' Turold roared. 'What are we waiting for?'

Ronan and his men were already mounting up, and with a firm motion of his arm he led them off westward. As they left the little hamlet behind, he turned to see the three priests looking much happier than they'd been when he arrived.

They were not far along the road west through the fens before Turold had kicked his horse alongside Ronan's. He rode in silence for a mile or so, but it felt inevitable he would not be able to keep his peace.

'You seem well informed about these marshland rebels, Dol-Combourg. How so?'

Ronan shrugged. 'Rebels are much the same all across these lands. Though the ones in the fens have proven much more elusive than their northern brethren.'

'Is that so.' Turold looked around at the surrounding flatlands. 'Perhaps the king should be more harsh in his dealings with them then.'

Ronan affected a smile. 'That does not sound very godly of you, Turold.'

The new abbot returned his grin. 'I doubt it will make any difference whether I am godly or not. These eastern marshes are filled with superstitious peasants. Godless, the lot of them. But they will bow to their Lord and their king, or they will be cast down like the Canaanites.'

Ronan was surprised at the sudden zealotry in his voice. 'How very rousing.'

Turold grinned wider. 'I've been giving it some practice ahead of my new appointment.'

A group of fenlanders were walking toward them along the road, carrying circular boats on their backs. They stepped off the road before the column could reach them, wrenching the skull caps from their heads and bowing their respects.

'I doubt you'll have much trouble converting these bog waders,' Ronan said.

Turold chuckled. 'Maybe, maybe not. But I'll be certain to take as much pleasure in it as I can.' There was a wicked glint to his eye, and Ronan could only imagine the gruesome methods he might adopt to inspire piety in his flock. 'So, do you intend to join me at Saint Peter's Burgh? I could use a man who knows the lay of the land.'

'I do not,' Ronan was quick to reply. 'Once you are safely delivered to the abbey I will be returning to the king's side.'

'Not even if I was to insist?'

'Insist all you like. I am the king's servant.'

Turold raised his eyebrow with incredulity. 'Not a man of God, eh?'

'The king *is* God. At least in these forsaken lands.'

Another bellowing laugh from Turold, as he kicked his steed onward ahead of the column. 'We shall see, Dol-Combourg. We shall see.'

A maniac, overseeing the spiritual welfare of a whole region. Once again, Ronan wondered what this debauched bastard had done that King William would reward him with such high office.

Then again, maybe he didn't want to know.

25

Saint Peter's Burgh, England, June 1070

Every dwelling burned as the dawn sun peered across the marshes. The birth of a new day. The death of this place, whatever it had been called. When the monks within their abbey had refused Hereswyde entry, she had tried to reason with them. Tried to coax them from within their holy fortress. But they had defied her, and the Danes had exacted a fiery retribution.

Now the air hung heavy with the acrid stench of burning wood. The haunting cries of the dying echoed across the devastated hamlet as Styrkar made his way through. At first he had intended to join in with the pillaging, to murder any Franks that might defy him. He needn't have been so zealous, as the Danes fell on the place like wolves.

Styrkar had seen their wrath before when they had ravaged the coast. Had joined in with their frenzy. Now he had no stomach for it. No urge to exact reprisals on these people. They were merely victims. Condemned by the wilfulness of their holy men.

As he walked from the burned-out carcasses of those huts, he left the sound of dying behind him. The closer he drew to the abbey, the louder the noise of banging grew, the sound of Hereswyde imploring those monks to open their doors to her. He had tried to warn her. Tried to explain that the Danes did not share her goal of unseating the Franks, and only cared for plunder. It had taken the deaths of innocents for her to learn that harsh lesson.

'Aethelwold, this is senseless,' she snarled, rapping on the oak doors with the flat of her hand. 'I have tried to reason with you. This stubbornness will only lead to more needless killing.'

Silence from within, as Styrkar came to stand but a few feet from the doors. Surrounding Hereswyde were her most loyal – the Heron, Lightfoot, Ouri – all of them looking equally discontented with their current task. These men were all adherents to a vengeful god, and wary of the superstitions of these eastern lands. Each one would be ill at ease with ravaging such a sacred place, let alone robbing it of its treasures.

'I have no more patience for you, Aethelwold,' Hereswyde shouted, taking a step back. 'Remember you have forced me into this.'

With that she signalled to the Heron, who rested a long axe across his shoulder. Reluctantly, the hulking warrior stepped forward and raised the weapon. The rest stood by as the Heron went about his work with little relish. Those oaken doors were sturdy, and it took more blows than Styrkar could count to bring it down. All the while there were cries of protest from within, and without the Danes gathered, like hounds waiting to be fed.

When finally the doors fell, there was a howl of triumph. Asbjorn shouted at his men in the language of the Danes to gather their fill, and they needed no further urging. As Hereswyde looked on, they rushed inside, their avaricious cries echoing to the rafters.

As the last of them entered, a harried monk crawled from within the abbey on hands and knees. Tears stained his cheeks and he gazed at Hereswyde mournfully.

'I warned you, Aethelwold,' she chided.

The monk's face twisted in hate. 'Your uncle would be ashamed of what you've become, girl.'

Hereswyde leaned in close to the kneeling monk. 'My uncle is dead. And in his place there will be a Frankish lackey. I will not allow his oily hands to besmirch any of this abbey's relics.'

Aethelwold had no reply, seeming to shrink visibly in the face of Hereswyde's ire. Styrkar left the cowed monk where he knelt, and followed the Danes within the dark confines of the old building.

It was just a church, like so many others he had seen on these shores since he was a child, if a little more opulent than most. The morning sun peered through windows of stained glass, though it was hard to see what they depicted after the Danes had already flung missiles through them. The rows of wooden pews had been pushed over, holy books scattered, considered worthless by the warriors now ransacking the place. Despite the pillaging going on, Styrkar still felt the hallowing effect of the place. Everything about it was designed to inspire awe in its congregation, and he could understand how the old gods had been abandoned in favour of this new Christ. For how could those ancient idols of the woods and rivers and skies compete, when such structures as this dominated the landscape? Not that it gave the Danes pause.

Two of them growled and snarled like animals as they fought over the golden cross upon the altar. At first they seemed content to wrestle for the idol, until one of them struck the other with his fist. Then the treasure was forgotten, as they drew knives and began to struggle even more fiercely.

Styrkar ignored them. He had not come for plunder. He had come for... what? To spit his defiance in the face of the usurper? Or was it that he simply had nowhere else to go? Perhaps both, but he did know that sooner or later, if they plundered enough churches and cut enough Frankish throats *He* would come. Then Styrkar would have one more chance at a reckoning. One last chance.

As the Danes continued to ransack the place, Styrkar's hand strayed to the pouch at his belt. Opening it, he took out the tiny wolf he had carved so many days ago. He had taken pride over its crafting, and it might almost be considered a thing of value. While his ancestral countrymen stole all they could, with no thought to the wrath of their god, Styrkar took a candle from its place on a shelf, and placed the wolf in its stead. Payment for what they had taken. Old for new.

'Here,' came a cry from somewhere deeper within the abbey. 'I've found them, over here.'

A clattering of feet as the Danes rushed to see what had been discovered. All apart from the two still fighting over their golden cross, huffing on the ground, their reserves of energy almost spent.

At the cry, even Hereswyde entered, the distressed monk

Aethelwold scurrying along beside her. Styrkar followed deeper into the building, seeing a door torn open, Danes peering in and laughing at robed men on their knees. Already one of them had been dragged out by the hem of his cassock, begging for his life as he stared at the hulking brutes who had uncovered his hiding place.

'Do not hurt them,' Aethelwold wailed. 'They are men of the cross. Harmless custodians of this abbey's relics. They were only doing what I commanded.'

'We will not hurt your holy men, monk,' Asbjorn said. 'As long as they give us what they were hiding.'

Aethelwold shook his head. 'We cannot just give you our relics. If we hand them over who knows what repercussions we will face. The Frankish abbot may well exact a bloody toll.'

'And what do you think we'll do if you don't?' Asbjorn offered an ice-cold glare that left his intentions in little doubt.

Aethelwold looked to Hereswyde, but she had only a shrug for him. Again, the old monk's eyes looked on with venom. 'You would leave us to our fate at the hands of these invaders?'

Before she could answer, Asbjorn stepped closer. 'You could always come with us, monk. I know my brother the king would welcome you at his court in Danmork. You and your people would be safe there.'

Already his men were tearing the relics from the arms of the monks within their transept. Styrkar could see Aethelwold was considering the options laid before him. Stay and perhaps die. Be taken over the sea, and at least they would live. No choice at all.

'Very well,' he answered, suddenly bowing his head to Asbjorn as though he were some saviour. 'We will. We will come with you.'

'No,' a cry went up from within the chamber. 'They will not have it. They will not.'

More commotion from within the transept as one of the monks wrenched a casket from the greedy hands of a Danish warrior, and staggered from the chamber.

'Brother Lang,' Aethelwold said desperately. 'Do not defy these men.'

Lang shook his head, gripping the casket close to his chest as though it were a swaddled babe. 'This is our most precious relic. We cannot give it to them. We cannot. It must be defended with our—'

Asbjorn slapped Lang's cheek with a meaty hand, and the monk gasped. 'You'll give it here or you'll be left behind for the Frankish dogs.'

There were tears in Lang's eyes, but he still shook his head in defiance. Before Asbjorn could bear down on the hapless monk, Styrkar moved between them, taking hold of the casket.

'Come now, little priest. Whatever is in that casket cannot be worth your life.'

Gently he eased the prized possession from Lang's grip and handed it to Asbjorn. The Dane took it, quickly flipping open the clasp to see what treasure it contained. On seeing its contents, his lip curled in disgust.

'What is this?'

Lang reached for the casket, but Styrkar held him back, lest he stir Asbjorn's ire further and end up a carcass.

'It holds more value than you could possibly comprehend,' Aethelwold said.

'It's a rotting arm,' Asbjorn replied, showing all around what the casket contained.

He did not lie. Styrkar felt his stomach churn at seeing the decomposed limb resting within its metal box.

'The sword arm of the sainted King Oswald,' Hereswyde said, as though she had known all along what the casket contained. 'Slain by Penda, the last heathen king of these lands. It is said to hold healing properties.'

'Is it?' Asbjorn replied, sceptically. 'Well I hold no store by superstition. They can keep it.'

He slammed the lid shut and handed it back to Lang, who took it gratefully, smiling through his tears. Before he could speak his thanks, Hereswyde prised the box from the monk's arms.

'No. I don't think they can. I will take this prize. It will not be left for the Franks and their new abbot.'

Asbjorn shrugged. 'As you wish.' Then he turned his attention back to his men, and the treasures they were still pillaging from the place.

One by one, they led the monks from the abbey and out into the acrid air. When the abbey was suitably ransacked, they went back to their ships and pushed off from the bank. Styrkar watched, Hereswyde still at his side, still holding tight to that casket and its desiccated contents.

'I should have listened to you, Red Wolf,' she said, as they watched the Danes leave with their booty. 'I should never have trusted King Sweyn. He cares only for riches.'

'It is of no matter now,' he replied. 'We are no worse off than we were yesterday. Only now you have the arm of a dead king. For what it's worth.'

Before she could answer, they heard quiet weeping from

behind them. The monk, Lang, sat on the grass in the shadow of the abbey as the morning sun crested the spire. He had refused to travel with his fellow monks, electing instead to remain behind. The contents of the casket may have just been rotting flesh and bone, but clearly it had value to him.

'Don't be such a baby,' the Heron snapped, as he marched past the monk. 'And remember what we told you to say if you're questioned by the Franks. I'll know if you don't do as you're told.'

Lang nodded, compliant and cowed.

Hereswyde smiled up at Styrkar and gave her new treasure a pat. 'Worth much to some. Worth nothing to others. Now we will see how much it is worth to the usurper king.'

Styrkar felt a swell of excitement. Every day they provoked him was another day closer to his reckoning. It could not come soon enough.

26

He had come to sense it in his time travelling across this cursed land. That dread feeling of death hanging in the air, long before he could see it or taste it.

But of course, the abbey had been ransacked.

What should have been a simple task, to transport the new abbot to his seat in the fens, had gone awry before he even arrived. The abbey despoiled. The surroundings ravaged.

Of course they were. For the path of Ronan of Dol-Combourg was perpetually strewn with dog shit of the most putrid kind.

The smoke had barely cleared by the time they reached it. Wailing still audible from somewhere among the black ruined carcass of the town. At least the abbey looked to be in one piece, despite its smashed doors.

'Looks like they beat us to it,' Serle grumbled, looking altogether unaffected by the devastation.

'Looks like they did,' Ronan breathed in reply.

'Sacrilege!' bellowed Turold. 'I'll excommunicate every last fucking one of them.'

Ronan wasn't sure whether the powers of excommunication came under an abbot's purview, but that didn't seem to matter to Turold. While the priest ranted amidst the carnage of his new home, Ronan surveyed the surroundings. It was flat land, but he had come to expect that. An altogether indefensible position, and one he would hardly have chosen to position a church of such significance. Nevertheless, defend it he must.

'Serle, have the men set up a perimeter. Dig as deep a trench as you can; make sure there is a watch set up in every direction. Especially along the river.'

His man nodded in reply, before reining his horse around to bark orders at the men under their command. Wymon remained sitting in his saddle, eyes narrowed at the surrounding marshes as though he expected trouble. Ronan could only hope he was just being cautious.

'This is your fault, Dol-Combourg,' Turold growled from his horse.

Ronan regarded the fat man on his fat pony. 'How so?'

His face had reddened considerably from the first time they'd met. 'You were supposed to protect this place. Protect me.'

'We travelled here with all speed, Lord Abbot, despite your objection. Had we arrived any sooner it's highly likely we would be as burned and blackened as these houses. So consider yourself lucky. And… you are welcome.'

Turold seethed, but his whining ceased. As the rest of the men began to dig their trenches and find what wood they could for a makeshift palisade, Wymon climbed down from his saddle as though he had spotted a rabbit in the undergrowth.

Ronan watched him stalk toward the base of the abbey, where hawthorn and cotoneaster had been growing in abundance. Slowly he unsheathed his sword, staring into the bushes until he drew back his arm as though to strike.

The hedge ruffled, and someone burst out wearing a threadbare robe and raising his hands high.

'Please,' the vagabond cried. 'Don't kill me, please, I beg you. I am just a monk of this abbey. I'm the only one left.'

Wymon grabbed hold of the man by the collar, caring little for his protestations, or claims to being of a holy order. Sword still drawn, he dragged the man forward, and drove him to his knees in front of Ronan's horse.

'Do you have a name, priest?' Ronan asked as the man cowered.

'Yes… Lang… my name is Lang.'

'And where are your fellow monks now?'

Lang stared, almost too afraid to speak. When finally he did, his hands were clenched as though in prayer, voice quavering like a child being scolded. 'They took them. The Danes took them.'

'Danes?' Ronan asked, feeling his gut suddenly roil. 'The Danes are here?'

He had gone to great lengths to rid these shores of those raiders. If they were back, the king would surely have to know about it.

'Yes, they have joined with the silvatici of the marshes.'

'The what?' Turold spat, his patience for this coward all but run out. 'What are you talking about, man?'

'The rebels, your holiness,' Lang replied, bowing his

head. 'They fight still. Striking from the fens and forests. They are led by a… by a man named Hereward. A lord of these lands before the new king took them from him.'

'Ah, I knew it,' Turold said, clambering down from his horse. 'I knew this gift of the king's would end up being a poisoned chalice. Not only do I have to bring these Saxons to the faith, but I have to fight rebels too. I knew it. No wonder he did this to me. No wonder I was sent to this armpit.'

As he stalked off toward the abbey, Ronan could only wonder once again what Turold and William had agreed. Clearly the king's beneficence was not all it had first appeared.

With Wymon still standing over the cowering Lang, Ronan slipped down from his saddle, stretching his aching back and flexing his leg. He looked down at the beleaguered monk, feeling an unexpected note of sympathy.

'You're a lucky man, Lang. Not to be carried off by those savages.' Then he looked to the broken doors of the abbey through which Turold had disappeared. 'Although there might soon come a time you'll wish they'd taken you along, with your brother monks.'

He signalled for Wymon to let the man go free, before he followed Turold toward the abbey. Curiosity was getting the better of him, and he wondered what state they had left the place in. Seeing the new abbot's reaction might also offer some amusement into the bargain.

As he crossed the threshold, he heard Turold's noisy outrage as he bellowed to the vaulted roof. His fury echoed through the abbey, and Ronan found it hard to suppress a grin. The place was in disarray – the pews little more than kindling, everything of value stripped, the coloured glass of the high windows smashed to an indecipherable mosaic on the floor.

He was careful as he made his way through the mess, expecting at any moment to find a bloody corpse left behind by the Danes, but there were none. When eventually he passed a shelf, and saw the small wooden token abandoned upon it, he struggled to catch his breath.

With a trembling hand, Ronan reached out and plucked the tiny wooden wolf from its resting place. He had seen its like before. This could be no coincidence, not here, not now.

The Red Wolf still lived, but Ronan could hardly be surprised by it. That man would have clawed his way from Hell itself to exact his vengeance. And now he was back, in the only place left in these lands offering a vestige of defiance to the king.

'The king must know about this,' Turold shouted, all too close. 'I want him here, Dol-Combourg. I want his armies at his back. I want these rebels hunted down and slaughtered. Burned in the righteous fire of our Lord God. I want—'

'Do stop shouting, Abbot Turold.' Ronan secreted the wooden carving in the pouch at his belt. 'You will bring the roof down. Fear not, the king will hear about this – I can assure you. However, I don't rate your chances of having him come here to root out these silvatici himself. He is a very busy man officiating two kingdoms.'

'Then you must do it.' Turold glared, his flabby cheeks reddening by the second. 'You must take your hundred and fifty lances and root out those peasant bastards. Burn as many hamlets as you please, I will absolve you of any sin.'

Ronan matched Turold's glare. 'It will take more than

a single abbot to forgive my sins, Turold. But even if I was enticed by an offer of absolution, a hundred and fifty men would never be enough. These rebels know the land. Have the loyalty of the populace. They will be impossible to find. And if I get close I will be ambushed long before I even spot them.' His hand brushed the pouch containing the wooden wolf. 'Besides, if they have recruited who I think, then even a thousand men would be inadequate for the job.'

'Coward,' Turold spat.

Ronan's smile did not waver. 'Yes. And it has seen me survive this long where bolder men have perished.'

Turold opened his mouth to speak again, when there came a shout of alarm from outside. Ronan ignored the incensed abbot, and made his way back outside, to see that his men were pointing across their half-dug defences. Ronan limped closer, in time to see a group of villagers approaching from the marshlands.

As they drew closer he could see they were covered in filth, each one looking desperate and forlorn. Most likely they had fled for their lives when the Danes arrived, abandoning the rest to be slaughtered.

'My lords,' one of them called, raising a withered hand. 'My lords, thank Christ you have come.'

They stopped just beyond the hastily constructed boundary. Perhaps a dozen, men and women. No children though, and Ronan guessed they might still be hiding out among the rushes.

Normally he would have turned such vagabonds away, but perhaps this was a chance to turn the situation to his favour. Still, he had to be careful. These Saxons were a deceitful bunch, as much likely to stab their rescuers as laud them with praise.

'Come.' Ronan beckoned for them to approach. 'You are safe now. All you need do is demonstrate your fealty to the king, and you will have his protection.'

The one at their head immediately dropped to his knees. 'You have it, my lord. The king, I mean. We are loyal subjects all. None of us expected the Danes. We thought it was just—'

'Shut up, Maccus,' another one snarled. 'Your tongue flaps when it should be still.'

Maccus bowed his head at his friend's chiding.

Ronan leaned in closer. 'Fear not, Maccus. You were not about to tell me anything I do not already know. That you thought it was just the rebels. That they follow a fallen thegn named Hereward.'

Maccus looked up with mournful eyes. 'Yes, that's right, my lord. We were supposed to be under their protection. But when Aethelwold refused to open the doors to the abbey, those Danes—'

Another hiss from the second Saxon. 'Maccus, shut your—'

'I'll not, Hidda. I'll be silent no longer. We've kept our secrets for too long now, and look where it's got us.'

Hidda leaned closer. 'I'm warning you, hold your fat old tongue.'

'What you gonna do?' Maccus snapped. 'Go and tell your friends on the isle?'

Both men suddenly stopped. Clearly the loose tongue of Maccus had flapped a little too much for either of them.

'Isle?' Ronan asked, trying to remain as calm and unthreatening as he could.

It didn't do the trick, and immediately both men turned tail to flee back across the shallow trench. On instinct, Serle wrenched the sword from his scabbard, hacking Maccus across the top of his skull and felling him in an instant. Wymon was second to react, leaping atop his horse and galloping after Hidda as he foundered through the swampy ground. Ronan was about to shout that they should take him alive, when Wymon flung his lance, impaling Hidda where he stood.

Ronan sighed despondently. At his feet, the rest of the survivors knelt cowering. Did any of them know about this isle Maccus had mentioned? Was it that important?

No, it wasn't. Ronan had risked his life before pursuing fugitives, and for nothing. Had risked his life to track the Red Wolf and ended up cowering in a pig pen to survive.

His reward had come when he'd been found lying in a whore's bed. If he'd learned one thing, it was better to let opportunity come and find you, rather than hunt it down at risk to life and limb. Let some other man search out his glory in the marshes. If the Red Wolf was here, he wasn't going anywhere. And should the king finally decide to end all resistance in this damp and dismal place, then Ronan was sure he would tag along... with an army at his back.

27

Hammer, tap, tap. Hammer, tap, tap. That rhythm was spellbinding. Singing in Styrkar's head as he was lulled by the heat of the forge and skill of the smith. Weland was a master, and it was often that Styrkar would come here to watch him work. Of course, Weland was not his real name. He had chosen it from an old poem, and it fitted him well enough, so why not wear it. Doubtful anyone would care.

A final hammer and Weland plunged the steel back into the fire. He wore the thick gloves of his trade but even so Styrkar found it incredible how he could endure the heat. Then they waited, waited, until that metal was white hot once again and Weland went back to the hammer.

It would be a fine blade; Weland had promised that much. Styrkar could not doubt him. He had wielded blades made by this smith before – perfectly balanced, keen, hardy. Never before had Weland made a sword just for him though. It would be far from the layered and twisted steel of a thegn's blade, but Weland could hardly be blamed for that. He had neither the resources nor the time to make a beautiful sword of legend. It would be a reliable weapon though. And in times such as these, that was a more valuable commodity than beauty.

A shout from outside. Weland did not even look up from his labours as Styrkar turned and stepped out into the daylight to see what the commotion was about. He squinted in the sun, looking across the fort to see the western gates were open, men watching on as their Danish allies made ready to leave.

Styrkar's jaw clenched as he watched them busying themselves. Those treacherous bastards were abandoning these men in their time of need. Without thinking he made his way closer, forcing down the anger, but he had been abandoned once too many times by these pretenders. By these men who claimed to be brave, but were only out for what they could rob and pillage.

It reminded him of years before, when as a child he had travelled with the followers of Harald Sigurdsson. Back then they had laughed and told tales of their courage and their prowess. When tested, they had fled in the face of danger, craven and cowed. Now, it looked like the followers of Sweyn were doing the same.

As he drew nearer he saw the king leaning on a barrel as his men carried their booty to their ships. Asbjorn stood beside him, along with Hereswyde, dwarfed by those tall Danes.

'We had a bargain, King of Danmørk,' he heard her say.

Sweyn shrugged, offering that stare only kings and killers were able. 'Bargains change. As with all things.'

'So you would just abandon us? Take your booty and leave? Tell me what has changed? Did you strike another bargain with the Franks?'

'No bargains, lady. I have reconsidered what it is possible to gain in these lands. And I have decided there is nothing I want.'

'Nothing you want?' She stepped closer, almost threateningly despite her stature. 'No lands? No throne?'

'Throne?' Sweyn almost laughed. 'You talk as though there is still a chance the usurper will be separated from his crown. Look around you, woman. You are all that is left. A rabble in the marshes. You would need an army to topple the king from his seat, and you do not have it. I cannot risk my people for such folly.'

Styrkar reached their side, and the pair went quiet. Asbjorn stiffened, expecting trouble, as well he might.

'Abandoning your oaths for a second time,' Styrkar breathed.

Sweyn shrugged like a man without a care. 'Oaths are made. Oaths are broken. As well you know, Red Wolf.'

Before Styrkar could answer, Asbjorn stepped between them. 'Make no trouble. This would be a fight even you won't survive.'

It only stoked the fire within Styrkar to brighter flame. 'What is a second son to do but carve his name in glory? Those were the words you spoke to me once. Where is the glory in this, Asbjorn? Abandoning your allies to their fate while you sail away with what riches you could loot from a place of holiness. And not for the first time.'

'I am too old to die in a swamp,' Asbjorn replied. 'Alone and forgotten. If that is the fate you wish for yourself,

Styrkar, then stay by all means. But know there is an oar on my ship for you, should you wish to take it.'

'I would not,' Styrkar replied through gritted teeth. 'I pulled an oar once before for men who claimed themselves heroes, but turned out to be craven.'

King Sweyn clamped a hand to his brother's arm before he could lunge forward. Likewise, Hereswyde stood in front of Styrkar, using all her weight to hold him back.

'Enough words have been spoken,' Sweyn said. 'It would be a shame to ruin our parting with violence. Don't you agree?'

'I do,' Hereswyde replied, shoving Styrkar back with surprising strength.

Still, he and Asbjorn stared at one another as Sweyn dragged his brother toward the open gates of the fort. The Danes swiftly finished loading their vessels. Along with the riches plundered at Saint Peter's Burgh, Aethelwold and his monks also joined them. Styrkar had no idea what fate awaited them across the sea, but he could only hope it would be better than anything the Franks would offer. Somehow he doubted it would have been much different.

'You should have let me kill him,' Styrkar said, as they closed the gate on those Danes.

'And then where would I be? With even fewer men to face the usurper. Though perhaps Sweyn was right. Perhaps this is folly and I am only leading these men to their deaths.'

'So what will you do? You have no lands, no family. Will Hereswyde of the Marshes go and find a husband to lie with and raise pups?'

Her eyes darkened, as though that were indeed a fate

worse than death. 'No, Red Wolf. I will fight to the end. Even if I am alone.'

'You will not die alone. That I promise you.'

Before she could reply, a harsh cry cut the newly quieted air. The Heron was glaring at the closed gates, venting his anger. Surrounding him were other men – Lightfoot, Duti and Kite – all squabbling their discontent. Though Styrkar could not hear their words he recognised men panicking. Fear was infecting them, which in turn manifested as anger.

Hereswyde made her way closer. Styrkar followed as those men shouted ever louder.

'We are lost,' the Heron growled. 'Our last chance at salvaging victory sails away across the seas. We are left without allies. Only a matter of time before the Franks find us. We must—'

'What must we do, brother Wulfric?' Hereswyde asked. At her word the men went silent. 'What has the Heron decided for us?'

A twitch of doubt on his face before he set his jaw. 'There is nothing left here. Nothing but death. We must flee.'

'And you have decided this? You have decided to lead these men off into the woods and marshes, never to be seen again?'

'And where have you led us?' the Heron snarled, raising his hands to the high wooden walls. 'To this... this fortress? This prison? You think we can stand against the king and his knights forever? No one is coming to help us. All the Saxon lords are dead or on their knees. Every new moon another castle of stone rises to dominate the English horizon. And here we sit, waiting for the day they will finally come for us.'

'We stand because we have no other choice,' she replied. 'Because we are the last of our kind, and we do not kneel.'

A sneer twisted the Heron's face, and he barked a bitter laugh. 'No, Hereswyde, daughter of Eskil. We do not kneel. Other than to you. You who have led us here to our deaths.'

He pulled his sword from its scabbard. The rest of the men stood back, and Styrkar grasped the axe at his side. Hereswyde glanced over her shoulder toward him, raising her hand to stop him interfering. With no desire to undermine her authority in front of these men, Styrkar took a step back.

'Don't do this, Wulfric,' she said, and there was genuine grief in her voice. 'We have faced so much together. It would be—'

The Heron howled like a berserker, surging forward and hacking down with his blade. Hereswyde, dodged aside, narrowly avoiding that sweeping sword as she wrenched her seax from its scabbard.

She faced him with emotionless intent, but Styrkar was still unsure whether she would be able to deal a killing blow to one who was once so loyal. The Heron had no such qualms, bellowing again as he swept his sword from side to side, putting Hereswyde on the back foot.

Wulfric's bellow echoed all through the fort, his blade audible as it swooped left to right and back again, but Hereswyde bided her time, picking her moment. He struck at her again, and after letting that blade sweep past, she darted forward, seax piercing the hulking warrior's chest.

The bellow was caught in his throat as she wrenched her weapon free. His arms dropped to his sides, sword falling to the ground as he looked down at the open wound, crimson spreading across his tunic.

'Damn you,' whispered the Heron, before he pitched forward into the dirt.

All eyes regarded that corpse. Styrkar gripped his axe, in case any of the others decided to pick up where the Heron had left off. If any of them were inclined, they lacked the courage to do so.

'Anyone who doubts me can leave,' Hereswyde said, still staring at the corpse of her once loyal follower. 'Or you can face me now, should you have the courage. If you want the burden of leadership, just draw your sword and take it.'

She dragged her eyes away from Wulfric's body and scanned the crowd. Those who had previously voiced their discontent were silent. No one was up to the challenge.

'I gathered you all here with common purpose,' she called out, voice raised so they could all hear her now. 'We were turned from our lands. Our people slaughtered. Raped. The north is a wasteland because of the usurper king. No one dares to oppose him now. No one but us. It is time to provoke this false king. Time to draw him to us, and make him waste his knights at our door. And if we die here, at least they will say that we made a stand. We did not run away into the fens like a scattered flock, too afraid to fight. We died for this place, with weapons drawn. Spitting our curses as we fell so that in a hundred years, a thousand, they will still speak of us.'

A cheer went up from somewhere across the fort. It was

joined by another, and another. Soon that noise gripped the fort, ringing out across the flatlands.

With a final glance at the Heron's body, Hereswyde turned away, cleaning her blade on her sleeve before sheathing her seax.

'What now?' Styrkar asked as she walked by.

'Now I have an old score to settle,' she replied, without stopping.

28

They watched from the cover of woodland. Across the marsh stood a fort, imposing in the twilight. Outside it a peaceful lustre was cast, lapwings and curlews still visible as the sun went down, their evening calls pealing across the fens. The inhabitants of that fort had no idea what waited within the woods – thirty killers on the hunt, come to exact their leader's revenge. To fall on that place like wraiths and leave none alive, before sinking back into the wetland.

'Is it as you remember?' Styrkar asked as he stared across the boggy ground.

Hereswyde stepped forward, her skin covered in dirt, eyes white and wide as they peered from a blackened face. 'The palisade is higher. The gate stronger. But what lies within will be much the same. Other than the one who lives there.'

The Frankish lord who had taken it as his residence. The one who had ordered the murder of Eskil, Hereswyde's father. Styrkar had heard her tale of vengeance. How she had poisoned his killers and set her hounds on them. How she had murdered them all with arrow and sword. But the one who had ordered her father's death had not been among them. Now it was time for that debt to be paid in full.

She drew her blade, and on that unspoken signal two dozen more hissed quietly from their scabbards. Styrkar drew his own sword, newly forged by the smith of Ely. Its weight was perfect. Grip leatherbound and fitted to his hand. Now he would have a chance to test its keen edge against Frankish flesh.

Hereswyde led them from the trees and waded into the marsh. The rest followed, thigh-deep as they went, careful not to disturb the wading birds lest they give them away with their sudden flight. A pale moon lit the way, all eyes focused on the fort looming ahead.

There was light from within the fort, but it did not penetrate far into the night. Styrkar held his breath as they trod more solid earth, moving to within the shadow of the palisade. Lightfoot knelt, shouldering his bow as he covered his mouth with both hands. He whistled through his fingers, mimicking the warbling call of a jack snipe. Then they waited.

Styrkar watched the lip of the parapet, at any moment expecting to see a helmed head peer over it and spy the thirty crouching there in the dark. For the cry of alarm to go up. For them to be assailed by a torrent of arrows.

Instead he heard the sound of a wooden bar being moved, the quiet creak of the gate as it was pushed open. From within the fort came rushing several figures, gripping their cloaks tight about them. Men and women scampered off into the night lest they become victim to the inevitable violence. Not one of them said a word, already forewarned of what lurked beyond the walls of the fort, only too eager to see their Frankish masters murdered in their wake.

Once they were gone, Hereswyde led the way through the open gate. In they slipped, thirty wolves on the hunt, using the night as their cloak. Fires burned within, and Styrkar heard the sound of revels from within a longhouse of stone and wood. Upon the parapet were two warriors patrolling, but their attention was focused on the surrounding marsh, and not what might lurk within.

Hereswyde signalled her archers. Lightfoot, Duti and the Hedge-Sparrow all nocked arrows to their bows. A hum of the strings, a hiss of air, and the sentries upon their parapet were silenced.

Styrkar could hold himself back no longer, striking out from the group to find quarry. He did not have to search long, spying someone staggering away from a pit that acted as privy for the fort. Clearly the man was in his cups. A disadvantage that would be his downfall, though sober he would have ended up just as dead.

A knife would have been the best tool for work such as this – silent work in the night – but Styrkar was too eager to test his blade. He gripped it tight in both hands, stalking ever closer, focused on that man's neck. His victim only saw him at the last moment, a wild phantom come to send him to the next life. Styrkar saw the man's eyes widen, his mouth open to scream, but his head was cut from his shoulders before he could utter a word. A keen blade indeed. Styrkar would be sure to commend Weland upon his return to the Isle of Eels.

As he looked around for another kill, he could hear the quiet sound of men dying across the fort. More arrows whispered through the air. More men struck with sword and axe before they could call for aid. This was not the way Styrkar would have preferred to go about his labours. Give him an open field to charge across. A blue sky to rage beneath. Brothers to fight beside. But he did not get to choose his battlefield, and for now this one would have to suffice.

As he rounded a hut he stopped in his tracks, his wandering thoughts almost getting the better of him. A man stood not five feet away, hand on his sword, eyes wide with fright. His hair was shaven in the Frankish style, and he looked almost too terrified to cry out, eager not to give away his position to the raiders who had come to the fort.

That fear left him as he shouted in his foreign tongue. Styrkar darted forward to silence him as he bellowed, but before he could reach the man, two arrows struck him. Styrkar froze, watching the man grasp one of the arrows jutting from his throat as he fell to his knees, gurgling his last.

Across the fort, Hereswyde's followers stopped, listening for any sign from the longhouse that the man's cry had been heard. When a laugh bellowed from inside, they sighed in relief and Hereswyde signalled for them to move closer.

Styrkar was close to her shoulder as she neared the front of the building. Other men slowly rounded the structure, searching for entrances at the side and rear. Hereswyde did not wait, pushing open the main doors and striding through.

There was laughter at first, merriment that was cooled by the evening breeze blowing in off the marsh. One by one the men turned toward her. One by one their laughter ceased. Brows creased in confusion, then rose in concern, then furrowed in anger. Before any of them could reach for a weapon, the door to one side burst open, and in rushed grizzled killers. Then another door to the rear.

Axes swung. Bows thrummed. The Franks dropped their cups of ale, drawing knives, raising chairs, anything they could find to defend themselves, but they were already too late. Styrkar was in no mood to be left out, darting forward, letting his fledgling blade sing. Wherever a man moved to face him that sword struck. Two heads fell severed one after the other, as the walls were spattered with gore. Where there had been raucous laughter only moments before now were bellows of anger and pain, screams for mercy, groans of the dying.

One man, better dressed than the rest in a jerkin of fine black velvet and gold thread, crawled his way from the melee. As he cowered with his back to the far wall, Styrkar advanced. They locked eyes, the Red Wolf savouring that fear before he struck…

'Not him,' Hereswyde shouted, before Styrkar could finish the slaughter.

He stayed his hand. The longhouse had fallen quiet now but for the whimpering of one wounded man, quickly silenced by the thud of an axe. All were dead but for the one in his fine garb.

'Bind him,' Hereswyde ordered.

Her men were quick to obey, dragging the man across the floor and shoving him into a chair, before binding his hands to the armrests. He offered no resistance, staring about him with wide eyes.

'Wait,' he pleaded. 'Before you kill me you should know who I am. My name is Frederic of Oosterzele-Scheldewindeke.

I am a lord of note in these parts. And I have gold. Lots of gold.'

'Frederic what?' Lightfoot laughed. 'Sounds like a right mouthful.'

Hereswyde came forward, glaring at the bound man with undisguised hate. 'Mouthful or not, this is the man I have come to see. We have business he and I.'

Frederic looked confused, head shaking. 'No. There must be some kind of mistake. We have never met, I am sure of it. Whatever business you have must be with someone else. I am sure we can come to some arrangement in any regard. I am brother by marriage to Earl Wilhelm of Warenne. He is adviser to the king. He will—'

He went silent as Hereswyde raised a finger to her lips. 'You sit in the house of Lord Eskil. Remember that name?'

Frederic swallowed hard. 'I have heard it yes. But I never met the man.'

'No. I imagine he was dead long before you arrived. Take it from me, he was a great lord. A fair leader. Loved by the local people. Murdered for his trouble.'

Frederic shook his head. 'I know nothing of that. Nothing, I swear it.'

Hereswyde made a tutting sound. 'Be careful how you blaspheme. I know you speak lies. I was here, those years ago. I questioned Lord Eskil's murderers, before I in turn killed them. They spoke of the one who gave them their orders. Of a Frederic.'

'But… but that could be anyone. There are lots of Frederics throughout this kingdom. I am not your man, I promise you.'

'Oh but you are, Frederic brother of Wilhelm. And we both know it.'

'No. No I'm not. I never even met this Lord Eskil. It wasn't me. I am no one of importance.'

She leaned closer. 'On that we can agree.'

Hereswyde turned, making her way toward the door as Frederic continued to plead.

'Burn it down,' she ordered, as she crossed the threshold.

Despite Frederic's cries of protestation, the men began to pile kindling all about the longhouse. Styrkar left them to it, abandoning the sobbing Frederic tied to his chair. Outside, Duti had already thrown torches onto the thatch. As Lightfoot skipped through the open door they flung the rest of their torches inside.

It did not take long for the wooden structure to catch flame. Frederic's panic rose to a frenzy as he begged for his life, but those gathered to watch him burn were deaf to it. Four hard years they had suffered at the hands of his ilk. His screams of anguish were like music to them.

When he looked at Hereswyde he could see no relish in her eyes. Something within them was haunted, but that was little surprise. This had been her childhood home. The place her father had sat her at his knee. The place he had been murdered. She must have cherished memories of this place, but now they were aflame, just like the longhouse. Fading like the cries of the man they had come to kill.

No words would soothe her now. Not even vengeance could do that, as Styrkar knew only too well. But it did not stop them in its pursuit. It could not.

29

Ely, England, October 1070

Autumn mists had descended over the isle as the weather began to turn, shielding it from the prying eyes of the outside world. For some it might have offered some blessed relief, but for Styrkar it only added to his frustration. Still the king had not come. Yet again his reckoning was delayed. His last oath to Gytha still unfulfilled. What might they have to do to provoke the usurper? So far, harrying the surrounding land had accomplished little. Surely it was only a matter of patience, but then the Red Wolf had never been a patient beast.

Styrkar had even considered striking out from their fortress isle during the long nights. Had planned to slink through the fens like a predator, to seek out the king and slit his throat in the night. It had been a fanciful idea. One more likely to see him killed before he ever set eyes on the tyrant, than to satisfy his thirst for vengeance. Besides, he was no footpad. He was a warrior born, and he would face his foe with a bellow of rage, not stab him in the back like a coward.

He walked the fort, taking in the mundanity of it. Routine was good for most of the men, keeping them preoccupied as they waited, but for Styrkar the high walls of their island were like a cage. He yearned for this to be over. For all this to end in rage and steel, but for now he had to satisfy himself with the banal sound of idle chatter and that familiar woodsmoke smell of the fens.

Without thinking he took the worn stone stairs up to the old shrine. The place was overgrown, its roof rotted through, but there was still something hallowed about it. The statue of Aethelthryth stood on its plinth of gathered rock, and for the first time Styrkar appreciated how much it suited this band of outlaws. A rag-tag saint for its rag-tag worshippers. He could only hope she was watching over them, for they needed the help of gods more than anyone.

Somewhere, across this land in a distant place, his daughter was in a holy place such as this, though he hoped it at least had its roof. She would be two winters by now. Able to walk and talk and pray to a god that was not her own. She would not know her father's name. Perhaps not even her mother's.

Styrkar had not allowed himself to think on that too much. It would not do for the Red Wolf to wallow in self-pity. He had put such thoughts away, instead replacing them with all his hate and anger. But now, in this place, it was all that came to mind.

Mercifully someone else made their way up the stone stairs, and Styrkar pushed those thoughts to the back of his mind, deep in the vault where he kept them. Hereswyde appeared from below, looking not a little surprised to see him here.

'When you first came to Ely, you refused to make your vow on the shrine of Aethelthryth,' she said. 'Now I find you here of your own free will.'

'I did not mean to trespass.'

Hereswyde looked unconcerned. 'You may worship your own gods in this holy place, should you wish to. It matters not to me.'

Styrkar gazed toward that worn statue. 'I am not sure if the gods are even listening.'

He expected her to show more devotion, to assure him her saint would protect them, but instead she nodded in agreement. 'Neither am I. But I have to believe. For the sake of the men and women under my protection, if not for myself. One thing is sure – the Franks believe. And they grow more pious every day.' She raised a folded piece of parchment, words scrawled across it in black ink. 'The abbot Turold has sent a missive demanding the return of his relic. The arm of Saint Oswald.'

'And your answer?'

'I have not sent one yet. But I think you can work out what I will say.'

'Perhaps you should say yes. It might buy you some mercy when the Franks finally come.'

She raised her eyebrows in surprise. 'You really think that will work?'

He shook his head. 'No, I don't. The king does not know the meaning of the word. The people of these lands have paid a high price for mercy over and over again, and still he has never shown it.'

She turned and patted the metal box where it sat beside

Aethelthryth's altar. 'Then we shall keep it. At least until someone mighty enough comes to claim it for their own.'

The distant sound of the bell rang. Before either of them could make their way down from the shrine, they heard the sound of approaching feet, and someone calling Hereswyde's name.

Lightfoot appeared, bearing a worried look on his handsome face. 'Hereswyde. Someone is here.'

'The Franks?' she replied, a little relish in her voice.

'No. Saxons, from the north.'

They followed him down from the shrine, and out into the dreary daylight. Across the fort the doors had already been opened, boats moored beyond it, but these were indeed no returning Danes. Styrkar recognised the stout figures of bearded Saxons, their flaxen hair and beards unkempt, but still they carried themselves with dignity.

As they drew nearer, Styrkar recognised the one at their head; broad-shouldered and piercing of eye as he stared from a noble face. Morcar had changed little since they had last met, though perhaps now those blue eyes of his harboured more shadow. He waited patiently, surrounded by the others as they watched Styrkar and Hereswyde approach. When they were close enough, he forced a smile on that bearded face.

'They told me the Isle of Eels was a last bastion against the foreign cur,' he said as he watched them come closer. 'I didn't believe it until I arrived.'

'And you are welcome here, Earl Morcar,' Hereswyde replied. 'I am—'

'I know who you are, despite the rumours this place

is marshalled by a man, bold and fierce.' His eyes fell on Styrkar. 'And it is no surprise that the Red Wolf fights with you.'

Styrkar glared back. 'The surprise is why you have come at all, and not accepted the scraps thrown by your Frankish masters.'

Morcar's eyes darkened. 'I have played their games long enough. I will play them no more.'

'And what of your brother Edwin? Does he still dance to the usurper's tune?'

'No,' Morcar said through gritted teeth. 'He dances to no tune but a dirge now. He is dead. Murdered by his own warriors when there was nowhere left for him to flee. They slaughtered him on the banks of a northern river in return for their own lives.'

Styrkar was suddenly reminded of his first campaign, when Harold had warred against the Welsh. Their king, Gruffydd, had also been murdered by his own men in return for mercy. A reminder that loyalty only got you so far. Styrkar would have offered sympathy, but he had never liked Edwin, nor Morcar for that matter.

'So you have come to the last place in all England that might offer you a reckoning.'

'I have. But I do not come alone.'

Hereswyde stepped forward. 'Indeed you do not. And we are grateful for it. Who are these men?'

Morcar turned and gestured to a tall broad figure on the far side of the group. Styrkar immediately recognised his bald head and bushy beard.

'I have brought Siward Barn, thegn of the northern hundreds, come down from the safety of Alba to reclaim what was stolen from him.' Styrkar offered Siward a nod of welcome, which the man duly returned as Morcar continued. 'With him are other powerful men cast down by the Bastard Duke. Here Turkill Thorkelsson.' He gestured to a huge warrior who resembled a Dane, his arms bound in brass rings, beard braided. 'Ordgar and his son Alwine.' Two stout bearded men who barely looked any different considering they were father and son. 'And my own cousin, Corby.' He patted the closest man on the shoulder, and he nodded his shaggy head. 'All bring their own housecarls and fyrd. All ready to fight to the last.'

Hereswyde smiled in reply. Styrkar had not seen her do so for many days, and he could only imagine her relief. Where there had been despair, now was perhaps a glimmer of hope.

'Welcome,' she said. 'All of you, welcome to Ely. You have my thanks. And what hospitality we are able to offer.'

'This is not all,' Morcar said, gesturing for the men behind to step forward. 'With us are priests of the cloth. They will offer us absolution in our fight against the foreign scourge. This is Abbot Thurstan.' He gestured to a gaunt man, his hands in his sleeves, who still managed to look pious despite his pauper's robes. Then a second figure stepped from behind the others, and Styrkar felt the wolf stir within. 'And this is—'

'Ethelwin,' Styrkar growled.

The priest's eyes went wide at the mention of his name. Styrkar felt his lips curl back from his teeth, and Morcar frowned in confusion.

'You know him?'

Styrkar took a step toward Ethelwin, who cowered back,

but had nowhere to go. 'We met in Dun Holm. He rode at the head of a Frankish army, before Edgar and the northern lords slaughtered them to the last man. This priest would have damned us all, and he will damn you.'

Ethelwin shook his head with vigour. 'No… no that's not true. I was only trying to keep the peace. To save lives, as is my duty to the Lord God.'

'You will betray us the first chance you get.' Styrkar laid a hand to his sword.

Morcar got between them, as the surrounding men became agitated at the prospect of a priest being murdered. 'Easy, Red Wolf. I have heard the tale of Dun Holm. Ethelwin had no choice in his actions, and he has pledged himself to our cause now.'

Styrkar dragged his murderous gaze away from the fearful Ethelwin, to stare deep into Morcar's eyes. 'And what about you? The man who fled the field in the face of Harald Sigurdsson. Who failed to join us at Senlac Hill. Who spurned the chance to join the Aetheling in his rebellion? How can I trust your word now? We have already been betrayed by the Danes once. How will you demonstrate your loyalty?'

Morcar took a step back and drew his sword. The men around him flinched, but none reached for their own weapons. Styrkar tensed, expecting the worst, but instead of attacking, Morcar knelt before Hereswyde.

'You have my blade, lady,' he said, raising his sword in both hands as an offering. 'I pledge myself to your cause. For it is the cause of us all. The duty of every Saxon to oppose the usurper king to our dying breath.'

Hereswyde could not quell a grin of satisfaction. 'Put

away your weapon, Earl Morcar. You will need it soon enough. I accept your vow. Your men are welcome. From this day all our old quarrels are forgotten. We are one, standing against our common enemy.'

Morcar stood. 'To the last man.'

Some of those who had come with him repeated Morcar's words. Both Ethelwin and Thurstan made the cross gesture of their god.

'Good,' Hereswyde said, loud enough for all to hear, then slapped Morcar on the shoulder. 'Then come. You must be in need of food and ale after your journey. And we have both.'

She led the group away, and Styrkar watched them go. He would put aside his disdain for Morcar so that they might fight their common enemy, but supping with him was a gesture too far. Siward did not join them either, instead running a hand over his bald pate as he stood beside Styrkar.

'I did not think to see you again, Red Wolf.'

'Nor I you,' Styrkar replied. 'I would have thought the safety of Alba was too tempting. What word of Edgar and Máel? Will they be making the journey south to join our fight?'

Siward looked at the ground, as though in sorrow, and Styrkar braced himself for the worst news. 'While you were here in the fens, William took his armies north to subjugate the troublesome king of Alba. Máel could not hope to oppose him. He and Edgar live, but they are powerless to help us.'

'So the usurper has been distracted all this time? That would explain why he has not turned his eye to this isle, no matter how I have tried to provoke him.'

Siward looked up at Styrkar gravely. 'He is distracted no longer.'

The Red Wolf almost smiled. 'Good. Then together, Siward, we shall cause such mischief as to bring him running to our door. Then I will kill him.'

Siward's stern look faded, and the two men shared a smile. 'If any man can, Red Wolf, then it is you.'

Part Four

Finem Ludum

30

Ronan was no stranger to hard winters, but in this land they had always seemed that much harder. This year's though had seemed less harsh than the others. Less chill somehow. A time for feasting and merriment rather than fighting and killing. It had been a welcome relief.

The months afterward had also brought with them a calmness he had never felt on these isles, as winter snows had melted away to be replaced by the blooming of spring. Now summer was here, all that changed.

Once more they gathered their arms and mounted their heavy horses. Once more they travelled north. Once more they prepared to face an enemy that simply would not yield, no matter the burning wrath they poured upon its head. And once more, Ronan of Dol-Combourg found himself thrust in its midst, like a sheep in a bear pit.

He tried to sit tall and proud as they trotted toward the fort. Serle and Wymon had both stripped down to thin linen shirts in the baking sun, but Ronan still wore his jerkin.

There was no telling who he might bump into on his way to the king's muster. As it was, all he met was a camp full of stinking knights.

They surrounded the fort, covering the lowland all around it. More than he could possibly count, but they certainly numbered in their thousands. He had not seen so many since the battle on the hill, when the Saxon king had fallen. Now they gathered to quell the last vestige of defiance in these lands, almost five long years after.

'Hope there's spitted pig waiting,' Serle grumbled, as much to himself as anyone else. 'Can anyone smell cooking?'

As they approached the open gate to the fort, all Ronan could smell was the prospect of violence. Compared to the men massed without, within the compound of the fortress boundary there were few men. Ronan reined in his horse, taking in the sight, realising the king's leopard standard was not flying. He was not here yet.

'See to the horses,' he said to Serle, sliding down from the saddle. 'And see if you can find us something to eat if you're so hungry.'

Serle nodded, grumbling all the while. Wymon was his usual silent self, as the men dismounted and led the horses to a makeshift stable.

Ronan made his way to the wooden steps that led up onto the parapet. His leg protested slightly, but in the warmth of summer it did not give him such trouble as it did in winter cold. By the time he reached the top there was a sheen of sweat on his forehead from the hot sun, and he began to regret wearing his jerkin.

Looking out across the wooden defences he took in the sight of the marsh. Not two miles hence, through the heat haze that hung over the grass-covered waters, he saw it in the distance. The fortress they had come to quell.

From what he could see, it was an entire island amid the fens. A sprawling town surrounded by a wooden wall, which would be easy to miss on a day more gloomy than this one. From such a distance, it looked as though it posed little threat. He doubted it would look so benign if he were up close, and knee-deep in the surrounding bog.

As his eyes were drawn along the parapet, he saw two men standing across the walkway from him. They were locked in conversation, and as soon as Ronan saw who they were it brought a grin to his face. It had been well over a year since he'd seen Mallet and Giselbert. More than a year since he'd negotiated their freedom from the hands of those Danish raiders. For all the thanks he'd received.

He made his way closer, and the men saw him coming. If he'd been expecting a warm welcome, or even a little gratitude, he was sorely mistaken. Mallet's brow darkened, and he turned, striding away on his long legs, not offering so much as a cursory nod of acknowledgement. Giselbert looked a little more welcoming, remaining behind to greet Ronan with a smile.

'You are well, Dol-Combourg?' he asked as Ronan came to stand beside him.

'As well as can be expected, under the circumstances. Is Lord Mallet not feeling well? He doesn't look well.'

Giselbert shared Ronan's grin. 'You know as well as I that his humiliation in Yorke is an insult he demands redress for. Seeing you only reminds him of that ignominy.'

'Yes, I imagine owing me his life stinks more than shit in his moustache.'

Giselbert slapped a hand to Ronan's shoulder. 'Be careful, Ronan. You are the king's favoured… for now. But it still would not do to make an enemy of Mallet.'

'Fuck Mallet. I have more pressing things to worry about than him.' He gestured out across the marsh. 'I have that to worry about for a start.'

'As do we all,' Giselbert replied, squinting across the flat land. 'That bastion is the last part of this country left to conquer. An island four miles long and seven miles wide, and it is the last place in these lands to stand stubbornly against us. Over the past six months it has been a staging point for more raids than we can count. If it is not destroyed it will become a beacon for the Saxons. A light to which they will flock in resistance.'

'Surely it will not be so hard,' Ronan replied. 'It stands isolated enough. And there can be no more than a few hundred defenders.'

Giselbert gripped the spiked wooden palisade. 'Word has it the rebel lord, this Magister Militum, Hereward, has now recruited Earl Morcar, along with many others. They are fanatical. They will never surrender.'

'Who can blame them after what we did to their lands in the north,' Ronan replied, the memory of it returning to plague him, making his stomach squirm.

'Who indeed. But blame is not the issue. We are not here to repent the king's wrath. We are here to exact it. And this will be more difficult than burning a few farms and salting the land. That fortress is surrounded by water on all sides. Some of it disguised by patches of flag-iris that hide the treacherous footing beneath. Inaccessible to cavalry. Any boats that try to approach would be vulnerable to artillery. The place is all but impregnable.'

'That does sound like a quandary, Giselbert. I hope someone has a plan.'

'So do I. That is what we have gathered here to discuss.' His eyes shifted to look down into the courtyard of the fort. 'And it looks like that discussion is about to begin.'

Ronan followed his gaze. Riders were entering through the open gates, one of them carrying the king's standard, and another the holy cross. At their fore rode King William, his head uncovered, visage dark, but then it had reason to be. There was still rebellion within his kingdom after all these years. After everything he had done to quell it.

With him was a knight Ronan recognised – Wilhelm of Warenne. He was a fearsome warrior both by reputation and from what Ronan had seen with his own eyes. During the battle at the hill he had rode at the vanguard, assaulting the Saxon lines again and again. When the pretender had been defeated, the king had wasted no time in showering Warenne with gifts of land and riches.

Beside them came another knight Ronan did not recognise. His features were pinched, eyes beady, but he had the broad shoulders of a seasoned warrior, and a scarred face to match.

'Who rides with the king there?' Ronan asked.

'Him?' Giselbert said, squinting down at the knight, who wrenched his reins sharply to halt his horse. 'That is Ivo of Taillebois. A man who carries a cruel reputation.'

Ronan could well believe it from the look on his face. But it was a look he had seen on many faces across these lands. 'Don't we all.'

'I mean it, Dol-Combourg. Be careful around that man. You do not want to get on the wrong side of him.'

'I am sure. Unfortunately, for one reason or another, I often end up on the wrong side of most people. But I will take you at your word, Giselbert.'

'Good. Then let us go and greet our king.'

They made their way down from the walkway, reaching the courtyard just as William was dismounting his horse and handing the reins to a squire. He glared around the fort, seeing the men gathered – Mallet, Giselbert, Ivo, Warenne and Ronan.

'Now we are all here,' he grunted. 'Let us waste no time.'

He turned, entering the keep as one of his knights opened the door for him. Ronan followed the procession as they made their way up the creaking wooden stair to a single room. The fire was dead in its hearth, a slight breeze blowing in through the window to relieve them from the stifling air.

King William sat himself in the single chair, shrugging off his cloak and pulling off one of his boots before emptying out whatever had been troubling him. The rest of them stood around in silence. Mallet and Giselbert of Gant stood side by side, chins raised. Wilhelm of Warenne leaned casually against the window frame, letting the breeze blow at his back, at ease in the king's company. As for Ivo – he lurked in the shadow, leering from it and moving his weight from one foot to the other, as though waiting to strike like a nocturnal hunter.

He put Ronan ill at ease, and it was obvious Giselbert had not been joking. Already Ronan would rather have been anywhere but near this man.

Before the king could speak, the stairs creaked, and a boy

appeared carrying a tray with cups of wine. He offered one to the king first, then went around the room as the others took them one by one. When finally he passed Ronan there were no cups left. Typical.

'You all know why you are here,' the king said after wetting his lips. 'There is one last vestige of resistance in my lands. One last weed that must be rooted out. And together we will see it destroyed.'

He paused, taking another drink. Ronan looked around at the others, none of whom had anything to say as they slaked their thirst. With no drink of his own, he took the opportunity to make his own suggestion.

'Has no one tried to offer these rebels terms of surrender, my king? It was a tactic that worked with the Danes. And they plague our shores no longer.'

The king didn't even look at him, simply staring ahead as he squeezed his cup in white-knuckled fingers. 'No. It is too late for that. These are not mercenary Danes to be bought off. This is an enemy dug in with nowhere to flee. They cannot be bought. Only when the last of them is dead, or on their knees in chains, will this be at an end.'

'I for one will offer them no clemency,' Warenne said, a sneer on his lips. 'These are the men responsible for the brutal murder of my wife's brother, Frederic. Burned alive in his own dwelling. Gundred, my bride, is inconsolable. I would offer her their heads.'

It was obvious there would be no easy end to this. Again, a creaking on the stairs before they could continue. The boy appeared once more, bearing a platter covered in hunks of roast capon. This time as he handed it out to the gathered men, Ronan didn't even try to take himself a piece.

'They have no need for gold anyway,' Ivo said, tearing off a bite of chicken. 'Rumour has it their island fortress is filled to the brim with booty from a hundred raids.'

William rose to his feet, discarding the chicken bone after devouring its meat. 'And every man who helps me take this island will get their share. As always.'

Those words rang hollow in Ronan's ears. Though his fortunes had risen of late, he had yet to receive the riches he so coveted. 'Could we not merely wait them out? Cut off their lines of supply?'

The king shook his head. 'Not possible. The Saxons have access from every direction by boat. There is no way we could block every waterway in and out. They could feasibly stay within their fortress indefinitely. Launching raids at will. No, this fortress must be taken. Its existence is an insult; I will tolerate its defiance no longer.'

'With all due respect, my king, how do we achieve this?'

He glanced toward the window. Over Warenne's shoulder the island fortress was just visible in the distance. 'I will construct a bridge to it. A causeway across the marshes. Once it is built, we can ride right up to the front door. Their surroundings will offer them no advantage.'

Ronan glared through the window. It seemed such a long way to that fortress. And across such unforgiving marshland. 'But it is—'

'Any arguments?' the king asked, glaring at each of his lords in turn.

Slowly they shook their heads. Ronan had plenty, but he too shook his head.

'No, my king. It is a sound plan.'

'I am glad you think so, Dol-Combourg. Because I have decided you shall have the honour of riding at the vanguard.'

Ronan swallowed, that old familiar sense of panic rising up within. 'I... I can assure you, such an honour is not necessary.'

'Nonsense,' said the king. 'You have no need to be so modest. Don't think I haven't noted how loyal you have been these past months. It is the least I can do for such a faithful servant. And besides, you will have first claim on all that gold.'

He took a step closer, staring right into Ronan's eyes. Those eyes that brooked no refusal.

'Thank you, sire,' Ronan said.

It sounded meek. He didn't care.

31

Ely, England, July 1071

The abbot, the one they had called Thurstan, stood proudly in the centre of the square. One hand was raised and in the other he held a battered old book. Styrkar heard his litanies echoing across the wide-open space, the words uttered in a language he did not understand. An ancient language of conquerors he had heard holy men use in a score of holy places. He hoped they were blessings he was spewing, though it was doubtful anyone knew the truth. He could have been prattling inanities for all these kneeling Saxons could tell.

Nevertheless, kneel they did, and they prayed as he spoke. Styrkar walked past them, doing his best to ignore the din. He had no need for prayers. His gods were not listening, if indeed they ever had. And if they were, they did not care to answer him. He needed the boon of Odin and Loki. Of Thor and Tyr. Even Fenrir, the wolf his mother had said spawned him. But none of them had helped him so far. They had not spared him the loss of Harold or

Edith. Had not stayed the hand that murdered Gisela. Neither had they seen his enemies brought low. That had been the Red Wolf, which lurked within Styrkar. He had been the one to do that, and more besides. Styrkar needed no blessings from gods. Not even the one that ruled over these lands, and dwelt in the hearts of its people. Or at least most of them.

As he left Thurstan and his flock behind, he saw others praying in their own way. An old man they called the Diviner preached to a flock of his own. He used water to douse the heads of some of his followers, saying blessings in the old forgotten dialect of the fenlands before he made some sign on them, and had them drink of the tepid waters.

Perhaps a pointless exercise. Perhaps not. If it gave those men bravery in the face of what was coming, then what did it matter? Real or imagined, if it offered them courage it was worth the effort.

Styrkar left them all behind, those heathens and Christians, and mounted the defences. Here was his altar. Here was where the Red Wolf would make his offerings in the blood of his enemies.

At the top they were waiting – Hereswyde, Morcar, Siward. And each was looking out across those marshes at what was making its way closer. Inch by inch, day by day those earthworks drew nearer. What had started as a distant flurry of activity now had become more ominous.

It had not taken them long to work out what was coming. The king's men were building foundations. Filling in sections of the bog into which they could sink props. In turn ropes were set between and logs tied in place to create a floating bridge of sorts. It would be sturdy, of that there was no doubt. Sturdy enough to carry an army of horses? Styrkar looked forward to finding out.

'How long do you think?' Morcar said, still staring across the fenland. 'Before they reach the shore?'

Hereswyde did not adjust her gaze. 'It will be days rather than weeks, by the speed they have reached this point.'

From further along the defences someone let loose an arrow. It fell painfully short of the builders. Another man shot his bow, this one doing a better job, but only hitting the wooden barricade floating upon a pontoon. It seemed those Franks had thought of everything.

Days before Hereswyde had sent out saboteurs to try and cut the ropes and saw down the props, but they had failed. The invaders kept watch night and day, and those men had only just managed to escape with their lives. The king was determined to end them this time. He had brought his knights in numbers. It was only to be expected.

'We do not have enough men to defend these walls when the Bastard Duke arrives,' Morcar grumbled.

Styrkar had to resist the temptation to throw him over the palisade. 'Show some mettle for once, Morcar.'

The earl rounded, darkness in his tired eyes, but then none of them had slept much these past days. 'I will not balk when the fighting starts. No matter what you think.'

'You have no idea what I think, Morcar.'

'Enough,' said Siward, standing between them. 'We will all rise to do our part. Fighting amongst ourselves will do no good. Not here, at the end.'

'Then we are decided,' Hereswyde said, still staring out across the marsh as though willing them to come faster. 'Every one of us will fight to the last.'

'And your people?' Morcar asked. 'Will they stand with you until the end?'

'Have no fear of that. Now your priests are here to offer them absolution, they will die atop these walls with joy in their hearts. We all will. These men of the fens are made of hardy stuff. They would rather that than die on their knees begging.'

'Then let them come,' Morcar said. 'Let them build their bridge. We are ready.'

Styrkar did not need to voice his agreement. None of them did.

32

He had never seen its like. A causeway wide enough to ride two horses abreast stretching from east to west for a mile or more across the marsh. Wood, stone and faggots lashed together, and fastened underneath with sand-stuffed sheepskins to keep it all stable. How they had managed to construct it in so little time was nothing short of a miracle, though Ronan was well aware of what could be achieved when people were sufficiently motivated. And motivate them the king had.

Promises of gold, land, mutilation. He had resorted to them all, and in the end the bridge to the Isle of Eels was finished. Now all that remained was to ride across and take that fortress. And as luck would have it, Ronan was to receive the honour of riding at their head. Oh, happiest of days.

His horse whickered beneath him. It was nervous, but of course it was. The thing wasn't stupid – it most likely knew exactly what they had planned. There was a simmering atmosphere of excitement around him, mixed in with reluctance. The surrounding knights, armed and armoured to the proverbial teeth, had all heard of what awaited in that castle. Gold beyond any dreams of avarice. The only thing holding them back was the wooden causeway. It was untested. A new-built bridge that they would ride their heavy horses across in all their regalia. Anything could happen, and Ronan could well understand their reluctance, but the longer they waited, the more that reluctance was drifting away like the morning mist, to be replaced by greed and lust.

'You know, I envy you, Dol-Combourg.'

Ronan flinched at the words. When he looked down, he saw Ivo of Taillebois standing not too far from his steed. He stared out across the causeway toward the fort in the distance.

'Really, my lord? Then why didn't you say so sooner? It could be you waiting to lead the charge in my place.'

Ivo hawked and spat into the water, as though he hadn't heard Ronan's reply. 'Taking your pick of all those riches. You will return a wealthy man.'

As he quietly calculated how far he had to ride across that wooden path, being a wealthy man was the last thing on Ronan's mind. 'I will be sure to bring you back a treasure befitting your status, Lord Ivo.'

Taillebois turned his narrow face toward Ronan. There was menace in his eyes, just for a moment, before his face creased into a humourless grin and he barked a laugh.

'God be with you, Dol-Combourg.'

With that, he turned and made his way back through the mass of waiting horses.

'God has never been with me, you son of a fucking whore,' Ronan breathed, sure that no one else could hear him above the stamping of hooves and heavy breathing.

'I don't like that man much,' Serle said, glancing over his shoulder. 'Looks like he'd cut your throat sooner than say hello.'

'You're a good judge of character, my friend,' Ronan replied. 'If I die in this treacherous endeavour, you have my permission to slit his throat, if the opportunity presents itself.'

Serle tipped his helmed head in acknowledgement. Ronan turned his attention back to the island they were about to assault and gripped his lance tighter. Looking across the row upon row of riders he could see other knights likewise checking their weapons. More men were arrayed behind carrying ladders to assault the fort's high walls. Yet more carrying parts of artillery machinery that would be hastily constructed to supplement the assault.

If they could advance in good order this would be a straightforward siege. Ronan had done this before; he knew how it worked. But even as he waited to give the order, it all started to crumble.

Someone shouted shrilly, something he couldn't make out. Then another shout, demanding to know what they were waiting for. The discontent travelled like a wave.

Ronan yelled for them to be calm, but he was already losing the lead riders. One of them kicked his horse ahead, its hooves clacking on the wood of the causeway as he tested its sturdiness.

'Who is with me?' the man cried. 'Who will come claim the riches of Ely.'

Again, Ronan shouted for them to wait, but too late. Too slow. Too quiet.

A roar went up now. A clangorous shout that was taken up as the lead riders started their journey along the mile or so to the location of their treasure. Ronan shouted again, but the mass of horses was already moving as one.

Desperately he looked over toward where a standard bearer held up the king's flag. He was to signal that flag bearer for them to advance, but hadn't had the chance.

'That gold won't gather itself,' shouted someone from their midst.

Already the lead riders had sped their steeds from walk to trot to canter. It wasn't long before they increased to a gallop, hooves clacking on the causeway, drumming as they charged.

Ronan was caught up in the frenzy, forced to follow along that bridge, and he felt it sway beneath the weight as his steed began its advance. He wanted to shout for them to slow, to tell them they should approach one at a time, but it was too late now. No one was listening, their lust for those riches overcoming their good sense. This was madness, but then the promise of wealth would do that to some men. Especially when they had been fighting long and hard for the promise of it.

They were some distance from the shore now. Ronan glanced about, looking for any sign of Wymon or Serle, not that they could help him now. Then he looked down, quickly realising his mistake as he saw the black depths of the marsh only feet away.

There was nothing else for it – they had to get across with all haste. He could already hear those unsteady timbers cracking beneath the weight of scores of horses. Already feel the bridge listing from left to right.

Ronan shouted for them to charge, digging spurs to his horse's flanks as he galloped along with the rest. There was a sudden splash, an animal shriek, and he caught sight of someone pitching off the bridge from the corner of his eye.

There would be no rescue. No stopping to help. That would have been suicide. Though they rode on as a mass, in reality each man was on his own now. Each responsible for his own survival, if it had ever been another way.

Another crack beneath the hooves of his horse, this time louder than the others. His steed stumbled, almost losing its balance, and Ronan lost grip on his lance. He grasped the reins in both hands, for a moment thinking of wrenching back on them to halt his gallop, but that would have been madness. He was caught within the maelstrom now. He just had to hold on for dear life and see where it took him.

They charged on, and he passed another horse foundering in the water, half claimed by the marsh. Its rider clung onto the lip of the causeway, but the mud of the bog was sucking him down, clad as he was in heavy mail. Then he was gone as they raced past, onwards toward the fort growing ever larger before them.

A whip of the air as something flew past his head. Another, then another, followed by the scream of a man to his left. A quick glance and he could see an arrow protruding from the eye of another rider who was lurching back in his saddle. It took a moment for him to realise it was Wymon.

Ronan dragged his gaze away. Wymon had been a close companion. Not quite a friend, perhaps, but close enough. Now he was dead, but if Ronan had learned one thing it was not to get too close to any man, lest he be torn from you, leaving a space that could not be filled. Aldus had taught him that. His big friend, lost to this endless fighting, now no more than a memory.

Ahead a glimpse of salvation. Solid ground at the foot of the fortress. It was barely a hundred yards away. Not long now and the lead horses would be able to—

A resounding crack of wood. This one deafening in its finality.

Ronan felt the bridge give way beneath his horse, heard that chorus of whinnying screeches as the animals realised their doom. Men yelled all around him, their screams louder than the cracking noise of the bridge. The entire structure collapsed ahead of him, sliding into the mire, but there was nothing Ronan could do to halt his advance. Nothing he could do to stop the charge behind him, as his horse raced headlong into the boggy pit.

It slid beneath the surface up to its neck. Before Ronan could think what to do, another horse careened into the bog beside him, splashing mud in his face. The deafening sound of hooves had halted now to be replaced by shouting men, flailing and desperate.

Quickly Ronan tried to slide his feet from the stirrups, his good leg freeing itself with ease, but his accursed crippled one not moving at his command. He plunged an arm into the murky waters, desperate to free himself, tasting the bog on his lips as he gasped feverishly. More horses plunged into the marsh around him. More screams as his mount sank deeper.

He managed to grasp his foot, pulling it free, before he scanned the scene around him, desperate to find something to hold on to, some spot of firm ground on which to find safety. All he saw was a sea of mud and horses and men flailing desperately as the marsh sucked them down.

The water was up to his waist, and he could feel it creeping through his armour, weighing him down. Up ahead was the shore, not twenty yards across a lake of mud and dying men. A cheer had gone up from atop the palisade as the fort's defenders saw their enemies claimed by the marsh, but Ronan had no time to lament that. Their delight in his demise was all too premature.

His horse was almost submerged. Ronan lurched forward, grabbing the beast's mane in his mailed fists and dragging himself toward the shore. The weight of him pushed the steed further down, and the last thing he saw was the white of its panicked eye before it disappeared beneath the surface. A wooden plank from the causeway was just ahead and he clawed his way closer, then dragged himself on top of it.

'Help me,' someone shouted almost in his ear.

Ronan looked to his right, seeing Serle, head half submerged, arm reaching out for help. He could have reached him, could have grabbed Serle's hand, maybe even pulled him to safety. But it was just as likely Serle would have pulled them both to their deaths. Ronan turned away as his friend shouted for help again. Ignoring the noise, clawing his way across that piece of wood, as Serle's shout turned to gurgling shriek. Then silence.

No time for mourning, or someone would be saying prayers for him. The sudden thought almost made him laugh. Who would say prayers for Ronan of Dol-Combourg's passing?

Another horse was struggling in the mud ahead of him,

its rider already consumed by the bog. Ronan grabbed its saddle, dragging himself ever closer to that shore. As he did so he wrenched the helm from his head in a seemingly futile attempt to make himself lighter. But then he was desperate. Any chance he had to avoid drowning in the mud he would take.

The horse sunk fast beneath him, but Ronan clawed on. He had to make it to the shore. It was only feet away... almost within his grasp.

Something caught on his belt. Ronan gasped, panic gripping him as he looked back, expecting to be snagged on something, but instead he saw a mailed fist holding him back. A knight, eyes wide in fright, desperate not to die – and who could blame him.

Ronan reached for his belt, grabbing the dirk from its sheath before stabbing at that mailed hand. He heard the man cry out, high-pitched as he released his hold on Ronan's belt. He cursed, eyes turning from fearful to accusing, but the marsh was already sucking him under. Then he was gone, as Ronan turned away, continuing his own fight, crawling for his life.

He let go of the knife. It would do him no good now. Solid ground was only ten feet away. Surely there were shallows. Surely he could wade his way to safety.

Ronan lurched forward, flinging himself into the mud. Immediately the marsh took him, pulling him slowly to his doom.

'No,' he murmured, reaching out desperately for the shore. 'No, please.'

The mud seeped into every link of mail. It felt like he was encased in solid iron as it dragged him under to his chin, to his lips, into his mouth, into his nose. All that was left was to spit and gurgle, as he blindly reached for the shore.

The mud was in his throat. He would have kicked his legs, but they were held fast by that marsh, firmer than any manacle. His other arm sunk below the surface, and he only had one left to reach out with. One last desperate act of defiance before...

A firm grip around his wrist. Someone pulled so hard it almost dragged his arm from the socket. The marsh squelched its annoyance at losing another victim, as Ronan was hauled from the boggy ground, dragged onto the mud of the shore where he floundered like a landed trout.

He gasped. He sobbed. He would have offered his eternal thanks. But as he managed to wipe the mud from his eyes, and saw those grim-looking Saxons leering down at him, he thought perhaps thanks might be a little premature.

33

They had watched as those horses approached from over a mile away. Listened to that thunderous storm as they drew ever closer – a trail of mounted might on its way to crush them in their fortress. The Franks had come looking for battle, and the fens had consumed them as hungrily as any god of the sea.

Styrkar had stood at the palisade, his grim visage not wavering as they drowned before him. He had been surrounded by clamour. Shouts and bellows of sheer joy. The relief that it had been the marshes that had done their work for them, as the men of Ely watched in rapture. Those knights had drowned in their hundreds as Hereswyde's army laughed. The Red Wolf could take no great joy in it though. The marsh had robbed him of his reckoning. At least for now.

The revels lasted well into the night. The songs and prayers rising up from out of the marsh as those corpses rotted beneath the water. Carrion birds feasted on the

273

bloated remains, desecrating those muddy graves, as the Isle of Eels rejoiced.

Still, Styrkar felt no desire to join them. He was offered no solace by this. Took no pleasure in it. Not until he had heard of their single prisoner.

One of the knights had survived, plucked from the muck like a razor clam off the beach, and brought within the safety of the fort. At first, he had thought nothing of it. Then he had learned of the man's malady. His crippled leg, a wound not caused by his charge against them.

But surely it could not be him. Surely fortune had not presented Ronan right to Styrkar's door. He had to know for sure.

There was a makeshift dungeon dug beneath the foundations of their fortress. One that had lain empty since all this began, for they had taken no prisoners in their raids. The men on guard nodded at Styrkar as he made his way into its depths, and as they pushed back the door to that single cell, he held his breath. When he saw Ronan's face it almost caught in his throat.

Men surrounded him, but Ronan sat unmolested on a bed of straw. His armour had been stripped, his face filthy and mournful. When he saw Styrkar entering his prison, that look turned to fear then... hope? Did he see a familiar face and think there might be mercy?

Styrkar stood, looking down in silence as the rest of the rebels waited for him to speak. Ronan glimpsed from one face to another, perhaps wondering what fate awaited, before gazing back at the ice blue eyes of the Red Wolf.

'Well,' he said, with a familiar nonchalance. 'I must admit, this is a very intimidating situation.'

'Leave us,' Styrkar breathed.

Without a word of protest, the other men filed out of the dank cell. The door clanked as they shut it behind them, and Styrkar continued to glare at his prisoner. One he had yearned to find, to kill, and now he was here. In turn, Ronan looked back, his false confidence never wavering, as though he expected death to come. As though he wanted it.

Finally, Ronan was forced to swallow. If he tried to do it quietly he failed, instead making a sound like the amorous call of a toad on heat.

'Have you come to kill me?' he asked.

Such a simple question, but one Styrkar struggled with. He had come to see if the rumours were true. If the man they had captured was his one true enemy. Now it was…

'I do not know yet.'

Ronan nodded his understanding. 'I see. Because I'll admit, I have no idea why I'm still alive. If you're thinking about torture, please let me reassure you that it will not be necessary. I am more than happy to tell you everything I know.'

Cowardice, so brazen in its familiarity. Styrkar could have laughed at how predictable he was.

'I have no desire to learn anything from you.'

Ronan's brow creased in confusion. 'Really? You don't even want to know where I have hidden your daughter?'

The thought had crossed Styrkar's mind from time to time, but he had pushed it down. Quelled it. Kept it closed within an iron casket lest it begin to plague him. To divert him from his true purpose.

'I do not need to know. It would do me no good even if I did. I am trapped here on this island. Bound by oath to myself and others. I will stay until I am dead, or your king is defeated.'

That seemed enough to satisfy Ronan's curiosity and again he nodded his understanding. 'So... what do you want?'

There were so many things. Desires he had not allowed himself to consider. Had he the power he would have demanded Gisela back. To turn back the days and take her away from this land, as he should have when she asked him. Begged him.

'There is only one thing left for me. To face your king one last time. To stand victorious over his dying body and show him who has killed him.'

Ronan's eyes widened in surprise. 'Is that all? Well, in case you hadn't noticed you will have to fight your way through an army first. The king fought against you on the hill, but that was then. He rides at the head of no army, now that he sits on a throne. He has other men to do that for him.'

'Then I will cut my way through them,' Styrkar spat. 'I will bathe in the blood of every Frank who stands in my way, and build a bridge to Valhöll with their skulls.'

The echo of his outburst rang through the tiny cell. Ronan looked distinctly unimpressed.

'Listen to yourself. It's as though you believe the myth of the Red Wolf. But that's all it is... a myth. None of it is true, Styrkar. You are a peerless warrior, for sure, but you think you can take on an army and live?' He shook his head. 'Don't waste your life. Think about that daughter of yours. I could take you to her. Right now. All you have to do is get me out of this cell and put me on a boat. We could row it together through this damned marsh and leave this place in our wake. What is there to stop us?'

Styrkar could barely hide his contempt for the creature sitting before him. The coward, with the sharp tongue.

'You talk only to spare your own life.'

'Do I?' Ronan snarled, a hint of desperation in his tone. 'Yes… yes I do. I won't lie about that. But it isn't the only reason. I owe Gisela. I owe that little girl who I saw birthed into the world. She deserves a father. Even if that father is you.'

'So you would atone for all you have done? You would seek to wash away the stain of your misdeeds with this one act?'

Ronan darted forward, but stopped short of rising to his feet. 'Does it fucking matter? There is no one in this godforsaken land who deserves atonement. Who in this bloodstained country has not killed just to stay alive? Or murdered for profit? We are very much the same, you and I. The only difference is you kill for revenge where I do it to raise myself from the mire. Tell me, Red Wolf, which is the nobler cause?'

Ronan stared defiantly, despite the filth that covered him. Despite his precarious position.

'You think yourself noble?'

Ronan thought on that one, his expression changing from deep thought to self-satisfied amusement. 'I think myself a survivor.'

Perhaps the truest thing he had said so far. 'And how much longer do you think that will last?' Styrkar asked, almost tempted to prove his words wrong. 'How long do you think your lies and schemes will keep you out of a lonely grave?'

Ronan's lips turned to sneer, to grin, before he laughed in Styrkar's face. 'Before I met you, I imagine I could probably have gone on for quite some time. Now, things don't look so good anymore. I did try to change; you must know that. I turned my back on those plans for the promise of another life, but it was snatched from me before I even had a chance to pursue it. But this land is not made for good men.' He looked deep into Styrkar's eyes. An earnest look that could not be denied. 'But you already know that better than anyone.'

The words cut sharp. 'Yes. I do.'

'You see, just like I said – we have much more in common than you'd care to admit, Red Wolf. We are both men set to serve in a land to which we do not belong. A land that has robbed us both.'

'This land gave me everything until you and yours arrived on its shores.'

Ronan shook his head, frustration writ on his narrow features. 'Stop dwelling on the past, man. Think of what remains. Think of the daughter who awaits you. The life you could seize. Are you too blind to see the chance you have left?'

'I see it,' Styrkar replied, through gritted teeth. 'I see it every night in my dreams. But it is always just beyond my reach.'

'Then we should go. It's not too late. Cut these bonds. Get me out of here, and together we will find her. Take her far from these shores, never to return.'

So tempting. To abandon all his oaths and just do what was right. To take his daughter away from here, and beg forgiveness for his broken vows later. But there would never be any forgiveness. Not for the Red Wolf. Besides, that little girl would still be better off far away from him. Safe in that holy priory, surrounded by pious women who would care for her better than Styrkar ever could.

He took a step closer to Ronan. The cripple did not shrink, but bravely raised his chin.

'Tell your king that I am coming.'

A flicker of doubt across Ronan's mud-stained brow. 'You're… letting me go?'

'Your god smiles on you, this day.'

Before Ronan could answer, the door creaked open. Abbot Thurstan stood in the doorway, his battered book in his hands.

'It appears he does,' Ronan breathed.

Thurstan stepped into the cell. 'I have come to offer absolution to the prisoner. Before he meets his fate.'

Styrkar was still looking down at Ronan, still wondering if this was the right thing to do. 'Pray all you like. Then take him back across the marsh. He has a message to deliver.'

34

He could barely see five feet in front of him as they guided him out of the fort. The surrounding marshland was black as pitch, still as a corpse. All he could hear was the sound of his bare feet squelching through the mud, and the shuffling of the men with him.

Two of them were burly, shaggy, smelly. Just the kind of undesirables he would expect to dwell in this godforsaken place. The third was the priest in his threadbare cassock. Thurstan they called him. Some old Saxon of note, apparently, though Ronan had never heard of him before. His presence was unnerving. Why would he be here, other than to say the last rites over a condemned man?

Still, they took him to the water's edge, where a tiny rowboat waited. He was bundled in, and not gently, those two burly men taking up their oars as Thurstan climbed aboard with them. It wasn't until they pushed off from the shore that Ronan began to believe he might make it through this in one piece after all.

He listened to the gentle swish of the oars as they proceeded into the murk. The fires flickering from atop the fort receded until they were surrounded by nothing but darkness. Only the crescent of the moon lit their way through the reeds, and the further they went, the more he found himself glaring into the dark waters. More men than he could count had drowned in there not two nights ago. At any moment he expected Serle's accusing face to pop up and admonish him. Ronan clasped his hands together to stop them shaking. He had enough to worry about, without thinking on wraiths and boggits and ghosts coming to torment him.

Looking across the boat he saw that Thurstan was equally troubled. The old man stared mournfully into the gloom, clutching that battered book in his hands.

'You look worried, Abbot,' Ronan said, breaking the silence. He half expected one of the rowers to tell him to be silent, but they carried on their work without a word.

Thurstan's mouth twitched, and he shook his head. 'I am not worried,' he replied, and it sounded like the lie it was. 'I just thought I might accompany you back to firmer ground. Ensure you were kept safe.' He glanced at the rowers, as though accusing them of ill intent.

'You wish to ensure my safety? That is befitting a man of your status.' Ronan leaned in closer. 'Would you in turn feel safe if we were to talk in the Frankish tongue?'

Thurstan glanced toward the rowers, before nodding his head. 'Yes.'

So, perhaps more to his presence than it appeared.

'Then tell me,' Ronan continued in his own language. 'What are you doing on that island with a bunch of rebels?'

'It is my holy duty,' Thurstan replied.

'To die with your flock?'

'To…' Thurstan looked down at his worn Bible. 'To try and end this. We have all fought for too long. It is time to bow to the king. All of us. I just… I don't know how to persuade them.'

From the vehemence of his outburst, the abbot had clearly been thinking on the subject for some time. He sounded desperate, like one of those men drowned in the mire.

'If you were to help end this, the king would surely offer you clemency.'

'And I would take it. But… I just don't know how.'

Ronan laid a comforting hand on the old man's shoulder. 'I am sure a man in your position would be able to persuade some of them. Were you to leave in the night, row away just like this, the king would more than welcome you into the fold. Then, with you gone, it might persuade the others to throw down their arms. To end all this needless violence.'

The rowboat cruised through a patch of tall reeds, before bumping into the shore. The men put up their oars and stepped onto solid ground.

'Out,' one of them said, pointing into the darkness. 'Carry on that way, half a mile.'

Ronan struggled to his feet, and stumbled onto dry land.

'Remember what I said,' he cast back at Thurstan, before staggering away from the men and their boat before either of them could change their minds and leave him dead in the bog.

He was lost in mere moments. Looking back, he could no longer see the men or the priest or their rowboat, and he pressed on regardless through the dark. The going was hard, his feet slopping in the mud, and at any moment he expected to stumble into a boggy pit and be sucked down to his doom.

Something screeched in the distance, and it set his heart aflutter. Maybe they had abandoned him here on purpose. Maybe they knew the marsh would claim him.

Just as he was about to cry out in desperation, he heard voices in the distance.

Lights flickered across the fens. Ronan increased his pace, ignoring the screeching pain in his leg as he staggered on, huffing in air, determined not to weep. He could see the silhouette of a fort looming up ahead. Hear the lamenting song of men around campfires. Smell the delectable aroma of food on the air.

'Stop there,' a deep voice shouted.

He did as he was told, holding up his hands, trying to stop them shaking.

Two men approached from the firelight, spears pointed right at him. Without so much as a by your leave, one of them grasped him by the throat.

'What the fuck do we have here? A spy?'

Ronan tried to pull the hand away from his throat, but it held on tight. 'No... I am...'

'Just gut the bastard,' the other one said. 'It won't redress what we have lost, but it'll be a start.'

Ronan managed to unknot the fingers from his throat and staggered back. 'Do you think I am some bog-trotting Saxon bastard?'

The men's eyes widened as they heard their fellow countryman. 'You're... one of us.'

'I am Ronan of Dol-Combourg, returned from the dead. Now take me to the king.'

The men nodded, helping Ronan from the edge of the marsh and guiding him through the camp and into the fort. There was a subdued atmosphere within, as men stared forlornly into the fires. Easy to understand why after witnessing what happened at the causeway.

Nevertheless, Ronan headed toward the tower with eagerness, seeing Giselbert rise to his feet as he made his way past, a shocked look on his face as though he had seen a ghost. Not surprising. Most likely they thought he had perished along with the rest.

He made his way up the stairs of the keep, the single knight on guard opening the door ahead of him. Inside the king's chamber he saw someone already standing there – Ivo was talking to the king, who reclined in a half-barrel bathtub. If King William was mournful over the loss of so many knights he was hiding it very well, wallowing as he was in the water, a plate of eels resting on his chest.

When Ronan entered, looking like he had just been dragged from the mire, Ivo stopped mid-sentence. The king cast his eyes up and down the bedraggled figure before him.

'Dol-Combourg? You're alive.'

'That I am, sire. Although I am in need of a good scrub-down. Apologies for my attire.'

'Think nothing of it,' William replied, plucking a slick eel from the plate and swallowing it down.

Ivo glared at Ronan, his eyes looking almost feral in the torchlight. 'I take it you didn't bring me anything back from the fort after all, eh Dol-Combourg.'

He grinned a gap-toothed grin. Ronan swallowed down the jibe as best he could.

'Unfortunately, I was too busy swimming for my life, before my capture.'

That stopped the king as he plucked another eel from the plate. It slipped from his fingers as his brow furrowed. 'Capture? And you escaped?'

'Not exactly, sire. They… let me go.'

'They what?'

'Yes, sire. In fact, they were quite accommodating.' He remembered the message Styrkar had told him to deliver, but thought it best to keep that to himself.

'Then God is clearly with you. But not with us. I lost many men in that charge. So now, Ivo and I are just planning the next step.'

'Are you indeed?' Ronan looked up at the brute that was Ivo of Taillebois, wondering what possible plan he could have other than slaughter.

'Yes,' Ivo said. 'I was just telling the king of a pythoness I have heard tell of. A witch of the marshes. One who could lay a curse on these superstitious fenlanders.'

'A curse?' It sounded preposterous. 'You think a witch will defeat the Saxons where a hundred knights have failed?'

'Don't underestimate the power of superstition, Dol-Combourg. Especially not around these parts. I've known these Saxons long enough to understand how they think.'

'Really?'

Ivo leaned closer, his eyes turning dark. 'Yes, really.'

'Then why don't you bring this pythoness here so we can see her cast this curse.'

Ivo turned his gaze away.

The king laughed. 'Lord Ivo believes this woman's power to be real. Don't you, my skittish friend?'

Ivo did not answer, and Ronan almost laughed. 'So what do you propose, sire? I mean... I can always treat with this woman on your behalf.'

King William shrugged. 'Right now, I am willing to try anything. What can it hurt?'

'Then as soon as I am washed and dressed, we shall go. Shan't we, Ivo?'

The menacing Ivo suddenly looked much less a threat. 'Yes, I'll take you to her, Dol-Combourg. But be careful what you offer in trade for her service. It would take a braver man than me to try and bargain with a witch.'

'And it goes without saying...' Ronan smiled '...that I am a braver man than you.'

Ivo leered, but did not speak any insult. His silence was more than enough reward for Ronan.

35

Cildeford, England, July 1071

They rode south for half a day. Ivo started off cheerfully enough, but the closer they got to their destination, the quieter he became. They had only brought two other knights, but Ronan had been assured they were reliable. But how reliable did they need to be to face one mad old woman?

As they travelled, he found himself glancing toward them, half expecting to see Wymon and Serle riding close by. But those men were gone, their absence a constant reminder that it was not a good idea to try and make friends in these lands. That friendship was fleeting, and often more trouble than it was worth.

When Ronan looked back upon the scarred and grim face of Ivo Taillebois, it was reassuring to know he wouldn't be making any friends there, even had he wanted to. The knight was one of those unpredictable types. You could just never tell what he would do at any given moment. Ronan had met enough of those men to know they deserved a wide berth. By God, he had been one of those men once. And now… who knew what he had become. For now, a messenger. Later, a warrior. Eventually… with luck, a valued companion to the king, and a wealthy man. All he had to do was live long enough to reap his reward.

'So how did you learn of this woman?' Ronan asked, growing tired of the silence and the endless road. 'This pythoness? Have you become friendly with the locals, Ivo?'

Taillebois leered, as though suddenly inspired by a particularly lascivious memory. 'After a fashion. I was told the tale by a Saxon whore who made my acquaintance. They all flap their mouths when offered the appropriate reward.'

'True,' Ronan replied. 'It must have cost you quite the sum.'

Ivo's grin grew wider. 'Only the length of my cock.'

He laughed at that as though it were the funniest thing he'd ever heard. All the while, Ronan couldn't help but feel sorry for that whore, whoever she was. He doubted Ivo was in any way a considerate lover.

'So where are we headed?'

When Ivo had finished his laughter, he pointed further along the road toward the base of rolling hills. 'There is a cave up in the moorland.'

Of course it was a cave. Where else had he expected this witch to dwell? 'You have a map to it?'

'No. But I have a rough idea where it will be.'

'What? You think there'll be a signpost to show us the way?'

Ivo raised a calming hand. 'Have a little faith, Dol-Combourg. I know what I'm doing.'

Somehow Ronan doubted that, but he had no choice

but to follow anyway as the sun began to dip, and they approached a small village at the edge of a stream. After crossing a stone bridge beside a mill, they found themselves at the centre of the burgh. The inhabitants were understandably wary, but a few came out to greet them as they stopped their horses by the village well. The stench from it was enough to deter Ronan from taking a drink.

'Greetings,' Ivo said from atop his horse. 'We have come on the king's business. We seek the woman in the hills. Your hedge-witch and healer. She is said to live close to this place.'

The villagers looked at one another conspiratorially, but no one said a word. If they were trying to protect this woman with their silence, they weren't doing a very good job.

Ivo pulled a coin purse from the saddlebag at his side and jangled the contents. 'What about now? Anyone have any idea?'

One of the villagers stepped forward, surprisingly young and handsome considering the company he was in. 'I might do. Depending on what's in that purse.'

Casually, Ivo gestured to one of his men, who raised a crossbow from his side and loosed. The bolt hit the young man square in the chest and he pitched forward without a word.

A scream went up. A flurry of panic as a woman fled and an old man dropped to his knees and begged. Pretty much the usual reaction to when they murdered someone. Ronan had long since grown immune to the horror of it. Although as he watched the blood pool from beneath the prone body of that young man, he began to wonder if he had. Or if his sense of everything had become dulled. His feelings inured to the atrocities he bathed in day in and day out.

'Any of you remember now?' Ivo shouted.

One of the old men stepped forward, wringing his hands, nodding his head so the flaps of his cap bobbed back and forth. 'Yes, lord. I do, lord.' He pointed along the road from the village with a trembling hand. 'Go west. Through the wood. Her cave is halfway up the side of the tor. You can't miss it.'

Ronan expected another crossbow bolt for the man's trouble, but instead Ivo nodded his thanks, before stowing away his coin purse. They turned their horses, as innocent villagers cried and mourned in their wake.

'You see,' Ivo said. 'I told you to have a little faith.'

'Don't you think that may have been a little harsh?' Ronan replied, surprising himself with his sympathy.

Ivo looked incredulous. 'You think I should have paid them?'

That did seem a little over the top. 'You could always have offered the length of your cock.'

A cloud of confusion descended over Ivo's hard face, before a smile slowly crept up the side of his mouth. He laughed hard again. Probably harder than he had at his own joke.

They continued on, with night descending by the time they rode from the woodland and found themselves at the bottom of the tor the old man had directed them toward. By the moonlight, they could see the cave entrance a hundred yards up the face of it, surrounded by rock.

Ivo and his companions hung back as Ronan led the way. At first, he felt like mocking them for their caution. This was, after all, one old woman. But as they drew closer, he couldn't quell an overwhelming sense of foreboding. When he drew to within a few feet of the cave entrance, he saw that corn dollies had been placed upon some of the rocks. They were twisted into stark depictions of spreadeagled men, and in the moonlight they looked as though they might almost spring to life at any moment.

Ronan pulled his horse up, and Ivo rode up beside him. There they sat in the silence, just staring at that gaping hole in the hill.

'Well then,' Ivo whispered. 'Off you go.'

Ronan gently slid down from his saddle, resisting the temptation to draw his sword. 'Thanks for the help.'

Ivo shrugged his reply, as Ronan approached the cave. There was flickering light within, and as soon as he crossed the threshold he saw candles glowing dully on the ground, lighting his path deeper. Carefully, Ronan limped on, gritting his teeth as he was greeted by bones and skulls tied together with twine and hung from the roof. Strange symbols had been chalked onto the walls, and everything about the place seemed designed to unnerve.

He had to convince himself this was the contrivance of an old charlatan. It might work on these Saxon peasants, but Ronan of Dol-Combourg was made of sterner stuff.

'Someone calls upon me in the dead of night.'

The words struck Ronan right in the heart, and he shivered to his bones. It was a hiss of a voice. A slither under his flesh. The kind of voice he had dreaded hearing as a little boy, alone in his bed.

'Am I in danger?' the woman asked.

It seemed ridiculous that someone who sounded so

ominous would think they were the one in danger. Ronan had to tell himself that this was just an old crone, hiding somewhere in the dark. No matter what she sounded like, she was no danger to him.

'No, you are not.' He tried to sound as confident as he could, but with all the shadows and the symbols and the fucking bones it was difficult. 'In fact, I come with an offer. I come with silver in return for a favour.'

'A favour?' She sounded as though she were savouring the word. As though it tasted sweet on her lips. 'It is true that I can heal the sick. But what ails you… is beyond even my power to repair.'

This was getting stranger by the second. 'No, crone, I have not come for you to make me walk as others do.'

Movement in the shadows before she slid from the dark like a cat from an alley, eyes tiny, nose long, flesh wrinkled and shining in the light of a hundred candles. A smile widened on her lipless mouth, and he could see all but one of her teeth was missing, and that one was misshapen and yellow.

'I wasn't talking about the leg.' She pointed a long and cracked fingernail at him. 'I was talking about what ails you inside. So much loss. So much pain. So much—'

'Spare me, woman. I do not need your charlatan's riddles. I come on behalf of King William. I was told you hold a position of power within these fens. That you are known. That you are feared.'

Her eyes narrowed as her mouth widened in a grin. 'You flatter me… bastard son.'

His breath caught in his chest. 'How… how would you know that?'

'I know many things. I have many ways. Isn't that why you're here?'

Ronan cleared his throat, hoping it would also clear his mind of all the thoughts roiling within it. Surely this was not real. This woman was no witch, whether the Saxons believed it true or not. This was just some mad old crone peddling curses and potions... wasn't it?

'The king will offer you riches beyond imagining,' he said quickly. 'Anything your heart desires will be yours. You could live like a queen.'

The crone threw back her head, mouth opening wide as she screeched a laugh that filled her cave. Ronan almost had to clamp a hand to his ears.

'I already do, boy. Look around you.'

Despite his better judgement, he did as she asked, unsure of what he was supposed to be looking at. On a shelf nearby was a toad that stared at him sullenly. Every stone seemed slick, every chair worm-ridden. 'Yes, so I see. But you would have the king's gratitude at least. Anything you wanted would be within your grasp.'

She stepped closer, seeming to slide across the ground like an eel from the marshes. 'And all I would have to do is betray my people. Betray the guardians of the fens.'

'The what?'

She stared deep into his eyes. For a frightening moment, Ronan thought that perhaps once this woman might have been beautiful. That those eyes might have enchanted a score of men and lured them to her bed.

'There is power in this land. Power that ruled supreme before the Romanus brought their one god. Before the Jutes and Angles brought many. Before you came.'

Ronan shook his head. The smell of her was bewitching, like incense in a church.

'You could help to end this needless slaughter. You could bring peace. Cast your enchantments and the rebels at Ely will flee in fear.'

She raised a razor-thin eyebrow. 'Yes, they will.'

'So… we have a deal? You'll do it? Just name your price.'

'My price?' She moved even closer. Now he could smell her breath and it was not the fetid stench he had expected. It was somehow sweet, despite her rotten gums. Like clove and cinnamon. 'Maybe I do have a price in mind, boy. Are you willing to pay it?' Her ragged shawl slipped from her shoulder, revealing a not altogether hideous bone structure.

For a moment, one fleeting moment, Ronan thought perhaps it would not have been an altogether unpleasant sacrifice to make for his king. Then again, he still had standards.

'I appreciate the offer, but no. Silver will have to do.'

She reached out, her hand brushing his leggings, uncomfortably close to his crotch. 'Come now, boy.'

Ronan reeled back, as though a spell were broken. His knife was out of its sheath before he realised it, blade pointed at her neck. She giggled in the back of her throat, making a wet sound that made his stomach lurch.

'A beast circles you,' she whispered. 'It stalks you. Covets your flesh. And soon—'

'I'll show you a fucking beast, woman,' he snarled, shaking the knife as threateningly as he could manage.

It only amused her more, her shoulders shuddering with the mirth of it. 'That blade won't help you, child. Nevertheless, I will help your king. And I will take his silver.

Expect me at the Isle of Eels in a tenday. And cook me something juicy, eh, bastard boy. I'll be hungry.'

Ronan nodded as he backed away, but he kept that blade to hand until he felt the chill night air on his neck. Once he'd sheathed it, he turned to see Ivo waiting atop his horse.

'So how did that go?' he asked.

Ronan mounted his steed as fast as he could manage. 'She is everything you said she'd be. And oh so much more.'

As he reined around his horse to face down the hill, Ivo leaned in closer. 'You look ill, Dol-Combourg. Are you sure she didn't steal your soul?'

Ronan glared back, ignoring his insipid grin. 'We have no souls to steal anymore, Taillebois. You know that as well as I.'

36

It had taken them eight days to erect the tower. Its foundations were sunk deep into the marsh, a few hundred yards from the fortress walls. Stakes marking out a path to the foot of it leading to solid ground a half-mile distant. Those defenders must have expected a siege, as Ronan had watched them fire their arrows in vain, trying to stop the workers as they toiled ankle-deep in the mud. In retaliation, ballistae had fired back, keeping the rebels quelled while level upon level the tower had risen, until it looked over the palisade.

Now it stood ready, Ronan wondered if it had all been for nothing. They were hanging so much on heathen superstition. Still, too late to turn back now.

'This had better work.'

The king's voice rumbled behind him. Ronan felt the sudden urge to remind him that it had been Ivo Taillebois, and not Ronan of Dol-Combourg who had come up with this scheme. Perhaps not the right time though.

Taking his cue, Ronan limped toward the canvas tent

where she was waiting, and pulled back the covering. He was hit by the sudden stench of her – the earthy stink of the bog, mixed with a heady essence of something he couldn't quite identify. As she stepped out into the twilight, silence fell over the surrounding knights.

She was bedecked in rags, bones tied to them with catgut and hanging from her like a rattling curtain. Covering her hair was a headdress of briar and thorn, two ram's horns protruding from it, adding to her menace.

'Are you ready, woman?' Ronan asked, trying to sound like he was the one in command.

She took in her surroundings at leisure, until her eyes finally fell upon Ronan. Then she sniffed the air, as though it might give her some clue as to where her quarry lay, as though she were about to hunt some terrified game.

'Now is a good time, bastard boy.'

'This way then,' Ronan said, swallowing down his fear.

He led her across the boggy ground toward the marsh, not looking back. Armed men lined the way, raising their torches to light the pathway. Beyond the tower he could see the palisade of the island fortress in the distance. For now it was silent. Its defenders should have been quaking in fear, but then they could not possibly have known what was in store for them. If indeed this worked at all.

They reached the bottom of the scaffold, timber stairs leading up to the summit. Ronan stopped, gesturing for her to continue, but she paused. Before he could ask what was wrong, she reached within her ragged shawl and produced a grey coney. At first he thought it was dead, but then it twitched and spasmed, as though it might be able to escape her clutches. All in vain.

In her other hand she conjured a curved blade from within that shawl, and in one swift motion opened up the rabbit's belly. Its entrails flopped forth, dangling there as the rabbit's twitching ended.

She was whispering, eyes rolled back in her head, and it was all Ronan could do to stay and watch. His stomach was turning, nausea creeping up on him like a spectre. He considered praying, but doubted any holy communion could save him from whatever this was.

A fox shrieked amid the distant fenland. Then a flock of blackbirds were startled to flight, crossing the sky above the isle. The incessant hum of insects that infected these marshes like a canker gradually waned, to leave the place silent as death.

The rabbit's corpse slipped from her fingers to slap on the ground. 'You should hide away now, bastard boy.'

Ronan's jaw ground as he was determined not to show any fear. 'I will stay.'

The smile didn't waver from her lips. 'Suit yourself.'

She turned, taking the stairs up to the summit of that tower.

Night had fallen, and with it was an eerie sense of foreboding. Styrkar had stood upon the palisade and watched for the past eight days as they had built the tower. It hadn't taken long for them to work out it was no siege engine. The tower was too far to lob artillery beyond their wall, but close enough for... something. As darkness had cloaked the surrounding marsh, and they had lit the scaffold with torches, he knew whatever they had planned would happen soon.

'What do you think they're doing?' Hereswyde said quietly, as though she were afraid to besmirch the uncanny silence.

He shook his head. 'I do not know. But I have an ill feeling. Do you sense it?'

She nodded almost imperceptibly. 'It is too still. Too quiet. No animals nor birds to make a sound. It is as though the fens have been hushed somehow.'

A torch sparked into life atop the tower. Then another, and another. Styrkar squinted, spying a figure standing in the midst of that light, bedecked in a horned headdress, arms raised.

'Isle of Eels,' a cry went up, carrying across the marsh. The voice struck dread into Styrkar's heart, as though it were the dead that spoke. 'You have stood defiant for too long. You have thumbed your nose at the rightful king. Until now, the guardians of the fens have watched over you. They watch over you no more.'

Wenoth and Gille had come to stand beside them now, with Winter and Lightfoot and Ullicus. All silent as they looked out at the tower, the only thing they could see through the blackness of the marsh.

'With every new breath you draw, let the air be tainted,' that fell voice continued. 'Let the taste of despair linger on your tongues. Let the walls that shelter you crumble as an ancient ruin. Let it mirror the weight of your futile resistance.'

Morcar had joined them, and he snarled his defiance before turning to the abbot Thurstan. 'Do something. Before this witch infects us all with a malady. Before these men lose their nerve and flee into the marsh.'

Thurstan nodded, turning from the palisade that looked down upon the courtyard beyond. There, more men had gathered, their faces forlorn as they listened to the haunting voice from across the marsh.

He flicked open the pages of his battered book, as though searching for an appropriate verse, but whether he could not read it in the dim light, or could think of no appropriate passage, he closed his book once more.

'Listen to me,' Thurstan called, trying to drown out the witch upon her scaffold. 'Listen, men of Ely. Listen to my prayer.' Below there was still disquiet, but all eyes turned to the abbot as he began. 'O merciful Father, whose divine light pierces the darkest of nights, we beseech thee in this hour of tribulation. Thy grace, a beacon of hope, illuminates our path through the encroaching shadow. Grant us strength, o Lord, to withstand the curses of the heathen, which seek to enshroud us in malice.'

Styrkar could see some of the men were desperate to listen, but others were grasping holy symbols, or their own pagan trinkets, in fear.

Thurstan realised he was losing them, and he raised his hand to the moonlit night. 'Thou, who art the shepherd of our souls, guide us through this tempest of malevolence. Let the light of faith dispel the encircling dark, and may our hearts remain steadfast in the face of—'

'Let the waters that surround you turn to poison,' the witch shrieked, her bellow drowning out Thurstan before he could continue. 'Let it choke the life from every fish that swims, let it taint every drop you drink. May the river that cradles this isle become an abyss that reflects the darkness that will consume your souls.'

'No,' Thurstan called out. 'Do not listen to her. Listen to me. Look to the Lord God. He will protect us. He will grant solace to your hearts, though they are burdened with fear. Grant courage to those who still stand, righteous and untainted. He is the shield. The bulwark against sin that shall guard our humbled sanctuary.'

'Your crops shall wither and rot beneath this fetid and barren soil. Famine will whisper its way on the wind. The very land that sustains you shall turn to dust, yielding only thorns and thistles in place of once-bountiful harvests. Despair, men of Ely. Despair.'

'With thy mercy, O Lord, turn this tide of deviltry. Let the light of dawn herald not only a new day but a triumph of righteousness over darkness.'

'Let the bonds of kinship fracture. Let mistrust and betrayal fester like a fetid wound. May friendships crumble like ancient stones, alliances unravel like the threads of a rotting tapestry…'

'Bestow upon us the strength to heal the fractured bonds that have come asunder. May unity be our shield, and compassion our sword against this threat of doom. Let forgiveness blossom where seeds of discord were sown, for in thy grace, O Lord, lies the power to heal…'

Thurstan's voice gave out as the witch continued her tirade. To Styrkar's eye it was like watching warriors fight until one of them faded. On this occasion it was Thurstan who had been bested.

There were tears in the abbot's eyes, and Morcar glared at him in fury. Styrkar could only feel sympathy with the holy man as he slunk away, and the witch was left to continue her tirade uninterrupted.

Helplessly, they stood and they listened as the long night drew on. She damned them for all that time as some men prayed and others wept. The hunger they had suffered for weeks, the prospect of a grim death, all adding to their misery.

For his part, Styrkar waited and watched atop that palisade until the dawn appeared, shedding light, and not a little hope on the isle. With the sun came silence, and in the distance, the witch made her way down from the scaffold, and was escorted away by the Franks.

'Do you think that's it?' Hereswyde asked. She had stood with him for most of the night.

'I don't,' Styrkar replied. 'How are the men?'

'They won't last long with that screaming at them all through the night. Lightfoot tells me a dozen have already fled. At this rate there will be no man left to defend this place within ten days.'

'So we must act.'

She gazed up at him. 'What do you suggest?'

'I'll think of something. Have no fear on that.'

'Well think fast. The days grow shorter.'

With that she left him to look out onto the marsh. As he did so, he heard a familiar caw, the only animal sound he had heard since the previous day.

Turning, he saw it there along the palisade, looking at him with a baleful eye. The valravn, waiting to claim him. Waiting to seal his fate.

'Not long now,' the Red Wolf whispered. 'Then you will have what you seek.'

The valravn took to the wing, satisfied with his offer.

Happy to wait for its prize.

37

The night was still, when rain or blow would have served them well. Nevertheless, they could not wait any longer. Could not allow that prating crone to strike further terror into the heart of Ely.

Styrkar slipped into the cold waters, Hereswyde alongside him. They were both stripped bare, daubed in mud, and armed only with a blade each, and Hereswyde's bow. At first the water took his breath away, but he suffered it, slipping deeper into the marsh, becoming a part of it so he might swim unseen toward that huge scaffold.

He could still hear her screaming, though the words had become indistinct. It was best not to heed them, lest he be stricken by whatever witchcraft she was spreading.

Yard after chilling yard they waded toward the shore, both silent as they neared their goal. When they eventually reached it, they crawled among the reeds, peering the short distance across dry land to the base of that wooden tower. Armoured men waited at the foot of it, spears and shields gripped tightly, five of them watching for any sign of an approaching boat. For Ely to send its fighter to silence the screaming woman atop her perch. But death was not coming on a boat. It was coming silent and cold from the depths of the marsh.

An eel slithered past Styrkar's leg as he waited, silken and bulbous. He didn't react, keeping his eyes fixed on those armed men, doing his best to ignore the howling bitch atop her tower. The moon was fat, and it was so easy to see in the light it shed. One sound, one movement might give them away as they waited. But they did not have to wait for long.

A distant shout pealed across the marsh. At first it was indistinct as the crone continued her rant, louder than ever. Styrkar focused for a moment on her words, and immediately regretted it.

'I hear you beg to your false god. Let the winds carry your lamentations, unheard and unanswered. May the heavens close their gates to your pleas.'

He gritted his teeth at the sound of her dread voice, concentrating instead on the shouts that grew louder in the distance. Peering through the reeds, he saw a flicker of light across the fens, as beside him Hereswyde took the line of hemp she had kept in her mouth and silently strung her bow.

Shouts grew louder as that flicker reached higher in the sky, and flames lit the night. The fires rose, Hereswyde's men having done their part and set light to the dry reeds close to the Frankish camp.

The Frankish guards at the base of the scaffold looked around in confusion. They spoke to one another in their foreign tongue, panicked and unsure of what to do. One of them gestured toward the rising flames across the marsh, before three of them darted off to help. Only two left. It would not be enough to stop the Red Wolf.

Styrkar slipped from the water, drawing his sword in silence, clinging to the shadow that surrounded the base of the tower. He worked his way close, could almost hear the nearest knight breathing as he stared into the dark. Without so much as a snarl of rage, Styrkar darted forward. The man had hardly enough time to raise his spear, his eyes growing wide as Styrkar struck. His blade sunk deep, just above the armour of his throat and below his chin. The thrust so perfect it burst from the mail at the back of his neck.

As his enemy fell, Styrkar wrenched his blade clear, looking to the second knight. He was alert, raising shield and spear, making himself a harder target, and here was the Red Wolf all but naked. They began to circle one another, and even with the advantage of armour the Frankish knight looked afraid. He didn't look it for long before there was a hiss from the shoreline, and his back was impaled by an arrow. His face took on a pained expression, as though he had been betrayed. The spear fell from his limp fingers, shield lowered enough for Styrkar to dart forward and finish him quick.

Hereswyde stalked from the shadow, and they both approached the bottom of the scaffold. There they paused for a moment, listening to the shouts in the distance that were almost drowned out by the screams of the crone above. The fires were only growing higher, the flames licking the night sky for all to see, including that witch.

'Let your fires writhe like serpents,' she shrieked. 'May its smoke become a shroud, choking your breath and blinding your eyes. The very air you inhale shall carry the scent of damnation.'

Hereswyde shouldered her bow, drawing her curved seax. Styrkar led the way up the wooden stairs, his feet silent, though his weight caused the scaffold to creak. As he reached the top she was waiting, watching, as though she expected death to come for her and didn't care.

The pythoness grinned a toothless greeting. 'What is this? Have you come to make me an offer too?'

'I offer you a swift death, woman,' Styrkar replied, taking a step closer.

'Do you, Red Wolf?'

He stopped in his tracks. 'How do you know my name?'

She sniggered. 'I know many things. Some that have happened in the past. Some that will happen in the days to come. I see your end, Red Wolf. I see you howling amid a ring of ancient stones. A howl that echoes through the mountains for eternity.'

Styrkar had lowered his blade. He felt suddenly stricken by the woman's words, her portent cutting him deep. It was almost his end, as the crone stepped closer, producing a blade of her own.

He reeled back as she slashed at him, but Hereswyde was faster. She darted forward, seax clashing with the witch's curved dagger. The crone dodged back out of range, before slashing again.

Styrkar shook his head, clearing it of whatever enchantment this creature had placed on him. As the women cut and slashed at one another, he grabbed one of the torches that illuminated the scaffold.

Hereswyde dodged back, avoiding a wayward slice of the crone's knife. The Red Wolf darted in, thrusting the naked flame at the woman. Her rags caught alight, the fire spreading rapidly up her body, the dried thorns and briar she wore about her head igniting like kindling.

She screeched her defiance, but the flames did not heed her. Styrkar and Hereswyde staggered back from the heat as the old woman went up like a pyre, screaming all the while. As her dying screams echoed out across the fenlands, she pitched backwards, tipping over the side of the scaffold and plummeting to her doom below.

All went silent but for the distant shouts of the Franks vainly fighting the marshland fire that was consuming their camp. Styrkar went to the edge of the platform, looking out. Lit up in the distance, he could see the Franks had gathered. They barked their warnings, gesturing frantically to the scaffold and the pythoness still burning at its base.

'They're coming,' Hereswyde breathed.

'Then we'd best be swift,' Styrkar replied, already making his way toward the stairs.

'Grab the buckets,' Ronan cried.

That wall of fire was moving ever closer. The wind was not a strong one, but it was enough to spread the flames inexorably toward them.

Men rushed all about, desperate to move their belongings, their weapons, their horses from the path of the conflagration. Before Ronan could shout any further orders he heard cries of alarm from across the camp.

Turning, he saw the distant scaffold lit up by torches. The pythoness was no longer on her perch, but there was movement atop it. Damn the Saxons, and damn his stupidity for not seeing this coming. The fire was merely a diversion. Such a simple ruse, and yet they had fallen for it.

Before he could decide what to do, he heard a thump of hooves against the soft earth. Mallet rode up beside him on the back of a black warhorse, his sword drawn, though he'd had no time to don mail.

'The rebels have struck out from their fort, Dol-Combourg. Are you going to just stand there and let them escape?'

Another steed stood close by. It was so tempting, but then it was also such a dangerous idea. But could he just stand there and let Mallet shame him? The man who had badgered, and hectored and threatened him for so long?

Of course he couldn't.

Ronan grasped a lance from where it was skewered in the ground. His sword was already strapped to his side; in recent days he had realised it was best not to be caught without it. Grabbing the horse's reins, he dragged himself into the saddle.

Mallet offered him a sideways grin, before digging his heels to flanks and setting off toward the tower along the path that was staked out. Ronan turned to the others, seeing half a dozen men stricken with shock, doing nothing to help with the grassfire.

'You men, grab some weapons,' he snarled. 'The Saxons have attacked the scaffold. We cannot let them thumb their noses at us without reprisal.'

It did the trick, and the men raced to take up their

weapons. Ronan kicked his horse, quick to follow the galloping Mallet, who raised his sword and bellowed, as he had done at the battle on the hill. That day he had distinguished himself. Set an example for them all. Now there was only Ronan following in his wake, but he would have to do.

The scaffold reared up ahead as his steed ate up the yards. Mallet had already spied his quarry: two figures descending the stairs from the platform, both covered in mud, a man and a woman. On seeing the mounted knight charging at them they stopped, the man brandishing his sword.

Mallet galloped straight at him, and Ronan got a familiar sinking feeling as he recognised the dark warrior's gait, his huge frame, his blue eyes piercing from within the mud-covered face. He would have warned Mallet, but there was no time as his horse raced to trample his foe.

The woman rolled aside, her bowstring already nocked. She drew it back before letting fly, and the arrow struck Mallet's horse in the neck. It went down without a sound, Mallet toppling from the saddle to land in a heap.

Ronan reined back his own steed, lifting his lance to fling it at the Red Wolf, but the woman had drawn another arrow and nocked in a single motion. She let fly, and Ronan lurched back as the arrow flew wide. His sudden motion spooked the horse beneath him and it reared…

Next thing he met the cold ground with a thump, his lance falling from his grip. As he scrambled to his knees, he just had time to see his horse bolt, before Mallet staggered to his feet. The famed hero of Senlac Hill looked about for a weapon. The Red Wolf provided him a blade of his own as he loomed from the dark, sword swinging.

Mallet's head toppled from his body and bounced on the ground.

Another arrow hissed past Ronan's head, fuelling him with the impetus to stand, to wrench his own blade free of his scabbard. The woman nocked for a third time, but Styrkar raised his hand.

'Wait,' the Red Wolf demanded.

They stared at one another, those cold eyes made even more piercing in his mud-covered face. Though the sword was reassuringly heavy in Ronan's grip, he knew it would never be enough. But then Styrkar had stayed the woman's hand, perhaps even saved Ronan's life. Not for the first time...

His daughter. It could only be the knowledge Ronan carried of her whereabouts that curbed the Red Wolf's killing rage. Perhaps there was something human in there after all, beyond berserk fury.

A shout from behind. The men he had provoked into action at the camp were on their way.

'We have to go,' the woman hissed.

For a moment Ronan thought that Styrkar might ignore her. Might stay to fight and die, but instead he turned and bounded into the darkness. Ronan could only watch as they raced off toward the safety of the marsh.

'Lord Mallet,' one of the men said as he reached Ronan's side. 'Lord Mallet is... he's dead. But... how?'

Ronan had no response. Mallet had proven himself a hero, but heroes died just as readily as cowards. It wasn't until he heard the sound of hooves, and a horse reined in beside him that he drew his gaze away from the darkness of the marsh. Looking down at him was Ivo, face blackened from the soot of the fires.

'Is that the pythoness?' he asked, gesturing to the charred remains at the foot of the scaffold.

Ronan nodded. 'I think we may need a new plan.'

38

Ely, England, August 1071

He slept soundly for the first time in what seemed an age. A dreamless sleep untroubled by the nightmares of his past or present. It was not to last, and he rose to the sound of troubled voices.

Styrkar made his way from his humble shack, taking up his sword, wondering if today would be the day the Franks found a way into their fortress. But there were no men at the palisade. No sound of thunderous cavalry from beyond the walls. Instead, the noise of discontent echoed from the central square, where it looked like all the remaining men of Ely had gathered.

Hereswyde and Siward stood at the centre of the squall surrounded by the rest. Men Styrkar recognised were shouting in dismay, demanding to know what they might do now. When he saw the Hedge-Sparrow standing at the periphery, Styrkar made his way closer.

'What has happened to provoke the men?'

The Hedge-Sparrow shook his blond head. 'The Earl

Morcar has fled, and his men have gone with him. Also Thurstan the abbot. They left in the dead of night taking their boats and all they could carry.'

'Cowards,' Styrkar breathed.

'Cowards who have doomed those of us that remain. How will we hope to prevail against the Franks now?'

A valid question, though one Styrkar had never thought to ask himself. He had abandoned any idea of prevailing over the Franks when the Aetheling gave up his campaign for the crown. Instead, he had satisfied himself only with thoughts of vanquishing one man. A man who now seemed impossibly far away.

Styrkar moved forward, pushing his way through the press of men. When he reached the front he saw several of them raging, making their discontent clear for all to hear.

'Surrender is our only chance,' Gille snarled, a burly man with one eye who had been one of Hereswyde's most loyal. 'We have done enough. If we throw ourselves on the king's mercy now—'

'The king has no mercy,' Siward argued, his few remaining housecarls nodding their agreement. 'At best he will take your hands for defying him. At worst, your eyes too, if not your lives.'

'So what do we do?' asked Rapenald, a tall rangy archer.

'We fight, as we have done for these five long years.'

Perhaps there might have been a time when Siward Barn's words would inspire these men of Ely. When they would have followed this northern magnate to their deaths. But weeks and months and years of endless fighting for little reward had taken its toll. The hunger that grumbled within their bellies was made vocal on their tongues, and they shook their heads at the idea. It seemed the prospect of imminent defeat, no matter how glorious, was one they did not cherish. Now that even the abbot Thurstan had seen fit to flee, there was no one to offer them the rousing word of their god. All hope seemed lost.

Styrkar made his way from the crowd as they continued to argue, and made his way into the shrine of Aethelthryth. The place was solemn as it always was, but it stirred little reverence within the Red Wolf.

The casket lay in its usual place of honour upon the altar, and he took it from its resting place before offering the statue of their saint the most cursory of nods. When he left the shrine their argument had become more heated. No more could he discern words as Hereswyde and Siward were shouted over and argued down. It seemed their rebellion would end here and now with the murder of its leaders.

'Men of Ely,' the Red Wolf roared. His voice echoed through the square, and silenced their argument in an instant. All eyes turned to Styrkar, standing tall with an iron casket in his grasp. 'My brothers. Warriors I have fought beside. Bled beside. I understand your despair. I have felt it too. But now I do not fear. Now I know my fate is the same, whether I fight or I flee. We are all bound for the earth. All destined to be laid in the mud. That is not in question. The only thing you must ask yourself is what manner of death you will have. One of regret? That you did not fight until the end? For the only certain thing is that if you do not fight you will still die.'

They were looking at one another hesitantly. Heeding the Red Wolf's words as readily as they had joined him in battle.

'Here is the relic of your Saint Oswald. Together we stole

it from the cathedral of Saint Peter's Burgh. So many saints. So many places. So much misplaced reverence.'

Styrkar flung the casket on the ground. It cracked open, spilling the rotting arm onto the ground before them. Some of the men looked on in shock. Others appeared unmoved.

'Have no more reverence for these meaningless idols. They will not protect you from what waits. The arm of a dead king will not help you.' Styrkar drew his blade. 'Only your own sword arm will give you the end you desire. Your own strength. Your own legend. Go not to your graves cowed, men of Ely. Join me in glory.' He stepped forward, glaring into the faces of those men. 'You, Lightfoot and Duti. You, Winter and Wenoth. You, Grugan and Gille. Hogor who keeps us fed. Leofred, Liveret and Rapenald. Alsinus and Ullicus. Starcolf and Toste. You are all brave men. I have seen it with my own eyes. Will you flee now, so close to the end? For what is there to flee to but shame and misery and a life under the Bastard King's heel?'

'No,' said Wenoth. 'We will not flee.'

'We stand with you, Red Wolf,' answered Ullicus.

'We follow Hereswyde to the end,' shouted Grugan.

And a cheer rose, filling the fortress isle and echoing out across the palisade. As the men gave their oaths to one another that they would fight to the end, Styrkar was surprised to see the bishop Ethelwin, standing to the edge of the crowd. He moved closer, and Ethelwin flinched as Styrkar loomed over him.

'You did not think to run with Morcar and the abbot?' Styrkar asked over the sound of chattering men.

Ethelwin shook his head with vigour. 'Despite what you may think of me, I am no coward.'

'No? Or is it they just didn't want you along with them? Either way, you are the priest of this place now.'

He turned back to the gathered army. The remaining rebels who stood against the king of these occupied lands.

'Now we are of one mind,' he shouted, silencing them once more. 'Let us build about ourselves a greater fortress. Dig trenches and fill them with spikes into which their horses will flounder, build walls of stone from behind which we can stifle their charge. Build a castle among the marshes that will force the Franks to fight for every yard should they breach our walls. Our own kingdom, for which we will fight to the last.'

Again the men of Ely cheered, and the Red Wolf felt hope in his heart once again.

Hope for a death worthy of their legend.

39

From the top of the hill, Ronan could see for miles. It wasn't common for him to appreciate the bleak beauty of this landscape, but today he found himself feeling some benefit from it. The blue sky and its slow-moving clouds had a soothing effect he had sorely been missing. Green fields rolling off to the west presented a pastoral idyll he had never really appreciated before. Of course, his lightness of mood was enhanced by the two prisoners driven to their knees at the feet of his dark steed.

This felt like just where he belonged – atop a warhorse, with a Saxon lord and prominent priest bowing before him. He could well get used to it. When he'd heard the men had fled the fort at Ely and offered their surrender he could barely believe his luck. Now as he sat looking down, waiting for the king to arrive, it felt like it had been the only possible outcome. A stroke of fortune Ronan hadn't allowed himself to appreciate in years.

Thurstan glanced up, looking as though he wanted to

speak, but he held his tongue in Morcar's presence. When they had last been together in that little rowboat, Ronan had offered him some hope to cling onto. A notion that King William might offer mercy were the priest to fling himself upon it. Whether Thurstan had been a fool to trust him, they would find out soon enough.

'Are we to wait here all day?' Morcar asked gruffly. 'We've surrendered, haven't we? What more humiliation is there to suffer?'

'The king has some questions,' Ronan replied, taking not a little pleasure from looking down upon the fallen nobleman.

Morcar looked around in confusion. 'Here? On top of a hill?'

Ronan did his best to curb a smile. 'What can I say, kings move in mysterious ways. Just like God, eh, priest?'

If Thurstan had any opinion on that he didn't bother to express it. Morcar continued to glare, but, bound and kneeling, there was little he could do about his situation. The way he kept glancing at the downcast priest beside him, it was obvious Thurstan had persuaded him that surrender was the best option. Clearly, he had not expected such shoddy treatment.

'You know we've met before,' Ronan said, unable to hold his peace. 'At Waruic. By strange twist of fate, you offered your surrender on that occasion too.'

Morcar sneered his disdain. 'Is that so? I don't remember you at all.'

Ronan leaned forward a touch in his saddle. 'No? Well, you'll remember this time, won't you.'

Before Morcar could snipe back, there came a sound of

beating hooves. It heralded the king's handsome steed as it carried him to the top of the hill, and he reined in beside Ronan.

'Now would be a good time to bow,' Ronan suggested, as William regarded his prisoners.

Thurstan leaned forward, his nose almost touching the dirt. Morcar merely inclined his shaggy head, not taking his eyes from his captors.

King William held the rein in his right hand. In his left was a fistful of cobnuts, one of which he proceeded to flick into his open mouth and crunch down on.

'Morcar... again,' he rumbled, looking down his nose at the two men. 'How many times much I teach this errant bastard obedience?'

'Unless I have missed my guess, sire,' Ronan replied. 'This is most likely the last time.'

'Who is the priest?' William asked, before tossing another cobnut in his mouth.

'The abbot Thurstan. Part of the rebellion, and the man who saw me to safety from the island.'

If the king was swayed by Thurstan's act of benevolence toward Ronan, he made no mention of it.

'It seems errant priests are as common in these lands as errant lords. Like pockmarks on a leper's arse. Let's see if they can be of any use. Ask them how I breach the isle's defences and enter the fort. They must know of a way.'

Ronan regarded the prisoners carefully. Though he had little pity for either, he thought it only fair to offer them every opportunity to comply with their king's wishes.

'King William has a request. He would ask a favour of you, in return for his leniency. If you wish to find yourselves in his good graces, he would know a way into this Isle of Eels, as you call it.'

Thurstan opened his mouth to speak but before he could, Morcar struggled to his feet. 'Tell your king we will not betray our countrymen. This usurper will have to satisfy himself with our capture. It is the only prize we offer.'

Ronan turned to King William, who was chewing on another cobnut. 'He says no.'

'Not altogether surprising,' William replied, before gesturing to one of his men who stood at the edge of the hilltop. The knight turned, waving to someone at the foot of the hill.

Thurstan crawled forward a little on his knees. His hands were clasped together. Where his battered Bible was, Ronan had no idea. 'My lords, please. We were offered mercy. The Lord God knows it, and he will be the final judge of us all. I would ask that you find it in your heart to offer clemency, and you will be bestowed His blessing.'

'What does the priest mumble about?' William asked. 'Anything I'd want to understand?'

'Definitely not,' Ronan replied, as there came movement from the edge of the hilltop.

A dozen of the king's spearmen led a group of bedraggled Saxons in their midst. They approached with heads down, faces hidden beneath their mass of hair and beards. Clothes little more than rags.

'What is this?' Morcar demanded on seeing his few remaining housecarls being driven to their knees. 'I have surrendered to you. I was told there would be clemency. Whatever you're planning—'

'Please,' Ronan said raising his hand for silence. 'We

know you have surrendered, and now you are at the king's mercy. He offers you your life, and in return he only asks that you tell him how we might be able to enter Ely.'

Morcar gazed at his men, teeth gritted, before he turned to the king. 'You tell him he can go to Hell.'

'Disappointing,' Ronan said, gesturing to one of the spearmen.

He nodded, before grasping the hair of the first housecarl in a mailed fist. A second knight approached, dirk drawn.

'My lord,' the prisoner cried, as the knife came closer. 'My lord Morcar, please.'

His pleading turned to screaming as he was swiftly parted from his eyeball. Blood spattered his face as he shrieked, and his eye was cast to the ground. Ronan found himself wincing at the mutilation, as Thurstan clasped his hands tighter and began to mumble prayers to the grassy atoll.

'You don't have many men left, Morcar,' Ronan announced. 'And they only have two eyes each. Once those are gone, the king will have his torturer move on to other appendages.'

Morcar lurched forward. 'The king can go fu—'

Ronan offered another casual gesture to the man with the dirk. Once more the housecarl was grabbed by the hair, his pitiful yelling ignored as his one remaining eye was cut out and the squealing sounded more like a pig being castrated.

'You're cowards,' Morcar railed. 'Bastard cowards. I should never have trusted you.'

As he raged, Thurstan struggled to stand. 'Please, stop this. I will tell you what you want to know.'

Ronan smiled at the effectiveness of the plan. 'Ah, the priest finally finds his voice.'

'Hold your tongue,' Morcar snarled.

Again, Ronan gestured to one of the knights, and Morcar was struck in the gut with the butt of a spear. He fell to his knees, struggling for air, as Ronan turned back to Thurstan.

'Well? You may speak freely, Thurstan. And in the king's own tongue, if you will.'

The priest's hands shook as his eyes darted between Ronan and the king. 'I will. I will tell you, but I must have guarantees. Sire, you must spare the defenders of Ely if you are able. They are Christian souls, and each one must be allowed a chance to throw down their arms and come into the light of God's mercy.'

There was silence but for the crunching of cobnuts, as King William considered the abbot's words.

'Very well, priest,' he replied eventually. 'All those who offer themselves in surrender shall be spared. All those but the rebel, Hereward. He alone shall face my wrath, one way or another. I will have his head as an example to any others who would think to raise arms against the rightful king of these lands.'

Thurstan was almost weeping now, the burden of betrayal weighing heavy on him. 'There is a path, through the marsh to the south of the fortress. I... I can show you where.'

Ronan found the priest's words dubious. 'The river shields the fortress to the south, and the fenland is impassable.'

'The river can be forded,' Thurstan insisted. 'At a certain point. And there is a path along which you could bring your horses to within fifty yards of the fortress gates. But the isle is still surrounded by its moat. There is no path for you to cross that final obstacle.'

Ronan turned to his king, who had now finished

crunching on his afternoon meal. 'There you have it, sire. Nothing that can be done about the moat.'

King William offered him a shrug. 'That is in hand, Dol-Combourg.'

'Really?' Ronan asked, his memories of the disaster on the causeway coming back to him in an unwelcome rush. 'Then what is to be done with our errant lord here?'

The king leered down. 'Morcar?'

At the mention of his name, Morcar gazed up once again at his captors. There was hate in his eyes, along with defiance. 'What about me? Am I to be mutilated now? Executed? Do it then. See what happens. See what further rebellion you enflame throughout the north. My name will become—'

'He will live out his days in a cage,' the king interrupted, bored of the fallen noble's rant. 'One suitable for a man of his standing.'

'What was that?' Morcar demanded. 'What did he say?'

'Rejoice, Lord Morcar,' Ronan said. 'The king has decreed that you will live, at least. But otherwise... you're fucked.'

'What...? Does he realise who I am? What power I—'

But the king had already turned his horse and started making his way back down from the hilltop. Ronan followed with the sound of Morcar's raving in his wake.

When they reached the bottom, Ronan could keep his peace no longer. 'Sire, when Thurstan mentioned Ely's moat you said it was in hand. May I ask what you meant?'

'You may, Dol-Combourg. And I will do better than answer you. I will show you. Come.'

With that he kicked his horse's flanks, speeding from

trot to gallop, leading the way along a straight road beside the woodland. Ronan was at pains to keep up, getting the impression that riding free rein was something the king no longer got to do often, and took pleasure in when he could. They rode east for a mile or more, until the road dipped through the wood. There was a sound of running water beyond, and eventually the king led them out onto the banks of a river.

William reined in his horse, gesturing to where men stood at the opposite shore. 'Something Giselbert has been cooking up.'

Ronan could see labourers were stripped to the waist, making ready a bridge of sorts that spanned the river. Pontoons had been laid side by side, wide enough for a single horse but almost forty or fifty feet in length. Planks were secured across their hulls, making a bridge across the span, and strapped together to form a solid platform on the water.

'This looks... just like the causeway we built,' Ronan breathed.

A sound of another horse approaching, and Ronan turned to see Ivo Taillebois riding nearer. He reined in close by, a wicked grin on his face.

'Not quite, Dol-Combourg. You are just in time. Care for me to demonstrate?'

'We have already tried this?' Ronan said, the prospect of galloping across those pontoons filling him with dread.

'You did,' Ivo replied, with a gap-toothed grin. 'Not I. Let me show you how it's done.'

Without pause for a command from his king, Ivo kicked his steed. The horse bucked, racing for the shoreline and the waiting platform. At any moment Ronan expected the beast to refuse or, at best, throw Ivo to the riverbank. Instead, it leapt onto the first pontoon, hooves clacking as it rode right across as though along solid ground.

When he reached the other side, Ronan could see the king smiling his approval. His final plan was most definitely in hand. The moat that surrounded the island would offer no protection.

Soon, Ely would fall.

40

They stood at the southern rampart, watching torches winking in the distance as the sound of hammer on wood drifted on the breeze. The Franks worked through the night and all the day, building their earthworks from which they would launch their final attack. The king had forded the Alreheda River over a week before, erecting towers on the solid ground beyond. And for seven days he had battered the walls of Ely with catapult and ballista, assaulting the fortress and keeping its occupants quelled while he forged a stage from which he would claim his final victory.

The Isle of Eels had remained defiant. Those few men who remained were stalwart in the face of the relentless barrage. It would not be enough. Their few hundred would never be able to hold back the tide once it breached the wall. They had counted as best they could. Over a thousand Franks milling just beyond the river. No doubting now that this would be their end; it was only a matter of when.

'Tell me,' Hereswyde said quietly, as she looked out beside him. 'Who do you think you might have been had the Franks not come and stolen King Harold's crown?'

Styrkar thought back to those years he had spent at his master's side. To the battles they had fought. Of the one he had lost.

'I was to be given lands. Most likely I would have become a thegn. Found a wife. Grown grey and fat.'

'You do not sound regretful.'

'I have learned it is best not to regret a life you never had.' But that was a lie. He had thought often about the life he might have had with Gisela. The one taken from him.

'It is a wise way to be,' Hereswyde replied. 'Most likely I would have been married off to some local lord. Though I do not know if I regret it.'

Styrkar looked down at her, that ferocious woman, as scarred and brooding as any housecarl he had ever met. 'How would any man have tamed you?'

There was a twinkle of light in her eye as she thought of that life unled. 'Perhaps I would have let him. All I would have asked in return is that I be allowed to hunt with my hounds every now and again. Play my lyre to soothe away the cold dark nights.'

'You make music? I never knew.'

That light in her eyes died, to be replaced by a look of regret. 'I put aside such things a long time ago.'

So much sadness in her words. So much remorse. 'It is not too late for you, Hereswyde. You could still escape what is coming. Take your men and vanish north into the marsh. The Franks are not at our door yet, and there is still time enough to abandon this place.'

She turned to him, all notion of sorrow disappearing from her features to be replaced by grim acceptance. 'And leave you to defend this wall alone? I think not.'

'I will die here. It will make no difference whether you are with me, or gone into the fens.'

And as he spoke those doom-laden words, he was certain they were true. Styrkar had no intention of leaving this place alive. The king was coming, and he might not have another chance to face him. He glanced along the palisade, expecting to see the dark silhouette of the valravn eyeing him expectantly, but for now it was hidden.

'Destiny is a fickle master to follow. It can offer either glory or despair. It seems the Red Wolf has accepted both.'

Styrkar knew that his end had been written long ago. His path would always have led him to this place at this time. 'I began my journey as a slave. When given my freedom I made an oath to follow one man. After he was gone, I made more oaths and let them lead me. And sometimes I broke them. The last one I made was to a girl in a foreign land. A girl destined to be a queen. That oath has brought me here, to you. It is the last one I shall make, and I intend to keep it.'

'And you will keep it for what? All for nothing in the end, but to spit in the eye of the usurper before we all die.'

He sensed a note of sorrow there for the first time. Hereswyde showed no fear, but he was sure he could see her eyes glistening, as though she might weep for the life she had never led. 'Perhaps you should have raised children. Instead of an army of rebels.'

Hereswyde's smile was bitter. 'I could say the same to you.'

Her words brought back thoughts of a daughter he had

never seen. A little girl so near, yet she may as well have been on the other side of the world.

'I... I could have. Perhaps I even should have. But my daughter is better off without a man like me to raise her.'

'You have a child somewhere?' Hereswyde asked, as though the notion were an impossible one. 'The Red Wolf has a cub?'

'Aye, he does. But I know not where. And even if I did, it is too late to claim her now.'

Hereswyde looked back out toward the darkness of the marsh. 'It is not too late. Not until you are dead, Styrkar the Dane.'

With that she left him alone upon the high rampart, with the chill breeze, and thoughts of a child he would never see. The hammer sound on wood clinked softly in the distance, the torchlight winking ever nearer as the nights went by, bringing doom to Ely.

41

The crisp air of the fens carried that familiar smell of rot. A stench he'd never grown used to, just like he'd never quite grown used to the pain in his leg. Even now it ached, reminding him he was alive. Reminding him he had to stay that way, no matter what it took.

The pontoons were stretched out before them, spanning the deeps of the marsh. A bridge all the way to the shore at the foot of the island fortress. Its moorings were secured on the far bank at the foot of the ramparts, kept safe from sabotage by ranks of artillery. Ronan remembered well how he had waited at the causeway, the mile-long bridge that was supposed to carry them to victory months ago. He hadn't believed it would work then. This was no different.

A glance to his left and he saw Wilhelm of Warenne, sitting tall and proud, glaring ahead with jaw set. To his right, Ivo of Taillebois, picking something from his teeth, as though they'd just reached the end of a feast. Ronan could not have found himself wedged between two more different men, but they were here on common purpose. One that would reach its end today, one way or another.

Ronan allowed himself a brief glimpse over his shoulder, a difficult feat when encased in mail. The king sat astride his black war steed, leopard standard billowing beside him, eyes dark as they stared at the fort of Ely. It had defied him, as so many others had. Now he would see it fall, as every other rebellion had fallen before it.

'How I have missed this.'

Ronan turned back to see that Ivo had stopped picking at his brown teeth and was looking almost lovingly across the lashed pontoons.

'The waiting?' Ronan asked, slightly bemused.

Ivo nodded. 'It is the best part. All that riding and killing goes by so quickly, you never really get the chance to appreciate it. This though, this moment of anticipation, is to be savoured.'

'Is that what I've been doing wrong all this time?' Ronan asked, no less bemused. 'Not savouring things when I have the chance?'

There was no savouring to be had. All Ronan felt was arse-clenching fear. When he heard a squeak of wheels as the ballistae were rolled to the fore, he felt no less terrified of what was to come.

'A man who takes pleasure in any part of this has truly fallen far from the sight of God,' Warenne said disdainfully. 'None of this should be savoured. We are doing God's work and securing our king in his position on the throne. It is a grim business and should be performed cheerlessly.'

Ivo spat something from his mouth. 'Don't be so dour, Warenne. You are about to avenge the murder of your wife's brother. If nothing else, it should put you in her good graces. Imagine what she'll let you do to her when you return to her bedchamber.' He grinned lasciviously, as though he were picturing it in his mind.

Warenne glared across darkly. 'Don't ever mention my wife again, Taillebois. Or I'll—'

'Gentlemen,' Ronan interrupted, raising a hand for there to be peace. 'We are perhaps about to ride to our deaths. Can we save the quarrelling until afterwards?'

Before either man could disagree, the shout went up to, 'Prepare arms.'

There came a jangling of barding and rattling of harness, as a thousand knights checked their swords were loose in scabbards and shields were firmly attached to arms. Lances were gripped tight, and reins held loose as the breathing of man and beast grew heavier.

Ronan heard the strain of a dozen ropes as ballistae and catapult were braced.

'Load!' came another shout.

Now to begin…

The call drifted across the marsh as Styrkar looked down from the rampart. The enemy siege weapons were in position, and men scurried forth with ammunition.

He looked across to where Hereswyde stood with bow in hand, and offered her a nod. She replied with one of her own, before turning, and rushing lithely across the walkway.

'Prepare yourselves, men of the fens,' she cried. 'They are coming.'

Across the rest of the isle, the defenders were moving into

position. The shield wall was already forming. Beyond that, a low wall behind which hunkered a row of archers. In the far distance were stones ripped down from the ruins of the abbey and stacked as a makeshift barricade. There awaited Siward Barn with his men. Their last line of defence against what was coming.

Styrkar had no time to consider if it would be enough, before he heard the first rumble of siege weaponry. A boulder soared toward the wall, accompanied by the sharp thwap of ballistae.

He ducked as the boulder soared overhead. The huge spear-sized arrows flung by the ballistae thudding into the wooden palisade. Along the rampart, the archers ducked, too fearful to show their heads lest they be skewered by an errant missile.

The barrage continued unabated, as the Franks at their siege weapons began to focus their eye. The catapults concentrated on the main gate, and it rumbled again and again as more rocks were flung against it.

Styrkar made his way down from the rampart. He would do no good up there. All that was left was to wait for the gate to fall. Then he would have his chance.

The men at the shield wall made room for him as he came to stand at their side. Leofred and Wenoth nodded their welcome as he took up a spear in readiness.

'Lock your shields, men of Ely,' the Red Wolf bellowed, as the gate rumbled once again. 'Do not falter. We hold this line until I give the order to fall back.'

'Yes, Red Wolf,' a few of them cried in reply, though some were too distracted by the gate as it shuddered before them.

Styrkar glanced up at the rampart, seeing Hereswyde and

the other archers waiting, bows already nocked. Everyone glaring at the gate.

With the next barrage, it fell…

No sooner had that great gate collapsed than the order was given. Ronan was holding his breath as a hundred horses rode at the vanguard, striking out toward the pontoons. Hooves clacked in a chorus, the platform lurching beneath them, but despite his fears the boats held the weight of those warhorses and the armoured riders they bore.

They drew closer to the fortress all too swiftly, his fellow knights riding toward the breach in the wall with zeal. Ronan couldn't turn back now even had he wanted to… and he wanted to, oh so much. Around him echoed yells of anger and fear, horses snorting at the prospect of battle. No sooner had his steed leapt from the pontoon onto dry land than they were assaulted by a conflagration of arrows.

Shafts whipped past them. Horses whinnied as they were struck. He heard the familiar sound of men screaming in pain, but by some miracle not a single one hit him. Only a few riders were ahead of him, already crossing the threshold, their steeds flattening the fallen gate. Why did he always find himself near the fucking front, where the fighting was most brutal? Why was he never near the back, giving the orders from behind the safety of a stout shield?

No time to consider that now, as he tightened his grip on his lance, and saw what awaited them within the high wooden walls.

A barricade had been erected to either side of the entrance, funnelling the riders toward a shield wall directly ahead. Their horses galloped heedless at that waiting mass of shields, and Ronan got the overwhelming sense they were being led right into a trap. It didn't matter – they were committed now, no turning back.

The first of the charging knights was met by a forest of spears, his steed turning as he vainly tried to strike at the Saxons with his lance. More riders followed in his wake, racing across the face of the shield wall, looking for a target to strike. Then it was Ronan's turn, his lance jabbing at anything that moved as he passed so many shields, those spearheads thrusting toward him as he galloped.

Ahead of him he heard a sharp cry, as the rider in front was speared. He toppled from his saddle, wooden shaft still embedded in his side as his warhorse galloped on.

As Ronan wheeled about, yet more riders entered the gates, these ones led by Ivo himself. He yelled for the men to follow as he kicked his horse into a frenzy, reining it headlong into the centre of the shield wall.

They rushed past Ronan in a wave, crashing into the defenders, buckling the centre of their wall, but immediately losing the impetus of their charge. There they stood, jabbing at shields, desperately trying to deflect the mass of spears aimed at them.

Ronan could not just sit and watch. Despite the madness of it all, he kicked his steed, tugging on the reins and driving it toward the centre of the melee. A growl issued from his throat as he joined the rest, his lance jabbing frantically, arm jolting as the shaft hit those solid wooden shields. There was a scream when he eventually managed to strike flesh, but among the mass of growling bearded faces he couldn't see who he had struck.

An arrow slammed against his shield. Another whistling past his head. A spear thrust at him, but was turned by his mail.

Ronan screamed, caught up in the violence. Consumed by the madness. Giving himself over to it.

For what else could he do?

He could smell the stench of horse, feel the billowing breath of those steeds. One of the beasts turned in a panic, almost knocking Styrkar off his feet, but he managed to keep his footing in the fast-churning earth.

The sound of hammering weapons and bellowing men was deafening as he jabbed with all his might, thrusting that spear at the enemy, hoping it might make a difference.

A shrill cry beside him, as someone was smashed in the skull by a sword. Was it Wenoth? Leofred? He had no time to find out as he was forced to raise his shield and deflect another blow. The steel slammed into the wood, splintering the shield's edge, spraying shards into his face, and he snarled in defiance.

Another yelp of pain and the man beside him collapsed, his shield falling atop him. Styrkar was quick to stand astride the corpse, plugging the gap in their shield wall, as a Frankish lance thrust down. It skewered his shield, the Frankish knight dragging it out of Styrkar's grip as his horse carried him away.

With only his spear remaining, he raised his arm and flung the weapon. It clattered off a knight's shield, enraging Styrkar further. All thought of their shield wall, of defending the line, vanished from his mind.

The Red Wolf snarled as he leapt forward, grasping a knight by his sword belt and dragging him from the saddle. He fell to the ground with a thud, as Styrkar reached for the sword at his side, but before he could pull it clear of the scabbard his victim was stabbed by a spear. Another defender jabbed his weapon at the floundering man, and his mail was punched full of holes as more spears impaled him where he lay.

With sword in hand, Styrkar surveyed the scene. The shield wall had fallen into disarray. Horses milled about the place, hooves stomping the softening earth, as the defenders of Ely did their best to hold them back. Even as he watched he saw more than one man fall, easy prey to the mounted knights. It would not be long before they were all slaughtered.

'Retreat,' he bellowed above the din. 'Back to the wall. Hear me, men of Ely.'

There were cries of acknowledgement as they began to disengage, and race back across the open ground. Styrkar yelled for retreat again, as he withdrew, sword swinging to batter an errant lance aside. One man, Alsinus, was still determined to engage, and Styrkar dragged him away, and the defenders began to rush toward their second line of defence.

As they ran, Alsinus suddenly stumbled and fell beside him. An arrow had pierced his side and he gasped in agony. Styrkar snapped the shaft, before picking Alsinus up and dragging him on. Behind he could hear the stomping sound of hooves closing in, and Alsinus seemed to weigh more and more with every step.

Just as the hooves grew deafening, he turned to face down

the rider, but he was no longer alone. Hereswyde raced to his side, drawing her bow back to her cheek before loosing, the arrow humming as it flew from the string. The charging knight was forced to tug on his rein, horse veering as he ducked the arrow. Styrkar reached for Alsinus once more, but realised the man had breathed his last.

'Are you still with me, Red Wolf?' Hereswyde shouted above the din.

'I am with you,' he replied, before they raced toward their next line of defence.

The rebels were fleeing, but the knights to the fore of the Frankish vanguard were more preoccupied with clearing up the stragglers, rather than pursuing their foe. Among them, Ivo Taillebois could be seen, sword raised as he mercilessly hacked the last few pathetic defenders to meat.

A cry went up from Wilhelm of Warenne, demanding their attention as he frantically gestured with his shield.

'Form a line,' he bellowed. 'We charge their position as one.'

'Wait,' Ronan urged, gazing along the path that would lead them directly to a low wall, behind which a few defenders crouched. 'We should be cautious. This could be—'

His voice was drowned out by the sound of stomping hooves and yelling men as they heeded Warenne's words. Ivo galloped to join them, yelling like a dog catching the scent of its quarry on the wind.

'Come,' he screamed. 'They are right there.'

Without waiting for the rest, Ivo burst forward, his steed churning the ground. In no mood to be left behind, others followed, their horses kicking up the soft earth. Ronan hung back, his uneasy feeling only deepening as those knights charged.

When the first warhorse leapt the wall there came a crunch of reeds as the ground beneath it collapsed. The horse screeched as its rider was pitched from the saddle. Unable to stop the impetus of their charge in time, other knights followed, the earth collapsing beneath their steeds.

Horses foundered beyond the wall. Ronan could hear wounded knights screaming for help, as the rebels fell upon them.

'Now,' Warenne yelled. 'Follow me now.'

He led the second rank. This time their advance was measured as they trotted closer. Ronan kept with the main group as they rode faster and faster toward the wall. Ahead of him the first rider leapt the wall, using the corpse of a dead horse to bridge the pit dug just beyond it. Men were still crawling from the deep gully, while others had already been speared by the frenzied rebels. Further on, more men were retreating, but they would not get far.

A shout went up for the knights to charge.

Pulling his sword from its sheath, Ronan kicked his horse, eyes fixed on the wall, hoping the ground beyond would not swallow him when he leapt it.

They had filled that trench with spikes, and some of the horses still squealed in agony. Their ruse had worked all right, but it would not stop the tide that was coming.

'To the ruins,' he heard Hereswyde cry, as if any of them had forgotten the plan.

They ran, no one looking back as the last barricade loomed ahead. Styrkar could hear their hot gasps of desperation now. All thoughts of valour were gone, replaced by the desperate need to survive.

Ahead, stones had been piled high to stop the advance of the warhorses. Behind them, the thunder of hooves rumbled once again as they galloped ever closer. Above, arrows flew like hail, whipping the air as the archers did their best to give the fighters as much time as they could to find shelter.

'Men of the north,' Siward bellowed from atop a stack of rocks. 'Steel yourselves. Now is the time to show these Frankish bastards some Northumbrian grit.'

Styrkar and the others flew into the maze of stones. Here the warhorses would be forced to break their ranks, making them easier to pick off, but even as he grippped his sword tighter, and mounted the fallen masonry, he could see the deluge that was falling upon them would never be stopped.

Hundreds of them had come. Warhorses snorting their hate, knights bedecked in mail, helms shining, shields braced. The rebels could never win. But winning had never been the intention. Their king was here – he had to be – and Styrkar would not spurn the chance of sealing this final victory himself.

The Red Wolf raised his blade, as those mounted knights charged...

Towers of stone stood ahead like colonnades. The knights at their head were funnelled into that labyrinth, the impetus of their charge stifled by the unexpected barrier.

Arrows rained, peppering the ground and shields and horses. Squeals of pain, the thump of falling steeds, the yell of men as their bodies were crushed beneath.

Madness upon madness, poured upon yet more madness. He was riding into the mouth of Hell itself, but for Ronan of Dol-Combourg it was too late to rely on luck to save him now. His teeth were gritted, eyes focused ahead, his only thought to kill. To vanquish these bedevilled Saxons once and for all.

A hiss. A thud. A grunt of pain and he saw Wilhelm of Warenne leaning back in his saddle. The shaft of an arrow protruded from his shoulder, and he pitched from his steed, falling to the churned earth.

No time to think about helping, as Ronan looked up, seeing a woman standing astride the relic of a shattered building, already nocking her bow again. He lifted his shield, hearing the sharp thud of impact as his horse galloped on, heedless of the danger. Ahead, riders milled among the piles of rubble, unsure of how to proceed.

Ronan reined in his horse, and it stomped its hooves, spinning as it churned up the dirt. Ivo was gone. Warenne was gone. There was no one but Dol-Combourg to lead. No one but a crippled, duplicitous coward.

'Onward,' he found himself yelling. 'Onward for the king. Onward for Christ and the crown.'

No one was more surprised than him, when those words instilled courage in the foundering knights. He was answered by cheers and growls and yells of defiance. As one, the riders reined their horses around, slamming spurs to flanks as they bolted into the maze to take the fight to the cowering Saxons.

Ronan allowed himself a small smile of satisfaction, before urging his own horse onwards. For the first time he let himself think of victory. Of glory. Of—

An axe slammed into his shield, as a bald-headed warrior appeared from nowhere. He was standing on a clump of rock, elevated enough so his blow hit Ronan dead centre.

The sword fell from his hand as he pitched backward, his steed racing on, the ground smacking him full in the back. All the wind in his lungs was slammed free, and he was left gasping for air. Hooves thundered by as the rest of the knights continued their charge, leaving him behind.

Ronan rolled onto his front, desperate to breathe. Frantically he unbuckled his helm, wrenching it from his head. He couldn't speak, couldn't see anything for the splatters of mud being flung up by a score of horses as they trampled past.

Desperately he clawed his way through the dirt, eager to escape.

Fuck victory.

Fuck glory.

All he wanted was to live.

A hand grabbed his arm, pulling him from the mire. Ronan almost fought, but he could barely suck in enough air to breathe. When he saw it was a Frankish spearman who had hauled him to his feet, and not one of the Saxon rebels, all thought of resisting left him.

The man guided him to a rock, and sat him down. His lips were moving as he spoke, but Ronan couldn't hear anything other than a sharp ringing in his ears. He glanced about, expecting to see that bald axeman coming at him, but there were only mounted knights now, galloping their horses into the ruins of Ely.

'Are you all right?' the spearman's voice echoed all too loud and all too suddenly.

Ronan focused on him, his lungs finally filling, as anger welled within. He grasped the man's spear and wrenched it from his grip.

'I will be when the last of these bastard rebels is dead.'

With that he stood, limping after the horsemen as they raced toward their final battle.

There were so many of them. Styrkar had never seen horses in such numbers, not even at Senlac when they had raced up the hill in an all-consuming wave. From his elevated position he spotted yet more entering the fort, galloping in through the fallen gates, charging alongside spearmen and archers.

They were done. There was no arguing it. No amount of rage and fighting would see them victorious. No lives would be spared. This fortress would become a tomb to them all.

'You have to run,' he shouted above the din of rampaging horses and the clashing of steel.

Hereswyde had drawn her bow, but she stopped, looking at him in disbelief. 'What did you say?'

'Take your men and go. While you still have a chance. There are boats moored beyond the western rampart. Save as many as you—'

'No. We made a pact, Red Wolf. I will die here, by your side.'

Styrkar shook his head. 'We talked of my destiny. Of my

fate. But yours is not written yet. You must go and tell the tale of this place, or the Franks will tell it for you. Do it now, Hereswyde. There is no more time to think on it.'

She lowered her bow, gazing at the force of arms now overrunning the Isle of Eels. She knew there were only two outcomes to this – death or flight.

Hereswyde looked back at him. No words to say. No platitudes. She knew his fate as well as he.

Styrkar watched for a moment as she turned, yelling to her men that they should retreat to the western palisade. That their only hope was the postern gate to freedom. They needed no further encouragement, following her as she danced across the ruins, and out of sight.

A sound of thunder rang in his ears, as the Red Wolf turned back to the fray. The smell of death was in his nose, a taste of murder on his tongue. He could sense the violence before he saw it, and it pulled him closer, drawing him like the scent of quarry.

Lips curled back from gnashing teeth and he snarled, moving faster toward the stink of battle. He ran along the ridge of ruined stone, high above the rampant horses, glaring down upon his prey, picking the right one to strike. There, a rider in a green surcoat, mail flashing bright, lance raised high.

Styrkar leapt, sword arcing down, but the rider saw him at the last moment, raising his shield as the blade struck. The impact jarred his arms before they both tumbled. The knight fell back to the ground, the Red Wolf thudding to the earth beside him. He rose quickly, as the knight fumbled his sword from its scabbard. Before he could raise it, Styrkar struck the side of his head, helm denting, mail sheared through by the blade's keen edge.

Chaos raged around him in a hot wind. Before Styrkar could find another foe, he felt the lashing pain of a spear jab at his shoulder. He growled his curse, as the sword fell from his hand, and he stumbled. Horses stamped close by, and he scrambled from the path of two galloping riders. A fallen axe lay but a few feet from him, and he scrambled forward to grasp its haft.

As he rose, another lance came stabbing at him, and he only just managed to lurch out of its way. In that moment, a gap opened amid the charging horsemen, and he saw a rider approaching beneath a leopard standard. He was flanked by knights, carrying no weapon, but his face was unmistakable. Those arrogant eyes, a sneering lip beneath his moustache.

King William had come.

The Red Wolf bellowed as he charged, axe raised. A rider galloped across his line of sight, and he swung, knocking the knight from his steed. He ignored the fallen man, desperate to reach the usurper, his only thoughts on vengeance as the storm whipped around him.

A sting of agony lanced up his leg. An arrow protruding from his thigh. He snapped off the haft, ignoring the white-hot heat as he staggered on…

Teeth rattled in his skull as he was struck in the head, but the Red Wolf managed to stay on his feet, tasting blood, vision blurring for a moment before he focused once more on the one man he had come to kill.

Only a few feet more and he would meet his prey. The king had not yet seen the Red Wolf amid the carnage. Had not yet realised his doom…

A blade lashed Styrkar's arm, and the axe grew impossibly

heavy. It fell from numb fingers, as he lost his footing, falling to his knees. The world slowed as horses milled about him. The clink of barding and stomp of hooves filled his ears, knights wheeling about him, weapons poised to strike.

Styrkar looked up and realised he was kneeling within a circle of huge rocks, relics of a dead age, and the words of the pythoness crept up on him with cold wraith-like fingers.

I see you howling amid a ring of ancient stones. A howl that echoes through the mountains for eternity.

He drew in a lungful of air, determined to fulfil that prophecy. To bellow his last defiant breath. But there was no breath left to muster. Instead, he knelt amid a sea of horses, panting and defeated. Seeing lance after lance and wondering which it would be to end his days.

'No,' he heard cry above the din.

Through the horses someone was moving closer. Though shadow was descending over his vision he could make out an armoured figure struggling nearer... a face he recognised. The last one he wanted to see here, at the end.

Ronan of Dol-Combourg looked down on him, as the Red Wolf bled on his knees. He stared back for as long as he could, blood on his lips, agony in his bones...

Then all was shadow.

42

He could see nothing through the mist. Hear nothing but a whispered promise carried on the breeze. The promise of a life unlived. One that had slipped through his grasp...

Through that white haze he heard the valravn call. It had come for him as he knew it would. Come to take him for its own, but before that it would show him that life. Reveal the future he would miss with his passing on the battlefield. Show him glories unseized, victories that would never be his.

On dark wings he was cast aloft, flying on warm winds, across seas, across verdant fields and white-tipped mountains. Soaring to a land of warring nations far to the south. And in that land the valravn suddenly became his to protect. No longer his ever-watchful nemesis, but his burden to care for. One he would have given his life to save.

And in that land over the sea he would have fought in searing heat. Would have pledged himself to new masters *who spoke many languages. Would have battled alongside a man who would become a legend, and who he would call both friend and foe...*

The screech of a hawk, and that vision of a life that would never be was shattered.

Now he was in service to an emperor. Not a king and his kingdom but a warlord who ruled many nations, and he became his trusted wolf. His protector and the guardian of his family, and in turn became part of that family, and the valravn along with him.

For a year and a day he would serve that emperor, until a new warlord arose. One who sought to cast his master down. One he would fight against in a mighty battle... and be defeated. From there, enslavement would be his prize. In shackles before a warrior woman, the warlord's bride, one who would sell him into the bondage of a new master...

Another screech, as he was pulled from the wings of the valravn, and conveyed many hundreds of leagues to the east. Pressed into service once more, but this time on pain of death in an unfamiliar land with unfamiliar customs.

Here he would be set to guard another family, an adviser to kings, and he would walk many miles across the desert to see them safe from killers. Killers without faces, who might strike from the shadows. Who might give their lives in the service of death itself, and yet he would prevail.

And so, in his victory he would be offered freedom. And the valravn would return after seeking him for many years. It would bargain and lie and offer itself to seal his freedom, until a deal would be struck. One that would see him fight a final battle, and when it was won, he would fly once more on raven's wings, returning to the side of his emperor.

But peace would be short-lived. An armada would rise to destroy his master, and he would set sail to face those ships with an old friend whose face he could not see.

He would hear of Ulf, his dead master's boy, imprisoned in a far-off land. And he would enter Hel to free that boy, now a man, and in time they would both flee to a fortress city under siege.

And years after, when they had escaped. When that long-elusive peace seemed so close, he would be called back to the shores of England. Where old friends and old enemies dwelt. And there he would fight. And there he would die, bellowing his last upon a mountaintop surrounded by stone...

A hawk screeched...

Styrkar opened his eyes.

The world was spinning, and he fought to focus. He was sure he was about to fall, but he quickly realised he was already sitting on a floor, hard and cold, a stone pillar at his back.

Somewhere a bell jangled.

He tried to raise his arms, but his wrists were manacled to chains looped around the pillar behind him. Chains that felt so heavy, weighing him down, leaching all the strength from his limbs.

A cool breeze blew in from an open arch and made him shiver.

A voice spoke nearby in no language he could understand.

He felt sick, but swallowed it down, as gradually the spinning slowed and he could focus once more. There was a man not too far away with his back turned. Beside him rested a falcon upon its perch. Tenderly, the man fed it a sliver of chicken, the hooded bird snapping at the morsel before gobbling it down. Then a sliver of chicken for the falconer, the two sharing their meal like old friends.

Someone spoke again in that alien tongue, but Styrkar couldn't see where they were in the shadowy confines of the cold chamber. The man beside his falcon turned, and Styrkar felt like puking all over again.

The king, the usurper, the Bastard Duke, turned to look at him. It was a casual glance of disregard. One you might give while passing a stallholder selling wares of no particular value.

Styrkar strained against his bonds once more, the chains rattling, holding him fast. He was weak and he knew it. Even had he not been chained he doubted he would have been able to fight. His arm was numb, blood crusted in rivulets down to his elbow. His hair was likewise matted with blood. The shaft of an arrow still protruding from his thigh.

King William spoke, looking directly at him as though he might understand. This king, this conqueror, who had not even bothered to learn the language of the people he now ruled.

Before Styrkar could spit his defiance from parched lips, a shadow fell over him. He looked up, knowing who it would be before he took in those familiar features, regarding him with feigned concern.

'You have caused us quite the dilemma,' Ronan said. 'The king is at a loss. We have simply no idea what to do with you. He has made a promise, you see. And to a man of the cloth, of all people. A promise that he would spare the rebels of Ely... all but the ringleaders, that is. They are to be punished. Maimed, obviously. Made eyeless, or handless, or something equally gruesome – I forget the details. But you? What to do with you? Are you a ringleader, or just a hapless follower? I never quite know with you.'

Styrkar glared back, with all the fire he could muster. They both knew what he deserved. That an eye or an ear or a hand would never be enough to pay back the insult he had dealt the king over the years. Only death would satisfy that debt.

Ronan knelt down, leaning closer. 'I am not even sure the king knows who he has in chains,' he whispered. 'The elusive Red Wolf. Scourge of the Franks. Shield Breaker. Witch Killer. I mean, if he did know then surely it would be, er...' He gestured with the flat of his hand as though cutting his own wrist. 'Personally, I think—'

'Just fucking kill me,' Styrkar croaked.

Ronan looked almost offended. 'What?'

'I have already heard enough of your horseshit blabber. I am in chains, bleeding my last. What does it matter what the king believes? I am dead anyway.'

Ronan struggled to stand again, unsteady on his crippled leg. 'You're not playing the game, my old friend.'

'I am done with games. I am done with—'

'No. That is not how this works. We have both walked a long road to get to this moment. Now you are here, and I am here, and you will beg me for your life. Beg me to tell you where I have hidden your daughter. Beg me—'

'Go to Hel.'

Ronan narrowed his eyes, head jerking forward as he

prepared to spit something at Styrkar, but he stopped when the king spoke again. William gestured at Styrkar, looking annoyed for a moment before turning his attentions back to his falcon.

'Your king loses patience,' Styrkar taunted.

'He is not the only one,' Ronan hissed in reply. 'You will die, Red Wolf, if that is what you yearn for. But unless you beg me, I will travel to the priory where I hid your daughter. I will take her from that place of safety, and I will cut her little throat.'

There was grit in his eyes, but it wavered. His face showed steel, but it was a mask.

'You will not. It's not in you. Not anymore.'

Ronan's lip quivered as he fought for the words. 'Then… I will send someone to do it. I have that power now. I have the will to—'

'No, you don't. You never had the will. Not really. All the things you've done, all those wicked deeds committed, were done to get you where you are.' He gestured toward the king, still enamoured of his falcon. 'Beside that man over there. Now you have everything you want, apart from my submission. And you will never have that. So, tell your king what you must, but whatever you do, make sure you kill me. Because if I am set free…' he leaned as close as he could, straining on those chains '…I will kill you all.'

His last words echoed through the chamber, startling the falcon so much it flapped its wings in desperation to take flight. King William turned, regarding them in confusion before speaking more words in the Frankish language.

'Does your king want to know what I have to say?'

Styrkar asked Ronan, who was unsure how to proceed. 'You should tell him.'

Ronan shook his head. 'No, he gets the idea. He only asks why you, of all people, hate him so much when all he wishes to do is rule in peace.'

Styrkar stared at the king, who looked back with no emotion. When he spoke, he knew the king would not understand his words, but he had to speak them anyway. Had to unburden himself one last time before the end.

'Because you took everything from me. My master. My lover. My child. You stole everything from this land, murdered its people, desecrated its sacred places. All for a crown that was never yours to claim.'

The king stared for a moment, before looking at Ronan as though he might want him to translate. Before he could, William turned, unhitching his falcon from its perch, and made his way through the arch as though he didn't care after all.

'I offered you a chance,' Ronan said quietly, when they were finally alone. 'Remember that.'

Then he followed his king, leaving Styrkar chained, with nothing but the cold.

43

They had wasted little time rounding up the ringleaders. How his fellow knights could discern between the real agitators, and those commoners caught up in the rebellion, Ronan had no idea, but nevertheless the maiming had already begun. The king was true to his word, and already scores of peasants had been set free to return to their farms or hovels or wherever they dwelt in the fenlands. Those important enough had also been granted clemency – Morcar already resided in his prison, with the bishop Ethelwin and Siward Barn not far behind him. For the rest, there remained only a fate worse than death.

A score of men were in chains, kneeling at the edge of the fortress courtyard. This place they had taken such pains to defend now acting as their gaol. They were beaten, wounded, malnourished. Some might have said that was punishment enough, but not so the king. These men would serve to send a message. An example to all who might think of sparking the flames of rebellion once more, just as examples had been made again and again over the past years of strife. Why anyone thought it would be different this time, Ronan had no idea, but the king was nothing if not persistent.

In the centre of the mud-strewn space a rock had been placed and one of the prisoners lashed to it, his arm stretched across the flat surface by a rope. Blood covered the stone, and the men chained around it had all seen what was to be their fate. But subdued as they were, beaten as they were, they made no noises of lamentation. No one begged for mercy or deliverance. All that remained was grim acceptance, and a little part of Ronan could only admire them for that.

'Where is your rebel lord, Hereward?' asked Ivo Taillebois.

How he had survived the battle, Ronan had no idea. The last he'd seen, the man's horse had been pitched into a pit full of wooden spikes. Heedless of the peril, Ivo had managed to crawl out of it unscathed. Or perhaps slither, as snakes were wont to do. Despite surviving almost certain death, his appetite for more cruelty and slaughter had not been abated. In fact, it appeared it was only piqued.

'Tell me where he is, and you will be freed,' Ivo assured his prisoner.

The man lashed to the rock looked in no mood to offer any assistance, even if he did know where the elusive Hereward had gone. 'Fuck off.'

Ivo let out a despondent sigh, stepping back from the stone lest he be spattered, and signalling to the knight standing by with his axe. Chop and thud and sever and scream. A sequence that they had been repeating all morning. Ronan should have been hardened to it by now, but the shrill noise still went right through him like a winter wind.

A tourniquet was fastened around the whimpering man's wrist before his foot was bound and stretched across the rock. No time for him to gather his wits before Ivo leaned in close and asked again, 'Where is Hereward?'

Before Ronan could listen to the man's defiant answer, a slight figure joined him at the edge of the courtyard. Giselbert smiled politely as he witnessed the ordeal before them. There was some discomfort in his eyes, as though he would rather have been anywhere else, but he endured it nonetheless, as the axe came down once more and the screaming started all over again.

'Good to see you looking so well, Dol-Combourg,' he said when the noise had subsided slightly. 'This has been a long ordeal. God has truly been looking down on us.'

His use of the word 'us' was a little rich since Giselbert had not been involved in any of the actual fighting. 'Not all of us, my friend. I saw poor Wilhelm unhorsed right in front of me as we rode toward the Saxon defences. An arrow right through his mail.'

Giselbert's expression brightened a little. 'You'll be pleased to learn that Wilhelm of Warenne survived his wound. He is weak but alive.'

Ronan wasn't sure if that was good news or not. 'How fortunate for him.'

'Fortune smiles on us all. Now this last rebellion has finally been quelled we can take time to consolidate our holdings and build our castles. Before we look to expansion beyond the borders of England.'

Though Ronan could never admit it, the prospect was not one he relished. 'So, it does not end here.'

Giselbert offered a knowing smile. 'As you are aware, Dol-Combourg, our king is an ambitious man. He has already subdued Alba to the north. Éire is next. Then who knows?'

A familiar sense of dread began to tighten in Ronan's gut, squeezing bile up into his throat, which he quickly swallowed down. 'So this is not the end. There will be more battles, more rebellions. More murder, more executions.'

As though to punctuate his thoughts there resounded another thud, followed by its requisite scream.

'That is why we are here,' Giselbert said, gesturing to the grim spectacle in front of them, as though Ronan hadn't noticed. 'To conquer. To subjugate. And, by the will of God, reap the rewards.'

Ronan turned away from the bloody stone, as another tourniquet was tightened around another severed limb. 'Yes. And some of us are still waiting patiently for those rewards to arrive.'

Giselbert clapped a hand to Ronan's shoulder. 'It won't be long, my friend. I am sure of it.'

With that he made his way from the courtyard as the moaning and bleeding continued. Ronan found it hard to share in his optimism. It had been five long years since he had come to these shores on the promise of wealth and status. In that time he had certainly risen, but also fallen, in more ways than one. Now, at the king's side, it appeared he had almost reached the summit, but still...

A jangle of chains from across the open courtyard, as men in mail dragged a prisoner out into the open. Ronan almost didn't recognise Styrkar, his head bowed, hair bloodied and matted, limbs hanging limp as he was dragged bodily toward where the other prisoners awaited their mutilation.

It should have been easy for him to let this happen. Even to stay and witness the act. Ronan had been plagued for years by the Red Wolf. This should have been the final triumph. So why did it feel so empty?

Styrkar was beaten. Was that not humiliation enough? Add to that the fact Ronan had been his prisoner not so many weeks ago, and he had been set free. Offered mercy by the one man with more reason than any to offer him none.

As they dragged the sorry prisoner past, Ronan held up a hand to stop one of the knights. 'What is that man's fate?'

The knight looked confused, as though the answer were obvious. 'He's one of the ringleaders. His fate is the same as the rest – hands, feet and eyes.'

They had dumped Styrkar at the edge of the courtyard, as the man in the centre was parted from his eyes with a shrill yell of agony. It was an ignoble fate for anyone. To live out his sorry life relying on others. Begging for charity, while wallowing in his own shit. An unfitting fate indeed for the Red Wolf.

'No,' Ronan said. 'He is a commoner of no import. Set him free with the others.'

The knight's brow creased in confusion. 'A commoner?' He gestured to where Styrkar sat, leaning against the ruined wall. Even battered and beaten, he was still a specimen to behold. 'Look at him. He's at least—'

'I said he's a commoner,' Ronan interrupted. 'Would you argue with the king over it?'

'No… but I—'

'Then don't fucking argue with me. Unchain him and let him go.'

The knight looked as though he might try and protest further, but instead he shrugged. 'All right, if that is the king's will. He'll soon be dead of his wounds anyway. Killing him might be a mercy, but…'

With that he approached the other knights, conversing briefly before they did as they were bid and cast off Styrkar's chains. It took two of them to lift him and carry him toward the ruin of the fortress gate.

All the while, Ronan watched from the shadow, in no mood to be seen. He was not even sure he had done the right thing. The Red Wolf had vowed to kill them all. It wouldn't be out of character for him to return, healed and ferocious as ever to carry out his promise. Living up to his legend.

Ronan almost laughed at that. There were no legends here. Only condemned men. Only beaten cripples. Only misery.

44

He staggered on into the marsh, through shallows to his ankle and deeps up to his waist. Any moment he expected the fenlands to claim him, to suck him down to their depths forever, but for some reason they spared him that fate. Allowing him to wander aimless, where so many others had perished.

He had no idea why the Franks had let him go. Perhaps he looked too pitiful for them to bother with. Too pathetic even to face an axe. Styrkar did not think on it as he wandered on. It did not mean the gods were smiling on him. They could just as easily have spared him one grim fate just so he could face one a hundred times grimmer. That was if his wounds didn't finish him first.

The shaft of the arrow still protruded an inch from his thigh, searing pain shooting into his bones with every laboured step. With the rank waters he was wading through it would not be long before it became infected. He should have cut it free by now, but with no blade to hand the task was beyond him.

His head still throbbed, though the bleeding in his scalp had stopped, his hair dry and matted and crusted to his face. The slash in his arm had been bound well enough, but he was sure he could smell its stink, most likely rotten already. Styrkar didn't have long, no matter what happened.

Just as he thought on that, on whether it might be best for him to find some spot of dry land among the marsh and lie down for his final rest, he spied life through the morning mist. A town stood up ahead, thatched roofs just visible, torchlight winking as someone led pigs along the road.

Styrkar focused as hard as he could on those dwellings, the ground beneath him hardening, marsh giving way to a stone-laid path that wound right through the centre of the town. His breathing grew heavier, step after step slowing, his body cheating him of one last reprieve. He would not make it.

When he heard the tinkle of a river nearby, it was all he could do to turn his head and face it. The water flowed by gently, the bank thick with grass that looked so soft he could not resist stumbling from the road and sitting himself down.

So close to that town. To someone who might have helped.

It didn't matter now.

As he sat and listened to the river he was struck by an ancient memory. Of when he had sat by a river with his king, his master... his father. That day he had talked with Harold as an equal, not as a slave. He had been set free and presented a gift.

Styrkar raised his hand to his neck to touch the iron torc with its wolf heads. It was not there, and he could not remember when last he had worn it. Had he lost it at Yorke when the bridge had cast him into the icy waters of the river? Had it been in a battle since, in the cold north or on the wall of Ely?

It didn't matter anymore. The thing was just a memory. As everything was a memory, soon to be nought but dust.

A voice close by, followed by laughter. At first he ignored it, but as those voices drew closer he recognised them as foreign. He should have moved, or at least tried to hide himself, but he no longer had the desire nor the strength to flee.

The clop of hooves on the road came ever nearer, until they stopped. Styrkar turned his head, seeing two riders in jerkins rather than mail. Their heads were uncovered, hair shorn in the style of Frankish knights. Both regarded him suspiciously, as they shared wary words.

One of them jerked his head up, in case Styrkar was in any doubt who they were talking to. 'You. Where you come from?'

At least this one had taken the effort to learn a few words of the country he had come to sully. Commendable, but not so much that Styrkar would offer a reply.

The knight turned to his fellow and they exchanged a bemused look. Then they argued in their sing-song language, one of them obviously keen to be on his way, where the other was not satisfied.

He turned back to Styrkar, climbing down from his horse and moving closer before gesturing south across the marshland. 'The fort? You are rebel?'

Again Styrkar offered no answer, which only served to anger the knight. He slowly drew his blade, caring nothing for Styrkar's wounds or his sorry visage, and prodded him with it. As he did so, the knight on the horse exclaimed something in protest, keen to be off, but the other would hear nothing of it.

'Up. On your feet, rebel.'

A quick end might have been a good one, all told. It was peaceful here, after all. But there was enough of the Red Wolf still alive in Styrkar to stir his ire. Perhaps enough for him to howl his fury one more time.

Gingerly, he struggled to his feet, wincing at the pain in his leg as he tried to balance on the riverbank. He knew he was beaten already, but it still could not quell one final curse.

'I will kill you,' he growled. 'Weapon or none.'

At first the knight glared, his anger stoked, but then the side of his mouth twitched into a smile. He sniggered, looking to the one on the horse, who seemed much less amused by Styrkar's defiance. That snigger turned to laugh, then to bellow, as he sounded out his mirth.

Then the mirth was gone, replaced by dead-eyed certainty. A look of murder Styrkar had seen time and again, all across these isles. The knight raised his sword to strike.

A snake hiss whispered in the air, before stopping dead with a thud. An arrow appeared beneath the swordsman's arm, through his rib. He froze, as the one still on his horse fumbled for the sword at his side.

Another hiss. And another. More arrows – one in the rider's neck, one in his chest. He slid from his saddle, weapon still in its scabbard. The one holding his sword aloft slowly sank to his knees, staring at Styrkar all the while, his look of murder replaced by despair.

From out of the nearby scrub came men with bows. As they drew nearer, Styrkar recognised them as Lightfoot and Winter. Hogor the cook was with them too, gripping a knife he'd only ever used for filleting. He ran up beside the kneeling knight and opened his throat as though butchering swine. Styrkar barely noticed the gush of blood across the knight's jerkin as he keeled over into the long grass.

The three men stared at him, unsure of what to say, to do. It took Hereswyde to appear and gesture at them swiftly, before they grabbed the warhorses, and Hogor dragged the second corpse from the path and onto the riverbank.

'I did not think I would see you again,' Hereswyde said.

Styrkar wanted to answer her, but he could think of no words. He would have embraced her, but he had not the strength. Instead, he staggered forward, and she grabbed him, holding him up.

'Get him on a horse,' she said.

Winter and Lightfoot took hold of Styrkar and eased him gently into a saddle, before Hereswyde climbed up behind him. She took the reins, guiding the steed from the path and into the marsh as the others followed.

The day flowed by in a haze as Styrkar drifted in and out of consciousness. Their path took them through tall reeds and sparse copses. Skirting settlements and fording shallows, until eventually they reached a camp deep in a patch of woodland. The sun was setting as Hogor and Winter helped Styrkar down from the horse and laid him beside a tree.

Quickly a fire was lit, and Hereswyde brought beer to wet his parched lips. He could see Hogor was kneeling by the fire, heating his knife in the flames, as Lightfoot began to clean the wound on Styrkar's scalp.

'Why are you not leagues from here?' Styrkar asked.

'I was waiting to see if there were any other survivors,' she said as she unbandaged his wounded arm. 'But it seems most have already fled.'

Hogor approached and knelt down, looking nervous at what had to be done. 'I am sorry, Styrkar,' the cook whispered.

Styrkar nodded for him to proceed. Winter and Hereswyde gripped each of his arms as he gritted his teeth. Hogor cut swiftly, digging the knife into the flesh of his thigh to help remove the arrow shaft. Despite his quick work, Styrkar growled in his throat, feeling dizziness almost take him, but he managed to cling to consciousness as the arrow was removed. Lightfoot and Hogor then worked to bind his arm and thigh, as Hereswyde offered him more beer, which he gratefully accepted.

'We will find more of our people eventually,' she said, as he gasped in relief at his thirst being quenched. 'You are welcome to join us.'

She looked determined, as though the weeks of suffering and eventual defeat had never happened. Styrkar took her arm, squeezing it with all the strength he could.

'It is done. I am done. No more, Hereswyde.'

She shook her head. 'I don't believe that's true. I don't believe the Red Wolf would just give in.'

'The Red Wolf is dead. It is over – you must understand that.'

He could see the determination in her eyes but it was wavering. She looked to the others, but it was obvious they did not share her zeal, and none of them could hold her gaze. A tear welled in her eyes and she quickly wiped it away.

'I do understand. But... what now?'

'For you? Perhaps it is time to pursue that life you did not lead. For me, there is only one thing I have left to do. But I will need your help to do it.'

'Anything,' she said, taking his hand and squeezing tight.

'I need you to find me a ship and a crew willing to sail far from these shores. Have it waiting at the port where the Black River meets the sea. Give me... ten days. If I do not come by then, I am not coming at all.'

She nodded. 'I can do that. But you will need to rest first, before you do whatever it is you have to do.'

Styrkar thought about standing, to prove he was well enough to face any task. Thinking better of it, he nodded his agreement.

'Perhaps you're right. This can wait until morning, at least.'

He closed his eyes, and for the first time in so long, sleep came easily.

45

The doors to the hall had been flung wide, despite the cold. Fires burned as knights danced and skipped with more abandon than Ronan had never witnessed before. The surrounding barrack huts echoed with laughter as men divvied up the spoils and shared their mead, and the meat from a half dozen spitted pigs.

A knight pranced by holding a huge golden crucifix as though it were his dance partner. He was followed by another who wore an ornate golden helm upon his head. Others paraded the treasures and relics they had pillaged from Ely, showing little in the way of respect for their heritage. Ronan was only glad William was not here to see this, how his honoured knights had devolved to drunken sots, but he had returned south to deal with other matters of kingship.

For Ronan there was no such merriment. He watched from the periphery, as he always did. Feeling no part of this group. He had ridden with them, all right. Shed blood with them. Shared their victory. But even now, after all he had done with these men, he still felt as though he was not one of them. There was no shared kinship. No feeling of brotherhood. Just a strange emptiness.

'You should be joyous,' said a familiar voice, before the ugly face of Ivo Taillebois loomed from the darkness. 'Have a drink, Dol-Combourg. We won.'

Ronan raised a hand to refuse the proffered bottle of mead. 'We did win. This time. And so we celebrate, but what then? You get to return to your estates and servants. And I...'

Ivo slapped him hard in the shoulder. 'And you get to stand beside our king as his most trusted retainer. Most of these men would give their eye teeth for such an honour. Is it not good enough for you?'

Ronan looked out at those frolicking knights, and wondered how true it was that they would have desired to change places with him. 'It will have to be.'

'Your problem, Dol-Combourg, is that you're not belligerent enough. Did you stake your claim on any of Ely's treasures? No. And that's the thing – you just refuse to seize what is yours by right. Because if you don't seize it, someone else will.'

'I tried that once... taking what's mine.' Ronan thought back to the few days he had spent with Gisela and her child. Days when he had allowed himself to believe his life could be different. 'It didn't work out too well.'

Ivo rolled his eyes in frustration. 'So what will you do? Mope like a lovesick maid? We are the victors, and now we claim the spoils. You think just because you have not been handed a castle and half the county that somehow the king has robbed you of what is yours by right? That you are not valued?' He leaned in closer, eyes narrowing. 'If you wish to be valued then you must either be a favoured son or a lord. You, Dol-Combourg, are neither. So learn to live with it, or dig yourself a deep hole and bury yourself within.'

Ronan was starting to wish he'd accepted that drink. 'As ever, Ivo, our conversation has been most invigorating.'

'You know what's invigorating? Drinking and whoring. Perhaps you should try it – you could well be dead tomorrow.'

With that he walked off into the dark, to join the rest of the revellers. Ronan couldn't help but feel relieved to see the back of him, but there was also a pang of envy left in Ivo's wake. That man might well have been a cruel simpleton, and simple in his cruelty, but he lived life to the full. Perhaps that was what Ronan was missing.

'My lord?' He turned to see a squire approaching. 'My lord Ronan?'

What now? Did someone's arse need wiping? Maybe he was required to fetch more ale for the real knights.

'Yes, what is it?'

The boy gestured up to the keep looming on its hillock. 'Lord Giselbert wishes to speak with you.'

Ronan couldn't keep in his despondent sigh. 'Of course he does.'

Leaving the squire behind, he made his way across the bailey to the flying bridge. Up and up he limped, over the bridge and into the keep and up those torturous stairs. At the door to the main chamber he paused for a moment to catch his breath before knocking. Giselbert answered immediately, bidding him enter, and Ronan opened the door, half expecting to see the man taking a bath exactly where the king had been some weeks before.

No bath this time. Only a table, and a single chair upon which Giselbert sat, poring over parchments by candlelight. The last time Ronan had seen a sight like this they had been in Yorke. It felt like they were a long way from Yorke now.

'Thank you for coming,' Giselbert said immediately, without making Ronan wait a moment more than he had to. A pleasant surprise, all told.

'What can I do for you, Lord Giselbert? Only I hope it's nothing too taxing – there is apparently mead to drink, and those spitted pigs won't eat themselves.'

Giselbert said nothing, instead plucking a sealed scroll from the table and offering it.

Ronan took the scroll with trepidation. 'More orders I take it?'

'Why don't you open it and find out.' Giselbert sat back, with an odd look of satisfaction on his face that did nothing to ease Ronan's nerves.

He looked down at the scroll, seeing the wax seal upon it. The king's seal: a knight riding atop his horse, surrounded by the words, *By this seal recognise William, Chief of the Normans.*

The wax broke crisply, and he unrolled the vellum. Within, the words filled the entire scroll from top to bottom, written by a scribe no doubt, since the king could neither read nor write. Ronan scanned the contents. Then he read them again, more carefully. Then once more, just to make sure he wasn't imagining any of it.

'Well?' asked Giselbert, before Ronan could read the letter a fourth time. 'Is it what you had hoped?'

'The king...' His hands were shaking at the news. News he could not quite believe. 'The king has pledged me both land and title. With sale and soke, and toll and team.' Ronan couldn't take his eyes off the cross at the bottom of the script – the sign-manual of the king himself. 'This is...'

'Everything you asked for, and more,' Giselbert replied with a knowing smile. 'Congratulations. Now you are a name of note, lord of an estate, and will benefit from the power it brings you.'

'I... I don't know what to say.'

Giselbert sat back in his seat, smiling as though he had just won a bet. 'I'm sure you'll think of something, sooner or later. You always do.'

'Thank you, Giselbert.'

He shrugged. 'Don't thank me. Thank the king. Now, I suggest you go and enjoy yourself with the rest of the men. And perhaps don't mention what you've just been granted. I doubt they'll be pleased with a few looted trinkets when they find out what the king has given you for your loyalty.'

Ronan nodded his agreement and rolled the scroll up tight before securing it within his jerkin. A last nod of appreciation to Giselbert, and he left the keep, limped his way down the ramp and across the bailey. All the while his mind roiled with thoughts of a lordly manor. Of serfs, and land across which he could ride. Land he owned, that no one but the king himself might take away.

This time when he returned to the revelling knights, he did not refuse to join in. And as he drank his fill of mead, and ate sweet white meat from a spit, he found himself laughing for the first time since... he could not remember.

So much mead, so much meat, and Ronan was full in

the belly and light in the head. He was overwhelmed by the weight of it all, this reward he had waited so long for, and as the night drew on he eventually wished for solitude, so he could toast those he had lost along the way.

With the air growing crisper, he wrapped a cloak about his shoulders and carried his cup out through the open gates of the fort. The moon lit up the surrounding marshes, the hills rolling off to the west, the river winding south. Though his foot ached he still stood, gazing up at the moon before he raised his cup.

'If you are up there, Aldus, my old friend... we did it.'

The crack of a twig behind him, but he was too slow to turn, too drunk to realise the danger until that giant shadow fell upon him. He staggered, dropping his cup as someone grabbed him about the neck. Ronan grasped the thick arms corded with muscle, first feeling dread, but then hope as he felt his assailant weaken slightly.

Then a hand was clapped to his mouth to stifle any cry for help.

A foot kicked his crippled leg, and he screamed in pain, but it was a muted sound that would not be heard amid the singing and laughing still resounding from the fort. The arm grew tighter about his neck, the hand releasing its grip on his mouth.

He opened it to scream, to beg, to barter...

Metal cracked his skull so hard, none of that mattered anymore.

46

Travelling northwards again, despite the great pains he had suffered to avoid it. All his plans, all his schemes, but it seemed there was just no getting away from fate. Now he rode ever further into the bleak chill of the countryside, and he could think of no way back.

Ronan's head was pounding, his hands bound tight in front of him, gripping the reins of the horse Styrkar had thrust him upon. They had ridden all night and all day, their steeds plodding on side by side, and now the road's end was within reach. Of course, his travelling companion had remained mute for the entirety of the journey after commanding Ronan to take him to his daughter. At first the silence had been a blessing, but now panic was starting to set in. The prospect of this all coming to a sudden stop, and then there would be no more use for Ronan of Dol-Combourg. He knew with grim certainty what that would mean.

'You look almost ready to drop,' Ronan said, as

conversationally as he could manage, with the gut-wrenching fear that clutched at him. 'Perhaps it might be a good idea to rest awhile?'

No answer. But of course, no answer.

Styrkar's arm and leg had been bandaged, the arrow removed from his thigh. His hair had been tied back at least, but there was still congealed blood visible on his scalp. He was pale, dark shadows shrouding his eyes. The mighty Red Wolf looked just about ready to fall from his saddle.

'I'm sure there is a village not far from here. Maybe we should go there. Take advantage of their friendly northern hospitality. Eat a meal, perhaps? Wash the stink of the road away?'

Nothing. Not so much as an acknowledgement he had even heard. Ronan glanced back over his shoulder, wondering how far he might get if he grasped the reins and turned the horse. Looking back, he saw the axe at Styrkar's side. It looked sharp. Sharp enough to stop him thinking about escape... at least right now.

'I don't suppose we could pause our journey for just a while. At least long enough for me to relieve myself?'

No answer to that either.

'Why don't you just piss in your saddle,' Ronan continued, mimicking Styrkar's accent and gruff tone. If the hulking Dane thought it an insult, he made no issue of it.

Before he could carry on with his taunting, he spied another traveller on the road ahead. A horse-drawn cart was trundling its way toward them, drawing relentlessly nearer. Upon the cart's single seat sat an old, balding man, his grey beard drooping down to his chest.

Ronan felt a sudden flutter of hope. Perhaps this might

be his saviour. This old man could carry word of his capture to Frankish ears and he would be saved. Thank the Lord for small mercies.

When they reached one another, the old man tugged on his reins, halting the sorry-looking nag that pulled his even sorrier-looking cart. Styrkar halted his horse, and Ronan was forced to do the same.

'Good day to you,' the old man said, touching a finger to his forehead, where years before he might have tugged at a forelock when he had one.

'And to you,' Styrkar replied.

Ronan leaned closer to him. 'So it does speak,' he whispered.

'Where you bound for?' the old man asked, ignoring Ronan altogether.

'A long way from here,' came the gruff reply.

The old man nodded knowingly, as if that was where he was heading too. 'I don't blame you, friend. Not after what's been done to this country. After what they done.'

'All right, old man,' Ronan said. 'Enough of this aimless chatter. I can offer you a rich reward if you head to the nearest fort and tell them I am held prisoner. This man wishes me ill. You will find favour with the king himself if you aid me.' The old man didn't answer, nor even look in Ronan's direction. 'There is no need to be afraid. This red-haired beast might look fierce, but he will not harm an innocent man. My name is Ronan of Dol-Combourg, and I am—'

'Anyway,' the old man said loudly, 'you have a safe and pleasant journey.'

'And you,' Styrkar said, as the old man slapped his reins to the horse's flank, and his cart trundled on.

Abandoned. But what had he expected? That he would

get any help from the people of these lands? After all he and his countrymen had done to the place, especially in the north, he was lucky that old man hadn't spat in his face.

On they rode, and as the day wore on, so Ronan's dread grew. As long as the road lay ahead of them he was useful, and he would live. As soon as it ran out...

'I feel it my duty to warn you,' he said, trying to divert his thoughts from a bloody demise, 'the nuns at the priory we are heading to are not the most welcoming. I am not entirely sure they will be willing to simply hand over a child to some dishevelled Dane on a whim.'

If Styrkar had any opinion on that he did not share it. Whatever he had planned, he certainly didn't intend to reveal it to Ronan. He was left to sit and endure his thoughts once more, consoling himself that at least this time as he trod this road it was not in a blizzard. In fact it might almost have been considered pleasant, had it not been for the sense of impending doom.

'You know, it is nowhere near as cold as the last time I made this journey,' he said, no longer caring if Styrkar was listening or not. 'Though I have to say, the company is much different. Back then I rode with a man named Mainard. You might have liked him, but I am afraid he met with an untimely end. What was it that happened to him? Oh yes, I remember now... you cut his head off while he was taking a bath.'

'Is that the place?' Styrkar said, as though he hadn't heard a word.

Ronan peered ahead, seeing the slate roof of the priory peaking above the hilltop. 'It is indeed. The Priory of Bigger, or Begger. Some saint or other – I forget which. And your daughter lies within, safe and sound, just as I said.'

Styrkar nudged his horse into a trot, and Ronan's followed suit. The priory loomed ahead as they skirted the hill, and the closer they got the more panic began to set in.

'Fact is, I have kept my end of this arrangement. You don't need me anymore, so it might be best for us to part ways.'

No answer, but then there was no way it was ever going to be so easy.

The horses veered from the road as they reached the gate to the priory's courtyard. Hooves clopped on cobbles until they were almost at the front door. Styrkar looked across, his unspoken order for Ronan to dismount, no doubt.

As he struggled from the saddle, wincing as his leg touched the ground, Ronan heard the noisy caw of a bird. Looking up, he saw a raven perched on the porch roof. Styrkar stared at the creature with an expression Ronan found impossible to read. Was it hate? Fear? Either way, the Dane dragged his eyes away, and slid down from the saddle.

'You first,' he ordered, gesturing to the front door.

'Of course,' Ronan replied graciously.

This time, when he pushed the rotten door, it opened with a creaking sigh. Crossing the threshold, he said a silent prayer to whoever was the saint of this place, that the prioress had heeded his words the last time he was here, and the child he had left behind was safe and sound.

He offered the valravn one last glance, before following Ronan inside. The corridor within smelled stale and dank. A wholly inappropriate place to raise a child, but then so was this entire land.

Noises echoed from deeper within. Women spoke in what could only be the language of priests. Their words were parroted back to them in a chorus of children's voices. He didn't have to follow Ronan for long before they crossed paths with one of the nuns of this place.

She stopped ahead of them, staring wide-eyed for a moment, before rushing off into the depths of the priory. When they reached the end of the corridor, Ronan stopped.

'Maybe we should wait here. I'm sure they won't be—'

A woman appeared in an archway, taller and older than the first. She glared at Ronan with recognition, her eyes showing the contempt of someone who'd had the misfortune of meeting him before.

'You,' she breathed.

He smiled back. 'Yes, me. And a friend.' He gestured to Styrkar. 'We have come to look in on the infant I delivered into your care. And for both our sakes, yours and mine, I hope she is well.'

The woman looked confused. 'She is. But what—'

Styrkar stepped forward, and the woman fell silent. 'My name is Styrkar. I am the child's father, and I have come to claim her.'

The nun looked closely at him, as though searching for something, and it didn't take her long to find. 'Yes... I see. I am the prioress Beyhilde, and it has been my duty to care for the girl these past years. But... I cannot simply hand her over to you. Not unless I can be sure she will be protected, and raised to know the word of the Lord.'

Ronan offered a sideways glance. 'I tried to warn you this would be difficult.'

'Do you doubt that the child is mine?' Styrkar asked, ignoring him.

Beyhilde looked for a moment as though she might try to take issue with his claim of fatherhood, but thought better of it. 'No. That much is obvious.'

'Then will you deny my right as a father? To protect her? To raise her as I see fit?'

The prioress narrowed her eyes, searching for something. Perhaps an excuse to say no. Perhaps a reason to say yes.

'Sister Truda,' she called out. A girl came scurrying through the arch, head bowed. 'Fetch Adney.'

As Truda rushed off into the depths of the stone building, Ronan stepped closer to Styrkar. 'Look, I have kept my side of the bargain. Now would be a good time for me to leave. I have no doubt this will be an emotional reunion for you, and I—'

'Reunion?' Styrkar said, feeling the wolf spark to life inside, and leashing it. Telling himself this was not a time for anger. Not yet. 'This is not a reunion. I have never laid eyes on my daughter before. That was a blessing you stole from me.'

Ronan took a step back as the nun Truda returned, carrying a child in her arms. She placed the little girl down before him, and Styrkar knelt, looking into a pair of piercing blue eyes that mirrored his own, though her hair was covered by a wimple of white.

'This is Adney,' said the prioress.

Styrkar gently reached out and removed the wimple from the girl's head. A mass of thick red curls fell about her shoulders as he took in the sight of her. Eyes blue like the winter sky, hair red as flame. There was no doubting that she belonged to him... and he to her.

'Hello, child,' he said, and she looked back at him with no fear. 'I am your father. I have come to take you home.'

He stood, turning to the nun, Truda. 'Take her outside and wait there for me.'

The woman obeyed, picking up his daughter and making her way toward the courtyard. Styrkar turned to regard Ronan, who had shrunk back to the shadows, no doubt hoping they would conceal him. Slowly, Styrkar drew the axe from his belt.

'Wait...' Ronan pleaded, trying to back away.

'This is a priory of the Lord God,' Beyhilde said in protest. 'There can be no bloodshed here. If you are—'

Styrkar raised his hand for her to be silent. She looked at him for a moment, mouth opening to speak before she thought better of it. Then she looked at Ronan, offering nothing but disdain, before she turned and left them alone.

'Wait, don't leave,' Ronan pleaded, but she had already gone. He turned back to Styrkar, holding up his hands as though they might stop an axe. 'I gave you back your daughter. I did what you asked.'

'Kneel,' Styrkar commanded.

'I gave you—'

'Kneel.' It was more of a snarl. More of the Red Wolf than Styrkar.

Ronan lowered himself to the floor, gripping tight to the wooden pillar he had backed into. 'I'm sorry. I am, truly. I never wanted her to die. I tried... Please, God, I never wanted any of this...'

Styrkar stepped forward and raised the axe high.

His swing was true, the axe head embedding in the wood of the pillar an inch above Ronan's head. The Frank's eyes remained shut and he whimpered, expecting that killing blow to come. It would not. Styrkar was done with that now. Done with this pitiful excuse of a man. He had wasted too much of his life on the bitterness Ronan had caused. He would waste not another moment.

He turned, eager to leave the stifling confines of the priory. Outside, Truda was waiting in the chill air, holding that little girl tight in her arms. Styrkar climbed atop his horse, and the nun gently handed his daughter to him. After he had sat her in front, he wrapped her in a fur and grasped the reins.

The valravn cawed, before he could put heels to the steed's flanks. Styrkar regarded it, one final time. Then he rode away.

There was no way of knowing how long he clung to that wooden post. It could have been mere moments. Could have been half a day. When eventually he opened his eyes Styrkar was gone, having left his axe behind, buried in the wood an inch above Ronan's head.

Slowly he clawed his way to his feet. His hands were shaking. Tears filling his eyes. In the archway he could see the nuns were watching him, Beyhilde at their fore. She had nothing to say to him as he turned away and staggered to the door.

Out in the courtyard, the air was crisp, and mercifully the horse he had ridden here was still waiting for him. With some difficulty he struggled onto its back, gripping the reins.

He was free. All he had to do was put heels to the beast's

flanks and take the road south. Just ride as fast as the steed could carry him, and claim the lands and title that were rightfully his.

A harsh caw.

He looked up, seeing the raven glaring down at him. Judging him. Accusing him. Reminding him of that stain. The one that covered them all. The one that no amount of land and riches could wash away.

'I know,' Ronan whispered back at the creature. 'I know.'

47

Styrkar uncorked the waterskin he kept on the horse's saddle, offering it to the girl. She took it in her tiny hands and drank. When she was done, he fished out the last of the bullace he had foraged and offered it to her. She took the tiny plum from him and began to eat.

He had kept the coast on his left for a night and day, skirting villages and burghs, determined to reach the Black River as soon as he could. The fruit had been the only thing he could forage, but thankfully a passing trader had offered them some carrots from the goodness of his heart, quite taken with the flame-haired little girl riding with her father.

They could not be far away now. Just a little longer and he would be able to take her away from this place of dread and misery.

She glanced up at him, and he forced a smile. 'I know nothing about the raising of children,' he reassured her. 'But I promise you I will do my best.' Though she had not said a word since he had taken her from the priory, he was sure she could understand him, at least a little. Perhaps, perhaps not, but either way his words raised a smile on her red-stained lips, and she offered him the rest of the half-eaten bullace.

Styrkar smiled in return. 'I see you will be my guardian as much as I am yours.'

He took it from her, biting down on the underripe fruit and wincing at its sourness. Not once had she complained about the taste. He thought it best to do the same.

As the morning wore on, and the wind began to whip up from the sea, it was with relief that he spied the port at the foot of their sloping path. His horse plodded on until he rode into the settlement, smelling the welcome aroma of fires and cooking. Everything looked so mundane, but then he had learned a long time ago that ordinary settlements like this cared little for the battles of kings and rebels.

Before he could think to find food and warmth, he saw Hereswyde approaching from the dock. She was wrapped in furs, hair flattened to her head to cover the shaved scalp that might mark her out. The fury he had always seen flickering behind her eyes had died, and she looked just like any other woman in this place.

'Your ship is waiting,' she said as she took his horse's reins. 'It sails soon on the high tide.'

Styrkar gathered up his daughter and slipped down from the saddle. She gripped him tight as he balanced her on his hip. 'Where are the others?'

'Hiding,' Hereswyde replied. 'We thought it best to split up. Draw less attention. I told them we might meet again in Grentebrige after a few days. I doubt any of them will come.'

'And if they don't? What will you do then?'

There was a sadness to her now. An acceptance of things she had no control over. It would have hurt Styrkar to see her fall so low, but he knew there was no other way. All that remained for them both was to accept their fates.

'I... haven't decided yet. But I have thought on your words, long and hard, and perhaps you are right. Maybe this fight is done.'

'I know it is done. To accept that is for the best. There is no need for either of us to lose more than we already have.'

'And I see you have found a treasure of your own.' Hereswyde smiled at the girl, pinching her cheek. An act of tenderness Styrkar had not thought possible from this warrior woman. 'What is her name?'

Styrkar thought back to the priory. Thought back to the name the nuns had given his daughter. To the valravn sitting atop its porch. But he knew now what that bird was. It was no portent of death. Rather it was a spirit guiding him, watching him, reminding him of his daughter and eventually leading him along the path to where he would find her. Maybe it was what had kept him alive so long where so many others had perished.

'Her name is Revna. Revna Styrkarsdottr.'

Hereswyde leaned in closer, offering a wide grin. 'Hello, Revna.'

'Hello,' the little girl replied.

So she could speak. Styrkar would have to ensure he worked on that in future. Before he could try and tease more words from her, Hereswyde turned at the sound of a whistle. Across the settlement, someone waved from the dock.

'They are leaving,' she said. 'Your passage has been paid. You will reach the shores of—'

'I will find out when we arrive. Then our new life will begin. And who knows, perhaps we will meet again, you and I.'

'Anything is possible, Red Wolf.'

When she spoke that name it sounded as though she were talking of someone else. 'Goodbye, Hereswyde.'

She nodded her own farewell, and he walked by, through the open marketplace where fish were being gathered, and onto the wooden jetty. The *skeppare* mumbled his welcome as Styrkar stepped onto the deck, and his crew were quick to cast off. Men grasped oars, and for a moment he wondered where he might sit, and which oar was his. But no. Styrkar had come a long way since he was made to be an oarsman. This was the first day of a new life.

As the ship cruised along the Black River, he watched the land he had adopted as his home slip away into the mist. It was in the hands of a tyrant now, one he had failed to vanquish. One who had taken everything from him, but Styrkar had claimed something more precious. Not only his daughter, but his destiny.

The Bastard Duke had slain the Red Wolf.

All that remained was Styrkar.

It would be enough.

About the Author

RICHARD CULLEN originally hails from Leeds in the heartland of Yorkshire. *Oath Bound*, his debut historical adventure novel, was longlisted for the Wilbur Smith Adventure Writing Prize. As well as being a writer of historical adventure, he has written a number of epic fantasy series as R.S. Ford.

If you'd like to learn more about Richard's books, and read free exclusive content, you can visit his website at wordhog.co.uk, follow him on Twitter at @rich4ord, or join him on Instagram @thewordhog.